Aeschylus

Anatiposi

F. A. Paley

Aeschylus

Reprint of the original, first published in 1871.

1st Edition 2023 | ISBN: 978-3-38212-576-9

Anatiposi Verlag is an imprint of Outlook Verlagsgesellschaft mbH.

Verlag (Publisher): Outlook Verlag GmbH, Zeilweg 44, 60439 Frankfurt, Deutschland
Vertretungsberechtigt (Authorized to represent): E. Roepke, Zeilweg 44, 60439 Frankfurt, Deutschland
Druck (Print): Books on Demand GmbH, In de Tarpen 42, 22848 Norderstedt, Deutschland

AESCHYLUS

TRANSLATED INTO ENGLISH PROSE

BY

F. A. PALEY, M.A.

EDITOR OF THE GREEK TEXT.

SECOND EDITION, REVISED AND CORRECTED.

CAMBRIDGE:
DEIGHTON, BELL, AND CO.
LONDON: BELL AND DALDY.
1871

AESCHYLUS.

TO THE READER.

THIS Translation of Aeschylus,—an entirely new one,—is designed as an Appendix to my edition of that Poet in the *Bibliotheca Classica*.[1]

In some respects, an author's meaning and the connexion of his ideas are more satisfactorily conveyed by a translation, giving the context entire, than by notes, rendering only occasional words and phrases. I am not without hope that this book will be found acceptable to those students who are willing to use, not to abuse it; for to turn the verses, and especially the choral verses, of a poet so figurative and obscure as Aeschylus into anything like readable prose, really is a very difficult task.

In carrying out this design, I have knowingly laid myself open to the charge of departing pretty frequently from that

[1] I have made very many alterations in this (the second) edition, but nearly all in the way of simplifying and abridging the language, where that could be done without detriment to the sense. I may here cite, not inaptly, the words of Professor Max Müller, ("Chips from a German Workshop," i. p. 137,) "If Scholars who are engaged in these researches are bent on representing their last translation as final, and as admitting of no further improvement, the public has a right to remind them that 'finality' is as dangerous a thing in scholarship as in politics."

exact verbal rendering which is generally known as a 'literal translation,' and attending at least as much to the author's meaning as to his mere words. I am no advocate, as my numerous pupils, past and present, will attest, of lax construing or mere paraphrasing; but I contend that, if anything that deserves to be called readable English is to be produced, and if anything like justice is to be done to an author who is not supposed to write nonsense, such a licence, moderately used, must be conceded to a translator who is fully conscious of the fact (not to say the law) that the idioms of an ancient inflected and compounded language are widely different from those of a modern one of auxiliary and complementary word-forms.

The best translation is but a kind of compromise: as a proof of which may be mentioned the fact, that on an average fifty words of the Greek require about a hundred of the English to convey their full meaning. In cases where I have been compelled to paraphrase either quaintly-worded or involved sentences, I have generally given the *exact* sense in a foot-note; and I have also added, in the briefest form, occasional comments in explanation of the author's meaning.

CAMBRIDGE,
1871.

CONTENTS.

SUPPLICES.

PERSONS REPRESENTED.

CHORUS, THE DAUGHTERS OF DANAUS.	PELASGUS.
DANAUS.	HERALD.

Chorus. May Zeus the patron-god of Suppliants regard with favour this our voyage from[1] the finely-silted mouths of the Nile. For we left the divine land closely bordering on Syria, and are flying, not because we were sentenced by a vote of the citizens to exile from our own people for any deed of blood, but by an effort on our own parts to escape wedlock, and loathing as unholy a marriage with the sons of Aegyptus. And Danaus our father, the author of our counsels and the leader of our company, arranging for us this plan, determined on the best of evils,[2] that we should flee with all speed through the waves of the sea, and put-to at the land of Argos, whence our race, sprung from the divine touching of the brize-driven heifer, and from the life-giving breath of Zeus, has been brought into being.

What land then could we come to more kindly disposed to us than this, with these suppliant badges in our hands, the wool-tufted boughs? O city, O land and clear water, and ye, gods supreme, and powers of wrathful vengeance possessing the tombs[3]; thou too, Zeus, who art wont to be

[1] Literally "our naval expedition that started from," &c.

[2] The least bad of two alternatives. Martial has *optimus malorum*, xii. 36.

[3] *i. e.* the local heroes, ἐγχώριοι δαίμονες, whose power for evil was much dreaded.

invoked Third as Preserver, guardian as thou art of men that reverence thee; may ye all receive as suppliants this company of women with the merciful spirit of the land; but that lewd band of many males, the sons of Aegyptus, before they have set a foot on this low marshy coast-land, send seaward with their swiftly-rowed galley; and there, by a pelting hurricane, by thunder and lightning and rainy winds, having met with a wild sea, may they perish, ere ever they obtain selfish possession of the daughters of their father's brother, and ascend the unwilling couch from which the law of heaven keeps them away.

And now I invoke the divine offspring of the heifer to be our protector here across the sea,—that child of a flower-browsing ancestress, that touch that followed the amorous breath of Zeus:[1] and the time allotted by fate went on to its full accomplishment in a name suited to the event, and she gave birth to *Epaphus*. Him then I call to my aid; and now, while on these very pasture-grounds of our mother of old I recall to mind her former woes, I will show for the present sure proofs of my descent to the settlers in this land, and other proofs, mayhap, though unlooked for, will appear. And people will know the truth of my words in due time.

And perchance, if any one skilled in birds dwells near in this land, he will fancy, when he hears our piteous plaint, that he is listening to the voice of Tereus' sorrowing bride, the hawk-chased nightingale. For she too, constrained to leave her native haunts and streams, mourns with a strange wild moan for her woodland home, and makes music of her child's sad fate, how that he perished by her own hand, having suffered the wrath of an unnatural mother. So too do I, indulging my love of grief in these soft Ionian strains, rend my tender Nile-summered cheek, and [vex] my heart steeped in boundless tears. And I am ever gathering the flowers of sighs, in fear respecting my own relations, that some of them are interested in this my flight from yon dim

[1] *ἔφαψιν* seems here used for the offspring born by and through the touch, as conversely *γέννημα* must mean *γέννησις* in *Prom.* 869.

hazy land.[1] But, O ye gods who guard the sacred rights of Race, hear me, favourably regarding the cause that is just, and not conceding to impetuous youth to have its desires fulfilled beyond what is right: but show a prompt hatred to outrage, and be fair to us in the matter of our marriage. Even for those who flee hard-pressed from war an altar is a protection from harm,[2] an object of regard to the gods.

May the god in all truth cause *good* to prevail![3] But the desire of Zeus is not easily discovered. It burns brightly everywhere, even in the dark, though attended with events unforeseen to mortal men. Nor does it fall vain and helpless, as a wrestler thrown on his back, if any matter has been solemnly ratified by the nod of Zeus. For[4] dark and bosky wend the ways of his mind, not to be seen into by human eye. And he hurls from their towering hopes frail mortals in utter destruction; yet to do this he arms no force: all that gods do is done without toil. He is seated aloft on his holy throne, and yet from thence he contrives means to work out his will. And now let him have in his regard the lewdness of these mortal men, with which the parent stem[5] is shooting anew with a view to our marriage; for it hath budded and blossomed with ill-devising thoughts, and is goaded on by maddened feelings from which there is no escape: but it shall know its folly by its disappointment.[6]

Such are the piteous strains of woe that I utter in my complaint, shrill in their tones, grievous, causing tears to fall: ah me, ah me! marked with dirges as of the dead. For, though yet living, I honour my own fate by lamentations. I invoke the favour of this Argive hill-country; and well, O land! doest thou understand my barbaric accent. And

[1] She appears to mean the sons of Aegyptus. But *φόβος εἴ τίς ἐστι*, &c., will also bear a negative sense, 'fear that none care for,' *i. e.* that we are left friendless.

[2] Much more to us, whose cause is more pure and just.

[3] There seems a play on the words *θεὸς* and *θείη*.

[4] This word '*for*' seems further to explain the preceding, "But the desire of Zeus" &c.

[5] Aegyptus, whose *ὕβρις* as it were *breaks out afresh* in his violent and headstrong sons.

[6] It shall feel too late its folly, when it finds its wish thwarted by heaven.

frequently, as I speak, I fall upon my linen garments or my Tyrian head-attire with rending. But to the gods holy offerings are due, following upon a happy end of troubles, where death shall have been escaped. Alas! alas! these trials are hard to explain: whither will this wave carry us out of our course? Our oars indeed, and the linen-sailed water-tight house of wood, took me over the sea without a storm by the aid of favourable breezes. I have nothing to say against that; may only the all-seeing Sire in due time accomplish a favourable result, that the august race of the awful Mother may escape the marriage-bed of these males, unwedded, unravished! And may the holy maiden daughter of Zeus look with a willing eye on one who seeks her protection, even Artemis who stands there by the sacred wall;[1] and may she a virgin, who has escaped uncaught in so many pursuits, put forth all her strength to rescue a virgin suppliant. For if she does not, we will appeal, a dark and sunburnt race,[2] with suppliant boughs in our hands, to the infernal Zeus of the dead, that most ready receiver of all who come to him, having died by the noose, should we fail in gaining the ear of the gods celestial. O Zeus, 'tis through thy rancorous spite against Io that the anger of the gods still pursues us; for I recognise in this the fury of thy heaven-subduing bride: a storm will follow after a stiff breeze. And then will Zeus be liable to a charge of unjust neglect, for slighting that child of the heifer, whom formerly he himself created, if he now keeps his face turned away at our prayers. But O may he hear us with favour from above when invoked!

Danaus. My daughters, there is need of discretion; and with a discreet father you have come, even this faithful old pilot of your voyage. And now also, taking forethought for you on land, I advise you to mark well my words, and to write them in the tablets of your minds. I see dust, announcing without voice the approach of some host. The

[1] She appeals to a statue of the goddess, possibly represented as escaping from some amorous advances.

[2] Meaning, perhaps, like black shades or ghosts; but with an allusion to the swarthy complexion of Egyptians.

axle-driven wheels[1] may plainly be heard; and now I descry a company half-hidden behind their shields and brandishing spears, with horses and hooked chariots. Mayhap the rulers of this land may be coming towards us to inspect, having heard of our arrival from messengers. But whether they have peaceable intentions, or are making this march upon us whetted for the fray and with relentless anger, 'tis better on every account, my daughters, to take your suppliant seat at the raised altar-mound of these gods of contest.[2] For an altar is a better defence than a tower,—it is a shield not to be broken. Go then[3] at once, and holding in solemn form with your left hands your wool-tufted suppliant boughs, the proper offerings to Zeus the god of mercy, reply to the strangers respectful yet mournful and urgent words of request, as befits new-comers; and explain to them in clear language that this exile of yours is caused by no deed of blood. And let your speech be attended above all by no bold word; then, let no immodest glance proceed from your sober brows and your tranquil eye. Be not forward in conversation, nor prolix in your account: the people here are very jealous of long speeches. And remember to be humble: you are an indigent stranger and a suppliant, and it becomes not those who are inferior to talk confidently.

Cho. Father, you speak sensibly to a daughter not devoid of sense. I *will* take care to remember these good instructions of yours; and O may Zeus the author of our race regard us!

Dan. May he do so indeed, and with a kindly eye!

Cho. I should wish under present circumstances to have a seat near to you.

Dan. Then loiter not, but whatever plan you propose, carry into effect.

Cho. O Zeus, pity me for my troubles ere I am quite undone!

[1] Lit. boxes or naves of wheels. So *Ag.* 496.

[2] *ἀγώνιοι θεοὶ* were invoked generally as gods of trial and difficulty, *i. e.* as bringing such to a happy issue.

[3] Perhaps *ὡς τάχιστ' ἀμβᾶτε*, *i.e.* ascend the stage. Compare *Ar. Ach.* 732.

Dan. If *he* will it, all shall end well.

Cho. . . . . . .

Dan. Invoke now also this bird,[1] the symbol of Zeus.

Cho. We invoke the bright rays of the sun that they may bring us safety.

Dan. Apollo too, the pure god; himself an exile from heaven.

Cho. Knowing this fate, he can sympathise with mortals.

Dan. May he sympathise with us indeed, and stand by us with willing favour!

Cho. Whom then of these gods must I further invoke?

Dan. I see a trident here, the mark of some god.

Cho. Well, as he has given us a good voyage, so may he give us a good welcome to this land.

Dan. Here also is Hermes, according to the usage of the Hellenes.

Cho. May he then herald us good tidings, as free guests of the land.

Dan. Reverence also the common altar of all these greater gods, and taking your places on holy ground sit there,—like a flock of pigeons in fear of hawks, birds of their own feathered race,—to be safe from relations[2] you hate, and who would pollute the sacred laws of kindred. How can bird devouring bird be free from defilement? And how could one who takes in marriage an unwilling child from an unwilling father, become holy?[3] Not even when dead in Hades shall the lewd man escape guilt, if he does that. For even there, as men say, another Zeus passes sentence on human sins by a last judgment among the dead. Be on the look out, and come here to this place, that the present affair may turn out all for the best.

King. Of what country is this band—a company in naught resembling the Greeks, gorgeous as it is with barbaric robes

[1] The cock seems to be meant, from a fancied analogy between ἀλέκτωρ and ἠλέκτωρ (ἐλκήτωρ), an epithet of the sun.

[2] In the Greek, "relations" is in apposition to "hawks"; but this cannot literally be put into intelligible English.

[3] *i. e.* by what rite of expiation.

and close wrappings—that we address? For this is not the Argive female attire, nor from any of the parts of Hellas. But how you ventured fearlessly to come to this land, not even announced by heralds, and without proxeni,[1] independently of guides,—that is a matter of wonder to me. Boughs however, according to the general customs of suppliants, lie beside you at the statues of the god of contests. In this point alone Hellas will agree with you in conjecture. And for the rest, there are several things one might have guessed at, were there not a living voice to inform one here on the spot.

Cho. You have spoken about my dress words that are true. And now whether do *I* address you as a citizen, or as one bearing the protecting staff of Hermes,[2] or as chief ruler of the city?

King. For that matter, you may reply and speak with confidence to *me;* for I am the son of earth-born Palaechthon, lord of this Pelasgic land, and it is after me their king that the race of Pelasgi who cultivate this soil is rightfully called. Of all the land through which the clear Strymon flows, in the part fronting the setting sun, I am sovereign: and I reckon as the limits of my empire the land of the Perrhaebi, the parts beyond Pindus, near to the Paeonians, and the hills of Dodona; and the [eastern] boundary of the watery waste cuts it off: all within those limits I hold under my sway. Now of the Apian land itself this plain has long ago borne a name in compliment to a man who practised the healing art. For Apis, arriving from Naupactus across the sea, a son of Apollo,[3] and an adept both in healing and prophecy, cleared this land from pestilent monsters, which Earth, defiled by the pollutions of ancient murders, sent up in anger, a dragon-swarm of hostile indwellers. Of these evils Apis effectually

[1] People of the country to speak in your behalf.

[2] A herald's wand. But the integrity of the text is rather doubtful.

[3] Physicians generally were called sons of Apollo, *e.g.* Pindar, *Pyth.* iii. 67. Here Apis (ἤπιος) is but another name for the healing god himself; and the legend records the introduction of some form of his worship from Epirus.

applied remedies, both by drugs and expiations,[1] to the Argive land, and so obtained of old our mention of him in prayers in place of a physician's fee.[2] As you now have the proofs on my part, declare to me your own race, and say on. A *long* speech however this city cannot endure.

Cho. Short and clear is our tale: we profess to be Argive women, offspring of the heifer that was blessed in her progeny. And all this I will establish as true by my account.

King. You speak words, strangers, that are incredible for me to hear,—how that this descent of yours is from Argos. For you more nearly resemble the women of Lybia, and not at all those born in this land. And the Nile might perchance nourish such a growth; a Cyprian stamp too, resembling yours, is impressed on female forms by male artists. I am told moreover that certain Indian women live as nomads on camels that are ridden like horses and carry burdens like mules,—a tribe inhabiting a land bordering on the Ethiopians.[3] Those unmarrying flesh-fed Amazons too, if you had been equipped with bows, I should shrewdly have guessed you to be. When informed I shall understand this the more, how your stock and your descent can be from Argos.

Cho. They say that Io formerly became a priestess of the temple of Hera in this land of Argos.

King. She was so assuredly, and the tradition very widely prevails. There was some story too, I think, that Zeus had intercourse with a mortal?

Cho. Yes, and those embraces were not concealed from Hera.

King. How then did these jealousies of the royal pair end?

Cho. The Argive goddess turned the woman into a heifer.

King. Then Zeus no longer approached her, as a heifer of well-shaped head?

Cho. They say he did so; with his form likened to a cow-serving bull.

[1] As a *μάντις*, and one of the *Λύσιοι θεοὶ*, Plat. *Resp.* p. 366. 13.

[2] Or perhaps simply, 'obtained in return.'

[3] See the note on *Prom.* 828.

King. What then did the powerful spouse of Zeus do in respect of that?

Cho. She appointed one who was all eyes to be a keeper to the cow.

King. What sort of shepherd-herdsman do you mean by this *all-seeing* one?

Cho. Argus, a son of Earth, slain by Hermes.

King. What other annoyance did she contrive for the poor cow?

Cho. A gad-fly that persecutes oxen and excites them. (Those by the Nile call it *oestrus.*)

King. Did this then drive her out of the land by a long course?

Cho. All this also you have said consistently with my story.

King. Did she not also arrive at Memphis and Canopus?

Cho. Yes, and Zeus who touched her[1] begot a son by the might of his divine hand.

King. Who then professes to be the child of this heifer that was sprung from Zeus?

Cho. Epaphus, truly called after the seizing of booty.[2]

King. . . . . . .

Cho. Libya, who enjoys the honour of having given a name to the largest continent.

King. What other offspring from her have you yet to mention?

Cho. Belus, who had two sons, and was the father of my father here.

King. Tell me now the name of this sage old man.

Cho. Danaus; and he has a brother with fifty sons.

King. Unfold to me *his* name also, and grudge me not the information.

[1] Throughout there is a play on the name Ἔπαφος as derived from ἐφάπτεσθαι, 'to touch.' It was a supernatural birth,—an incarnation of a deity without procreation; an ancient Egyptian doctrine of great moment and interest, especially as connected with ἐπίπνοια.

[2] I suspect this verse, which gives quite a distinct origin to the name Epaphus, is by a later hand, and was designed to make some kind of sense in a mutilated passage.

Cho. Aegyptus. And now, knowing my descent of old, fail not to raise from the altar this band of Argive origin.

King. Well, you *do* seem to me to have some ancient connexion with this land: but how did you venture to leave your father's home? What fortune befel you?

Cho. King of the Pelasgic race, the misfortunes of mankind are ever varying: you will nowhere see trouble assume the same appearance.[1] For example,—who ever expected that this unlooked-for flight would bring to the shores of Argos a kindred race formerly born there, by causing them to leave their home in haste through dislike of cohabitation in marriage?

King. What is it that you say you ask for in the name of these gods of contest, having in your hands newly-culled wool-tufted boughs?

Cho. That I may not become a handmaid to the race of Aegyptus.

King. On account of a family feud, or do you speak of an unlawful union?

Cho. Why, no one would purchase[2] relations for their masters.

King. 'Tis in this way[3] that family influence increases in the world.

Cho. Aye, and when matters go wrong, desertion is an easy matter.

King. In what way then can *I* act towards you[4] according to my duty?

Cho. Do not surrender us to the sons of Aegyptus at their demand.

King. 'Tis a grave request you make,—to undertaké a disastrous war.

Cho. Yea, but Justice ever proves the champion of her own friends.

[1] A metaphor from the varying plumage of a bird.

[2] viz. by a marriage-dowry.

[3] By intermarriages with kindred families.

[4] viz. if your cousins have acted undutifully.

King. Perhaps so, if she took part in the business from the first.

Cho. *Your* duty is to reverence the chief altar of the city thus crowned with woollen fillets.

King. I do feel awe, when I see these shrines overlaid with boughs.

Cho. Heavy, be assured, is the resentment of Zeus the god of suppliants. Son of Palaechthon, hear me with willing heart, king of the Pelasgi! Look at me, your suppliant, driven a wanderer from home, even as a heifer pursued by a wolf on a lone precipice, where trusting to his aid it lows, telling the herdmen of its troubles.

King. I see your company here before these gods of contests shaded with newly-cut boughs and with heads bent low to the earth. Well! may this affair of you claimants on our citizenship end without mischief! But we must take care lest, from unlooked-for and unforeseen events, a quarrel should arise to the state;[1] for *that* the government desires not.

Cho. Yea truly, may our flight bring you no mischief, but be favourably regarded by the suppliant-law of all-allotting Zeus. But now do you, though the senior, learn a lesson from me who was born long after you: if you show mercy to a suppliant you shall never want, [provided that there be paid][2] offerings to the temples of the god from a holy man.

King. You are not seated as suppliants at *my* house. If the city incurs guilt in its public relations, let the public concert together to provide remedies. But *I* will not conclude any pledge beforehand, but only after I have communicated with all the citizens about these matters.

Cho. *You* surely are the city, *you* the public; as irresponsible lord you have power over the altar, the hearth[3] of the land, by your own sovereign decrees; and so also, seated

[1] Perhaps, πολὺ νεῖκος γένηται. For the next verse ends also with πόλις.

[2] Two or three words have been dropped out of the text.

[3] The principal, or metropolitan altar.

on a throne of undisputed sway, you ratify all civil business. Beware of incurring guilt in the sight of the gods.

King. May the curse of guilt indeed fall on my enemies! but you I am unable to assist without harm. Yet on the other hand this is not pleasing to my feelings, to slight these prayers. In truth I am perplexed, and fear possesses my heart both in acting and declining to act, and in taking the chances.

Cho. Hold in regard Him who from high heaven regards others,—the protector of much-suffering mortals who, when appealing to others as suppliants, obtain not lawful justice. Know that the wrath of the god of suppliants remains, with difficulty appeased by the piteous complaints[1] of the guilty sufferer.

King. Why, if the sons of Aegyptus have a right over you by the law of their city, on the plea that they are the nearest of kin to you, who would care to oppose such arguments? You must of course urge in your defence, in accordance with the laws of your country, that they have no authority at all over you.

Cho. Never, O never may I become subject to the caprices of these males! I prefer, in truth, a flight by the light of the stars as a means of escaping the odious marriage. Take justice as your ally, and decide on that which is righteous in the sight of the gods.

King. The choice is not easily made; do not take me for judge.[2] I told you before also, not without the concurrence of the people will I act in this matter, no, not if I *have* authority. The people must never say, if something untoward should have occurred, 'By regarding these new-comers you ruined[3] your city.'

Cho. Zeus the patron-god of Relations regards both sides in this matter, but inclines to one of them. He awards injustice to the unjust, but the lot of the righteous to those

[1] Or, "remains implacable at the complaints of him who has been wronged," viz. as a suppliant.

[2] Though you have chosen me as *σύμμαχος* and *πρόξενος*.

[3] Perhaps *τιμῶντες ὤλεσαν π.*

who keep the law. Why, when these two cases are fairly balanced, do you feel compunction at doing that which is right?

King. Truly now do we require some deep salutary counsel,—we want a clear-seeing eye, and one not too much confused by wine, to reach the bottom like a diver, that this affair may turn out harmless in the first instance to the city, and also fortunately for ourselves; and that neither war-strife may seize on you as captives, nor we, by surrendering you thus seated at the altars of the gods, bring upon ourselves the destructive god of Vengeance to become a wrathful inmate of our land,—that god who not even in Hades sets free the (guilty) dead. Seems it to you that we do *not* require a salutary counsel?[1]

Cho. Take heed, and become to us, as in duty bound, a god-fearing patron. Surrender not one who is an exile,—who has been driven far from home by an unnatural banishment; nor suffer me to be dragged violently away from these altars of many gods, O thou who holdest the entire sway over the land! Take note of the lewdness of these men, and beware of the wrath of Zeus! Do not bear to see your suppliant led away captive from the statues in despite of justice, like a horse pulled along by the head-gear, and the rude clutches of my finely-woven robe. For be well assured, in whichever way you shall have acted in this matter, it remains for your own sons and your house to pay a like justice by war. Consider well these righteous commands from Zeus.

King. Well, I *have* considered them; and this is what the matter comes to:[2] from engaging in a terrible war either with one side or the other there is no escape: it is fixed[3] as fast as the hull of a ship jammed in the stocks. Without

[1] This last verse seems spurious, and is little more than a verbal repetition of the first. The concluding speech of the king has *ten* lines, as the preceding dialogue has uniformly had *five*.

[2] Lit. "the ship is stranded on this coast."

[3] Lit. "it has been fastened with wooden pegs."

some vexation there is no concluding the business.[4] Now, for wealth taken out of a plundered house, other wealth may come by favour of Zeus the god of Property, even greater than the loss, and sufficient to fill up a large freight. So too when a tongue has shot forth reproaches that are not seasonable, but causing pain and greatly exciting passion, one speech may make amends for another; but, if we would prevent kindred blood-shedding from taking place, we must assuredly sacrifice, and many victims must fall to many gods as a deliverance from harm. Surely by doing that I steer clear of the quarrel. But I shall be glad to prove an unskilled prophet of evil rather than a cunning one: may it therefore turn out well, even contrary to my judgment.

Cho. Hear now the summing up of these many appeals for mercy.[1]

King. I listen: speak on: it shall not escape me.

Cho. I have breastbands and girdles for the fastening of my robes.

King. These things are befitting the condition of women.

Cho. With these then, be assured, there is a ready way——

King. Say now, what language is this that you will utter?

Cho. Unless you shall give this company some good hope to rest on——

King. *What* is the contrivance of the girdles to effect for you?

Cho. To adorn these statues with a strange kind of votive offerings.

King. Your words are a puzzle. Come, speak plainly.

Cho. To suspend ourselves forthwith from these gods.

King. I hear a word that cuts me to the very heart.

Cho. You know my meaning, for I gave it eyes to see more clearly.[3]

[1] Lit. "a steering to shore." The naval metaphors in this passage are remarkable.

[2] Or perhaps, 'of my respectful address.'

[3] By a similar figure *βλέποντα δοξάσαι* is used in *Choeph.* 829. Or perhaps, "I made *your* eyesight more clear."

King. In many ways indeed there are troubles hard to strive with: and a flood of evils comes upon me like a river. I have entered upon a wide sea of calamity both bottomless and hard to cross; and nowhere is there a harbour of refuge from evils. For if on the one hand I should fail to perform for you this request, you have hinted at a pollution not to be surmounted:[1] but if on the other hand I should take my stand before the walls and try the issue of battle with your cousins, the sons of Aegyptus, surely the loss of lives becomes a sad one, when men for the sake of women shed their blood on the plain. Still, I am bound to hold in awe the wrath of Zeus the god of suppliants: for the fear of him is supreme with mortals. Do you then, aged sire of these maidens, take these boughs in your arms and lay them quickly at some other altars of the gods of this country, that all the citizens may see a proof of this suppliant visit, and let not a word be thrown out about me: for the people are fond of bringing charges against those in authority. It may happen that some of them, feeling pity at seeing these tokens, will detest the lewd insolence of the male company, and so the people will be more favourably disposed to your side. For every one has kindly feelings towards the weaker.

Dan. This is deserving of much gratitude from us, to have gained as a patron one who has proved himself so merciful. But send with us attendants and some of the natives to point out the way, in order that we may find the altars in front of the temples of the gods who protect the city, and their . . . . . . shrines, and that we may have safety as we go through the city. For the form that nature gave us is not of a kindred sort, since the Nile does not rear a race like the Inachus. Beware lest confidence should give rise to slaughter: 'ere now some have killed even their friends through not recognising them.

King. Go, men;[2] for the stranger speaks well. Lead

[1] Or, 'beyond any that can be reached by conjecture.'

[2] He speaks to certain mutes who re-appear as a body-guard to Danaus at the end.

the way to the city altars, the shrines of the gods. And you must not converse at length with those you may chance to meet, while you are conducting this seafarer to be the guest of the gods.

Cho. To *him* you have spoken, and as he has his orders, may he go. But how must *I* act? Where do you assign *me* a secure place?

King. In the first place, leave here your boughs, as a token of your distress.

Cho. See, I leave them at your beck and command.

King. Now turn for refuge to this open level space.

Cho. You do not mean that a public square can protect me?

King. Be assured we shall not surrender you to be ravished by winged kites.[1]

Cho. But what if to those who are more odious than fell dragons?

King. Let her who has been received with good words speak good words of others.

Cho. Yet surely 'tis not surprising if I am intolerant from alarm of mind.

King. But fear at all times is unsuited to the character of kings.

Cho. Then do you, as by your words, so also by your actions give encouragement to my heart.

King. But your father will not long leave you all alone: —I myself will convene the people of the country, and so talk over the assembly as to make it favourable to you; and I will instruct your father what arguments he is to use. Remain therefore for a time, and beseech by prayers the gods of the land, that you may obtain all that you desire. And now I will go to forward this matter. May persuasive eloquence attend me, and luck in carrying out my design!

Cho. King of kings, most blessed of the blest, supreme

[1] The male cousins called κίρκοι, v. 20.

[2] Ζεὺς Τέλειος, the Perfecter or Accomplisher. *Ag.* 946. Literally, "authority (or majesty) most perfecting of the Powers" (τέλη).

Cause[1] among all the powers above, blissful Zeus, hear, and let our prayer be granted! Avert from us the lewdness of the men by shewing a just hatred of it, and drown in the purpling sea that dark-benched pest. Regard with favour the women's cause, and recal the pleasing legend of our ancient race, as descended from an ancestress that was dear to thee. Yea, call it all to mind, thou that didst once lay thy hand on Io! We say that we are inhabitants of the divine land,[2] though we claim our origin from this. And I have come back to the old footprints of my mother, the scenes of her pasture-watchings by Argus, even the herd-feeding meadow-land from which Io once fled, plagued by the gad-fly, distraught in mind, passing through many tribes of men: and as, guided by her destiny, she clave the surging Bosphorus, she left apart on each side the boundaries of the opposite continents. And now she speeds across the land of Asia, through the very heart of cattle-pasturing Phrygia. She passes the Mysian settlement of Teuthras and the vales of Lydia; and hastening over the mountains of Cilicia and Pamphylia by ever-flowing rivers, [she reaches] the rich deep-soiled plains and the corn-bearing land of Aphrodite.[3] Then she comes, while her winged keeper[4] pierces her with his sting, to the divine fertile plain, even the snow-fed pasture-ground which the furious Typho wanders over,[5] and to the water of the Nile, untouched by disease; she comes, driven mad by her ignominious toils, and goaded to frenzy by the stinging pains inflicted by Hera. And the people who then were the inhabitants of the land shook with pale fear at the unwonted sight,—a heifer portentous of half-human form, in part a cow, in part a woman; and they were amazed at the prodigy. And who then was it that at length soothed the poor long-wandering fly-goaded Io? 'Twas Zeus,

[1] Ζεὺς Τέλειος, the Perfecter or Accomplisher. *Ag.* 946. Literally, "authority (or majesty) most perfecting of the Powers" (τέλη).

[2] Egypt; so called in v. 4. The construction is a little obscure; but I think the above gives the true meaning.

[3] Cyprus.

[4] The gad-fly.

[5] See Herod. ii. 156.

lord of ceaseless time. [For by him at length][1] she is stopped from her violent course by his unharming[2] might and the breathing upon her of his divine love; and she sheds the mournful modesty of tears. And so having conceived a burden in her womb that was truly from Zeus, she gave birth to a fair child, throughout long ages most blessed. And hence all the earth cries aloud, "A life-giving race, which of a truth is from Zeus himself: for who else could have stopped the sorrows caused her by the plots of Hera?" That was the work of Zeus: and in saying that this our race is from Epaphus, you will be right. Whom of the gods can I reasonably invoke for deeds more just? He was the father and author, the king who with his own hand brought into being our race, the sage mighty artificer, the director of every expedient, even Zeus. Neither does he, by sitting under the command of another, hold a sway less than superiors: nor does he worship below while another is enthroned above. And his action is as prompt as his word, to execute with speed anything that his counselling mind conceives.

Dan. Courage, my daughters! All is well on the part of the citizens. The people have passed full and effective measures for your safety.

Cho. All hail, aged sire, who bring most welcome news to me. But tell us, to what purport has this final vote been carried? How many hands[3] were held up in the majority that prevailed?

Dan. It was resolved by the Argives, not by a division of votes, but with such accord that I felt young again in my aged heart,—for in full assembly the air hurtled with right hands held up as they passed this resolution, that we should live as licensed aliens in this land, free and not liable to arrest, and with security from being robbed by men. Further, that no one, either of residents or strangers, should attempt to take us captives; and that, if he should apply violence,

[1] Two or three words have been lost in the text.

[2] Not aggressive, *i.e.* ravishing, but only touching her with gentle hand.

[3] The Schol. certainly read ὅση χεὶρ = ὅσαι χεῖρες.

any one of the landholders here who should have failed to bring aid should be made an outlaw and driven an exile from his people. Such was the purport of the speech which the king of the Pelasgi eloquently addressed in our behalf, warning the people that the dread wrath of Zeus the Suppliant-god would never in aftertimes allow the city to thrive, and telling them that a twofold guilt incurred both from strangers and citizens alike,[1] making itself seen by visible signs before the city, would be a food of calamity that would prove difficult to deal with. When the Argive people heard these words, they passed a vote by show of hands, without waiting for a herald, that these things should be so. And the people of the Pelasgi listened indeed to the persuasive clauses of the harangue, but it was Zeus who brought about the result.

Cho. Come then, let us recite over the Argives good prayers in requital for good. And may Zeus the patron-god of strangers direct the gratitude of a stranger's tongue, so as to have fulfilment, and to be brought to an issue in all things without reproach.[2]

Hemich. A. Now at length,[3] ye heaven-born gods, hear me pouring forth my prayers for the people, that this Pelasgic city may never be consumed by fire, nor raise the joyless cry of wanton Ares, who cuts off men's lives in other harvest-plains; for that they have shown mercy to us, and have passed a kind decree; and they hold in religious regard the suppliants of Zeus, this pitiable flock.

Hemich. B. And they have not given their vote on the side of the males, disregarding the cause of the women: but they have kept their eye on the divine avenging observer who cannot be overcome in war, and whom no house would care to have sitting like a foul bird on its roof; for he perches heavily on it. For they hold in respect their own kin, suppliants of holy Zeus: and therefore by guiltless altars they shall win the favour of the gods.

[1] *i.e.* from rejecting the suppliants in their double relation.

[2] The text here is doubtful.

[3] Perhaps εἴ ποτε, νῦν θεοὶ κ.τ.λ. Compare *Ag.* 503. *Il.* v. 116.

Hemich. A. Therefore from these lips of ours enshrined in olive-boughs[1] let the patriotic prayer go forth, "Never may pestilence drain this city of men! Never may sedition stain with the blood of native bodies the surface of its soil! But let the flower of their youth be ungathered; and may the paramour of Aphrodite, man-slaying Ares, not prematurely cut off the bloom!"

Hemich. B. And let the altar-steps that receive the aged priests blaze with offerings; so may the city be prosperously inhabited. Let them pay reverence to mighty Zeus, who by ancient law directs destiny. And we pray that fresh produce from the land may always be forthcoming, and that Artemis the Darter[2] may favourably regard the delivery of women.

Hemich. A. And let no man-slaying feuds ensue, ravaging this city by arming the author of tears, that enemy to the dance and the lute, the god of War, and [rousing] a call to arms among the people. But let the joyless swarm of diseases light far off from the heads of the citizens; and let the fierce destroying wolf-god[3] be propitious to all the youth.

Hemich. B. And let Zeus make the earth to render its tribute by the produce of all seasons; may the cattle of the country that pasture before the city become prolific, and may they receive all needful substance from the gods. And may bards raise strains of praise[4] at the altars, and let the jocund song that loves the lute go forth from chaste lips.

Hemich. A. May the people also, who form the strength of the city, guard with jealous honour the offices of state,—the government that prudently directs its counsels for the public weal.[5] And may they offer to strangers a ready satisfaction in disputed compacts, without mischievous consequences, before appealing to arms.

Hemich. B. And the national gods who protect the land

[1] The suppliant boughs were held up as a veil before the face.

[2] Who was supposed to kill women in childbirth.

[3] Apollo was thought to cause the sudden deaths of males, as Artemis those of females. See note on *Theb.* 132.

[4] Probably *εὔφημον*, not *εὐφήμοις*. The meaning however would be virtually the same.

[5] There is some corruption of the text.

may they ever worship with the ancestral honours of sacrifices and bay-bearing processions: for respect towards parents is written along with two other precepts among the decrees of most venerable Justice.

Dan. I approve of these your discreet prayers, my dear daughters; but do you not be alarmed at hearing from your father unexpected and startling news. I descry from my watch-post[1] on this asylum of suppliants, the barque of our pursuers. It is too well marked to escape my notice: there are the reefings of the sails and the side-guards of the ship, and the prow, seeing its course before it with its pictured eyes, too well, alas! obeying the steering paddle in the after-part of the ship, as being unfriendly to us. And now the men on board are in sight, with their black limbs in conspicuous contrast with their white attire. The other ships too, and the whole assisting squadron may be easily discerned: and see! the leading ship herself, now nearing the land, has furled her sails and is being rowed with all the hands. Well! you must look quietly and dispassionately at this matter, and be earnest in securing the protection of these gods. I myself will shortly return with persons to assist us and to advocate our cause: for perhaps a herald or an embassy may arrive, desiring to carry you off by laying hands on you as captives. However, nothing of that kind will really happen: fear them not. Still it is better, if we should be slow in procuring aid, on no account ever to forget this protection of the altars. Take courage: be assured that in time and on the proper day[2] one who shows contempt for the gods will be punished.

Cho. Father, I am in fear, for already the swift-rowed ships are here, and no long interval of time is left. A very great fear in truth takes possession of my mind, that there has been no use in all this long rapid flight of mine. I am faint, my father, with alarm.

[1] Either the altar, or perhaps some elevated steps on the side of the proscenium, to which there was an ascent.

[2] 'The day fixed for a trial' is the technical meaning of κύριος ἡμέρα, *e.g.* in *Dem. Mid.* p. 41. Comp. *Ag.* 740.

Dan. Since the decree of the Argives has been formally passed, take courage, my child;[1] they will fight about you I am well assured.

Cho. They are a desperate set, that lewd race of Aegyptus, and insatiate in fighting; and I say this to one who knows them well: and having procured a timber-built dark-prowed fleet, they have sailed hither with a rage bent on gaining its end, with their numerous and sable crew.

Dan. Aye, but they will find many here who have their arms well seasoned[2] under the heat of a midday sun.

Cho. But O leave me not alone, I do beseech you, father. A woman left to herself is nothing; she has no fight in her. And they are exceeding crafty-minded and crafty-counselling, with impure hearts, caring no more for the altars than do carrion-crows.[3]

Dan. That would be indeed favourable to our cause, my children, if they should incur the hatred of the gods as they have ours.

Cho. There is little chance that through any reverence for these tridents and altars[4] of the gods they will withhold their hands from seizing us, my father. Too proud are they in their unholy passion, possessed with lust, shameless as dogs, caring nothing for the gods.

Dan. There is however a saying that wolves can master dogs; and certainly the fruit of the byblus is not superior to the ear of corn.[5]

Cho. As they have also the tempers of lustful and unclean beasts, we must be on our guard against their boldness.

Dan. Do not imagine that the getting under weigh of a naval host is a speedy matter, nor the mooring of a fleet, nor the carrying safely to land of the stern-ropes; nor do the pilots of ships at once feel secure in their anchorage, especially when they have come to a land without harbours. When the

[1] Read *τέκνον*, not *τέκνα*.

[2] Lit. "filed down," *i. e.* hardened.

[3] Which snatch meat from the very sacrifice.

[4] Perhaps *θεῶν ἕδη*.

[5] *i. e.* Greeks are stronger than Egyptians.

sun is sinking into night, darkness is wont to beget anxiety in a wary pilot. Thus there is not likely to be even a favourable disembarking of the army before the ship has been made secure in her moorings. But do you resolve, as being in terror, not to desert the gods from whom you have gained protection; and the city shall have no cause to disparage a messenger who is old in years but young in eloquence.

Cho. O land of hills, just object of our veneration, what shall we now have to suffer? To what place in the Apian land must we fly, if there is anywhere a dark hiding-place for me? O that I could turn into sable smoke, near neighbour to the clouds of Zeus; or that flying upwards without wings, and vanishing entirely like the invisible dust, I might be dissolved. But without flight somewhere my heart can no longer abide, and it palpitates all steeped in gloom. My father's look-out has been my death: I perish with fear. Now could I wish for a fatal noose by hanging, before that odious man approaches to take possession of me. Rather may Hades be my master in death, than he. O that some one could give me a seat in upper air, in which the vapoury clouds turn into snow; or that there were some smooth inaccessible summit-hid solitary hanging rock haunted by vultures, to be witness of my plunge into the depth below, before I endure by violence a marriage that will rend my very heart. But *then* I object not to become a prey to dogs and to the vultures of the land; for death is freed from the evils that make us fain to mourn. Let fate come; better that should befal me than the marriage-bed. Or is there any other escape or deliverer from wedlock that I can find? Cry *woe woe!* with a voice reaching the gods even up to the sky; sing strains supplicatory and earnest, such as may procure me a release. Regard thou the conflict, father of the gods, beholding violence with just and not friendly eyes And hold in respect thy suppliants, almighty ruler of earth Zeus. For the race of Aegyptus, intolerable in their lewdnes born of the male,[1] are pursuing me in my flight with swi

[1] *i. e.* of the male sex. See *Choeph.* 493.

chase and with clamorous search, and are desiring to get possession of me by violence. But the beam of thy balance is held over all: what is accomplished for mortals without thy will?

Cho. Oh, oh! Alas, alas! Here comes the sea-plunderer to plunder on land! 'Ere that happen may you be shipwrecked! [may you never reach us][1] having landed here. I raise aloud a voice of woe. I foresee in their actions a prelude to violent treatment of me. Ha, there! fly quickly to the protection of the altars. His proud and overbearing gait is intolerable alike on board-ship and on land. O king, stand up for us as our patron!

Herald. Off! off with you, I say, to the barque, with all the speed of your feet!

Cho. Now indeed there will be tearings of our hair and goadings of our flesh, yea, even bloody and murderous cutting off of heads.[2]

Her. Off! off, ye wretches, with a plague upon you, to he barque!

Cho. Would that on your briny course over the flowing you had perished, with that imperious insolence and your fastened ship besides! . . . . . .[3]

er. I advise you to give up, despite of yourselves, that of a too foolish mind. Ho, there! Leave the altars to the ship. I am not bound to respect what is l in this city.

Never more do I wish to see that cattle-nurturing ence the life-giving blood that thrives in cattle is I am of ancient descent, and I occupy a sacred n.

en in the ship you shall embark speedily, ish it or not, by force, yea, by force. Go, that ffer evil, wretched one, by my hands.

the text.
in the ex-
ives.
hopelessly corrupt.

[4] The Nile.

[5] Corrupt.

Cho. Ah me! so may you perish without a hand to help you in crossing the watery waste, having lost your course off the sandy headland of Sarpedon by easterly breezes.[1]

Her. Sob and moan if you will, and call on the gods: for you shall not escape[2] the Egyptian barque, even though you pour forth a still more piercing cry of woe.

Cho. Oh woe for this insult! For you speak fiercely. . . . .[3] May the mighty Nile that nurtured you turn away your insolence, and bring the insolent to naught.

Her. I bid you go to the doubly-prowed barque as quickly as possible, and let no one loiter. For the haling of captives shows no respect for fine locks.

Cho. Alas! father, the protection of the statues proves only a bane. He is carrying me off to the ship, with the stealthy tread of a spider. A dream, a dark dream! Oh woe, woe! Mother Earth, mother Earth, keep away him whose voice inspires fear! O king Zeus, thou son of Earth!

Her. I stand in no awe of your gods here. They did not rear me when young, nor feed me in old age.

Cho. He is raging close to me, this two-footed serpent; and like a viper that bites the foot, he has got a firm hold of me. Alas, alas! mother Earth, mother Earth, avert him whose voice inspires fear! O king Zeus, thou son of Earth!

Her. If somebody will not go to the ship, assenting to what I say, a rending will show little mercy to the fabric of a tunic.

Cho. Ho! ye leaders of the city, ye chief men, I am being made a captive!

Her. It seems I shall have to drag you, tearing you away from the altars by the hair, since you do not lend a quick ear to what I say.[4]

Cho. We are undone! We are suffering violence unlooked for, O king!

[1] Wrecked off the promontory of Cilicia by a "Levanter." My emendation, for *εὐρείαις εἰν αὔραις*, though rather summarily rejected by Hermann, I venture to think a very probable one.

[2] Lit. "leap over." The metaphor is explained on *Ag.* 350.

[3] A corrupt verse.

[4] I believe this couplet to be spurious.

Her. Many *kings*, sons of Aegyptus, ye will soon behold. Fear not, ye shall not say there are none to govern.

King. You sir! what are you doing? with what ideas are you dishonouring this city of the Pelasgi? Think you that you have come to a city of women? For a stranger from without, you are taking too great liberties with Hellenes; while wrong in so many points you have conceived nothing right in your mind.

Her. Why, what of these matters has been wrongly done by me in disregard of justice?

King. In the first place, you do not know how to behave as a stranger.

Her. How not? I, in finding what I had lost,—

King. What proxeni of the country did you communicate with first?

Her. Hermes, the greatest of proxeni, the god who assists search.

King. If you told it to gods, you shew no reverence for those gods.

Her. The deities of the Nile are those whom I reverence.

King. And those here are nothing to you, as *I* understand you.

Her. I shall take these girls away, unless some one rescues them.

King. You shall suffer for it, if you lay a finger upon them, and that speedily.

Her. The words which I hear are by no means friendly to a stranger.

King. I owe no hospitality to strangers who are robbers of the gods.

Her. I shall go and report all this to the sons of Aegyptus.

King. That is a matter of no concern to my way of thinking.

Her. But, that I may speak more plainly with knowledge,—for it is the duty of a herald to report all the circumstances clearly,—how and by whom shall I say on my return that I have been robbed of the company of female cousins? Be assured that Ares does not decide such disputes by the evidence of witnesses, nor does he make up a quarrel on the receipt of money; but before that many a hero falls on the field, and there is many an agonised shuffling-off of life.

King. Why should I tell you my name? Time will teach it, and then both you and your comrades will know it. But these maidens, provided they are willing, you may take, if you act in a kindly disposition, and if arguments consistent with religion should induce them. Such an unanimous vote has been solemnly passed by the city in popular assembly, never to surrender by force a company of women. Through this a peg has been driven direct, so as to remain firmly fastened.[1] These resolutions are not merely inscribed on tablets (nor written in the folded leaves of books[2]) but you hear them plainly from a free-speaking mouth. And now betake yourself as quickly as possible out of my sight.

Her. This doubtless is *your* pleasure, to incur a disastrous war. Well! may the victory and the success be on the side of the males.[3]

King. But male inhabitants of this land you will assuredly find, who do not drink wine made of barley. And now do you, maidens, take courage, and go all of you with these friendly attendants to the well-fortified city, closed in with the device of lofty walls. And houses there are in plenty which belong to the people; but I myself have a palace built with no humble hand,[4] if you have a mind to dwell happily along with many others; but, if it is more agreeable, you may also occupy separate abodes. Of these alternatives choose that which seems best and which is most pleasing to the minds of the majority. I and all the citizens, —the same who pass this vote,—are your legal protectors. Why do you wait for others of more authority than these?

[1] A figure from affixing tablets of laws or decrees to walls.

[2] I believe this verse—the earliest instance of the word βίβλος — is spurious.

[3] Not to you and your women, he contemptuously implies. See v. 885.

[4] Perhaps this verse should be transposed to follow 938.

Cho. May you, in return for the good you have done us, abound in all that is good, noble king of the Pelasgi! But kindly send hither our stout-hearted father (Danaus, our adviser and the author of our plan),[1] for he must first be consulted as to where we may find houses to live in, and what place is agreeable to him. Every one is ready to utter slander against foreign women; but may what is best happen for us. And do ye, dear handmaids, with good repute and with the temperate[2] language of the citizens, take your allotted places on the spot, according as Danaus assigned to each daughter a fair slave for her dowry.

Dan. My daughters, you must offer your grateful vows to these Argives, and make sacrifices and libations as if to Olympian gods, since they have proved your preservers by their unanimous decree. And, while they heard with indignation against those obstinate cousins the course I had taken respecting them, they at the same time appointed these men to be my attendants and body-guard, that I might have an honourable prerogative, and might not be waylaid and secretly made away with by the spear, and so bring an undying curse on the land. When I obtain from them such privileges as this, it is reasonable for me to hold in yet higher honour and regard the kindly feeling of their dispositions. And these instructions you will take down in your minds, beside many other maxims of prudence from your father already written there, to the end that a company as yet strange may be tested by time. Every one, in the case of an alien, carries a ready tongue for slander, and the uttering in some way of a word that too easily leaves a taint. But you I exhort not to do discredit to me, possessed as you are of an age which is attractive to mortals. For tender ripeness is by no means easily guarded; the very beasts hanker after it as well as men: is it not so? Yea, and creatures winged and walking on earth. Cypris offers for sale her dropping fruits,[3] and

[1] These words seem interpolated.

[2] Not the hasty words usually addressed to slaves. This perhaps explains ἀμηνίτως in *Ag.* 1003.

[3] A metaphor from grapes bursting with ripeness. The next verse is corrupt.

. . . . . And at the delicate beauty of virgins every passer-by discharges a winning dart from the eye, overcome by desire. Wherefore let us take care lest we suffer those very evils, to avoid which so much toil (has been incurred), and so much sea ploughed with our ship; and lest we cause disgrace to ourselves, but pleasure to my enemies. An habitation even of two kinds is before us to accept (the one Pelasgus, the other the city offers,)[1] to live in free of rent. These are easy terms. Only remember these commands of your father, valuing chastity more than life itself.

Cho. In all other matters may we be favoured by the gods of heaven: but concerning my marriageable age have no fear, my father; for unless some harm to us has been designed by the gods, I will not depart from the former course of my thoughts.

CHORUS.

Hemich. A. Go, then,[2] to pay your devotions to the blessed gods who are supreme rulers of the city, those who have in their care the safety of the state, and those who are enshrined by the ancient stream of Erasinus.

Hemich. B. Take up, companions of our way, the strain; henceforth let this city of the Pelasgi be the subject of our song, and let us no longer adore the mouths of the Nile in our hymns.

Hemich. A. No; but rather those rivers which (as they flow) through the land pour their mild waters, causing increase, and satisfying the soil of this land with fertilizing streams.

Hemich. B. And may virgin Artemis look with compassion on our company, and may this marriage not be forced upon us by Cytherea: may *that* contest be reserved for my enemies.

Hemich. A. Not that this hymn of ours, which is friendly

[1] This verse seems interpolated. The king is nowhere by name called *Pelasgus.*

[2] Perhaps ἴτε νυν should be read for ἴτε μάν. The word γανδεντες (γανάοντες) is corrupt. The sense required is ὑμνοῦντες or τιμῶντες. qu. ἀγαλοῦντες?

to her, neglects Cypris: for she has power scarcely less than Zeus and Hera; and she is honoured as the goddess of crafty wiles for her influence over the nuptial mysteries.

Hemich. B. And ever at their mother's side, as sharers in her honours, are Desire and winning Persuasion, to whom nothing can be refused; Harmonia too has a share of Aphrodite's power allotted to her, and so have the gently whispering Loves.[1]

Hemich. A. But I have boding fears of their sailing against us as fugitives, and of sad woes to be endured; yea, of bloody wars, now that they have had a favourable voyage with their swiftly-wafted ships in the pursuit.

Hemich. B. Be assured that whatever is appointed by fate, that must happen: one cannot go contrary to the almighty absolute will of Zeus. May the end of this marriage turn out as many other marriages have to women of former times.

Hemich. A. May the great Zeus avert from me a marriage with the sons of Aegyptus.

Hemich. B. What is best for us may yet come to pass.

Hemich. A. But you would fain make light of that which is no light matter.

Hemich. B. But *you* do not certainly know what is in store for us.

Hemich. A. How am I to see into the divine will, impenetrable to human ken?

Hemich. B. Use now moderate words.

Hemich. A. What moderation are you recommending?

Hemich. B. Not to take too much to heart the dispensations of the gods.

Hemich A. May sovereign Zeus take from us an odious marriage with men who are our enemies,—that Zeus who freed Io from her woes, by happily checking her course with his healing hand, and effecting her deliverance by his benevolent power.[2]

[1] Read *ψεδυραῖς τρίβοις τ' 'Ερώτων.*

[2] Perhaps *εὐμενῆ* (or *πρευμενῆ*) *βίον κτίσας*, "making her life favourable."

Hemich. B. And may he award the victory to the side of us women. The better alternative of an evil lot, and one of mixed fortune,[1] I accept; and (may he grant) that the coming trial[2] be conducted justly, in accordance with my prayers, with means of deliverance from the gods.

[1] Escaping the marriage, and the removal to another land.
[2] The subject, probably, of the play that next followed.

PROMETHEUS BOUND.

PERSONS REPRESENTED.

STRENGTH (KRATOS).	CHORUS OF NYMPHS, DAUGHTERS OF OCEAN.
FORCE (BIA).	
VULCAN.	IO, DAUGHTER OF INACHUS.
PROMETHEUS.	HERMES.

Kratos. We have come at last to a remote spot of this land, the untrodden tract of a Scythian wilderness. 'Tis for you, Hephaestus, to attend to the directions father Zeus enjoined upon you, to fasten this malefactor to the steep craggy rocks in sturdy shackles of adamantine bonds: for 'twas *your* prerogative, the bright fire used for every art, that he stole and gave to mortals. For such a crime as that surely it is meet that he should give satisfaction to the gods, that he may be taught to bear with patience the sovereign power of Zeus, and to cease from his disposition to befriend the human race.

Hephaestus. Kratos and Bia, you have done your parts in carrying out the order of Zeus, and no obstacle remains to its completion; albeit I have not myself the heart to bind a brother-god perforce to a bleak rocky gorge. Still, come what may, I must summon up courage for this; for to disregard the commands of father Zeus is a grave risk. Lofty-scheming son of the infallible Themis! 'tis sorely against the will of both that I shall fasten you with forged fetters, not easily unloosed, to this inhospitable rock, where neither voice nor form of any mortal man will greet you,[1] but broiled

[1] It is difficult to express more literally in our idiom the ellipse of ἀκούσει.

D

by the clear flame of the sun you shall change the bloom of your complexion; so will you rejoice when starry-kirtled night shall hide from the world the light, and the sun shall again disperse the morning dews. And for ever shall the weary burden of a present evil afflict you: for if any one is to give you ease, he is not born yet.[1] Such are the rewards you have got from your friendly disposition to mankind. You were a god, and nothing daunted by the resentment of the other gods, you gave prerogatives to mortals beyond what was right. For which offence you shall stand sentinel at this dismal rock, erect in posture, without sleep, not bending the knee. And many unavailing lamentations and groans shall you utter; for the mind of Zeus is inexorable; and every one is stern, who has newly come to power.

Kra. Come now, why are you hesitating and wasting time in bootless pity? Why do you not show your loathing for a god who is most hateful to the other gods,—a god too who treacherously gave away your own prerogative to mortals?

Hep. Relationship is a powerful tie, and so is companionship.

Kra. I admit that it is; but to turn a deaf ear to the orders of Zeus,—how is *that* possible? Fear you not that even more?

Hep. Ah! *you* were ever relentless and full of cruelty.

Kra. Why, it is of no avail to bewail this wretch's fate; so do you not trouble yourself bootlessly about things that can do no good.

Hep. O much-detested handicraft!

Kra. Why do you hate it? Of the troubles, to speak plainly, which you now have, your *art* is in no wise the cause.[2]

Hep. Nevertheless I could have wished that some one else had possessed it.

[1] Hephaestus perhaps knows that Hercules is destined to liberate Prometheus. But the words are purposely ambiguous.

[2] *i.e.* Zeus must be blamed for them.

Kra. One may do anything but become king of the gods. No one is free except Zeus.[1]

Hep. I know it by the present strait, and I have nothing to say against it.

Kra. Then make haste to throw fetters round this rebel, that father Zeus may not see you lazy at the work.

Hep. You may see there the armlets ready to your hand.

Kra. Then take and rivet them on his arms with a hammer with a strong grasp, and nail him to the rock.

Hep. The work gets on, as you see, and is not undertaken in vain.

Kra. Hammer harder, clinch the rivets, leave not a loose link anywhere; for he is clever at finding a way even out of close straits.

Hep. *This* arm at least is fastened in a manner hard to undo.

Kra. Then clamp this one also securely, that he may learn that he is a trickster not quite so shrewd as Zeus.

Hep. Excepting *him*, no one could fairly disparage me.[2]

Kra. Now fasten the ruthless jaw of the adamantine wedge driven right through his breast by main force.

Hep. Alas, my Prometheus, I deeply grieve for your sufferings.

Kra. There you are again wasting time in hesitation, and in sighing for the enemies of Zeus! Mind that you have not yourself to pity some day.

Hep. You see a spectacle painful for eyes to behold.

Kra. I see here a rebel meeting with his deserts. Come, throw the girths round his sides.

Hep. Do it I must: let '*Nothing in excess*' be your maxim in ordering me.

Kra. Be assured I *will* order, aye, and press you on[3]

[1] We are all slaves to, and must obey the orders of the supreme god; for we cannot dethrone him, gods though we be. The old reading ἐπράχθη is here rendered.

[2] All but Prometheus would say I did the work well enough.

[3] Literally, 'shout at you too.'

besides. Go below, and enring his legs with a strong constraint.

Hep. See now, the work is done, and at no great cost of labour.

Kra. Now hammer the galling chains with main force; for I can tell you the judge of the work is a severe one.

Hep. Your tongue utters language resembling your form.

Kra. Do *you* turn soft, but object not to me *my* cruelty and sternness of temper.

Hep. Let us go now, since he has got the fetters on his limbs.

Kra. *There* show your insolent defiance, and steal the prerogatives of the gods to confer them on creatures of a day! How much of these tortures will mortals be able to remove from you? By a false name the gods call you *Fore-Seer;* for you want a foreseer yourself to inform you how you may slip out of *this* device of our art.

Prometheus (*solus*). O glorious brightness of heaven divine! O swift-winged breezes, sources of rivers, and countless dimpling of the ocean billows, and Earth, nourisher of all things!—yon all-seeing orb of the sun too I invoke. See what sufferings I endure, myself a god, from the other gods! Behold with what tortures racked I shall have to struggle through my term of ten thousand years! Such is the cruel bondage that this new ruler of the gods hath devised against me.

Alas, alas! not only the present, but the coming evil I deplore, when I think where (in the distant horizon of time) an end to these toils is destined to appear.[1] And yet what am I saying? I know full well beforehand all that is destined to happen, and no calamity can come upon me unexpected. Well! I must bear my doom as easily as I can, for I know to my cost there is no struggling against the force of necessity. And yet *this* is a fate that I can neither brood over in silence nor speak plainly upon. Yes! it was through my giving privileges to mortals that I have got fixed, wretch that I am,

[1] A metaphor from the rising of a star.

in these bonds. I obtained by stealth the source of fire, stored away in a fennel-stalk;[1] (that little spark) which has proved to mankind the teacher of every art and their great resource. Such were my crimes, and such are the penalties that I pay for them, fastened up here in fetters under the open sky.

Ha! what have we now?

What is this sound, this odour that has been wafted to my senses without any object in sight? Is it heaven-sent, or human, or is it made up of both? Has some one come to this remote mountain to be a spectator of my pangs, or with what purpose? Behold me in fetters, an unhappy god, the enemy of Zeus, and who has incurred the enmity of all the gods that are allowed entrance[2] into the court of Zeus, through my too great friendliness for mortals. Aha! what means this rustling of winged things that I hear near me? The bright sky whistles with the light strokes of pinions. Whatever it be that is approaching, it fills me with fear.[3]

Cho. Fear not: it is a friendly band that has come to this rock with rival fleetness of wings, having gained at last the consent of our Father:[4] and swiftly was I borne by the breezes that wafted me in my course. For the clang of the hammering of iron penetrated to the depth of my cave, and scared away my bashful reserve; and I came off at once[5] in my flying car.

Pro. Alas, alas! Offspring of prolific Tethys, and children of father Ocean who encircles with his unslumbering stream the whole earth, look at me; behold with what cruel bonds I am fixed fast, and shall keep a miserable watch on the topmost rocks of this mountain-gorge.

Cho. I see, Prometheus; and through fear a mist came over my eyes, filling them with tears at the sight of your body bleaching against the rocks in these galling fetters of

[1] Used even by the modern Greeks for transferring fire. Here Prometheus seems to speak of the pith as tinder.

[2] He satirizes them as κόλακες.

[3] He thinks it may be the dreaded vulture which is to prey on his vitals.

[4] "Having *talked over* our father's mind."

[5] "Without waiting to put on sandals."

cruel adamant. For new helmsmen hold sway in Olympus, and by new-fashioned laws, I see, Zeus capriciously governs, and the grandeur of the old empire he is now bringing to naught.

Pro. O that beneath the earth and lower than Hades the receiver of the dead he had hurled me into fathomless Tartarus, savagely putting me in indissoluble chains! *Then* neither god nor any other being[1] would have exulted in these my sufferings! But now, a sport of the airs of heaven, wretch that I am, I suffer a fate that my enemies rejoice to behold.

Cho. *Who* of the gods is so hard-hearted as to exult in these tortures? Rather, who does not share in your indignation at your ill-treatment, except perhaps Zeus? *He* indeed in continued ill-temper sets his resolution inflexibly, and holds subject the heavenly host; and he will not cease to do so, till either he has satiated his heart's desire, or by some crafty device another shall have obtained possession of his jealously-guarded dominion.

Pro. Yet the day will come when this lord of the immortals will have need of me, tortured though I am in sturdy fetters, to shew him the new plot by which he is to be despoiled of his sceptre and royal prerogatives: and then not by all the honey-tongued enchantments of eloquence will he coax me, nor by his stern threats will *I* ever be intimidated, so as to give information on this head, till he has released me from these barbarous bonds, and has consented to make me amends for this cruel ill-treatment.

Cho. *You* indeed are bold, and relax nothing of your anger for your bitter pangs; nay, you speak your sentiments even too freely. But *my* mind is harassed by a penetrating fear; for I am alarmed for your fate, what course you must pursue[2] to see an end of these troubles. For the son of Kronos has ways not to be reached, and an inexorable heart.

Pro. I know well that Zeus is stern, and keeps the law

[1] *i. e.* man.

[2] "Into what harbour you are to put your ship."

in his own hands; nevertheless, if I mistake not, he will some day be softened in his resolution, when he has received a crushing blow in the way that I have foretold. Then he will calm this unyielding temper, and enter eagerly into unison and friendship with me, who on my part will gladly meet him.

Cho. Reveal and speak out plainly the whole story, what was the charge on which Zeus apprehended you, and now tortures you so ignominiously[1] and with such bitter resentment. Inform us, if the relation does you no harm.

Pro. Painful indeed to me is the story to tell, but painful it also is to withhold it, and so in every way it is an unhappy affair. When first the powers above had commenced their quarrel, and a faction of one side against the other was being got up,—the one party wishing to eject Kronos from his throne, that Zeus forsooth might reign, and the other party eager to bring about the opposite result, that Zeus might never become king of the gods,—thereupon I, though counselling for the best, was unable to convince the Titans, children of Uranus and Earth. They accordingly, slighting the use of crafty wiles through pride in their strength, fancied they could become masters without a long contest and by main force. But I had more than once been forewarned by my oracular mother Themis, (Earth she is also called, being one person under several names), what the issue of the matter was destined to be,—that it was not by might, nor by an appeal to strength, but by cunning, that those who gained the upper hand would prevail. When I explained all this to them in words, they did not condescend even to look at me at all. Accordingly, it appeared to me the best of all the plans that then occurred to my mind, to take my mother into my confidence and voluntarily side with Zeus, who on his part would be willing to receive us. It was by my counsels that the murky abyss of Tartarus concealed the god of primeval birth, Kronos, with all his allies. Such are the benefits that this tyrant of the gods has received from me,

[1] *Chains* were considered a servile punishment.

and such are the ill returns he has requited me with. For, I know not how it is, there is this vice inherent in absolute authority, the putting no trust in friends. However, what you ask me about, for what charge he is maltreating me,—this I will make clear to you. As soon as ever Zeus had taken his seat on the throne of his father, he at once proceeded to award to the gods their several prerogatives, and began to arrange the scheme of his new empire. Of poor mortals however he had no consideration at all, but wanted to annihilate the whole race, and plant on the earth another new one. To these schemes no one opposed himself except me. I made the venture: I rescued mankind from being shivered by his thunderbolts and going to Hades. Know that it is for *this* that he would break my pride by such tortures, alike painful to suffer and piteous to behold. Thus having given mortals the first place in my feelings of compassion, I was not myself deemed worthy of obtaining the same, but have been thus mercilessly taught obedience, a spectacle discreditable to Zeus.

Cho. Iron-hearted must he be, and made out of rock, who does not share in your indignation at your sufferings, Prometheus. For myself, as I should never have desired to see such sights, so on seeing them I am pained in my heart.

Pro. Why, truly, in the eyes of *friends* I *am* pitiable.

Cho. Did you not go somewhat even beyond this?

Pro. Yes, I stopped mortals from ever looking forward to their fate.

Cho. By devising what remedy of that malady?

Pro. I caused blind hopes to dwell among them.

Cho. That was a great blessing that you conferred on mortals.

Pro. But beside all this, it was I that gave them fire.

Cho. And do those beings of a day now possess the bright element?

Pro. Yes, from which they will learn to practise many arts.

Cho. Is *this* then the nature of the charges on which

Zeus is maltreating you, and relaxes nothing from your sufferings? and is there no limit to this trial appointed for you?

Pro. No other truly, except when it may be his pleasure.

Cho. And how can that ever be? What hope is there of it? See you not that you did wrong? But *how* you did wrong, as it is not agreeable to me to tell, so to you it is a pain to be told. Well! let us drop this subject: seek rather some way of getting free from this trial.

Pro. 'Tis easy for one who keeps his own foot out of harm's way to advise and to lecture another who is in evil plight. I tell you, I knew full well how all this would end: —yes, knowingly I erred, and that I shall not deny: it was by assisting mortals that I myself incurred these sufferings. But I confess I did not expect that by such a terrible punishment as this I should wither away against a lofty rock, condemned to inhabit this solitary inhospitable mountain. However, weep no longer for my present ills, but alight on the ground and hear the fortunes which are in reserve for me, that you may learn the whole matter throughout. Comply with my request; comply, and act in sympathy with one who is now in trouble. 'Tis in this way that calamity ranges about, and lights now on one, now on another.[1]

Cho. Upon friends by no means unwilling you have urged this request, Prometheus. Accordingly I will leave with nimble foot my swiftly-borne car and the pure regions of upper air, the highway of the eagle,[2] and will come close up to this craggy rock; and of your exertions and sufferings I long to hear an account from beginning to end.

Oceanus. I have come to the end of a long journey which I have performed in a visit to you, Prometheus, directing by my will, and without using a bit, this fleet-winged courser through the air. And with your fortunes, be assured, I condole; for not only, I presume, am I bound by my relation-

[1] A metaphor from a bird or a bee. He hints that the like troubles may one day come on the Chorus, when *they* will require sympathy.

[2] Lit. "of vultures."

ship to do this, but, apart from the ties of kin, there is no one to whom I would give greater consideration than to you. And you shall have practical proof of the truth of this, for it is not in me to utter vain compliments. Come therefore, signify to me in what you would have me coöperate with you. For you shall never say that you have a stauncher friend than Oceanus.

Pro. So, now, what means this? Have *you* then also come to view my sufferings? How ever had you the courage[1] to leave your own ocean-stream and its natural rock-roofed grottoes, and to come to this iron-producing land? Or have you made a journey on purpose to take a look at my fortunes and to condole in my woes? Behold a spectacle,—me, the friend of Zeus, me, who assisted in settling his sovereignty,—with what sufferings he is bending me to his will!

Ocean. I do see it, Prometheus; and I wish to advise you for the best, trickster though you are. Know yourself, and adopt for yourself new ways; for new also is the ruler among the gods. But, if you shall go on uttering such rough and sharp words, perhaps Zeus, even though seated far aloft, may hear you; so that what you now endure from his anger will seem to you to be mere child's-play of sufferings. Come, my poor friend, dismiss the angry feelings you cherish, and seek a riddance from these troubles. Perhaps what I am going to say will seem to you to be a stale maxim: such however, Prometheus, are ever the penalties of a too presumptuous tongue. But you are not yet humble, nor do you submit to your misfortunes; but besides your present woes you wish to get others. At least, if you act on the lesson I teach, you will not stretch out your leg against the goad, seeing that a stern monarch, and one accountable to none, is in power. And now I shall go and try if I can deliver you from these troubles. Do you on your part keep quiet, and not talk too fiercely. Do you not know full well, exceeding wise as you are, that on vain talk a penalty is inflicted?[2]

[1] Ironically said. Prometheus fully appreciates the temporising and compliant character of his new friend.

[2] See on *Agam.* 386.

Pro. I like the idea of *you* being free from all blame, though you shared in the whole affair, and made the venture in common with me! And now drop the matter; let it not be any concern to you. Do what you may, you will not prevail with him, for he is not easy to persuade. But beware, lest you should yourself receive some harm by your visit.

Ocean. Truly you are by nature far better at advising others than yourself: by facts and not by words I infer it. But now that I am going, do not by any means pull me back: I am confident, quite confident, that Zeus will grant me this boon, so that I shall release you from these sufferings.

Pro. For these offers I thank you, and I will not cease at any time to do so; for you are not wanting in readiness to serve me. But do not trouble yourself: for you will be doing so in vain, without any benefit to me, if you still insist on taking trouble. So be quiet, and keep yourself out of the way; for I would not, because *I* am in misfortune, therefore wish that to as many as possible evils should happen. No indeed! I am afflicted enough by the fortunes of my brother Atlas, who in the regions of the west stands propping with his shoulders the pillar between heaven and earth,[1] a burden not easy to hold in the arms. The earth-born inhabitant too of the cave in Cilicia I saw and pitied, a hostile monster with a hundred heads, when they fettered him like a slave by main force, the furious Typhoeus, who rose in rebellion against all the gods, with horrible serpent-jaws hissing out destruction.[2] From his eyes also he flashed a light frightful to behold, as if he would ravage by force the empire of Zeus. But there came against him the sleepless missile of Zeus, the down-rushing thunder-bolt giving forth flame, which in a

[1] In the original fable, and much as Hesiod represents it, Atlas was *under* the earth and sea, propping up the vast metallic vault of heaven which stretched like a dome over the flat earth, and touched it, or the circumambient stream, in the far limits of the world. Another account made a huge mountain, *e.g.* Atlas, Etna, or the Peak of Teneriffe, prop up the heaven from falling on the earth. Aeschylus combines or confuses the two accounts.

[2] This is a very ancient superstition of pre-historic man. Typhoeus was the earthquake god, who caused the rumbling noises heard in deep caves, and who vomited forth fire and smoke from the craters of the mountains under which he was laid. Pind. *Pyth.* i.

moment knocked out of him his lofty-worded boasts: for smitten to the very vitals he was burned black and blasted in his strength; and now his helpless and sprawling form lies hard by the narrow strait of the sea, squeezed under the mountain-mass of Etna. And there on the topmost peak sits Hephaestus forging molten iron, whence some day rivers of fire shall burst forth, preying with savage jaws on the level plains and the fair vineyards of Sicily. Such fury will Typhoeus cause to boil up from the mountain depths, with eruptions of hot and unapproachable fiery deluge, even though[1] burnt to cinder by the bolt of Zeus. Now *you* have had experience of his anger, and want not me for a teacher: save yourself, as you well know how.[2] But *I* will go on bearing my present fate, until the proud will of Zeus shall have ceased from its resentment.

Ocean. Do you not then know this, Prometheus, that of a disordered temper arguments are the physicians?[3]

Pro. Yes, if at the right time one tries to soften the heart, and does not attempt to reduce an inflamed passion by violent treatment.

Ocean. But in being prudent and yet making a venture, what probable harm do you see? Let me hear.

Pro. Pains spent to no purpose, and the character of a weak-minded credulity.

Ocean. Let me go on suffering with *that* disease[4]; since it is best for one whose views are wise, to appear not to be wise.

Pro. This error of judgment will be thought to be mine.

Ocean. Clearly your reply sends me back home.

Pro. Yes, I fear lest your grieving for me should bring you into enmity,—

Ocean. Mean you with him who has lately taken his seat on the sovereign throne?

Pro. Take good heed that *his* heart be never vexed.

[1] That is, he refuses to yield even yet. This is a warning to Prometheus to be wise in time.

[2] By not advocating the cause of a rebel.

[3] That arguments may influence Zeus, and assuage his anger against Prometheus.

[4] The metaphor from surgery is kept up.

Ocean. Your own case, Prometheus, is my instructor.

Pro. Set off, take yourself home: cherish your present sentiments.

Ocean. I was just going when you added those words to hasten me. For my winged quadruped is flapping with his pinions the wide track of air; and glad he will no doubt be to rest his limbs in his stall at home.

Cho. I weep for you, for this is a hapless fate, Prometheus: and as I pour from my tender eyes a stream of teardrops, I drench my cheek with fountains of water. For these are sad times: Zeus rules by laws of his own, and is showing to the gods of the former empire an overbearing disposition. Already the whole country groans aloud and sheds tears, sighing for the glories of the grand old sovereign sway of yourself and your brother Titans: not only do the mortal races who occupy the settlements in fair Asia sympathise in the loud groans extorted by your sufferings; but the maiden dwellers[1] in the land of the Colchians, fearless in fights, and the Scythian hordes who occupy the furthermost regions of earth near the Maeotic lake;[2] the valiant youth of Arabia[3] also, a people who dwell in a citadel perched on precipitous rocks near Mount Caucasus, a warlike host, uttering defiance with a serried front of sharp spears.[4] The only other one of the gods I have as yet seen in trouble is Atlas the Titan, rendered tame under torturing bonds of adamant,—who ever sustains on his back with heavy groans the vast weight that is borne upon him, even the revolving vault of the heavens. And the ocean-surge roars in cadence, the abyss beneath moans, and the dark recess of the gloomy region of the dead rumbles under the earth; yea, the very springs of the clear-flowing rivers wail in pity for his pain.

[1] The Amazons.

[2] The sea of Azov, beyond which to the east the world was unknown to the early Greeks.

[3] Either *Arabia* is a corrupt reading, or (and more probably) Aeschylus was quite wrong in his geography. See however, Plautus, *Trinum.* v. 934, 'in Pontum advecti ad Arabiam terram sumus.'

[4] On referring to a popular translation of Aeschylus to see how this difficult phrase is turned, (literally, 'storming in sharp-prowed spears,') I find nothing more satisfactory than "clamouring amid sharply-barbed spears." But ἐν means "accoutred with."

Pro. Think not that from affectation or foolhardiness I hold my tongue. Rather it is by reflecting on my own case that I am vexed in my heart, when I see myself subjected thus to ignominy. Yet who was it but myself that completely defined for these new gods their several prerogatives? However, I say nothing about them; for indeed I should only be telling you who already know. But hear about the evils that existed among mortals,—how I made them, hitherto without reasoning powers, to have mind and to be possessed of intelligence. And I shall tell you this, not with any wish to disparage mankind, but by way of explaining the good feeling implied in my gifts. They in the first place though seeing saw to no purpose, hearing they did not understand; but, like the forms of dreams,[1] during all that long time they did everything in a confused and random way, and knew not brick-built houses turned to the sun, nor the craft of carpentry. But they used to dwell in holes made in the earth, like the tiny ants, in the sunless recesses of caves.[2] And they had no sign either of winter, or of flowery spring, or of fruitful summer to rely upon; but they used to do everything[3] without judgment, till at length I shewed them the risings of the stars and their nicely determined[4] settings. And further, numbers, the best of inventions, I devised for them, and the combining of letters, at once the origin of literature, and the means of recording every event. And I was the first to join together under the yoke the animals that served them for drawing and for riding,[5] that they might be used by mortals to relieve them in their severest toils. I brought too under the car horses, taught to love the rein, the ornament of luxurious wealth.

[1] As fickle, unstable, and inconsistent as dreams. Compare *Ag.* 82.

[2] Modern researches seem to show that at least some very primitive races of men really did live in caves, which they shared with the wild animals, just as Lucretius also states V. 955, 984. These traditions therefore are by no means lightly to be set aside.

[3] Sowing and reaping are principally meant.

[4] The true as distinguished from the apparent risings. Some knowledge of astronomy seems to have been the earliest intellectual achievement of man.

[5] 'Submitting themselves to collars and to (bearing) men's bodies'.

Besides, no other than myself found out for them the sea-traversing canvass-winged cars to convey mariners. Such were the contrivances I devised for man, and yet, unhappy wretch! myself have no cunning craft by which I may get rid of my present misery.

Cho. Your misfortune is discreditable to yourself: you lost your senses and went wrong, and then, like a bad physician, after falling sick you despair, and cannot find remedies to cure yourself withal.

Pro. When you hear from me the rest of my story, you will wonder yet more at the various arts and shifts that I devised for man. The most important was this: if any one had fallen into an illness, there were no remedies to avert it, either to be swallowed as food, or to be used as ointments, or to be taken as draughts: but for want of drugs they used to pine and waste away, till I showed them mixtures of soothing remedies, by which they keep away every kind of malady. Many ways too of divination I arranged for them: I first taught them to distinguish what sort of dreams would turn out true: the obscure import of ominous sounds I made clear to them, and the meaning of objects met on the way. The flight too of crooked-taloned birds of prey I clearly defined, both those which are lucky in their nature, and the unlucky ones: and what way of life they severally have, what likings and dislikings with each other, and what habits of flocking together. I showed them too what the smoothness of the liver[1] meant, and what particular colour it should have to be pleasing to the deities; and the mottled appearance of the lobe of the gall-bladder.[2] Further, by roasting the thighs enveloped in fat, and the long chine, I led mortals into the true way of an abstruse art.[3] The signs too of flame[4] I made them see clearly, though before they were hidden as by a film from their eyes. Such then were my services on these

[1] The absence or obliteration of the seams which divide the liver into *lobes*.

[2] The lobe of the liver nearest to which the gall-bladder lies, (*lobus quadratus* in anatomy).

[3] That of divination. Signs were derived from the roasting of the chine, as is clear from *Ar. Pac.* 1053 seq.

[4] See Eur. *Phoen.* 1255.

matters: but those great benefits to man which lie hidden under the earth,—copper, iron, silver, and gold,—who can assert that he had found them out before I did? No one, I am very sure, that does not desire to talk vainly. In fine, in a short statement hear the whole matter: *all* arts came to mortals from Prometheus.

Cho. Do not now benefit mortals beyond what is right and reasonable, and yet be careless of yourself in misfortune: since I for my part am of good hope that you will yet be released from these bonds, and be not less strong than Zeus himself.

Pro. These things fate is not destined as yet to bring about in this way; but after being bent to his will by countless woes and pangs, I am thus to get away from my bonds. For Art is weaker by far than Necessity.

Cho. Who then is the director of this Necessity?

Pro. The three Fates, otherwise called the Mindful Furies.[1]

Cho. Is Zeus then inferior in power to these?

Pro. Assuredly he cannot escape what is destined.

Cho. Why, what *is* destined for Zeus, except to go on reigning for ever?

Pro. That further information you cannot have, and do not press for it.

Cho. I suppose it is some grand secret that you keep so close to yourself.

Pro. Mention any other subject: for this one it is not by any means the proper time to tell you plainly about, but it must be covered up as much as possible; for it is by keeping this secret that I am to escape from my degrading bonds and bodily pains.

Cho. Never may Zeus the dispenser of all things set his authority in opposition to my will: never may I be tardy in approaching the gods with holy sacrifices of slaughtered oxen by the ever-flowing stream of my father Ocean, and never may I offend in my words. Firmly may this abide in me,

[1] See *Eumen.* 361, 920; supra 218.

and may it never melt away from my mind. 'Tis something sweet to spend one's long life in confident hopes, nourishing the heart's desires amidst cheering joys: but I am affrighted when I see you racked by countless pains. It was because you feared not Zeus, but, acting on your private judgment, shewed too much respect for mortals, Prometheus. See now, how thankless was the favour, my friend: say, where and what assistance can be found. What help is there from the creatures of a day? Did you not perceive the powerless and feeble estate, like to a dream, with which the blind race of mortals is hampered and bound? By no contrivance will the eternal fitness of things established by Zeus be overstepped by the schemes of mortals. I learnt this truth by looking on your unhappy fortunes, Prometheus. And the strain of opposite tones has now come upon me,—this, I mean, to that, when I sang the nuptial song at the bath and the bridal bed, on the occasion of your marriage, when you led our half-sister Hesione, having won her by your presents to become your bride and the sharer of your couch.

Io. What land is this? what people? Whom shall I say that I see here exposed to the inclement sky chained to this rock? In punishment for what offence are you being tortured to death? Inform me, to what land, poor wretch that I am! I have wandered.

Ah, ah! See, what have we here? A stinging gad-fly[1] again pierces my poor flesh. The spectre of the earthborn Argus! Keep him off, O Earth! I am full of fear when I see that herdsman with his ten thousand eyes. There, there he goes, with his crafty eye! Not even when dead can he rest in the earth, but he finds his way from the abodes of the dead and hunts me down, making me rove all hungry along the sandy sea-shore. And the wax-compacted reed accompanies with its shrill notes his drowsy strain. O me,

[1] Io is dressed up as a human being with a cow's head, and is represented as attended by a ghostly herdsman and tortured by a brize or gad-fly. When she feels the latter, she knows the former is at hand. The legend represents the ancient cow-worship of India, and the *βοῶπις Ἥρη* of Homer is but another form of it. *Argus* is the peacock, also an Indian bird.

alas! alas! Whither are these long and toilsome wanderings taking me? In what, O son of Kronos, in what did you find me sinning, that you harnessed me to these woes, alas! and that you so persecute a poor maiden to frenzy by fears of being driven by the gad-fly? Burn me with fire, or cover me over with earth, or give me for a prey to sea-monsters; refuse not to comply with my prayers, O king! Too much toil already my long wanderings have caused me, and it is not in my power to discover in what way I may escape from my woes. Do you hear the voice of one who is a young girl, albeit she wears the horns of a heifer?

Pro. Surely do I hear the brize-driven daughter of Inachus, who captivates the heart of Zeus with love, and now, becoming odious to Hera, is being violently exercised in these too lengthy courses.[1]

Io. Whence comes it that *you* utter the name of my father? Tell me, the unhappy one, who you are—who, I say, O wretched man, who accost so truthfully this poor wanderer, and have named the heaven-sent malady which is wearing me out by stinging me with maddening goadings? Alas! tortured by hunger I have come bounding along at a rapid pace,[2] unable to cope with the craft and the jealousy of Hera. What wretches are there, O me! that suffer as I do? But signify to me clearly what is yet in store for me to suffer, what I have not to suffer; what remedy there is for this malady, show me, if you indeed know it. Speak, declare it to the poor wandering girl.

Pro. I will tell you plainly all that you desire to know, not making up riddles, but in simple language, even as it is right to declare one's sentiments to friends. You see here the giver of fire to mankind, Prometheus.

Io. O you who have proved yourself the common benefactor of mortals, unhappy Prometheus, in requital for what are you suffering these pains?

[1] A metaphor from the stadium.

[2] "With the hungry tortures of bounding steps I have come furiously rushing, tamed by the wrathful plottings of Hera."

Pro. I have but lately ceased lamenting my own woes.

Io. Will you not then grant this favour to *me?*

Pro. Say what you require; for there is nothing you may not learn from me.

Io. Inform me who fastened you in the mountain-gorge.

Pro. The device indeed was that of Zeus, the hand that of Hephaestus.

Io. And of what crimes are you paying the penalties?

Pro. Thus much only I am content to make known to you.

Io. Nay, but beside this show me the end of my wandering, and how long the unhappy one is to be an outcast.

Pro. Not to be informed of this is better for you than to be informed.

Io. Pray do not conceal from me that which I am destined to endure.

Pro. Nay, 'tis not that I grudge you this boon.

Io. Then why do you hesitate to tell me plainly the whole matter?

Pro. Objection I have none: but I *am* reluctant to shock your feelings.

Io. Be not concerned for me beyond what is agreeable to myself.

Pro. Since you are desirous, I must tell you: hear me then.

Cho. No, not yet: give me too a share in the pleasure. Let us first acquaint ourselves with this maiden's wrongs, from her own account of her long and perilous wanderings; but the rest of what she has to undergo let her be informed of by you.

Pro. 'Tis for you, Io, to comply with the request of these maidens, and the more so, as they are the sisters of your father. For to give free scope to tears and lamentations at misfortunes,[1] in a case where one is likely to win a tear from the hearers, repays time and the trouble.[2]

[1] *i.e.* from relations, as in this instance. ἀποκλαῦσαι like ἀποθαυμάσαι in *Ag.* 309, is, 'to have a good cry over,' 'to give full vent to one's sorrow.'

[2] Lit. 'involves a delay worth the making.'

Io. I know not on what grounds I should refuse *your*[1] request; so in a plain straightforward[2] account you shall hear all that you wish further to know. And yet I feel ashamed even to mention the reasons for which this heaven-sent tempest and this alteration of my fair form came so suddenly upon me, wretch that I was! Well, nightly visions used ever to visit me in my virgin chambers, and talk me over with smooth words:—"O highly favoured maiden, why so long live a virgin life, when you might obtain a most exalted marriage? Zeus has received a smart[3] from you by the dart of desire, and would fain have you share in his affection;[4] so do not, fair maid, testily spurn the bed of Zeus, but go forth to the deep meadow of Lerna, to the herds and ox-stalls of your father, that so the eye of Zeus may have relief from its longing desire." By such dreams as this for whole nights together I was haunted and made unhappy, till at last I made bold to speak plainly to my father about these midnight visitants. He accordingly sent to Pytho and by the road to Dodona frequent messengers to the oracles, that he might learn what he should do or say, so as to act agreeably to the will of the gods. But they returned, bringing back ambiguously-worded oracles, vague in their import, and expressed in terms hard to interpret. At length however a clear response reached Inachus, plainly charging and directing him to turn me out of home and country, to wander forlorn over the uttermost bounds of the earth: and that if he did not obey, a fiery bolt would come from Zeus, that should annihilate his whole race. Induced by such threatening oracles of Loxias, he drove me forth and shut me out of his house, with reluctance indeed on the part of both; but the bit of Zeus constrained him to do this even against his will. Immediately then my human form and understanding were distorted;

[1] If I refuse Prometheus, I cannot refuse *you*.

[2] σαφὴς means both 'clear' and 'true,' *falsehood* involving the idea of complexity.

[3] τέθαλπται. See Soph. *Antig.* 1086, *Trach.* 1082.

[4] 'To take on himself Cypris (love) together with you.' A metaphor from two oxen under a yoke. The metaphor is kept up in μὴ ἀπολακτίσῃς, 'do not kick away.'

and with horns, as you see, under the pain of a gad-fly's sharp bite I rushed with frantic bounds to the fresh stream of Cerchneia and the springs of Lerna:[1] and a herdsman rose out of the earth,[2] Argus, fierce in temper, and followed me, gazing on me with his thousand eyes wherever I bent my steps. A sudden unlooked-for fate however deprived him of his life: but I, stung by the brize, have ever since b driven by a scourge divine from one land to another. hear what has been done; and now, if you are able to tell what portion of my labours yet remains to be borne, inf me, and do not through compassion deceive me as others have done[3] by false words: for I assert that got-up tales are a most discreditable evil.

Cho. Ah, ah! keep her off, there, alas! Never, O never did I expect that the discourse of a stranger would come to my hearing,[4] nor that woes and sufferings and horrors so sad to gaze at and so hard to bear would chill my soul with a piercing pang.[5] O fate, fate! I shudder when I behold Io's case.

Pro. 'Tis too soon to sigh, and be so full of fears; stop, until you have learnt also what yet remains.

Cho. Say on, inform me fully: to those in distress in truth it is a relief to know clearly beforehand the suffering that is yet to come.

Pro. The former request you obtained from me easily; for you wished first to learn from Io herself the narrative of her own trials. Hear now the sequel, what sufferings this young girl has to endure from Hera. And do you, daughters of Inachus, lay up in your mind my words, that so you may have a full knowledge of the extent of your wanderings.

First then, turning round from this spot towards the rising

[1] A cow tormented by flies seeks the water.

[2] γηγενὴς probably means, born out of the earth on that occasion. The ancient Indians may have fabled that the peacock was so produced.

[3] ξύνθαλπε. She perhaps means the 'smooth words' of the dreams, v. 665.

[4] The Chorus had expected only to converse with Prometheus, who was a relation, when they consented to alight, sup. v. 290.

[5] With a goad pointed at both ends. The language is figurative rather than strictly metaphorical.

sun, traverse steppes unploughed by man; and you will arrive at hordes of Nomad Scythians who live in wicker cots, raised above the ground on wheeled cars, and accoutred with far-shooting bows. To these approach not too close, but keep your track by the surf-beaten shores, and so pass out of the land. On the left-hand the iron-working Chalybes dwell, against whom you are to keep on your guard; for they are a wild race, not to be approached by strangers. You will then reach a river with violent current, not falsely named,[1] which you must not pass (for it is not easy to ford), till you have come to the Caucasus itself, that loftiest of mountains, where a river spurts forth its strong current from the very brows. Then, surmounting the passes of those peaks that seem to reach the stars, enter on a southward course, whereby you will come to the warlike Amazon host that shun wedlock, that host that at a future day will colonize Themiscyra by the Thermodon, where is that rocky inlet of the sea, Salmydessus, inhospitable to mariners, a stepdame to ships.[2] These will be guides to your journey right willingly. And you will come to the Cimmerian isthmus[3] close by the narrow entrance to the lake; this you must leave with good courage, and pass the channel into the lake Maeotis. And there shall be to all time a great record among mortals of this your passage; for it shall be called *Bosporus* after your name. Then, leaving the land of Europe, you will arrive at the continent of Asia. Does not now this ruler of the gods seem to you to be alike overbearing in everything? Because he desired, though a god, to cohabit with this mortal, he imposed upon her[4] these long wanderings. Alas, my girl, a rueful suitor this that you have got for *your* marriage! For the account you have now heard you must not think has yet even come to the beginning.[5]

[1] Hermann thinks the poet alluded to the name Ἀράξης, as if from *ἀράσσειν*. This whole account, though full of great geographical errors, is very curious and instructive as an effort of descriptive geography five centuries B.C.

[2] So called because shipwrecked sailors were there plundered or massacred.

[3] The Crimea.

[4] 'Flung upon her,'—again a metaphor from a yoke.

[5] It is, as it were, only a kind of preface.

Io. O woe for me, alas, alas!

Pro. Aye! you cry out now and indulge in suppressed sighs; what will you do,[1] I should like to know, when you hear the rest of your troubles?

Cho. Why, is there anything yet left for you to tell her about her misfortunes?

Pro. Yes, a stormy sea of grievous sorrows.

Io. What gain then is it to me to remain in life? Why do I not rather throw myself with all speed from this craggy rock, that so by being dashed on the ground I may be rid of all my toils? For 'tis better once for all to die, than all one's days to be suffering evils.

Pro. Methinks you would bear *my* trials sadly amiss, to whom to die is not permitted by fate; for that would be a riddance from my troubles: but as it is, no limit is assigned me for my toils, until Zeus shall have been expelled from his sovereignty.

Io. Why, is it destined that Zeus should some day be deposed from his rule?

Pro. You would be pleased, I daresay, at seeing that event.

Io. Of course I should, when I am ill-treated by Zeus.

Pro. Then you may rest assured this shall really be so.

Io. By whom will he be robbed of his imperial sceptre?

Pro. By himself and his own senseless schemes.

Io. In what way? Inform me, if there is no harm.

Pro. He will make such a marriage as he will some day repent of.

Io. Divine, or human? If it may be spoken, tell me plainly.

Pro. What is it to you what marriage? It is *not* allowed to declare this.

Io. Is it by a wife that he is to be driven from his throne?

[1] *που* is used as if he had said, *ἄλλο τι δράσεις που*, 'you will act differently, I daresay,' &c.

Pro. Yes; she will bring forth a son stronger than his father.

Io. And has Zeus no means of averting this fortune?

Pro. No indeed, until I shall have been released from my bonds.

Io. Who then is there who will release you, against the will of Zeus?

Pro. It is fated that he shall be some one of your offspring.

Io. What say you? Shall a child of *mine* rid you from your troubles?

Pro. Yes, the thirteenth in direct descent.

Io. *This* prophecy is not one that can easily be guessed at.

Pro. And do not seek either to learn your own troubles.[1]

Io. Do not first hold out to me a gain, and then deprive me of it.

Pro. With one or other of two relations I will freely present you.

Io. Shew me first *what* relations, and leave the choice to me.

Pro. I offer it to you then: choose whether I should describe to you plainly the remainder of your toils, or the person that is to release me.

Cho. Of these favours be pleased to grant the one to her and the other to me; and spurn not our requests. To her declare the rest of her wandering, and to me, him who is to loose you; for that is what I long to know.

Pro. Since you are both eager, I will not oppose your wishes by refusing to tell all that you desire further to learn. To you first, Io, I will declare your wanderings up and down over many regions; and do you inscribe them in the mindful tablets of your heart.

When you shall have passed the stream that divides the two continents,—keeping your face towards the path of the blazing sun in the east proceed straight on in that direction;

[1] As you cannot know everything about the fate of Zeus, so be content to let your own trials remain uninquired into.

and first of all you shall meet with blasts from the north, where you must beware of the roaring tempest that careers wildly over the land, lest it should suddenly take you off your feet and catch you up with its inclement whirlwind . . . . as you pass the booming surge of the sea, until you arrive at the Gorgonian plains of Cisthene, where dwell the daughters of Phorcus, ancient maidens, three swan-shaped sisters, possessing one eye in common, and each one tooth; monsters that the sun never looks upon with his rays, nor the nightly moon at any time. And hard by dwell three sisters of theirs, covered with feathers, with snaky locks, the Gorgons, hateful to the human kind, which no mortal shall look upon and live. So much for *this* caution that I give you.[1] But hear now of another portentous sight: for the pointed-beaked dumb hounds of Zeus, the Griffins,[2] are to be guarded against, as also the one-eyed host of the Arimaspi, riders on horseback, who dwell by the gold-washing stream, the river of Pluto.[3] To these come not near: after them you will arrive at a far-distant land and a black race, who dwell near the sources of the sun, where is the river of Aethiopia.[4] Along the banks of this stream proceed till you reach a cataract, where from the heights of the Bybline mountains the Nile hurls its holy and wholesome stream. By this you will be guided into the three-cornered land made by the Nile; where it is fated for you, Io, and your descendants to found your far-off colony. If aught of what I have said is indistinct or hard to make out, go over it again, and learn it from me clearly; for I have more leisure here than I care for.

Cho. If you have anything more to tell her, or anything to supply that has been passed over in the account of her long and weary wanderings, say on: but if you have told

[1] *φρούριον.* Probably *φροίμιον*, 'such is the introductory account,' *i. e.* such are the monsters I have first to tell you of.

[2] Assyrian sculptures of hawk-headed men and animals give rise to this legend.

[3] Πλούτων, the god of wealth; a play on, or confusion between, Πλούτων and Πλοῦτος.

[4] Both here and in *Suppl.* 282, Aeschylus confounded Aethiopia with the East Indies, of which the vaguest accounts had reached Greece either from merchants or from information obtained through the Persians.

all, then do *us* in our turn the favour we ask; and you of course remember it.

Pro. She has already heard the whole extent of her journey; but, that she may be assured she is not being told an idle tale by me, I will state clearly the toils she has undergone before coming here, giving her this very proof that my account is true. The less interesting part[1] then of the story I will leave out, and proceed at once quite to the end of your wanderings. For, after you had come to the plains of the Molossi and the parts about the lofty-ridged Dodona, where is the oracle and prophetic seat of Zeus the god of the Thesproti, and that portent, surpassing belief, of the talking oaks, by which you were plainly and in no ambiguous terms addressed as the damsel destined to become the renowned spouse of Zeus,—if ought of these incidents presents itself pleasingly to your mind;—from thence, I say, driven madly by the brize along the road by the sea-coast, you sped onwards to the great gulf of Rhea,[2] from which point you commenced your trying journey in the return.[3] And for all future time, be well assured, that gulf of the sea shall be called *Ionian*, a record of your journey to it for all mankind. Such are the proofs I give you of my intelligence, that it sees somewhat more than has been presented to view. What remains now I will explain to you and to her in common, returning to the same track of my former narrative.[4] There is a city called Canopus, at the furthest extremity of Egypt, close by the very mouth and alluvial bar of the Nile. There Zeus is to restore you to your human consciousness, by stroking you with his gentle hand and touching you, but no more.[5] And, to commemorate by a name the author of a race descended from Zeus, you shall bring forth a son, the swarthy Epaphus,[6] who shall possess all the fertile plains that the

[1] The commonplace part, ὄχλον, namely, that which might weary rather than amuse. The phrase hardly admits of a very close rendering.

[2] The Hadriatic.

[3] Or, 'in returning from which you lost your way in a storm.'

[4] The point where I before left off, namely, v. 834.

[5] See on *Suppl.* 17.

[6] From ἐπαφή, 'touch.' The above version, if rather verbose, appears to give the meaning of an obscure phrase. See however on *Suppl.* 45.

Nile covers by its inundations.[1] And the fifth in descent from him, a family of fifty female children shall return again to Argos, not of their own free will, but to avoid an incestuous union with their cousins; and they, with hearts incited by desire, like falcons in close chase after doves, shall come in pursuit of a marriage they ought not to pursue: but the god shall grudge them the possession of their persons. And the land of Argos shall give them refuge, after they have slain their husbands by an act of feminine vengeance,[2] emboldened by the security of midnight. For each bride shall deprive her spouse of life, by embruing a two-edged sword in his throat. So may Cypris visit all who are enemies of mine.[3] One however of the maidens love shall soothe so as not to slay the partner of her couch, but her resolution shall be blunted; and of two evils she shall choose this one, to be called a coward rather than a murderess. From her in Argos shall spring a race of kings: it requires a long account to go over this matter so as to make it clear; however, from this stock shall spring a hero bold, renowned in archery, who shall deliver me from my present toils. Such was the prophecy which my mother Themis, of ancient Titanian birth, recounted to me. But by what means and in what way,—to tell *that* a long account is needed; and you by learning it all will be no gainer.

Io. Oh helas! O woe is me! Again does the racking pain and heart-piercing mad-fit make me inwardly smart, and the sharp point of the gad-fly, not forged by fire, punctures me. My heart through terror beats against my bosom; my eyes spin round as in an eddying circle, and I am being carried out of my course by a violent gust of madness,[4] without the power to control my tongue: but troubled words keep up a random conflict against the waves of this hateful curse.

[1] 'Who shall reap as much land as Nile waters when it flows broad.'

[2] θηλυκτόνῳ Ἄρει.—νυκτιφρουρήτῳ, 'sheltered by the darkness of night.'

[3] *i.e.* 'may my friends be spared from such a marriage.'

[4] A confused metaphor between a racecourse and a ship's course.

Cho. Wise indeed, truly wise was he, who first weighed in his mind this truth, and declared it as a maxim with his tongue, that *to marry according to one's condition is the best course by far:* and that *one who is an artisan should aspire to marry neither among those who are conceited of their wealth, nor among those who make much of their high birth.* Never, O ye goddesses of fate, never may ye see me becoming a partner of the bed of Zeus, nor may I be wedded to any spouse of the heavenly host. For I am full of fear when I see Io's virgin estate, that recoiled from the advances of Zeus, so grievously distressed by the laborious wanderings imposed on her by Hera. But to me marriage, when indeed it is equal, is devoid of fear, and I have no anxiety about it: but never may the love of any one of the mighty gods regard me with an eye from which there is no escape. *That* is a war not to be waged, offering nothing but difficulties; nor know I what in that case would become of me, for I see no means of escaping the designs of Zeus.

Pro. Assuredly the day will come when Zeus, though full of obstinate pride, will be humbled; for he is even now preparing to make such a marriage as shall oust him from his sovereignty and throne, and bring him to utter nothingness: and the curse of his father Kronos shall then at length have its full accomplishment,—that curse which he imprecated on him when he was being deposed from his ancient throne. From these troubles no other god than myself would be able to shew him plainly the way to escape. *I* know it, and how it is to be done. Let him then sit confident on his throne, trusting to the clatterings he can make in the sky, and brandishing in his hands the fire-flashing bolt! For these will not help to save him from being hurled down in disgrace, never to rise again. Such an antagonist is he now arming against himself, a monster most difficult for him to contend with, even one who shall discover a flame superior to that of lightning, and a mighty crash surpassing that of the thunder; yea, who shall scatter in fragments the trident, the earth-shaking disturber of the sea, the spear of Poseidon: and when he has struck his foot against this calamity, he will learn how widely different is the being a slave from the being a king.

Cho. You, of course, make your own wishes the grounds of your rash talk against Zeus.

Pro. What will be accomplished, and also what I desire, do I give utterance to.

Cho. And are we to expect that some one will be lord over Zeus?

Pro. Yea, he shall have troubles more difficult to bear even than these of mine.

Cho. But how is it that you have no fear in blurting out such threats?

Pro. What should I fear, to whom it is not destined to die?

Cho. But he might find for you a contest yet more painful than this.

Pro. Let him do it then: there is nothing I may not expect.

Cho. Those who do homage to Adrastea[1] are wise.

Pro. Go on worshipping, praying, cringing to any one that is in power! Why, *I* care less about Zeus than nothing. Let him do his worst, let him hold us in thrall for this brief time, even as he chooses; for he shall not long remain king over the gods. But here I see this courier of Zeus, this servant of our new lord and master! Of course he has come to tell me some news.

Hermes. You, the mighty genius, you, that are too bitterly bitter, you, who sinned against the gods by giving prerogatives to ephemeral man, you, the fire-stealer, I address. The Sire orders you to declare plainly what marriage you are so loudly talking about, and by whom he is to be deposed from his authority. And to these questions, mind, reply not in ambiguous language, but speak out plainly each and everything: so do not, Prometheus, give me the trouble of

[1] A goddess who impersonated inevitable destiny. 'Those who submit to necessity are wise.'

two journeys; and you see that Zeus is not at all softened by such ways as these.

Pro. Finely-worded, in truth, and full of pride, is the speech, for a servant of the gods! Ye are yet young in your new empire, and ye think forsooth to dwell in the celestial citadel with nothing to rue. Have not I from that very citadel known two tyrants driven out? And a third I shall yet see (expelled) with my own eyes, even the present ruler, more disgracefully and more quickly than they. Do I seem to you at all to fear and to be cowed by your new gods? Far am I, nay, wholly short of such feelings. So do you go back in all haste by the road you came; for you shall learn nothing of what you are questioning me about.

Her. It was by such defiant words however that before too you brought yourself[1] into these present troubles.

Pro. For your slavery my own evil plight, be well assured, *I* would not exchange.

Her. No: of course it is better to be a slave to this rock, than to be a trusty-minded[2] messenger to Zeus.

Pro. So to insult the insolent is right and proper.

Her. You seem to me to wanton in[3] your present sufferings.

Pro. Do I? So may I see my enemies wantoning; and you I reckon of their number.

Her. Why, do you blame *me* at all for your misfortunes?

Pro. In plain words I hate *all* the gods who, having been benefited by me, ill-treat me unjustly.

Her. I hear by your words that you are raving with no slight mad-fit.

Pro. I would fain continue to be mad, if it is madness to hate one's enemies.

Her. You would be beyond endurance, if you were in prosperity.

Pro. Ah me!

Her. *That* word Zeus knows not.

[1] Lit. 'wafted yourself.'

[2] φῦναι πιστὸν, i. e. φύσιν πιστὸν εἶναι.

[3] Or, 'pique yourself upon.'

Pro. But time that is passing away teaches all things.

Her. And yet *you* have not yet learned to be discreet.

Pro. No, or I should not have spoken to you, who are but a servant.

Her. It seems that you intend to tell none of the things the Sire demands.

Pro. Why truly, I owe him a favour, that I should repay him one.

Her. You flout me, as if forsooth I were a boy.

Pro. Why, are you not a boy, and yet more senseless than one, if you expect to learn anything from *me?* There is no torture nor any contrivance by which Zeus shall induce me to tell him these secrets, until my galling fetters shall have been loosed. Wherefore let there be hurled at me the blazing fire-bolt,—let him with his white-winged snow-shower and his earthquake rumblings throw everything into ruin and confusion; for none of these will bend me so far as to inform him by whom he is to be driven from his sovereignty.

Her. Consider well now, whether this course seems likely to help you.

Pro. Long ago, be assured, all this has been considered, and my plans have been formed.

Her. Have the sense, O foolish one, do have the sense at last to take a right view of your present sufferings.

Pro. You tease me to no purpose; you might as well talk over a wave. Never let it enter your mind that *I*, through fear of the resolution of Zeus, will become woman-hearted, and humbly supplicate that greatly detested one, with feminine upliftings of my hands, to release me from these bonds. I am as far as possible from that.

Her. It seems that, however much I may say, I shall say it in vain; for you do not at all relent, nor are you softened in your heart by my entreaties, but, holding the bit between your teeth like a newly-yoked colt, you plunge and fight against the rein. However, you are playing the violent by a trick that will serve you little: hardihood, to one who is ill-advised, of itself avails less than nothing. Now mark well, if you fail to comply with my words, how terrible a storm, and how huge a wave of calamity will come upon you without escape. For first, the Sire will shatter this craggy ravine with his thunder and fiery bolt, and will bury your body in the ruins, and the arm of the rock shall support you.[1] And when you have completed a long period of time, you shall return back to the light; but even then, be assured, the winged hound of Zeus, the dusky eagle, shall fiercely tear up a huge piece[2] of your mangled body, coming as an uninvited banqueter for the whole day, and shall feed on your liver when gnawed black. Of such an agony as this expect not any end, until some god shall have consented to descend into the sunless Hades, and to abide in the gloomy depths of Tartarus. Wherefore take good counsel, since this bold threat is not invented, but even too truly uttered; for the mouth of Zeus knows not how to speak falsely, but will accomplish everything it says. So do you be circumspect and take thought, and not imagine that obstinacy is ever better than good counsel.

Cho. To us indeed Hermes seems to speak very much to the point; for he bids you give up your obstinacy and seek after the good counsel which is wise. Be persuaded: for to the clever it is a discredit to be guilty of a mistake.

Pro. With full knowledge on my part, be assured, hath this messenger dinned his orders into my ears. Well! for an enemy to be ill-treated by enemies is but fair play.[3] Wherefore let there be hurled against me the doubly-pointed zig-zag lightning; let the upper air be convulsed with the thunder and the rack of the wild winds, and may the earth be made to quake from its foundations by the blast even to its very roots, and the wave of the sea with its ruffian foam be heaped together upon the paths of the stars; yea, may he catch up aloft and hurl my body into murky Tartarus

[1] 'The rock shall clasp you in its tight embrace.' The figure is perhaps from a nurse carrying a child.

[2] Lit. 'a great rag of your body.'

[3] 'Is nothing unbecoming.'

with irresistible fling;[1] do what he may, he can never make *me* die.

Her. Such in truth are the counsels and the words one may hear from the crazed. For in what respect is this rebel's conduct short of insanity; in what does he relax at all from his fits of madness? But at all events do you, who condole with his sufferings, retire quickly to some place away from this spot, lest the harsh bellowing of the thunder should stun and stupify your senses.

Cho. Suggest and talk me over to some other course that you may succeed in persuading me to: for assuredly *this* proposal that you villainously made me is not to be tolerated. How can I, as you bid me, practise baseness? In company with him I am willing to endure whatever I must: for I was taught to hate traitors, and there is no malady which I loathe more than this.

Her. At all events remember what I forewarn you of, and do not, when overtaken by calamity, blame your fortune, nor ever say that Zeus cast you into an unforeseen calamity,—no truly, but that you cast yourselves: for with a full knowledge, and neither suddenly nor secretly, will you be entangled in the endless net of Atè through your own folly.

Pro. And now truly in reality, and no longer in mere threat, the earth rocks; the subterranean sounds of thunder rumble past me, the fiery zig-zag streaks of lightning gleam from the sky, the whirlwinds carry along the dust in eddies, and the blasts of all the winds leap wildly forth, showing a strife of conflicting gusts against each other; yea, the welkin has felt the disturbance along with the sea. Such a turmoil of the elements is now coming visibly upon me from Zeus, to cause me alarm. O venerable mother mine,[2] O ether, that carriest round[3] a light common to all, are ye witnesses how unjustly I am treated?

[1] 'With the unbending turnings-round of necessity.' The δίνη is probably the movement of the arm round before a throw is made.

[2] Themis.

[3] The upper air, *ether*, or bright fiery element, was believed to move round with the stars, as part of the πόλος or revolution of the sky.

SEVEN AGAINST THEBES.

PERSONS REPRESENTED.

ETEOCLES.	ISMENE.
A MESSENGER.	ANTIGONE.
CHORUS OF THEBAN VIRGINS.	A HERALD.

Eteocles. People of the city of Cadmus! a man ought to speak words that are to the point,[1] when he has the care of affairs at the pilot's seat in the stern, and manages the helm of the state without closing his eyelids in sleep. For should we have gained success, it is caused by the god[2]; but if on the contrary (which heaven forbid!) calamity should have befallen us, then Eteocles alone would be plentifully abused by the inhabitants all over the city in noisy songs and wailings, of which may Zeus the Averter become *averter*, as his name implies, to the city of the Cadmeian people. But for the present it behoves you—both him who is yet short of the full vigour of youth, and him who is past the period of manly strength, but still keeps up a vigorous growth of body, and each one who is yet in his prime, as is proper for you all[3]—to bring aid to your city, and to the altars of your country's gods, that their sacrifices may never become extinct, and to your children and your common mother the Earth, your

[1] Cic. *de Orat.* i. § 112, 'ipsum *dicere* nunquam est non ineptum, nisi quum est necessarium.'

[2] *i. e.* people are sure to say so.

[3] *ὥστε συμπρεπές.* The reading of the Medicean shows that the original writing has been tampered with, and Weil reads, with great probability, *ὥραν ἔχων ἕκαστος ὥς τις ἐμπρεπής*, 'as each is conspicuous for the age he has,' *i. e.* whether under age, or past the usual military ἡλικία, so long as he is not actually decrepit.—*ὥραν*, a time of life more or less near 'the prime.' It is so used by Plato, *Phaed.* p. 80, c.

most kindly nurse. For she it was who, when you walked in childhood on her friendly soil, taking upon herself the entire charge and pains of educating you, brought you up to be her colonists and trusty champions, that you might become such for an emergency like this. And thus far indeed, up to the present day, the scale of fortune turns in our favour: for though we have so long been beleaguered by the enemy, the war for the most part is going on well, by the goodness of the gods. But *now*, as the seer informs me, the feeder of fowls, on considering well, by hearing and intelligence,[1] without the use of omens by fire, the warnings of birds[2] by his infallible art,—he, I say, the possessor of such means of divination, declares that the greatest attack yet made by the Argives is being discussed in midnight council, and that they are plotting against the city. So now to the battlements and the gates of the martels depart all of you, hasten in complete armour, man the breastworks, take your stand on the floors of the towers, and staying firm at the outlets through the gates, be of good courage, and fear not too much an army of invaders: the god will cause all to end well. For myself, I have sent scouts and spies of the enemy, who I am confident are not going the journey in vain: and when I have heard their report, there is no fear of my being caught by treacherous craft.

Mes. Eteocles, most noble king of the Cadmeians, I have come bringing you precise news from the enemy's lines; and I myself am an eye-witness of their doings. For seven chieftains, dashing captains of companies, slaughtering a bull over a dark-banded[3] shield, and touching with their hands the creature's gore, swore by Ares, Enyo, and bloodthirsty Rout, that they would either bring ruin on the city and ravage the stronghold of the Cadmeians by force, or by their own death

[1] Teiresias, being blind, could only use *ears* and *mind*, but not *eyes*. Hence the poet adds *πυρὸς δίχα*, because the divination by *ἔμπυρα* required the faculty of sight. Weil reads, with Ritschl, *φάους δίχα*, 'without eyesight,'—an emendation rather ingenious than highly probable.

[2] Oracular or ominous birds.

[3] *δέρμα κελαινὸν ἀσπίδος*, *Il.* vi. 117.

would imbrue[1] this earth with their blood. And they were engaged in fastening with their own hands to the chariot of Adrastus[2] memorials of themselves for their parents at home, shedding tears, but no word of lamentation was in their mouths. For their iron-hearted resolve, burning with courage, breathed a spirit like that of lions when they flash fighting from their eyes. And the tidings of these doings have not been retarded by delay.[3] When I left them they were drawing lots, that each of them, as his place was assigned him, might conduct his company up to the gates. To meet this, fail not to marshal as quickly as possible at the outlets of the gates the bravest men selected from the whole city; for by this time the Argive host in full array is marching close up, is raising the dust as it comes; while the white foam is staining the plain with droppings from the panting mouths of the steeds. But do you, like a good pilot of a ship, strengthen[4] the citadel in her bulwarks before the blasts of war have swept over them with the force of a hurricane; for the land-wave of the army is roaring even now. And for doing this seize the opportunity that comes soonest. For the rest I too will keep an eye on them like a trusty sentinel by day: and if you are informed of the enemy's movements by a clear account, you will keep yourself unharmed.

Et. O Zeus, and earth, and gods that protect our city! thou too, great Curse, the mighty Erinnys of my father's spirit! destroy not, I pray you, root-and-branch[5] in a common ruin, this city taken captive by the foe,—a city which speaks the language of Hellas,[6]—and our native homes: and grant that they may never hold[7] in the yoke of slavery the free land and city of Cadmus. But become our protectors; and

[1] Literally, 'make paste of.'

[2] They had been told by Amphiaraus the seer that Adrastus would return safe out of the fight.

[3] *i. e.* 'I have come with all speed to tell you.' Others give *πίστις*, 'the proof of all this will soon appear in the action.'

[4] 'Make tight and trim.'

[5] Lit. 'grub up from its roots.'

[6] Not barbaric. So *ἑτερόφωνος στρατὸς*, inf. 159.

[7] The scholiast, who explains *μὴ ὑπεξελθεῖν* (*ὑπελθεῖν* Weil) *ζυγὸν δουλείας* seems to have read *ἐνσχεθεῖν*, 'to be caught in.'

I think that what I say is the common interest of us both; for a city that is in prosperity pays honours to the gods.

Cho. I utter loud tones of grief through fear. The army is let loose and has left the camp. A vast host of cavalry in advance is pouring yonder in a stream upon our city. The dust in the air convinces me by its sudden appearance,—that voiceless but plain and true messenger. Even yet the plains of my native soil, beaten by the hoofs of the horses, bring the sound of war to my ears. It is borne on the breeze, it roars like a mountain-lashing irresistible torrent. O all ye gods and goddesses, fend from us the coming evil! With a war-shout on the other side of the wall the white-shielded host is rushing in full array against our city. Who then will rescue, who will assist us, of gods or goddesses? To the images of which of these deities[1] must *I* kneel? Ye blessed beings, firmly seated on your thrones,[2] 'tis full time we should cling to your statues: why do we delay through excess of grief? Hear ye, or hear ye not, the clash of shields? When, if not now, are we to engage in the supplications of the peplus and of wool-tufted boughs? I am conscious of a loud din—there is the clattering of more than one spear. What wilt thou do—abandon to thine own land, Ares, ancient patron of our country? God of the golden casque, regard, favourably regard, the city which once thou didst hold well beloved! Ye gods, protectors of the land, come ye, come all, and see a suppliant band of maidens praying to escape slavery. For a wave of slant-crested warriors encircling the city roars like the surge on the beach, impelled by the blast of Ares. But do thou, O Zeus, almighty Sire, by all means avert capture by the enemy. For the Argives are environing the city of Cadmus: we are in dread of the foeman's arms. The bits strapped across the horses' jaws clink slaughter; and seven champions, conspicuous above the rest of the host for their

[1] Male or female. The Chorus asks what gods *they* are to appeal to, as women, *i. e.* whether the same or different from those Eteocles has just invoked.

[2] Not disposed to abandon the city. Cf. 207.

lancers' uniform, are standing at the seventh gate,[1] having had their places assigned them by lot. But do thou, war-loving power, born from Zeus, become the deliverer of our city, Pallas; and thou, equestrian god, ruler of the sea with thy fish-piercing trident,[2] Poseidon, grant, O grant us a release from our fears! Thou too, Ares—alas for our fate!—guard the city which bears the name of Cadmus,[3] and show thy regard for it by visibly interfering in its behalf. Cypris too, who art the ancestress of our race, keep them away from us; 'tis from thy blood that we are sprung; thee therefore we approach, raising our voices in heaven-moving[4] prayers. Thou also, O wolf-king,[5] become wolfish to a hostile army at the utterance of these sighs of ours: and thou, virgin child of Latona, hold in readiness thy bow. Ha! ha! the booming sound of chariots round the city strikes my ears: O queen Hera, the naves of the weighted axles creak: Artemis, goddess dear! And now the air hurtling with spears joins in the commotion. What is about to happen to our city? What will become of it? How much further is the god protracting the issue of the fray?

Ha! ha! a shower of stones is hitting the battlements: they are pelted to their very tops. O friendly Apollo, there is the clinking of brass-bound shields at the very gates: and from Zeus alone[6] can come a righteous end of the contest which this war is to decide. Thou also, blessed queen Onca,[7] enthroned upon our citadel, deliver thy seven-gated sacred seat. O ye deities, all powerful to save, efficient guardians of the towers of this land, both gods and goddesses, surrender not to an alien host[8] a city hard pressed by the spear. Hear

[1] Not having yet departed to their respective posts.

[2] The stabbing and slaughter of the enemy is compared to the harpooning of the tunny. See *Pers.* 426. The gods here are generally invoked in their *hostile* attributes.

[3] Cadmus had married Harmonia, daughter of Ares.

[4] 'God-invoking.' See on *Cho.* 639.

[5] One attribute of Apollo was that of a god of herds and wild animals (see *Agam.* 55), whence he was called Νόμιος. This is the origin of the legend that Apollo fed the flocks and herds of Admetus. He is λυκοκτόνος θεὸς in Soph. *El.* 6. See *Suppl.* 668.

[6] And there is nothing left for us, but that God may defend the right.

[7] The Phenician name of Pallas.

[8] To a host that speaks a dialect different from the Theban.

from virgins, hear, as in duty bound, their prayers offered with outstretched hands, ye friendly god; and by closing round our city as her deliverers prove that you love the land and people; be concerned for the public sacrifices, and through your concern assist us; yea, and be mindful, I pray you, of the solemn rites celebrated at the altars of the city.[1]

Et. I ask you, unbearable creatures that you are! do you think this the best course, and one likely to save the city, or to encourage the army beleaguered within these walls,—to fall down at the statues of the gods who preside over the city, and bawl and blubber, ye objects of hate to all who have common sense? Never, either in trouble or in dear prosperity, may I have to dwell with the womankind. For, if they have the upper hand, their impudence is such that one cannot keep their company; and if they are in fear, they are a yet greater nuisance to the household and the city. And so even now in the citizens, when you made these hurried flights through the streets, you caused by your noisy cries a cowardly faintheartedness. Why, you are forwarding in the best possible way the cause of the enemy without; we are being sacked by our own doings from within. Such are the blessings one gets by living with women. And now I tell you, if any shall refuse to obey my authority, whether man or woman, or if there be aught between the two,[2] a court-martial shall pass capital sentence upon them, and they need not think to escape being stoned to death by the people. For matters out-of-doors are the care of the man,—let not a woman have a voice about them: keep you at home, and so cause no further mischief. Do you hear, or do you not hear? Can it be that I am speaking to one that is deaf?

Cho. O dear son of Oedipus, I felt afraid[3] when I heard the din, the loud din of the rattling chariots, when the axle-boxes creaked as they went round with the wheels, and I

[1] *φιλοθύτων ὀργίων*, 'rites customary at sacrifices,' may be compared with *φιλοσπόνδου λιβὸς*, *Cho.* 284.

[2] He alludes to such persons as eunuchs, &c.

[3] This is apologetic.

heard the steering-gear[1] of the horses in their mouths, even the fire-forged bits.

Et. What then? did ever yet the sailor, by leaving the rudder and flying to the images of the gods in the prow,[2] find a means of deliverance, when the ship was in distress upon breakers?

Cho. I did but throw myself in haste upon the ancient images of the deities, trusting to the gods, when there was a roar of a deadly shower of stones falling thick and fast at the gates. *Then* indeed I *was* carried away by fear to say my prayers to the immortals, that they would extend their protection over the city.

Et. Pray that the towers may remain proof against the hostile spear.

Cho. Is it not then from the gods that this boon must come?

Et. Do as you like: but there is a saying, that the gods of a captured city depart and leave it to its fate.

Cho. Never in *my* time may this august assembly of gods desert us! Never may I live to see this city overrun by plunderers, and our[3] . . . being burned with hostile fire.

Et. Do not, in your invocation of the gods, pursue evil counsel; for obedience to authority is the parent of good order,[4] an offspring that is powerful to save. So the saying is.

Cho. It is so: but as yet the might of the god is above theirs; and often in the midst of evils it raises up[5] the helpless, even[6] when clouds of perplexing distress hang over his eyes.

Et. That is the part of men, to offer sacrifices and victims

[1] The guiding reins.—*ἄΐον*, 'I heard,' is Elmsley's conjectural reading for *ἀΰπνων*.

[2] 'By flying from stern to prow.'—*καμούσης*, lit. 'had foundered against a wave in the sea.' Plat. *Theæt.* p. 170, A., *ὅταν ἐν θαλάσσῃ χειμάζωνται ὥσπερ πρὸς θεοὺς ἔχουσι τοὺς ἄρχοντας, σωτῆρας σφῶν προσδοκῶντες.*

[3] *στράτευμα* is corrupt. The two first letters are written in the Medicean MS. by a later hand over an erasure. For *δαΐῳ* we should probably read *δαϊωθὲν*, from *δῃοῦσθαι*.

[4] Read *εὐταξίας*, not *εὐπραξίας*.

[5] Lit. 'sets on his legs again.' Read *ἀνορθοῖ*, or perhaps *νεφέλαν ἀπωθεῖ*.

[6] *καὶ* for *κἀκ* Weil, with Marcellinus *in vit. Thucyd.*

to the gods when foemen are making attempts upon a city; but 'tis yours, on the other hand, to be silent and to keep within the house.

Cho. It is through the agency of the gods that we live in a city yet unsubdued, and that the walls keep out the hosts of the foeman. What Nemesis is justly offended at this?[1]

Et. 'Tis not that I object to your paying honour to the gods; but, that you may not make the citizens fainthearted, keep quiet and be not so excessively afraid.

Cho. On hearing a sudden noise I came all in disorder with fear and dread into the Acropolis here, the august seat of the gods.[2]

Et. Do not now, if you should hear of any dying or wounded, hastily carry them off with lamentations. For 'tis on this that Ares feeds,—the slaughter of mortals.

Cho. Hark! surely I hear the neighing of horses.

Et. Do not, if you hear it, hear too plainly.

Cho. The fortress echoes from beneath,[3] as if the enemy were environing it.

Et. Well it is enough if *I* take measures about that.

Cho. I am in fear, and the battering at the gates increases.

Et. Do be silent, and say nothing about it in the city.

Cho. O associate powers, abandon not our fortifications.

Et. A plague upon you! Bear these dangers in silence.

Cho. Ye gods of the city, grant I may not suffer the fate of slavery.

Et. You yourself are making slaves both of yourself and of the whole city.

Cho. Almighty Zeus, turn against the enemy thy dart.[4]

Et. O Zeus,[5] what a race is this of women thou hast given us!

[1] At our praying to them on that account. Or perhaps, 'who is of so captious a spirit as to say he dislikes this?'

[2] Hoping the enemy would hesitate to drag away a suppliant from the altars.

[3] As if with the heavy tramp of an army without.

[4] Or perhaps, 'their own darts.' Sophocles, *Trach.* 1014, has ἐπιτρέπειν ἔγχος ἐπί τινι.

[5] He probably ironically imitates their tone of voice.

Cho. Bad enough—e'en as men when their city has been taken.

Et. Are you boding evil again, even while you have hold of the images?[1]

Cho. For terror carries away my tongue through faintheartedness.

Et. If you would but grant me a trifling favour at my request——

Cho. Say on, the sooner the better, and I shall quickly know.

Et. Be quiet, wretched woman, and alarm not your friends.

Cho. I have done: with others I will suffer what is fated.

Et. This word of yours I prefer to your other words: and beside this, keeping aloof from the images,[2] pray for the better fortune, that the gods may be our allies. And when you have heard *my* prayers, then do *you* chant a sacred paean of auspicious acclamation to the gods, as is the custom of the Hellenic people to raise a shout at a sacrifice,—an encouragement to your friends, tending to remove the dread of the enemy. I on my part make this promise to the gods of the country who protect the city, and those who occupy the plains and watch over the Agora,—to the springs of Dirce and the waters of Ismenus,—that if all turns out well, and the city comes safely out of the war, we will imbrue with the blood of slaughtered sheep the altars of the gods, and make a solemn offering of the trophies; while the garments of the enemy I will hang up before the shrines, set up upon spears in their holy temples.[3] This[4] is what you are to pray for to the gods, not with such fondness for sighs,

[1] The Greeks had a great dislike to mix evil with good. See on *Agam.* 620.

[2] They are to retire for a while, that Eteocles may address himself more directly to the gods.

[3] This passage has been tampered with by actors, grammarians, or transcribers. I have omitted a verse in the translation, which seems interpolated, *ταυροκτονοῦντας θεοῖσιν, ὧδ' ἐπεύχομαι.* This verse was inserted in consequence of the corruption of v. 262, by which *λέγω* could no longer govern the infinitives.

[4] Namely, *τὰ κρείσσω*, above, v. 255.

nor with vain and wild sobbings;[1] for you will not any the more escape what is fated. But I will go and post at the seven outlets in the wall, to oppose the enemy in their own grand style,[2] six champions. with myself for a seventh. before messengers in hot haste and quickly spreading rumours arrive, and set all ablaze by the urgency of the need.

Cho. I mind what you say; but fear does not let my heart slumber, for anxieties ever pressing round it keep alive my alarm at the host which surrounds our walls, even as a dove trembling at every sound and mindful of her callow young feels a dread of snakes, the fell invaders of her nest. For now some of them[3] are advancing against the towers with all their hosts and in full battle-array. What will become of me? Others[4] are hurling against the citizens assailed from both sides the rugged stone. By every means in your power, ye Jove-born gods, rescue the city of the descendants of Cadmus! And where will you get in exchange a plain in any country better than this, if you shall once have resigned to the enemy this deep-soiled land, and the water of Dirce, most wholesome to drink of all streams that Poseidon the earth-holder sends forth, and the daughters of Tethys? Wherefore, O gods that protect our city, cast upon our enemies without the wall a panic that shall cause them to lose their men and to throw away their own shields,[5] and gain for yourselves glory from our citizens. Yea, remain firm in your seats as deliverers of our city, moved by our piercing shrieks and entreaties. For it were a pitiable thing to send before its time to Hades a city so ancient, made a slave as the prize of war, and given up by the gods to be ignominiously laid waste by an Argive leader in crumbling ashes: that the women should be led away captives in chains, alas! both young and old, dragged like cattle by the hair, with their garments hanging in tatters about them: that the

[1] Exclamations of *πόποι*. From *ποι-φύσσειν* or *-φύζειν*, like *φεύζειν*, *οἰμώζειν*, *ὀτοτύζειν*.

[2] 'In that great way (of theirs).'

[3] The *ὁπλῖται*.

[4] The *ψιλοί*.

[5] *αὐτορίψοπλον* I have restored from the gloss of the Schol. Med.

plundered city too[1] should resound with cries for aid while captives are being ravished, their voices mingling with the uproar. Truly I foresee with alarm so grievous a fate. For it is lamentable for those just grown into girlhood, before the rites that cull the early fruits of virginity, to go through an odious journey away from their homes. What can I say? Why, that the dead fare better than they. For many dismal sufferings has a city to endure when it has been conquered in war. One man takes captive another, this man he slays, that house he even fires. The whole city is stained and blackened with smoke; and Ares, raving wild, quelling the courage of the people, fans the flame, violating religion.[2] Confused shouts prevail throughout the city, and against it is set a net to be thrown over the walls;[3] while man slays his fellow-man with the spear. The piteous cries of newly-born infants at the breast all stained with blood, resound, and plundering goes on, akin to the wild scurry through the streets. Plunderer has a lucky meeting[4] with plunderer, and the empty-handed invites the empty-handed, wishing to have him for a partner, —each alike desirous to get spoils neither less than nor in an equal[5] share with the rest. What have we reasonably to look for from this? Fruits too of all kinds thrown upon the ground cause pain at the waste, when they meet the eye, truly no cheerful one, of the housewives. The ample bounty of the earth mixed indiscriminately together is borne along in a worthless current; and the young slave-girls are filled with a new grief because the foeman has the upper hand, and is in possession of their unhappy captive beds. They only hope that the night of death may come in aid of their most woeful sufferings.

[1] Probably we should read *βοᾶν δὲ καὶ κενουμέναν πόλιν*, for *βοᾷ δ' ἐκκενουτένα πόλις*.

[2] *i.e.* burning the very temples.

[3] Forming a *στεγανὸν δίκτυον*, *Ag.* 349, as if to inclose the inhabitants. Or perhaps, 'a tower-clad enclosure,' like the wall investing Platææ, described in *Thuc.* iii.

[4] *σύμβολοι* were ominous objects on a journey, *Prom.* 495.

[5] *i.e.* 'but even more.' The passage is obscure, and the text uncertain. I have here rendered the old reading, *τί ἐκ τῶνδ' εἰκάσαι λόγος πάρα* (Schol. *ἢ πένθη καὶ συμφοράς*); but I fear it is corrupt.

Cho. (*A*). Here, if I mistake not, comes the scout to bring us, my friends, some new tidings of the army, plying in haste the racing paces of his feet.[1]

Cho. (*B*). And lo! here also comes the king himself, the son of Oedipus, at the precise moment for hearing the messenger's news: and *his* pace also is made irregular by its speed.[2]

Mes. I can describe, from full knowledge of them, the affairs of the enemy, and how each chief has been appointed by lot to his position at one of the gates. Tydeus, in the first place, is already shouting defiance at the gates of Proetus: but the seer will not hear of his crossing the ford of the Ismenus, for the sacrifices are not yet favourable. But Tydeus, furious and eager for the fight, utters angry cries like the hissings of a serpent in midday heat, and assails with reproaches the sage son of Oecleus[3] the seer, that he is shy of meeting his fate, and wishes to avoid the fray from a want of spirit. While he talks thus he nods a triple shadowy crest, his helmet's plume; and underneath the man's shield brazen bells clang forth fear. On the outside of it he bears this arrogant device, a sky wrought on it all blazing with stars; but a bright full moon in the centre of the shield, the queen of stars, the eye of night, shines conspicuous. Thus madly vaunting himself with his boastful accoutrements he stands shouting by the river bank, eager for the fray, even as a horse that pants violently against the curb that restrains him.[4] Whom will you appoint as champion against this man? Who is competent to undertake the defence of the gates of Proetus when the fastenings have been undone?

[1] The metaphor from the wheels of a chariot is untranslateable into English.

[2] For *οὐκ ἀπαρτίζει* Weil reads *εὖ καταρτίζει*, 'well brings his foot here at the right time.'

[3] Amphiaraus. The two characters are well contrasted: one all reckless and impatient, the other prudent and biding his time.

[4] The MSS. add a verse, which, from the false use of *ὅστις*, must be condemned as spurious, *ὅστις βοῇ σάλπιγγος ὁρμαίνει μένων*. This is a conjectural filling up of *-αίνει μένων*, written as a variant of *-αίνων μένει* above or under the end of the preceding verse.

Et. As for a man's uniform, *I* am not the person to fear it; nor do the devices he carries inflict wounds. Crests and bells bite not without the spear. And as for this night, which you say is pictured on his shield glittering with stars in the sky,—it may perchance become prophetic to him by a special meaning. For, if *night* should have fallen upon his eyes in death, then indeed to the bearer of it this arrogant device would rightly and justly sustain its own name; and so he will have his own insolence prophetic against himself. For my part, to Tydeus I will oppose the good son of Astacus here, as a champion at the gates,—a man right nobly born, one who holds in reverence the throne of Honour, and hates boastful words. For his practice is to abstain from base actions, yet by no means to play the coward. And from the heroes that sprung out of the sown teeth of the dragon, and were spared by Ares, his pedigree is derived,—and a thorough native he is, Melanippus.[1] Well! the issue Ares will decide by a throw of the dice: but he is being sent on the mission of justice, his kinswoman true, to ward off from the mother that bore him the foeman's spear.

Cho. May the gods now grant success to my champion, as he goes forth to fight for his city in the right cause! But I dread to see the bloody deaths of those who perish in defence of their friends.

Mes. To him may the gods give good fortune, even as you say. But Capaneus has obtained his post at the Electran gates,—a giant he, taller than the chief before described; and his boast breathes a spirit more than human, while he threatens our walls with horrors, which may fortune never bring to pass! For whether the god wills it or wills it not, he declares he will sack the city; and that not even the angry bolt of Zeus falling on the plain at his very feet[2] shall stop him. As for the lightnings and thunderbolts of the god, he likens them to the heat of the midday sun. And he bears as a

[1] Son of Astacus mentioned above.

[2] ἐμποδὼν, not ἐκποδὼν, is the reading of MS. Med.

device a half-dressed[1] man carrying a torch, and a lighted brand blazes in his hands ready for action; and he says, in letters of gold, *I will burn the city.* Against so dread a foe send,—who will confront him? Who will await the vaunting soldier without trembling?

Et. In respect of this (device) too[2] a gain accrues to the former gain: so true it is, that of men's vain conceits their tongue ever becomes a sure accuser. Now Capaneus threatens, with full resolve to act, in open contempt of the gods;[3] and exercising his eloquence with vain delight, though but a mortal wight, he is sending swelling words audibly up to heaven against Zeus. But I have full belief that against him *will* come, with the aid of justice, the fire-bearing bolt, in no respect resembling the hot rays of the midday sun. And now to oppose him, vain-boaster as he is, I have appointed a hero fierce as fire in his courage, the sturdy Polyphontes, a guard who will prove well able to maintain his post, by favour of Artemis the protectress and the aid of other gods. Now tell of another who has got a place at another gate.

Cho. Perish the man who utters proud boasts against our city! and may the thunderbolt stop his career, 'ere he burst in upon my chamber and carry me off captive from my virgin retreat with overbearing spear!

Mes. Well then, I will tell you of the man who has gained by lot his post at the next city gate. To Eteocles third in order the third ballot leapt from out of the upturned brazen casque, to bring up his company for an attack on the Neïstan gates. His mares, snorting fiercely in their head-gear, he is driving round and round, ready and willing as they are to fall dead at the gates. And the nose-pipes[4] make a whistling noise in eastern fashion, when filled by the breath of their loud-sounding nostrils. His shield too is blazoned[5]

[1] γυμνόν, lightly attired for active service.

[2] For κέρδει Weil reads κόμπῳ, which is probably true.

[3] Despising the thunders of Zeus.

[4] A kind of nozzle, or pipe, inserted in the nostrils of a horse to increase the snorting sound. It seems to have been an Asiatic invention.

[5] σεσημάτισται Weil, εἰσημάτισται MS. Med.

in no humble style; for a heavy-armed warrior is treading the steps of a ladder to scale an enemy's fortress, as if eager to sack it. *He* also[1] calls out, as one may spell in letters, that *not even the god of War shall force him to retire from the walls.* Against this man likewise send some one competent to keep off from our city the yoke of slavery.

Et. I will at once send this officer, and may he go with good fortune.[2] . . . . . And already there has been sent one whose boasting is in his hands.[3] Megareus, the offspring of Creon, of the race of Sparti,[4] who assuredly will not, through fear of the noise of rampant snorting horses, retire from his post at the gate: but either by his death he will repay in full the debt owed to his native land for his nurture, or, by capturing the man himself together with the warrior and city on his shield, he will adorn with the spoils his father's house. Now tell me of some other braggart, and grudge me not the account.

Cho. I pray for success upon *his* head, O champion of my home! but failure for the foe; and as they utter too arrogant words against our city, with frenzied mind, so may Zeus the awarder of Justice regard them with feelings of wrath.

Mes. Another, the fourth, holding the gate near the statue of Athena Onca, is standing by it with a war-whoop, the burly form and massive mould of Hippomedon. The ample disk,—the orb, I mean, of his shield,—made me shudder as he swung it round; I will not deny it. And the designer, whoever he was, proved himself to be no common artist, when he furnished this device on the shield,—a Typho sending forth through his fire-breathing mouth sable smoke, the flickering sister of flame. And the convex side of the bulging hollow shield has a groundwork laid down upon it by circling wreaths of snakes.[5] And he himself raised a

[1] Like Capaneus before.

[2] Some lines appear to have been lost, as this speech of Eteocles should contain fifteen verses instead of only nine.

[3] *i.e.* not on his tongue, nor on a blazoned shield.

[4] Those mentioned in v. 407.

[5] Those, namely, proceeding from the head and feet of Typhon or Typhoeus, a snaky monster (*Prom.* 363).

war-shout, and inspired by Ares is furious for the fight, like some bacchant, glaring terror from his eyes. Against such a man's attack we must be well prepared: for already defeat is being confidently talked of at the gate.

Et. In the first place Onca Pallas, as the patroness of our city, stationed close to her gate,[1] hating the violence of a man,[2] will keep him off as (a bird does) a fell snake from her brood. Next, Hyperbius, the valiant son of Oenops, has been chosen to oppose him, man to man, ready as he is to ascertain his fate at fortune's call, and neither in form nor courage, nor in the bearing of his arms, to be disparaged.[3] Truly, Hermes has matched them well; for not only is the man hostile to the man with whom he will be set to fight, but they will bring into the fray hostile gods on their shields; for the one of them bears a fire-breathing Typhoeus, while for Hyperbius father Zeus sits throned[4] on the shield as if holding his ground in fight, brandishing a flaming bolt in his hands; and no one yet has seen Zeus defeated. Such is the friendship of the gods on either side; and we are on that of the victorious, they on that of the defeated.[5] Nor can it be doubted that men thus matched against each other will also fare thus; since of course Zeus is mightier than Typho in the fight, while to Hyperbius, in accordance with his device, he is likely to prove a preserver, being painted so on his shield.

Cho. I do trust indeed that he who bears on his buckler the adversary of Zeus, the loathed form of the earth-born fiend, a portrait hateful to both mortals and to the everliving gods, will lay his head low before the gates.

Mes. So may it prove! But the fifth champion I next describe, appointed to the fifth, the Northern gate right

[1] Having her statue at the Ὀγκαῖαι πύλαι, (or Ὠγύγιαι, if Hesychius be right).

[2] There seems an allusion to the *Virgin* goddess (*Eum.* 707), and ὕβριν has a secondary sense, namely, that of violence offered to woman, as in *Suppl.* 96. Hence, probably, ἀνδρός is used, not τἀνδρός.

[3] 'A smart soldier,' we should say.

[4] Compare *Suppl.* 94, 589. Gr. 'sits standing,' *i.e.* as if unmoved in the fight.

[5] *Our* gods, Pallas and Zeus, are conquerors; *their* god, Typhoeus, is conquered by Zeus.

opposite to the tomb of the Jove-born Amphion. And he swears by the lance which he holds, and which he has the assurance to pay more regard to than to the god, and to value higher than his own dear eyes, that he will sack the city of the Cadmeians by the force of his spear.[1] So says the fair-faced offspring of a mountaineer mother, a stripling hero. And the whisker is just spreading over his cheeks,—for his youthful prime begins to make it grow,—the hair that is rising thickly upon them. But he, with savage intent, not at all bearing out his maiden name,[2] and with a terrible eye, takes his post there. Nor indeed without a vaunting device does he stand by the gate; for the reproach of our city (represented) on his brazen shield, the circular defence of his person,—the raw-feeding Sphinx fastened on to it by studs,—he was moving to and fro, a bright embossed form. And she is carrying off in her talons a fighting-man, one of the Cadmeians, so that most of the darts are aimed at this man.[3] And now that he has come, he seems likely to do no stint trade in fighting, and to bring no discredit on the long journey he has gone through, this Parthenopaeus from Arcadia. Such is the man, who though but a stranger in the land, still desires to repay Argos for rearing him to these fair proportions, and so he threatens these towers with a fate, which may heaven not accomplish![4]

Et. Well, if they do but get from the gods the same fate they intend against us, then truly, with all those unhallowed boastings of theirs, they will perish miserably in utter destruction. But against this man also,—this Arcadian you speak of,—we have a champion, not fond of empty boasting, but with a hand that has an eye[5] to what can be done, Actor,

[1] Or, 'in spite of Zeus.' (*βίᾳ Διὸς* Med.).

[2] Parthenopaeus from *παρθένος*. Weil transposes these two lines (531-2) to follow 523, after which he supposes a verse to have been lost containing the name of Parthenopaeus. But it is sufficiently implied in *παρθένων ἐπώνυμον*.

[3] His insulting device would provoke the Thebans to aim at him, Parthenopaeus, most.

[4] The foregoing speech, which is extremely difficult to translate, appears to have been tampered with, perhaps by actors who reproduced the play.

[5] Similarly *φρὴν ὠμματωμένη*, *Cho.* 839.

the brother of him I last mentioned.[1] *He* will not let words without deeds run fluently inside the gates[2] and increase the mischief, nor will he allow the bearer of the portrait of that most odious monster on his hostile shield to pass within the walls.[3] No! it shall stay outside, and complain of him who would fain carry it in, when it meets with many a hard knock under the city wall. In all which, if heaven wills, I shall prove a true prophet.[4]

Cho. Your words go through my breast, and the locks of my hair stand on end at hearing the loud threats of these loud-boasting impious men. O that the gods may destroy them 'ere they leave this land!

Mes. I proceed to describe the sixth chief,—a most discreet man, and at the same time most brave in fight, the seer Amphiaraus. He, posted at the Homoloian gates, abuses much with reproachful words the headstrong Tydeus, as 'the homicide', 'the disturber of the city', 'the chief teacher to Argos of all this harm', a 'summoner of the Fury', a 'minister of slaughter', and 'the adviser of these evils to Adrastus'. Then again he calls on your brother, the valiant Polynices, uplifting his eyes in reference to his father's death,[5] and twice reproachfully dwelling on the words of his name at the end of his address.[6] And this is the language he gives utterance to: 'Truly such a deed is well-pleasing even to the gods,—glorious too for posterity to hear of and talk about, —that you sacked your native city and the temples of your country's gods, by throwing in an army of alien race! As no plea of justice will staunch the fountain of a mother's blood,[7] so your native land, if once captured by the spear through your zeal, will never again fight on your side. I know then

[1] Hyperbius.

[2] 'He will not let this talker add to the talking already there, namely, by the women.'

[3] Weil reads *τεῖχος* for *θηρός*.

[4] This verse does not seem genuine.

[5] Shewing that he was shocked at the impiety of Polynices in being instrumental to the death of his father Oedipus.

[6] Ending his speech with *ὦ Πολύ-νεικες πολύ—νεικες.*

[7] Or perhaps 'tears.' Weil adopts *πληγὴν* from Seidler. But no poet could use such a phrase as 'extinguishing a blow': it is simply nonsense.

that for my own part, I shall enrich[1] this land, when I lie buried as a seer under a hostile soil. So let us fight: I look for no inglorious fate.' So spoke the prophet, as he wielded the well-turned circle of his shield all covered with brass: but there was no device on its orb. For he wishes not merely to *seem* best and bravest, but to *be* so, for he gathers his harvest from a deep-soil furrow through a mind, out of which those honest counsels grow. Against *him* I advise you to send both wise and brave antagonists: he is a formidable foe, who reveres the gods.

Et. Alas for the omen among mortals that brings the just man to share the same fate as the impious! In every affair of life there is nothing worse than fellowship with the bad; the crop is never worth the reaping; the field of folly[2] produces no fruits from it but death. For if a religious man embarks in a ship with hot-headed sailors and a set of evil-doers, he perishes together with the heaven-detested crew: or if he acts in any matter with citizens who are treacherous to strangers and unmindful of the gods, himself being honest, he falls, by the decree of justice, into the same snare with them, and dies stricken with that scourge of the god from which none can escape. Now this seer,—this son of Oecleus I mean, a discreet, honest, brave, and religious man, a great prophet too,—by joining with impious and bold-speaking men, who are making a long march in defiance of their own reason, will, if Zeus so chooses, be dragged down with them to reach that far-off city.[3] I expect then that he will not attack the gates at all:—not that he has no spirit, or through any cowardice of disposition, but he knows it is destined for him to perish in the course of the fight,[4] if the oracles of Apollo

[1] Lit. 'fatten,' namely, by his corpse; but alluding principally, perhaps, to the offerings which would be brought to his tomb, since he was destined to be worshipped as a hero-prophet.

[2] Contrasted with the field of good sense, in v. 589.

[3] Namely, from whose bourn no traveller returns. The fate of Amphiaraus, who was swallowed up alive with his chariot, is alluded to; otherwise the poet merely means *ξυναπολεῖται*.

[4] Schol. *οὐκ εἰς κίνδυνον ἑαυτὸν καθήσει*. He was *not*, however, to perish in the fight itself. Is the true reading *ἀλλ' οἶδεν ὡς χρὴ μὴ τελευτῆσαι μάχῃ*?

do not prove fruitless: and Apollo is wont to be silent, or to say what is to the point.[1] Nevertheless, we will post against him as a champion the mighty Lasthenes, a warder of the gate who is no friend to strangers, old indeed in wisdom, though he still has a growing youthful frame, a nimble eye, and a hand that is not slow to snatch the naked spear from the side of his shield. But it is the special gift of the god for mortals to succeed.

Cho. Hear, ye gods, our just prayers, and accomplish them, that our city may be successful, averting the horrors of war from us upon the invaders of the land; and may Zeus strike and slay them with his bolt from without the walls!

Mes. The seventh and last chieftain,—him at the seventh gate,—I will describe, even your own brother, (that you may know) what fortunes he imprecates with curses on the city. He prays that he may stand on the walls, and after being proclaimed king to the whole land, and having shouted over it a paean of joy for its capture, he may meet you in the fight, and slay you, if he falls dead by your side;[2] or that, if you survive, he may in turn banish you as the author of his disgrace, and requite you with exile,[3] in the very same way. Such are his words; and he calls upon the gods of his fatherland, the protectors of his race, to regard with favour his prayers.[4] And he carries a newly-made well-fitting buckler, and a twofold device affixed upon it: for the figure of a man, wrought in gold, represented to the eye as in full armour,[5] is being conducted by a female form, modestly leading him. *My name is Justice* (so the inscription says), *and I shall restore this man to his rights, and he shall regain his city and the range of his paternal home.* Such are the devices of the hostile chiefs. 'Tis for yourself now to decide whom

[1] Weil transposes this verse to follow 618.

[2] *κτανεῖν θανὼν* is restored from the Schol. Med.

[3] This passage is very obscure, and the reading uncertain. Perhaps, *ἢ ζῶν, ἀτιμαστῆρος ὣς ἀνδρηλάτης, κ.τ.λ.*

[4] The MSS. add a verse which I omit, as probably spurious, *τῶν ὧν γενέσθαι πάγχυ Πολυνείκους βία.*

[5] A *hoplite.*

you propose to send; for you shall never have reason to find fault with me for my messages. Do you, I say, decide how the state is to be steered.

Et. O house of ours, infatuated by the gods, and the object of their deep detestation! O family of Œdipus, all steeped in tears![1]—Alas, now indeed my father's curse is having its accomplishment.[2] However this is not the fitting time to cry or to lament, lest a yet more grievous[3] wail should be produced from it. But to him who so well sustains the import of his name, Polynices, I say it,—we shall soon know how the device on his shield will end; whether he will be restored to his throne by golden letters that babble on his shield, but have no sound sense in them.[4] Now if the virgin daughter of Zeus, Justice, had attended his actions and intentions, perhaps that might have been so; but never yet, either when he first came into light from his mother's womb, or while he was growing up, or after he had come to manhood, or in the thick tufting of the hair on his chin, did Justice have a word to say to him, or claim him for her own. Nor do I believe that, in the ill-treatment of his paternal land, she is now standing close by his side. In truth, Justice would be quite falsely named, if she consorted with a man all-daring in disposition. Trusting to these reasonings I will go and fight him myself; who else is fitter to meet him? I shall take my stand as chief against chief, brother against brother, enemy against enemy. Bring me at once my greaves, my safeguard against the spear and the throwing of stones.

Cho. Be not you, dearest of men, son of Oedipus, like in temper to that brother of yours who is called by the most ill-omened name; but be content that Cadmean should come to close fight with Argive men; for their blood may be expiated. But the death of men and brothers thus suicidally slain,—of *that* guilt there is no growing old.

[1] Or, 'in every respect to be bewailed.'

[2] He says this in reference to his resolve to meet his brother in person at the seventh gate.

[3] For the disastrous issue of the fight. Tears were omens of coming evil.

[4] Lit. 'combined with delusion of senses.'

Et. If a man should take some harm, at least let it be without disgrace; for that is the only advantage he can have in the grave. But from what is both harmful and disgraceful, you cannot say that any glory accrues.[1]

Cho. What is it that you are so eager for, my son? Let not a mad rage for war, filling you with fury, carry you away; but cast out the first impulse of a bad desire.

Et. Since this object is so earnestly forwarded by the god, let the whole family of Laius, under the ban of Phoebus, float away with the breeze, and be its portion the waves of the infernal River of Woe.

Cho. Too savage[2] a passion is impelling you to commit a manslaughter that will bear bitter fruits,—the shedding of unlawful blood.

Et. Even so; the unloving curse of a loved father coming to its fulfilment[3] sits upon my dry and tearless eyes,[4] telling me that the gain which comes first is to be preferred to the death which comes after.

Cho. But do not *you* be thus violently set against him: you will not be called a coward, when you have passed your life so well; the Erinys with her sable aegis will leave[5] the house, when once the gods begin to receive sacrifices from your hands.

Et. Methinks the *gods* have already resigned all concern for us: the only offering they care for is that of our deaths. Why then should we any longer be cowed by the prospect of our fate?

Cho. *Now* is your time,[6] when death stands close by you; for it may be that fortune will come with a milder breeze on your change of disposition, though it be a late one; but at present it boils.[7]

Et. Yes, for the curses of Oedipus made it boil up. O too true were the visions of nightly dreams, portending the sharing of our paternal property!

[1] This verse is corrupt.

[2] Lit. 'biting to the raw.'

[3] Weil proposes *μέλαιν' ἀρὰ*, as inf. 828. Eur. *Hipp.* 1236.

[4] Compare *βοῦς ἐπὶ γλώσσῃ*, *Agam.* 36. It weighs down the eyelids so that no tears can flow.

[5] *ἔξεισι δόμων* is Weil's admirable and certain emendation for *οὐκ εἶσι δόμων*.

[6] Namely, to repent.

[7] Namely, your *λῆμα*. The metaphor is from a troubled sea.

Cho. Take the advice of women, though you like them not.

Et. Tell me of something that is practicable;[1] but you must be brief.

Cho. Don't you go this road to the seventh gate.

Et. I tell you my mind is whetted, and you shall not blunt it by anything you may say.

Cho. But there *is* a victory,[2]—if not one of valour,—that the god holds in honour.

Et. No *soldier* ought to tolerate such a saying.

Cho. Do you then really wish to reap the consequences of slaying a brother?

Et. If the gods grant it, he shall not escape harm.

Cho. I dread that goddess who is the destroyer of families, unlike the other gods, that ever-true prophet of evil, a father's ban, a Fury summoned to accomplish the curses uttered by Oedipus in the bitterness of rage and with distraction of mind: for it is this *fury*,[3] fatal to the sons, that is urging them to the fray. And a stranger is the awarder of the shares between them, the Chalybian[4] settler from Scythia, the fatal arbiter in the division of their wealth, stern unbending steel, allotting them land to dwell in just enough for dead men to occupy, deprived of those large domains. But[5] when by mutual slaughter self-mangled they shall have died, and the earth's dust shall have drank up their dark-clotted gory blood, who then may give them expiations? who may wash them from their guilt? O new woes of the house, mixed in with the evils of old! For to the ancestral transgression I allude, which brought with it speedy vengeance, and abides even to the third generation,—when Laius, in despite of Apollo, who had thrice ordered him, in an oracle

[1] *i.e.* I may perhaps comply if you will say, and in few words, something reasonable.

[2] The being prevailed over to do what is right.

[3] There is a play on Ἐρινὺς and Ἔρις, as the Schol. Med. perceived. Compare that on the name Ἑλένη in *Ag.* 670.

[4] *i.e.* the inheritance will be divided by the sword,—they are fighting for the throne.

[5] Read *αὐτοκτόνως δ'*. The MS. Med. has *αὐτοκτόνωσιν*.

delivered from his central shrine at Pytho, by dying without offspring to prove the preserver of the state,—when he, nevertheless, overcome by the evil counsel of those dear to him,[1] begat a doom for himself, the parricide Oedipus,—one who dared to plant on an unhallowed field, where he was reared, a stock that should be steeped in blood.[2] It was a fatal blindness that brought together the infatuated man and wife. And now as it were a sea of troubles is bringing on a billow, one falling, while another with triple crest it is raising,—a wave that babbles and chafes at the city's stern. And between us a defence extends but a short way, even the thickness of a wall: I fear lest, together with its rulers, the city should be crushed. For now is being accomplished the sad reconciliation of the curse long ago uttered;[3] and a fatal crisis, when it arises, does not pass away.[4] The wealth of merchant-traders, too closely stowed, causes the loss of goods by throwing them out astern.[5] For what man ever was there that the gods held in such regard, or the worshippers at the common altar of the city, or the much-frequented meeting-place of the people,[6] as they then paid honour to Oedipus, after he had removed from the land that man-snatching pest [the Sphinx]? But when he became conscious, unhappy wretch, of his unfortunate marriage, impatient in his grief, with madness of heart, he perpetrated a twofold deed of horror;—with the hand that had before slain his own father he deprived himself of his . . . eyes,[7] and he launched against his sons curses, through rage at his scanty keep,[8]—curses, alas, of an angry tongue, even that they should some day divide their possessions with sword-wielding hand: and now

[1] Probably meaning his wife.—*ἀβουλιᾶν* Weil, Dind.; *ἀβουλίαν* Med.

[2] Who, by marrying his mother, had as an offspring two sons destined to slay each other.

[3] Namely, that by the sword.

[4] A general sentiment, founded on Greek Fatalism.

[5] Too much prosperity begets adversity. Compare *Agam.* 980.

[6] Weil's *πολύβατος ἀγὼν* (vulg. *αἰὼν*) *i.e.* the agora, is worthy of all praise. His happy illustration from Pindar, frag. 45. 3, *πολύβατον ἄστεος ὀμφαλὸν*, added to the requirements of the metre, leaves little room for doubt.

[7] The epithet *κρεισσοτέκνων* seems corrupt.

[8] See the Schol. on *Oed. Col.* 1375.

I fear lest the nimble-footed Erinys should bring them to an accomplishment.

Mes. Courage, maidens, mother's children[1] that ye are! Our city has escaped the yoke of slavery; the boasts of the fierce men have come to nought; the state is in a tranquil calm, and buffeted though it has been by many a blow of the waves, it has not let in the water. The walls are yet proof, and the single-handed champions whom we set as guards at our gates have redeemed their pledges. Our affairs generally are prosperous at the six gates; but the seventh gate the awful Seventh[2] chose for himself as the leader, king Apollo, bringing to pass for the sons of Oedipus the consequences of his ill-advised disobedience of old.

Cho. Why, what new circumstance has now occurred to the city?

Mes. The men have died by self-slaying hands.

Cho. *Who* have died? What is it that you say? I am beside myself through fear at your words.

Mes. Hear me now in your sober senses,—'tis the race of Oedipus.

Cho. Alas, unhappy that I am! I am a true prophet then of these evils.[3]

Mes. But you must not suppose that the one only was slaughtered by the other.[4]

Cho. And did they come even to *that?* Grievous are the tidings, yet tell me all plainly.

Mes. Even so as you say: by hands but too kindred were they slain.

Cho. Was their fate then thus common to both together?

[1] Without the courage of males.

[2] There is an allusion to the title of Apollo, *ἑβδομαγενής*, 'born on the seventh day.' The numeral contains an omen, precisely as *τρίτος σωτὴρ*, *Suppl.* 26.

[3] The Chorus had foreboded them, sup. 731.

[4] *ἀμφίλεκτος* probably meant 'picked out and set apart on each side'; thence 'chosen as an alternative,' which sense well suits *Agam.* 854. Hence also 'one thing placed apart from another,' 'at variance,' *Agam.* 1563.

Mes. Yes, and [the father][1] himself sacrifices the lives of his ill-fated offspring.

Cho. At such events one may fairly both feel joy and give vent to tears,[2]—that the city in the first place is prosperous, while its governors, the two generals-in-chief, have divided with the forged Scythian steel the entire property of their wealth. And they shall possess such a share of land as they have received in their burial, being carried along with[3] the wretched curse of their father.

[*Mes.*[4] The city is safe; but the blood of the two brother-kings the earth has drunk up bv a mutuallv inflicted slaughter.]

Cho. Great Zeus, and ye gods that protect the city, who now, as we see, are the deliverers of these towers of Cadmus, ought I to rejoice, and raise a shout of joy at the lucky escape of our city without hurt, or should I rather weep for those wretched and ill-fated authors of the war who have left no issue?—who rightly indeed and according to their names, men of *much strife,*[5] perished by their own unnatural devices. O dark and fully accomplished curse inherent in the family and uttered through Oedipus,[6] a chill settles on my heart at these evils. I composed a verse for the tomb like some Thyiad, when I heard of the gory corpses that had miserably perished;—*ill-omened indeed was this concert of the spear.*[7] The curse uttered by the father has worked out its purpose and not failed; the disobedient resolves of Laius have lasted till now. There is anxiety in the city, for the oracles are not losing their edge. O much lamented pair, this deed of yours surpasses belief; the lamentable woes arrived not merely in hearsay; here they are self-evident; what the

[1] Perhaps for *δῆτα* we should read *πατήρ,—αὐτὸς δ' ἀναλοῖ δύσποτμον πατὴρ γένος*, namely, by his curse. As the text now stands, *αὐτὸς* should naturally refer to *δαίμων*.

[2] See on *Agam.* 620. Lit. 'be suffused with tears.'

[3] Irresistibly suffering the consequences of. Compare 687, and 849.

[4] These two verses of the Messenger seem spurious.

[5] See above, 574.

[6] He seems to speak of ancient family curse revived and repeated, as it were, by Oedipus against his sons.

[7] Evil was the omen which matched the brothers against each other at the same gate. These words seem the burden of the *τύμβου μέλος*.

messenger reported in words is before our sight. A twofold woe, a twain evil of manly courage, self-slaying, bringing a double fate, fully accomplished are these sufferings. What can I call them? What, but troubles that haunt the very hearth of our homes?

But do you, friends, as you follow in the mournful train[1] ply about your heads the quick oar-stroke of your hands in the funeral procession, for such ever attends in its passage through Acheron[2] that unchartered dark-sailed mission-ship, that is not trodden for Apollo,[3] that knows not the sun, into the all-receiving and unseen landing-place. But stay,—here come Antigone and Ismene for a sad office, to sing a dirge over their brothers. With no difference of sentiment I expect that they will give utterance from their lovely deep-folded bosoms to a fitting grief. 'Tis our part, before the sounds of woe reach us, to sing the inharmonious strain of the Erinys, and to chant a dismal paean to the god of the dead. Alas, most unhappy in your brothers, of all who wear female attire,[4] I weep, I sigh, and there is no deception in the shrieks that proceed in truth from my very heart.

Hem. A.[5] Oh, oh! ill-advised, disobedient to their friends, and unsubdued by troubles,[6]—wretched brothers, who have got possession of their father's home by the aid of the spear.

Hem. B. Wretched indeed, in that they met with wretched deaths to the desolation of their family.

Hem. A. Oh, oh! you who have pulled down the walls of your own house, and seen monarchy but to your own destruction, now at length you have been reconciled, but by the help of the sword.

[1] Lit. 'down the gale of sighs.'

[2] Such lamentations escort the soul of the dead to Hades. The language here is so highly figurative as hardly to admit of being literally rendered.

[3] Not like the ship annually sent from Athens to Delos,—Apollo being the god of joy, *Agam.* 1042.

[4] 'who have the sash (*Suppl.* 451) thrown round their clothes.'

[5] It is unnecessary to remind the reader, whether of the English or the Greek, that for the next 150 lines there is little or nothing in the *sense* to interest. It was purely a *spectacle*, a recitative funeral strain, in which tone and impassioned action produced the entire effect.

[6] ἀτρύμων is that which has an edge not easily to be worn down. Compare ἀτεράμων.

Hem. B. And but too truly has the awful Erinys of their father Oedipus accomplished his curse.

Hem. A. Stricken through their left sides,[1] yea, stricken in those sides that sprang from one common womb. Alas, fiend-possessed pair! and alas for their accursed deaths by mutual slaughter!

Hem. B. Smitten they were, as you say, but in their family as well as in their bodies, by a home-thrust blow, with a fury that surpassed words to describe, and through an unlucky quarrel resulting from a father's curse.

Hem. A. And sounds of mourning have been heard throughout the city: the very towers mourn, the earth mourns for love of her departed heroes: but the possessions will be reserved for their descendants, through which the quarrel first came to the ill-fated pair, and ended in their death.

Hem. B. It was in a spirit of anger that they divided between them the property, so as to get equal shares. Therefore is the instrument of their reconciliation not unblamed by their friends, as the victory is no cause for delight.

Hem. A. Stricken by the sword so they lie; and by the stroke of the sword they have gained—one might well ask *what?*—shares in their ancestral tombs.

Hem. B. From the house a loud wailing[2] escorts them, a piercing groan spontaneously uttered, self-afflicting, harassing one's thoughts, no friend to joy, making tears to gush from true sorrow of heart, which as I weep seems to shrink within me, for the fate of these two princes.

Hem. A. And one may say over[3] the unhappy men that —they did much (evil) to the citizens, and to the ranks of all the foreigners who fell in numbers in the fight.

Hem. B. Ill-fated was she who gave them birth, yea, before all women who bear the name of mother. She took her own son for a husband, and these were the fruits of the

[1] Through the very heart.
[2] The text is here corrupt.
[3] By way of funeral oration over the bodies.

marriage; and such was their death by mutually-slaying brotherly hands.

Hem. A. Brothers they were indeed, even brothers in their death,[1]—in the unfriendly sharing, and in the mad contest which ended the dispute.

Hem. B. But now their enmity has ceased; and on the gory earth their life[2] has been mixed, so that they are now truly of *one blood.* A fatal reconciler of their strifes was that stranger from over the sea, that came forth from the fire, the whetted steel; fatal too and ill-starred was the distributer of their wealth, Ares, who caused the ban of their father to become true.

Hem. A. They have got their portions by sharing, O unhappy men for their heaven-sent woes! *Under* their bodies they shall have riches in land that will be bottomless.

Hem. B. O men who have made their own family to blossom with many woes! Over their fate now the Furies have shrieked their shrill death-strain, the whole race having been put to flight with utter rout. The trophy of their mad act stands at the gate at which they received the blow: and after overcoming the two, the evil genius of the house ceased from the contest.[3]

Antigone and Ismene.

Ant. You struck and were stricken.
Ism. And you died after killing your foe.
Ant. By the spear you slew.
Ism. By the spear you died.
Ant. Unhappy in your toil.
Ism. Unhappy in your fate.
Ant. Let sighs be uttered.
Ism. Let the tear be shed.
Ant. There you lie dead,—
Ism. After slaying your foe.

[1] *συνώλεθροι* and *διανομαῖς* are Weil's excellent emendations.

[2] Some of the Greeks, like the Jews, thought the blood was the life. See Plat. *Phæd.* p. 96, B.

[3] The metaphor is from the wrestling-school. See *Cho.* 852. *θείνειν* is used in this sense, Ar. *Ach.* 564.

Ant. Alas, alas! my soul is frantic with these groans.

Ism. And my heart sighs within me.

Ant. Oh brother that deserves the city's tears!

Ism. And oh you who are on every account wretched.

Ant. By a dear one you were slain.

Ism. And a dear one you slew.

Ant. A twofold horror to describe.

Ism. And twofold also to behold.

Ant. Double woes these, and from nearest kin.

Ism. Sisters are we, and by the side of brothers we stand.

Ant. Deeds of death to describe.

Ism. Deeds of death to behold.

Cho. O Destiny, dealer of afflictions and cause of misery, and thou, awful shade of Oedipus, black fiend from hell, thy power we acknowledge.

Ant. Alas, woes sad to behold—

Ism. Did you bring to my sight, on returning from exile.

Ant. But he did not come to the throne after he had killed his brother.

Ism. No, for after safely returning, he lost his life.

Ant. Lose it he did indeed.

Ism. And *him* too he slew.

Ant. Wretched family.

Ism. Wretched event.

Ant. Grievous cares for the dear objects of care.[1]

Ism. Soaked through (with tears for) the immensity of our loss.[2]

Ant. You indeed know it by going through it—

Ism. And you having learnt it not later—

Ant. As soon as you got back to your city.

Ism. Aye, to stand in arms against your own brother.

Ant. O troubles—

Ism. O woes—

Ant. To family and land.

[1] Lit. 'concern (mourning) bearing the same name as objects of concern.' There is the same play on the double sense of κῆδος as in *Agam.* 681.

[2] 'Triple' merely means 'very great.'

Ism. Yes, and for me too to look forward to.

Ant. Alas for the ruler of disastrous fortune!

Ism. O most deeply lamented of all men!

Ant. O brothers possessed by infatuation!

Ism. Oh where shall we lay them in the earth?

Ant. Wherever is the most honoured grave.

Ism. Alas for the wretched woman who married our father![1]

HERALD.

I have to report to you the measures which were passed, and are now in force, by the chief magistrates of this city of Cadmus. Eteocles here, in consideration of his right feelings towards the state, it was resolved to bury in a grave dug in friendly earth: for in keeping off her enemies he met his death in the city, and without sin against his country's religion or guilt of sacrilege,[2] he has died at that post where honour calls the young soldier to die. This is what I have been ordered to say about *him*. But as for his brother—the corpse of Polynices here—they have agreed to cast him out unburied, a prey to dogs, as one who was the destroyer of the land of the Cadmeians, had not some god made a stand against his spear: but not death itself shall release him from the guilt he has incurred from the gods of his fathers, in open contempt of whom, by throwing in a foreign host, he desired to take the city. And so it hath been decreed that this man, finding an ignominious grave in the winged vulture's maw, shall receive *his* reward; that no hand-raised barrow shall form part of his obsequies, and that no one shall pay honour to the place where he lies by shrill notes of woe; but he is to be refused the last office of burial

[1] Or, 'calamity caused by the marriage of my father.'—The above dialogue—which it is obviously hopeless to make readable in English—has at least this interest, that it is the most perfect specimen of a Greek κομμὸς, or form of passionate lamentation at a funeral, that has come down to us.

[2] 'Without blame on account of the religion of his fathers, being a holy man.'

by the hands of friends. Such are the decrees issued by the authorities of these Cadmeians.

Ant. Yea, but *I* say to the magistrates of the Cadmeians, that if no one else is willing to join me in burying this body, I will bury it alone; and I will play the dangerous stake by interring my own brother, nor do I feel shame at refusing to obey the city's rulers in this matter. 'Tis a strong tie, that common womb from which we are born, even though from an unhappy mother and a wretched father. Therefore, O my soul, do thou cheerfully share these woes with him who took part in them against his will, the living with the dead, with a sisterly feeling. But *his* flesh think not that any belly-pinched wolves shall rend;—let not any one suppose it; for a tomb and a grave I myself, woman as I am, will contrive for him, by bringing (earth) in the folds of my linen robe. And with my own hand I will cover him: let no one make a decree to the contrary. Courage, my soul! Means will not be wanting for carrying out thy design.

Her. I warn you not to act in defiance of the state in this matter.

Ant. I warn you not to give useless orders to *me*.

Her. Stern however is a people when it has escaped from evils.

Ant. Make it as stern as you please,[1] yet *he* shall not be unburied.

Her. What one whom the state abhors will *you* honour with a tomb?

Ant. Yes, for *he* is no longer held in honour by the gods.

Her. It was not so before he put this country in danger.

Ant. It was because he had suffered a wrong that he thought to requite it by wrong.

Her. But this deed was directed against all instead of against one.

Ant. Contention is the last goddess to finish a dispute. I tell you, I shall bury this corpse: waste no more words.

[1] Weil reads, after L. Schmidt, *τραχὺς δ' ἄθαπτος οὗτος οὐ γενήσεται*: 'And will not *he* become stern (in Hades) if he is unburied?

Her. Well, be headstrong if you will: I can only forbid you to do it.

Cho. O proudly-vaunting and family-destroying Fates, ye Erinyes, who thus root-and-branch have exterminated the family of Oedipus; what is to become of me? What shall I do? What plan devise? How shall I be so base as neither to bewail you nor to escort you (my brother) to the tomb? But yet I fear, and shrink from the feeling of terror[1] at my own citizens. *You* however will find many mourners; but he, the unhappy one, will go (to Hades) without a sigh, having none to sing a dirge over him but his sister. Who would care to obey the city in that?[2]

Hem. A. Let the city act or decline to act against those who lament for Polynices. *We* will go and join her in burying him; and thus do we head the procession. For this grief is common to the whole race;[3] and the city at different times takes different views of what is just.

Hem. B. Then *we* will go with *this* corpse, as the orders of the city and our duty to it conjointly require. For, next after the blessed gods and the might of Zeus, it was he who in an especial manner rescued the city of the Cadmeians from being overturned, and from being deluged by a wave of foreigners.

[1] Or, 'the object of the citizens' fear,' namely, the decree.

[2] So as to refuse him the small honour that I can pay him.

[3] Or, 'to us also as well as to his family.'

THE PERSIANS.

PERSONS REPRESENTED.

CHORUS OF AGED PERSIANS.
ATOSSA, THE QUEEN-MOTHER.
A MESSENGER.
THE GHOST OF DARIUS.
XERXES.

WE indeed, here present, bear the titles of Trusty Councillors of the Persians[1] who have gone off to the land of Hellas, and Guardians of the rich golden palace, whom king Xerxes himself, the royal offspring of Darius, chose according to seniority to be deputy-governors[2] of the country. But about the expedition of our sovereign lord and his army all glittering with gold, my mind with a strong presentment of evil begins now to feel disturbed from within,—for the whole[3] military strength of the Asiatic race is gone,—and to fret after our youthful hero; and no messenger, no horseman, arrives at the capital of the Persians. But they,[4] leaving the walled cities of Susa and Ecbatana and the old fortress of Cissa, went away, some on chariots, some on ships, and infantry with their measured step presenting a close rank of war. Thus did Amistres, Artaphernes, Megabazes, Astaspes, all generals of Persians, kings themselves, but subjects of the great king, set out on their march, inspectors of a vast army,—archers

[1] The genitive may depend rather on *ὄντα* implied, than directly on Πιστὰ, since they were properly councillors of the king; who however is included in *τῶν οἰχομένων*. Compare also v. 957—60.

[2] To be *ἔφοροι*, or superintendents. They were probably eunuchs in high trust.

[3] *All* of the *ἡλικία*, or military age, are gone, and none but the elder left to protect the land.

[4] *Οἱ δὲ*, (as suggested in my note), not *οἴτε*.

also and mounted horsemen, formidable to behold and terrible in fight for the courageous resolve of their souls: Artembares too, rejoicing in his steeds, Masistres, and the skilled archer, Imaeus, Pharandaces, and the driver of horses, Sosthanes. Others the mighty Nile, that supplies nourishment to many, sent out; (such were) Susiscanes, Pegastagon, an Aegyptian by birth, and the ruler of the sacred Memphis, the mighty Arsames, and Ariomardus, governor of the ancient Thebes: inhabitants of the marshes too, skilful rowers of ships, and in numbers countless. They are attended also by a multitude of luxurious Lydians, who are largely mixed up with[1] the entire native population of the continent,—forces which Mithragathes and the brave Arcteus, king-commanders, (conduct) and Sardis abounding in gold sends forth, mounted on many chariots, ranks with three and four horses yoked abreast, a sight formidable to behold. And the dwellers by sacred Tmolus are bent on throwing the yoke of slavery round Hellas,—Mardo, Tharybis, anvils of the spear, and the Mysian javelin-men: Babylon the golden also sends a mixed host in a long sweeping train, both those borne on ships and those who rely on their courage in drawing the bow. The sabre-bearing race likewise follows from every part of Asia, under the dread mandates of the king. Such a flower of the fighting-men of Persia is gone; and about them all the land of Asia that reared them is sighing with ardent longings, while parents and wives, as they count the days, tremble at the still protracted delay.

By this time hath the royal army, the destroyer of cities, passed over the straits into the neighbouring continent beyond, by cable-tied boats having got across the channel of Athamas' daughter Helle, and having thrown a peg-fastened pathway as a yoke on the neck of the sea. And the spirited commander of populous Asia is driving his flock divine[2] over the whole land in two main divisions, both with land-forces

[1] Schol. *οἱ διόλου τὴν ἤπειρον οἰκοῦντες.*

[2] These words are carefully used to represent the relation of subjects to the Persian king, according to the Greek view.

and by sea, confident in the stern discipline of his officers,[1] the godlike hero of the race that sprung from the golden seed.[2] And grimly[3] glaring in his eyes with the looks of a sanguinary dragon, with many hands and many ships, and speeding onward Syrian war-chariots, he is bringing against men renowned with the spear a force that is to conquer them by the bow.[4] And 'tis not expected that any one, by withstanding the mighty stream of men, will keep out by strong embankments the irresistible wave of that (living) sea. For dangerous to engage with is the army of Persians, and brave-hearted is its people. But the craftily-plotting deceits of the god what mortal man shall escape? Who that by nimbleness of step commands the art of leaping so as to alight on his feet? For Delusion, at first all smiles and flattery, coaxes men into her stake-nets;[5] but out of them 'tis not possible for a mere mortal to escape by surmounting the enclosure. For of old fate went against the Persians by the decrees of heaven, and put it into their minds to engage in wars for the storming of fortresses, in the turmoil of cavalry-actions, and in the overthrow of cities. They learnt too to look fearlessly on the briny waste of the broad sea, when whitened over by the strong blast, trusting to the tackle of slightly-built craft,—the plan for the transport of their hosts. 'Tis for these reasons that my heart, clothed in gloom, is rent with fear, Wah! for this Persian army of ours, lest the state should hear that this mighty city of Susa's land is bereft of its men, and the citadel of the Cissians should respond by heavy beatings of the breast, as the company of the women utters aloud this word, *Wah!* and rending should fall on their robes of fine linen. For the entire host both of cavalry and infantry, like a swarm of bees, have left their homes with the commander of the army, and have passed the bridge[6]

[1] 'Trusting in strong stern commanders.'

[2] Danae, visited by Zeus in a shower of gold, by which she became pregnant of Perseus, the mythical ancestor of the Persians.

[3] Lit. 'dark blue.'

[4] This is said rather from the Greek than the Persian view of the matter, and not without irony.

[5] See the note on *Agam.* 350.

[6] The bridge of boats, that juts out like a headland from either shore, till it joins in the middle.

projected from both shores and common to both continents alike. And the beds (of the forlorn wives) through longing desire for their husbands are filled with tears; the Persian ladies, luxurious even in their grief, each stricken with passionate regret for her lord, having sent out to the wars the valiant spear-armed partner of her couch, are left widowed at home. But come, ye Persians, let us take our seats in this ancient hall, and devise some sage and well-considered plan,—for need has come upon us,—(that we may know) how Xerxes our king, offspring of Darius, one of our race that bears the name of its ancestor,[1] really fares: whether it is the drawing of the bow that is getting the advantage, or the strength of the shaft-heading spear-point that has already prevailed. But here comes,—a light like that of the eyes of the gods,—the mother of the king, my queen. Let us do her obeisance. And it is further the duty of all of us to address her with words of greeting.

O queen, highest in rank of all the deep-waisted Persian ladies, aged mother of Xerxes, all hail, wife of Darius! The consort wert thou of one that was a god to the Persians, and the mother of a god thou art likewise, unless in some respect the ancient fortune has now changed for the nation.[2]

Atossa. It is for this that I am come leaving the gold-bedizened palace, and the common marriage-chamber of Darius and myself. *I* too[3] have a care that is rending me at the heart; and I will address to you, my friends, my remarks, though by no means without fears for myself, lest too great wealth in its hurried step[4] should kick against and overturn the fabric of prosperity which Darius raised, not without the favour of some god. On these grounds there is a twofold anxiety, too great for words, within my breast,—(a feeling) that as on the one hand we ought not to worship and honour a quantity of wealth without men, so on the other hand

[1] Persians, from Perseus.

[2] If unsuccessful in the war, Xerxes would forfeit his title of θεὸς Πέρσαις.

[3] κἀμὲ (as suggested in the note).

[4] Lit. 'having covered the plain with dust,' a figure from the invasion of a hostile army, as in *Suppl.* 176, *Theb.* 81.

on men who have not money the light of success does not shine in proportion to their military strength.[1] Now our wealth indeed is not to be disparaged; but about him who is the light of our eyes[2] there is some fear; for the eye of the house I consider to be the master's presence in it. Wherefore, such being the state of affairs, become for me advisers in this matter, ye Persians, aged councillors of trust. For all (my hopes of) good advice depend on you.

Cho. Be well assured, queen of this land, that you will not have to mention twice either word or deed, whatever matter authority may please to originate.[3] For devoted to your service are we whom you summon as your advisers in these matters.

At. For a long time past I have been haunted continually by nightly dreams, ever since my son got his army in marching order and went off to the land of the Athenians with the intention of ravaging it. Yet never saw I any vision so plainly as last night,—but I will tell it you. I thought that two female forms in fair attire,—the one dressed in Persian, the other in Dorian robes,—presented themselves to view, in size far more striking than women now are, and unexceptionable in beauty, sisters also of the same descent. As for the country they lived in,—one had obtained by lot the land of Hellas, the other the Persian.[4] These two, as I fancied I saw, were getting up a quarrel with each other. When my son was aware of it, he tried to restrain and soothe them, and putting them to his car he harnessed them to the yoke and put the collar-straps on their necks. One of them carried herself proudly in this guise, and had a mouth tractable under the reins; but the other was restive, and with her hands tried to tear in pieces the harness of the car, and then ran away with it by

[1] The meaning is, that if those who, like the Greeks, have men but not money, sometimes fail for want of the latter; yet mere wealth, which is the chief boast of the Persians, may equally prove inefficient, unless supported by valorous troops.

[2] *i. e.* Xerxes.

[3] In whatever matter royal command 'takes the initiative,' as the modern phrase is.

[4] To the Greek mind βάρβαροι meant 'easterns' generally. The word conveyed so little reproach, that Aeschylus does not scruple to put it into the mouth of the Persian queen.

force, without the bit, and snapped the yoke in the middle. And my son was thrown out, and his father Darius stood by pitying him: but when Xerxes saw *him*, he rent his clothes on his body. Well then, this was, as I say, my dream last night. So when I had risen, and duly dipped my hands in running spring water,[1] I took incense-offerings in my hands and stood at the altar, intending to pour sacrificial libations to the gods who avert evil, and to whom these rights belong. But suddenly I saw an eagle flying for refuge to the altar of Phoebus; and through fear I stood speechless, my friends. A moment afterwards I perceived a kite rushing at it with the full speed of its wings, and pulling out the feathers from its head with its talons. Nor did the eagle offer any resistance, but, as if completely cowed, it surrendered itself to the attack.[2] Now all these portents are, to me at least, alarming to behold, as they must be to you to hear. For be well assured, my son, should he succeed, would become a hero admired by all; at the same time, should he prove unsuccessful, he is not accountable to the city; and if he only gets back safe, he is not less than before the sovereign of the land.[3]

Cho. We do not wish, royal mother, either to alarm you too much by our suggestions, or to give you undue confidence; but make a visit to the gods with humble supplications, and implore them, if what you saw has any evil import, to cause *that* to be averted, but that the good may become fully realized both for yourself and your children, for the state too and all who are your friends. In the next place, you should pour libations to Earth and the departed Spirits; and supplicate your husband Darius, whom you say you saw in last night's dream, in kindly feelings towards you to send blessings upon yourself and your son from beneath the earth to the light of day; but that the contrary to these may be kept in durance

[1] 'And had touched with my hands a fair-flowing spring, with sacrificial hand, &c.

[2] 'But he (the eagle, did) nothing else than crouch down and surrender his body.'

[3] Though he would be a great man if he succeeds, he cannot be deposed if he fails.

under the earth[1] and obscured by the gloom. This course I recommend to you in friendly feeling, guided only by the dictates of sense;[2] and our judgment about the matter is, that it will bring about a favourable result, however the case may be.[3]

At. Well, certainly, as the *first* interpreter of these dreams, you have given the right meaning of them to my son and my family, with good feeling towards myself.[4] May then the good be fulfilled! As for these offerings, even as you enjoin us, we will make them all to the gods and to those friendly to us below the earth, so soon as we return to our palace. But with respect to the enemy,[5] I am desirous to be informed clearly, where in the world they say Athens is situated.

Cho. Far off towards the west, where sets the royal sun.[6]

At. Well, was this the land that my son felt such a desire to take?

Cho. Aye! for so all Hellas would become subject to the great king.

At. Have they so full a number of men in their army?

Cho. Yes, and an army of such a sort,—one that did mischief enough to the Medes.

At. And what else beside that? Have they wealth enough to last at their own homes?

Cho. They have a natural supply of silver, a treasure stored in the earth.

At. And is it the bow-drawing arrow that is the chief weapon in their hands?

Cho. By no means; lances used in close fight, and the accoutrements of shield-bearers.[7]

[1] Earth was regarded by the Greek Pantheists as a kind of sentient and active power, which could send up or detain at will the sentiments of the dead in Hades for good or for evil.

[2] Not being a regular or professional seer.

[3] That the course we advise will bring success, whether there are evils to be deprecated or blessings to be realized.

[4] The meaning is, 'my first interpreter is favourable to me, and I will accept his view of the matter as final and valid.'

[5] For this use of ἐκεῖνα compare inf. 397.

[6] The sun was worshipped by the Persians.

[7] ὁπλῖται, not ψιλοί.

At. And who is set over them as shepherd of the flock, and is the master to the army?

Cho. They call themselves the slaves[1] of no man, nor subjects either.

At. How then could they withstand an invading enemy?

Cho. (They *have* done so), so as to cut up a large and fine army.[2]

At. Truly, you speak grave words for the parents of those who have gone to think of.

Cho. But, if I am not mistaken, you will soon know the whole matter as it really is: for the rapid step of this man one may be sure is Persian from its appearance; and he (doubtless) brings the plain news of some success or disaster to hear of.

Mes. O stronghold[3] of all the land of Asia, O Persia, and O ample repository[4] of wealth! How by a single blow your great prosperity has been destroyed, and the flower of the Persians is fallen and gone! Woe is me! 'tis an evil to have to bring the first tidings of evil; but still it is necessary to unfold the whole disaster: I tell you, Persians, the entire army of the east has perished.

Cho. Grievous, O grievous calamity, startling strange, and dreadful, alas! Let not an eye remain dry, ye Persians, when ye hear of this disaster.

Mes. Be assured that all the hopes of the army are done for: indeed I myself had not looked for a safe return.

Cho. Too protracted for old men does this life of ours now appear, for to hear of this unexpected woe.

Mes. But as having been myself present, and not hearing the reports of others, I can give a clear account to you, my lords, of the evils that were sent us (by the god).[5]

Cho. In vain then, alas! all those hosts of light-armed

[1] Compare *Agam.* 1196.

[2] At Marathon.

[3] By *πολίσματα* Susa appears to be meant. It seems impossible that more than one city can be addressed. But this may be only a various reading in place of the next verse.

[4] The palace itself, called *πολύχρυσος* and *χρυσέοστολμος*, sup. 3 and 161.

[5] See *Cho.* 1029.

troops of mixed races went from Asia against a heaven-protected country, the land of Hellas.

Mes. Full of unburied bodies of the slain[1] are the shores of Salamis and all the adjoining coast.

Cho. Alas! they are the bodies of our own friends, sea-tost and dyed many colours,[2] that you describe as being carried in death by the waves on the two restless shores of the straits.[3]

Mes. For of no avail were their bows, but the whole army perished overcome by the impact[4] of the ships' beaks.

Cho. Raise a doleful cry of woe for those that have been unhappily slain; for (the gods) have caused a disastrous end of the whole affair in the destruction of the army.

Mes. O name of Salamis, most odious to hear! Oh how I groan when I think of that Athens!

Cho. Aye! Athens has good cause to be hated by her enemies. Truly, we cannot forget how many of the Persian ladies, who had done her no harm,[5] she made widows and husbandless.

At. I have kept silence all this time, unhappy that I am, being astounded at our disasters: for this calamity is of such surpassing horror that I can neither speak of nor ask about our sufferings. Nevertheless, mortals must bear misfortunes when the gods send them. Reveal therefore the whole extent of our loss, and tell me composedly, however much you are distressed at the sad events, who is *not* dead, and whom of the leaders of the host we shall have to mourn for, that was appointed to a post of authority, and by his death left desolate the ranks deprived of their leader.

[1] Compare *οὐκ εὐτυχῶς* in v. 327. *ἐφθαρμένος* includes, if it does not primarily mean, death by drowning. Cf. 453.

[2] As by blood, bruises, decomposition, &c. Cf. v. 319.

[3] Donaldson, *New Cratylus*, § 280:—"The *πλαγκτοὶ δίπλακες* appear to describe the *ἀντιπλῆγες ἀκταὶ* of the straits of Salamis. The epithet *πλαγκτὸς* is explained by a reference to the appearance of motion assumed by a coast, when the line of breakers keeps oscillating backwards and forwards." This nearly coincides with the Schol. *διαύλοις· τὰ γὰρ κύματα ἐκχεῖται καὶ ὑπονοστεῖ.* Some refer *δίπλακες* to ships' planks, others to folded garments.

[4] There seems a play on *βάλλειν* and *βέλη*, which is untranslateable.

[5] The Schol. rightly explains *μάταν* by *μηδὲν βλαψάσας*.

Mes. Xerxes himself yet lives and sees the light.

At. To my house you have indeed described a great light, yea, a clear bright day after a night of gloom.

Mes. But Artembares, commander of ten thousand horse, is being dashed about by the surf along the rugged shores of Sileniae.[1] Dadaces also, the leader of a thousand men, by the stroke of a spear, sprang with a light bound from off the deck of his ship. Tenago, the bravest of the Bactrians, and of the true old stock, is ranging (in death) the sea-lashed island of Salamis.[2] Lilaeus, Arsames, and Argestes besides, meeting with defeat by the dove-breeding island,[3] were butting with their heads against the iron-bound shore. Arcteus also, a neighbour of the sources of Aegyptian Nile,[4] Adeues, Pheresseues beside those two, and Pharnuchus, these all fell dead out of one ship. Matallus of Chrysa, commander of ten thousand men, and the leader of thrice ten thousand black-horsed cavalry, killed in the fight, dabbled his thick shaggy auburn[5] beard (in blood), and changed its hue by a deep purple stain. Arabus likewise, the Magian, and Artames the Bactrian, perished there, to take up a new abode in a rugged land. Amistris, Amphistreus, the wielder of no inactive spear, and the good knight Ariomard, causing grief to Sardis for his death,—Sesames the Mysian, Tharybis, the admiral of five times fifty ships, from Lyrna by descent, a comely man, lies a hapless corpse, unblest by the rites of sepulture: Syennesis likewise, foremost in courage, set as commander over the Cilicians, after giving more trouble than any one man to the enemy, died gloriously. Such are the leaders of whom I now make mention: but out of many evils that are before us I report only a few.

At. Alas! what I now hear is the crowning point of all

[1] *Σιληνιαὶ αἰγιαλὸς Σαλαμῖνος.* Schol.

[2] Schol. *πολεῖ εὐφήμως· κεῖται ἐν Σαλαμῖνι.* (A gloss that Dindorf has utterly misunderstood.) There is an allusion to the Athenian *περίπολοι*, horse-patrol, or coast-guards.

[3] Salamis, frequented by rock-pigeons.

[4] It was thought to rise in the far east, not in the far south. But the verses 310—315 can hardly be considered genuine.

[5] *πυρσὸς* was often applied to the colour of *young* beards.

our woes,—disgraces sustained by the Persians and cause for shrill wailings. But tell me this, going back in your account,—what was the number, now, of the Hellenic fleet, that made them presume to engage with the Persian force by an attack with their beaked vessels?

Mes. If it had depended on mere number, be well assured that the Persian would have been victorious in his ships: for to the Hellenes on their part the whole number amounted to ten times thirty ships; and of these ten were specially selected and set apart. But Xerxes, for I am well informed, had a thousand as the sum total of the ships he led, while those that especially excelled in speed were two hundred and seven: such is the reckoning. Do we seem to you to have been at all behind them in this fight? Rather it was some malignant power that thus destroyed the army, by depressing the scale with unequal fortune: the gods preserve the city of Pallas the goddess.

At. Is then the city of Athens still unravaged?

Mes. Yes, for while she has men she has a bulwark impregnable.

At. But the commencement of the set-to with the ships,—how was it? Say: who began the fight,—the Hellenes? Or did my son, presuming[1] in the number of ships?

Mes. The beginner, my queen, of the whole misfortune was some accursed fiend, or a malignant demon, I know not whence. For a Greek soldier from the Athenian host went and told your son Xerxes this story,—that if (he waited till) the darkness of night should set in, the Hellenes would not stay, but springing on to the benches of their galleys, one man in this direction, another in that, would endeavour to save their lives by a stealthy flight. But he, the moment he had heard this, not comprehending the crafty design of the Greek, nor that the gods were against him, issues this order to all his captains: so soon as the sun shall have ceased to light up the earth with his rays, and darkness shall have

[1] 'Through boasting against them about the (superior) number of ships.'

occupied the wide expanse of the sky, they shall marshall the close-packed fleet in three rows, to guard the passages out and the navigable sea-straits; while others (were to be posted) in a circle round the isle of Ajax;[1] for, if the Hellenes should escape a miserable fate, by finding some secret way of escape for their ships, it had been resolved that they should all lose their heads. Such orders he gave under the influence of a greatly deluded mind; for little knew he what the gods had in store for him. But they,[2] not in disorder, but with prompt obedience to command, made ready their midday meal, while each sailor looped his oar over the easy-rowing rowlock. But no sooner had the light of the sun gone down, and night began to come on, than every man who managed an oar went to his ship, and every one versed in the use of heavy armour. And one rank cheered on to the fight another rank of the long galleys; and they sail in the order each had assigned to him. And so all night long the captains of the ships kept their whole naval force sailing in and out. But now the night advanced, and no attempt at all was made by the Grecian host to sail stealthily off in any direction. As soon however as the morn with her white steeds had covered all the land, fair and bright to behold; at first with a loud clear note a shout from the Hellenes rang out like some joyous song, and in an instant a rousing cry of victory was sent back by the echo from the rocks of the island: and a sudden panic came on all the Persians, disappointed of their expectation; for it was not as for flight that the Hellenes then sang that solemn paean, but as exhorting each other to the fight with gallant daring of soul. And now the trumpet by its blast fired all the enemy's fleet: and instantly by the simultaneous dip of the plashing oar they struck the sea under the surface at the word of command. And very quickly the whole fleet stood out plain to view. The right wing in the first place, well marshalled as it had been, took the lead in

[1] Salamis.

[2] The Persians, who are about to intercept, as they suppose, the escape of the Greeks.

good order; and next after it the entire naval force came out against us; and you might then hear the loud shout of many at once,—*Sons of the Greeks! go, free your country, free your children, your wives, the temples of your fathers' gods, and the tombs of your ancestors! Now the contest is for them all.* But from our side too the deep hum of Persian voices went forth to meet it; and no longer was it the time for delay, but in an instant ship against ship dashed in its brazen cutwater. The attack was first made by a Greek ship, which broke off all the prow ornaments of a Phoenician galley, and then every one against some other directed his ship. At first then the continuous stream of the Persian host held out; but when a great many ships had been crowded in a narrow strait, and no chance of aiding each other presented itself,—then began they through their own clumsiness to break the entire side-banks of their oars, struck by[1] the brass-beaked prows, while the Hellenic ships, not slow to follow up the advantage, kept battering them on every side in a circle. Then hulks of ships were capsized, and the open sea could no longer be seen, crammed as it was with wrecks and slaughtered men. Nay, the very shores and reefs were filled with corpses, and in wild disorder every ship plied its oars for flight, as many as belonged to the Persian armament.[2] But they, as if (slaughtering) tunnies[3] or fish caught in a cast-net, with broken oars and fragments of wreck struck and broke the backs of our men; and groans and shrieks together prevailed over all the open sea, till the eye of dark night took away (the power to continue the fight). But the whole amount of our losses I could not, even if I should describe them in order for ten days together, fully inform you of.[4] For be well assured of this,—never in one day did so numerous a body of men meet their death.

At. Alas, alas! then a mighty sea of evils has indeed

[1] παίοντ' for παίοντα πρὸς, 'striking against,' as in *Prom.* 904.

[2] Both 423 and 425 are probably interpolations.

[3] See the note on *Theb.* 122.

[4] 'fill up the number of.'

burst its bounds to swamp the Persians and the entire population of the east.

Mes. Be assured of this now, that the evil is not yet half described. Such an accumulation[1] of calamity came on them, as to outweigh these by even twice as much more.

At. Why, surely no mischance could occur more disastrous than this! Explain, what is this new calamity which you state came upon the army, and which inclined the balance of evil still further against them.

Mes. As many of the Persians as were in the prime of life,—men bravest in soul and conspicuous for noble birth,—and to the king himself ever among the first in trust,—have perished dishonourably by a most ignominious fate.

At. O woe to unhappy me for this sad mishap! But by what kind of fate do you say that *these* perished?

Mes. There is an islet fronting the shore of Salamis,—small, affording bad anchorage for ships, but which the dance-loving Pan treads when he roves on its sea-beach. Thither did Xerxes send these men, in order that, when the enemy had lost their ships and were trying to find a safe escape on to the island, they might butcher the army of the Hellenes as an easy prey, and at the same time rescue their own friends from the sea-straits. But little did he know what was to come. For when the god had given to the Hellenes the victory in the fight, on that very day, having duly protected their bodies with brazen shields,[2] they leaped out of their ships and surrounded the whole island, so that our men were at a loss which way to turn; for they were often severely hit by stones thrown from their hands, while at the same time arrows from the bowstring fell on them and added to their destruction. And lastly, making a simultaneous rush upon them with a shout, they struck and made horrible butchery of the poor wretches' limbs, till they had

[1] συμφορὰ seems here to mean 'a bringing together,' a meaning acknowledged by the lexicons.

[2] The accoutrement of hoplites. Their ready change from mariners to heavy-armed infantry is eulogised.

utterly destroyed every living man. But Xerxes[1] shrieked out when he saw the depth of his misfortunes; for he occupied a seat commanding a good view of the whole army, a high hill near the open sea. Then, rending his garments and uttering a shrill cry of despair, he gave the instant order to his land-army, and rushed away in disorderly flight. Such is the calamity you have now to bewail in addition to the former one.

At. O cruel fortune, how hast thou then disappointed the Persians of their hopes! Truly my son devised to his own cost this way of taking vengeance on glorious Athens, and was not contented with the deaths of those Persians who before were slain at Marathon. Yes, my son thought to exact retribution for them, but instead of it he has drawn upon himself such a multitude of evils. But tell me, you,—those of the ships that have escaped destruction,—where did you leave *them?* Do you know, so as to inform me plainly?

Mes. The captains of the surviving ships spread their sails with all haste to the breeze, and took to flight in no order.[2] The remainder of the land-army miserably died out in the land of the Boeotians, some by the water-springs, distressed by thirst, others exhausted and out of breath[3] ..... we passed safely out into the territory of the Phocians and the Dorian land and the Melian gulf, where the Spercheus waters the plain with kindly drink. Thence the soil of the Achaean land[4] and a settlement of Thessalians entertained us when we had run short of food; there it was that the greatest numbers died from both hunger and thirst,—for both these we had to endure. Thus at length we reached the land of Magnesia and the territory of the Macedonians, as far as the ford of the Axius and the reedy lake of Bolbe and mount Pangaeus, in the land of the Edoni. But on that night the god sent a frost out of season, and froze the whole

[1] I have shown that these lines, 467—473, are spurious.

[2] 'In the manner of a hasty rout take up a disorderly flight the way of the wind.'

[3] A passage of some length has been lost from the original play. What follows, from 487 to 516, is a spurious and very faulty composition.

[4] Phthiotis.

stream of the clear Strymon. Then those who never believed in gods before addressed them in prayers, worshipping the earth and the sky.[1] But when the army had ceased their long invocation of the god,[2] they proceeded to cross the ice-encrusted ford. Those of us then who marched before the rays of the god were dispersed abroad, got safe away, (but not the others): for the bright orb of the sun lighting up the world with his rays penetrated the frozen river in the middle, warming it with his heat. And then they began to fall upon each other;[3] and happy indeed was he who soonest parted with the breath of life. But those who survived and met with a safe passage, after passing through Thrace with much hardship, arrived at last, having escaped every danger, but not many in number, at the land of their homes: so that the state of the Persians may well mourn in regret for the beloved youth of the land. This account is true; but I omit in my narrative many of the misfortunes which the god made to bear so heavily on the Persians.

Cho. O demon, hard to engage with, how very heavily did you trample[4] with your feet on the whole Persian people!

At. Alas, wretched that I am for the total destruction of the army. O nightly vision, but too clearly seen, of that dream,—how very plainly did you portend to me evil! But *you* interpreted it too lightly. Still, since your report on the matter did decide it in this way, I desire in the first place to pray to the gods; next, I will take liquid offerings from my house, as presents to the Earth and the Spirits of the departed, and return hither.[5] I well know indeed that it is all too late;[6] but it is with the hope that for the future

[1] They offered their prayers to the Elements in thanksgiving for so signal and unexpected a miracle as the freezing of the river, so as to afford a passage, at an unusual time of year.

[2] He means, that they lost valuable time in doing so.

[3] The ice was made slippery by the sun; the men could not stand on it, and in falling, probably, broke the ice and were drowned.

[4] ἐνάλλεσθαι, *insultare*, may be a figure derived from the *pancratium* or the wrestling school. See *Agam.* 1146.

[5] She does not say εἶμι ληψομένη, but ἥξω λαβοῦσα, namely, she will return to the grave of Darius.

[6] Lit. 'as upon things already done.

better things may happen. It is for you now, since this matter has ended so, to engage in faithful consultations with the royal councillors; and my son, should he come here before me, you must console and escort into the palace, lest he should add some further evil to the present evils.[1]

Cho. O sovereign Zeus, now hast thou destroyed the army of Persians boastful in their words and mighty in their hosts, and hast buried in gloomy mourning the city of Susa [and Ecbatana].[2] And many a maid, with tender hands tearing to tatters her head-tire, drenches with soaking tears the folds of her dress, sharing in the general grief; while the Persian matrons, daintily sighing,[3] longing to see again their newly-wedded lords, and having given up the finely-draped marriage-couches, the joy of their delicate girlhood, mourn with insatiable sighs. And I too take up dolefully as my theme the fate of the departed in the approved strain.[4] For now the whole land of Asia mourns for being emptied of its men. 'Twas Xerxes that led them, alas, and Xerxes that caused their death, and Xerxes that managed the whole affair imprudently by his sea-traversing barques. Why did Darius preside over the army as captain of the bowmen, once so harmlessly to the citizens, a leader loved by the people of Susa; while the land and sea-forces were taken out by these dark-prowed equally-rowed ships, and by (other) ships, alas! were destroyed,—the ships, I say, with the murderous impact of their beaks,—and by the hands of Athenian men? And the king himself, as we hear, has barely escaped by a route across the wintry steppes of Thrace. And they who perished first, left (unburied) of necessity, are besprent with brine on the Cychrean[5] strand, *Wah!* Lament and be stung with grief; raise a deep-toned cry of woe to the very heavens for our sorrows; strain your ill-boding voice to a loud shout of dire distress.[6] And cruelly bruised by the eddying currents,

[1] *i. e.* commit suicide.

[2] ἠδ' Ἐκβατάνων seems interpolated.

[3] ἁβροπενθεῖς, sup. 139.

[4] δοκίμως, namely, like public or professional mourners. It may be questioned if these two lines (548—9) are not interpolated.

[5] Κυχρεία was an ancient name of Salamis.

[6] Passages like this can only be rendered by paraphrasing, and even then they are with difficulty made readable.

ah, sad! they are gnawed by the voiceless brood of the pure element, *Wah!* And each house, bereaved of its head, is in mourning; childless parents, aged men bewailing their heaven-sent sufferings, now learn the full extent of their loss. And they in the land of Asia, forsooth, are no longer under the Persian rule;[1] no longer pay tribute at the stern command of a sovereign master; no longer will they prostrate themselves to the earth in humble submission to his authority; for the kingly influence is gone. Nor will mortals any longer keep their tongues in check; for the people are at liberty to speak their thoughts freely, since (say they) the yoke of constraint is removed. All blood-stained in its fields the sea-washed isle of Ajax has for its own all that once was Persia's.

At. My friends, whoever has had experience in sorrows knows that when once a tide of evils comes upon mortals, a man is wont to view everything with alarm; but, when fortune flows on in a tranquil stream, he is wont to feel confident that that same fortune will ever waft him on his course. (I say this now), for to me indeed at present all the adversities sent us by heaven seem in my eyes to be full of alarm; and there rings ever in my ears a dread note very different from the paean of Apollo.[2] Such harrowing tidings of misfortune affright my mind. For this reason I set forth on my return from the palace, as ye see, without carriages or my accustomed splendour, bringing for the father of my son, as propitiatory libations, such offerings as have power to appease the dead. There is sweet white milk from the pure cow, and the drop of the flower-working bee, the bright honey, with water drawn from the virgin spring: the unadulterated drink too from the wild vine that produced it, the sparkling liquor of old wine, is here: and the fragrant fruit[3] of the pale-green olive, which ever while it lives flourishes clothed with leaves, is before you, with chaplets of

[1] What adds to the bitterness of defeat is, that the Ionian peoples will begin to despise and disown Persian rule.

[2] The παιὰν Ἐρινύων of *Agam.* 628.

[3] εὐῶδες ἔλαιον, *Od.* ii. 339.

flowers, the children of all-producing earth. But do you, my friends, sing loud strains of good omen over these libations for the dead, and call repeatedly on Darius, who is now a spirit of power (in Hades). I on my part will head the procession to carry these earth-poured offerings in honour of the infernal gods.[1]

Cho. Royal lady, revered by the Persians, do you accompany these libations to the abodes beneath the earth, and we with hymns will beseech the conductors of the dead to be favourable to us in the world below. Do ye therefore, O holy powers, Earth and Hermes, and thou, king of the dead, send up from below a soul to the light; for if he knows any remedy that is good for our woes, *he* alone of mortals will tell us the way to get over them. Does our dear departed king, holding equal rank with the daemon-powers below, hear me uttering these varied dismal broken[2] appeals, so as to understand clearly my barbaric voice,[3] to convey to him through Earth the sounds of our all-doleful griefs? Does he hear me from below? But do thou, O Earth, and ye also who are rulers of the dead, suffer to depart from your abodes a mighty prince of the Shades, the Susa-born king of the Persians, and send up to us such an one as never yet the Persian land covered with the sod. Dear indeed was the man, and dear is his tomb; for dear was the character it hath hid from us. Aïdoneus, conductor of the dead to the world above, mayst thou send up the spirit of Darius! O what a king was he,[4] alas! For not only was he no destroyer of his people by foolish devastating wars, but he was called Divine Councillor to the Persians; and divine truly he was, since he governed his people prosperously. O king, ancient king, come visit us! come, I say, to the

[1] Lit. 'will conduct in front the earth-drunk honours.' It is difficult to deny, that the primitive notion of propitiatory sacrifices was simply that of *feeding* the hungry spirit in Hades. Hence, as here, the offerings, whether of flesh or fruit, are always such as constitute the natural and essential food of man.

[2] *δύσθροα*, the utterance of which is impeded by sobs.

[3] *σαφηνῆ*, sc. *ὥστε εἶναι*. Compare *Suppl.* 110.

[4] Corrupt.

topmost peak of the barrow, raising to earth the safron-dyed shoe of your foot, showing to our sight the crest of your royal tiara. Come forth, Darius, unharming father of thy people, come, ho![1] Appear, O master, that you may hear the new and disastrous calamities of our master. For now a Stygian mist flits over us, since all the youth of the land has perished. Come, unharming father Darius, come, ho! O woe, woe! O much deplored by thy friends in thy death, why, O lord of lords, by a twofold error[2] through thoughtlessness has all this land suffered the utter destruction of her three-banked galleys, now no galleys, alas!

Ghost of Darius. Ye trustiest of councillors, companions of my youth, aged Persians, with what distress is the city afflicted? The level earth groans, is cut up, and seamed (with wheels); and seeing my wife standing near the tomb I felt fear, and accepted the libations in a kindly spirit. But you are wailing as you stand by my tomb, and uttering loud cries and groans to summon my spirit from below you are calling on me in piteous strains. But to get out is no easy matter, especially as the gods below are better at receiving than at letting loose. Still, as I have held a post of dignity among them,[3] I have come: but be quick, that I may not be blamed for (exceeding) my time. What is this new disaster that has fallen heavily on the Persians?

Cho. I feel awe at the sight of thy countenance, and I feel awe to say what is unwelcome, through my ancient fear of you.

Dar. But, since I have come from below in compliance with your wailings, tell me by no means a lengthy but a concise tale, and describe the whole affair, laying aside this bashfulness of me.

Cho. I shrink from complying with your request, and I also shrink from speaking the truth,[4] by describing events painful for friends to communicate.

[1] *Δάρει', ἰαυοῖ,* Blomfield's correction, seems very plausible.

[2] The text here is corrupt.

[3] See *Cho.* 352.

[4] *ἄρτια,* which I have suggested from the gloss of Schol. Med. ἀληθεῦσαι, seems more probable than ἀντία.

Dar. Well then, since a long-familiar awe of mind is an obstacle to *you*,—come therefore, aged partner of my couch, well-born dame, cease from these tears and groans, and tell me something that I can understand; and of course human woes may befal human beings. For many mishaps by sea and many by land occur to mortal men, if their length of life should extend very far.

At. O thou who didst surpass all mankind in prosperous fortune,—who while you saw the beams of the sun were an object of envy to all, and passed a life of continued happiness, adored as a god by the Persians, now indeed[1] I hold you fortunate in having died before you witnessed the depth of our misfortunes. For the whole tale you shall hear, Darius, in a brief space:—the affairs of the Persians are utterly ruined, to say it in a word.

Dar. In what way? Did a sudden stroke of pestilence come, or a sedition to the state?

At. Not at all; but the whole army has been destroyed near Athens.

Dar. And which of my sons conducted an expedition thither? Inform me.

At. The impetuous Xerxes, taking out all the men from the level parts of the continent.

Dar. And was it with land forces or navy that the unhappy man made so mad an attempt as that?

At. In both ways: there was a double front of two armies.

Dar. And how did so vast a host contrive to pass on foot?

At. He bridged over the Hellespont by a device that enabled him to cross.

Dar. What, did he effect even this—the closing of the mighty Bosphorus?

At. So it was: and doubtless some malignant power affected his judgment.[2]

[1] νῦν γε, not νῦν τε.
[2] Or (as the Schol.) 'assisted him in his intention.' So inf. 738.

Dar. Alas! it was some mighty power of evil that came to make him act so foolishly.

At. (True): for we may see by the result what a mischief he brought to pass.

Dar. And pray how did they fare, that you so lament over them?

At. The naval host being discomfited caused the destruction of the land-army.

Dar. And has the whole host so utterly been annihilated by the spear?

At. Yea, so that in respect of the calamity the city of Susa in the first place bewails its lack of men——

Dar. Alas for so goodly a support and military succour!

At. And besides, the whole population of the Bactrians has perished in utter destruction, and not merely a few old men.

Dar. O foolish youth, what fine young allies he has lost!

At. And the army of Xerxes left all alone and deprived of assistance, they say, with no great number——

Dar. Comes to what end, and in what way? *Is* there any safety for them?

At. Arrived joyfully at the bridge which united the two continents.

Dar. And got safe to the mainland of Asia? Is that true?

At. Yes, a clear report of it prevails: in *that* there is no dispute.

Dar. Alas! quickly indeed has the fulfilment of the oracles come; it was upon my son that Zeus made the issue of the predictions to fall: but I somehow or other expected that the gods would accomplish these evils after a long time. But, when a man himself uses his best efforts, the god also lends a hand. Now does a fountain of evils appear to have been discovered for all my friends. But my son in ignorance brought all this to pass through the recklessness of youth, in that he expected to stop by chains, as if it were a slave, the sacred Hellespont from flowing, the Bosphorus, that stream of the gods; and he thought to alter for the better[1] its navigable strait, when he surrounded it with forged chains and made a spacious way for a mighty host. And though but a mortal, he fancied, by no means wisely, that he should get the mastery over all the gods, and even Poseidon. Must not this have been some malady of mind that possessed my son? I am in fear lest the vast wealth won by my labours should become for men the plunder of the first comer.

At. Such are the lessons that impetuous Xerxes learns by associating with those bad men; for they tell him, that *you* acquired by the spear great wealth for your children, while he, through want of manly spirit, fights his battles at home, and in no degree increases the fortune he inherited from his father. It was from hearing such reproaches oft uttered by worthless men, that he designed this expedition and this army against Hellas.

Dar. And therefore a deed has been done by them that is most terrible, never to be forgotten, such as never yet befel this city of Susa to drain it of its hosts, from the time that sovereign Zeus ordained this high prerogative, that one man should be ruler over all the pasture plains of Asia, holding the sceptre of government. A Mede was he[2] who first was head of the army; then another, his son,[3] completed his designs, for good sense directed the helm of his mind.[4] Third after him, Cyrus, a fortunate man, came to the throne and established peace for all his friends. The people of the Lydians and the Phrygians he acquired as his subjects, and the whole of Ionia he reduced by force: for the god was not hostile to him, such was his prudence. A son of Cyrus fourth in succession ruled the host, and Mardus fifth held sway, a disgrace to his country and the ancient throne; but him by the aid of craft Artaphernes the brave slew in his palace, with friendly conspirators to whom that duty had been

[1] To make a dry road out of a watery way.

[2] Astyages.

[3] Cyaxares.

[4] The Schol. Med. says there is a play on the name Ἀρταφρένης or Ἀρταφέρνης, ὁ ἀρτίας φρένας ἔχων. If so, this line is out of place; and indeed it gives no logical sense here.

assigned. [The sixth was Maraphis, and the seventh Artaphrenes.] And I too obtained the lot I desired, and made many expeditions with a numerous army: yet never did I bring so much mischief on the city. But Xerxes my son is young, and thinks like a youth, and does not bear in mind my orders. For be right well assured of this, my coequals in age; all of us together, who before severally held this sovereignty, shall be shown never to have caused by our actions so many calamities.

Cho. What then, king Darius? With what purpose do you bring your remarks to a close? How in this state of things may we Persian people yet fare for the best?

Dar. If you make not any expedition into the country of the Hellenes,—not even if the Median army should be greater than theirs. For the land itself is an ally to them.

Cho. What mean you by that? In what way, pray, is it their ally?

Dar. By killing with famine those whose numbers are greatly in excess.

Cho. But we shall send out a more manageable and select expedition.

Dar. But not even the army which has now staid behind in the regions of Hellas shall obtain a safe return.

Cho. How say you? Does not *all* the army of the east cross the Hellespont from Europe?

Dar. Few indeed out of many, if one may trust the oracles of the god, looking at what has now been done: for it is not that only some of the things predicted are coming true, but others not. And if this is really so, he is leaving behind[2] a chosen body of troops trusting to vain hopes. For they are staying where the Asopus waters the plain with his streams, a friendly fertilizer of the land of the Boeotians. There it yet awaits them to suffer the crowning miseries of all their misfortunes, in atonement for their insolence and

[1] 'To what port are you steering the end of your words?' See on *Suppl.* 436.

[2] Namely, those under the command of Mardonius.

godless designs. For when they arrived at the land of Hellas they felt no awe at plundering the sacred images of the gods, nor in setting fire to their shrines. But the altars have been levelled with the dust, and the images of the gods have been uprooted and overthrown from their bases, and lie heaped together on the ground. So it is that, having done evil, they are suffering not less,[1] and others they have still to endure, for not yet is the bottom of the evils reached, but they are still coming forth in greater abundance.[2] So thick will lie the gouts of gore from men slaughtered in the land of the Plataeans by the Doric lance. And heaps of corpses even to the third generation shall tell a silent tale to the eyes of men, that one who is a mortal must not hold too proud thoughts. For presumption blossoms and matures a corn-crop of delusion,[3] from which it reaps a harvest of tears. When then you see such penalties of these deeds, remember Athens and Hellas, and let no one, thinking disparagingly of his present fortunes, and enamoured of something else, waste like water his great prosperity. Be assured that Zeus is a punisher of overweening pride, and is ever by to exact a heavy reckoning. Wherefore do you instruct him, warned as he has been by the god to be wise in time, with lessons of prudence, to leave off sinning against the gods by a too boastful presumption. But do you, aged lady, the loved mother of Xerxes, go into the palace, and taking such attire as is becoming to him, go forth to meet your son: for all the clothes upon his body, through deep grief at his woes, have been torn[4] into tattered shreds of embroidered robes. Do you then discreetly soothe him by your words; for you alone, I am well assured, he will bear to hear. But I must depart into the darkness of earth below: farewell then to you, Elders, not the less though you are in troubles, and allow your souls such pleasure as the day affords; for to the dead there is no advantage in riches.

[1] See *Agam.* 516.

[2] ἐκπληθύεται, suggested in my note, satisfies the sense, and the explanation of Schol. Med. αὔξεται τὰ κακά.

[3] See on *Agam.* 745.

[4] Lit. 'are warp-broken.'

Cho. Many truly are the misfortunes, both present and in store[1] for the Persians, which I have heard with deep grief of heart.

At. God of heaven, what a host of painful evils crowd into my mind! Yet especially does this calamity afflict my heart,—when I hear of the woeful plight[2] of the garments on the body of my son,—that, I mean, which now invests him. I will go therefore, and taking a fitting attire from the palace, I will essay to meet my son; for those dearest to us we will not abandon in their misfortunes.

Cho. O heavens! 'twas a glorious and happy citizen-life that we then enjoyed, when the godlike old king Darius, all-sufficient in himself, unharming, not to be fought with, ruled the country. In the first place, we used to shew to the world that we had armies of good repute, and secure laws directed all things: safe returns too from wars brought the men back to their homes unworn by toil, without having suffered hardships, and successful. And what a number of cities he captured without passing the ford of the river Halys, or leaving his own hearth.[3] Such were the lake-cities[4] in the wide lagoon of the Strymon, close bordering on the Thracian settlements; and those without the mere on the mainland with fortified walls thrown round them, obeyed him for their king, both those which boasted of a site[5] by the broad stream of Helle, and the deeply-recessed Propontis, and the entrance into the Pontus. The islands likewise that lie off the headland of the sea, washed round by the waves but close bordering on this continent, such as Lesbos and olive-planted Samos, Chios, and Paros, Naxos, Myconos, and adjoining Tenos its close neighbour Andros. And the islands nearer the open sea, midway between the shores, he ruled

[1] Perhaps *κοὐ μέλλοντ' ἔτι.*

[2] This may be a satire on the Persian grandeur and love of dress: but it is to be feared the speech is spurious, and the Schol. Med. seems to ignore it.

[3] He seems to mean, without going into any other country than Asia, which was as it were the *ἑστία* of the great king.

[4] 'Acheloids.' Schol. *Ἀχελῷον γὰρ πᾶν ὕδωρ λέγουσιν.* The lake-habitations described in *Herod.* v. 16, appear to be meant.

[5] Perhaps from the natural beauty and advantage of the situation.

over, Lemnos, and the settlement of Icarus; also Rhodes and Cnidos, and the cities of Cyprus, Paphos, Soli, and Salamis, the mother-city of which is the cause of these sighs. The cities too, rich in possessions, in the Ionian district, populously inhabited by Hellenes, he ruled by his prudence; and he had at his command an unfailing supply of heavy-armed men and of mixed allies from every nation. But now all these things have been plainly turned against us by the gods, and we have to bear them, having received a terrible defeat in the wars by disasters at sea.

Xer. Alas! unhappy am I, having met with this dreadful fate when least expected! With what cruel intent has fortune set her foot on the race of the Persians! What will become of me wretched? For the strength of my limbs is relaxed when I see these aged citizens before me. Would that I too, O Zeus, along with the men who are dead and gone, had been shrouded in the darkness of death![1]

Cho. Alas, O king, for our brave army, and alas for the high honour of the Persian rule, and the proud ornament of her heroes, whom now fortune has cut off! For the land bewails the youth born on her soil, but slain by Xerxes, who has crammed Hades with dead Persians; for travellers to Hades are many men, the flower of the country, fighters with the bow; for a vast multitude[2] has perished out of the land. Alas, alas, for the brave forces; for the land of Asia, O king of our country, has had a terrible throw.[3]

Xer. You see me here, alas, an object of compassion, who have unhappily proved a curse to my family and my fatherland.

Cho. And such a strain[4] of doleful import will I send forth to greet your return, a voice practised in words of woe, even that of a Mariandynian mourner, a loud cry with many tears.

[1] 'That the fate of death had covered me over.'

[2] Corrupt.

[3] 'Has been made to lean on the knee.' See *Agam.* 64.

[4] Namely, not a song of joy, but a θρῆνος.—τοίαν for τὰν is conjectural.

Xer. Aye, weep and spare not the strains of grief interrupted by sobs[1]; for fortune hath thus changed and gone against me.

Cho. I too[2] will cry all dolefully, doing honour to the memories of those lately lost to the city by their defeat at sea, as one who mourns the loss of children; I in my turn will raise my voice in loud tearful wailings.

Xer. For the god of war, with all his array of ships, has ceded the victory to the other side, and met with discomfiture from[3] the Ionians; that fatal bay he has cleared of every living soul,[4] and that luckless shore.

Cho. Cry Oh! oh! and fear not to know the worst. Where are the rest of your many friends? Where those of your own staff, such as was Pharandaces, Susas, Pelago, Psammis, Dotamas, Agdabatas, and Susiscanes, who left Ecbatana?

Xer. I left them dead on the shores of Salamis thrown from a Tyrian ship,[5] beating on a rocky shore.

Cho. And where, oh! where is your Pharnuchus and the brave Ariomard? Where king Seualces, or the high-born Lilaeus, Memphis, Tharybis, and Masistras, Artembares and Hystaechmas? These questions too I would have answered.

Xer. Oh me! they saw the ancient, the fatal Athens, and they all with one convulsive struggle, unhappy wretches, were laid gasping on the land.[6]

Cho. And did you leave also that all-trusty councillor of the Persians, your own Eye of state,—him who counted his troops by tens upon tens of thousands, Alpistus, son of Batanochus, the descendant of Sesamas and Megabatas?

[1] The literal meaning appears to be, 'Send forth a dismal all-grieving broken-voiced utterance.' Such phrases are most difficult to render. I find the following in one published translation: "Pour ye forth a grievous all-lamentable sad-resounding voice; for this daemon hath made a turn back upon me."

[2] *κἀγὼ*, conjecture. Lit. 'Honouring the lately-endured sea-stricken heavy burdens of the city.' Another *χορευτὴς* is supposed to speak.

[3] 'Suffered evil from,' or 'felt the consequence of attacking,' &c.

[4] 'Having reaped the gloomy sea-level.' So *θερίζειν βροτοὺς*, *Suppl.* 628.

[5] Lit. 'gone dead out of a Tyrian ship.'

[6] Like fishes drawn alive out of the sea on to the beach.

The great Parthus too, and Oebares? Alas for the poor unhappy men! You describe evil succeeding evil[1] for the best of Persia's nobles.

Xer. You recal indeed to my mind the deep regrets I feel for my noble comrades and friends, when you speak of these dreadful ne'er-to-be-forgotten woes upon woes. My heart cries out in grief within my very breast.[2]

Cho. But there is yet another whom we miss: the Mardian general of ten thousand men Xanthus, and Anchares the Arian, Diaexis and Arsaces the commanders of cavalry, Kigdagates and Lythimnas, and Tolmus insatiate in fighting. I am astounded (by their loss): no longer on canopied cars[3] following in the royal train—

Xer. No, for they are gone who were the leaders of the host.[4]

Cho. Gone they are, alas! and their names are not heard.

Xer. Woe, woe!

Cho. Woe, indeed! for the gods have caused us an unexpected evil, conspicuous before all others,—such a one as Atè has watched[5] to its accomplishment.

Xer. We have received a blow, by such chances as seldom come.[6]

Cho. A blow indeed, that is plain to all,—

Xer. New griefs, yea, new griefs,—

Cho. By encountering Ionian sailors with ill-success. Unlucky then in its wars is the race of Persians.

Xer. Assuredly; in so vast an army have I, unhappy king, been smitten.

[1] Compare *γῆν πρὸ γῆς*, *Prom.* 700.

[2] "Thou dost in sooth call to my mind a lament for my excellent friends, while thou speakest of baleful, hateful, exceeding hateful horrors. My heart within me moans aloud, moans aloud for them unhappy." (Translation, Bohn's Classical Library.) This may serve to show the hopelessness of attempting word-for-word renderings in such passages.

[3] Carriages with umbrellas over them, as is frequently seen in the Assyrian sculptures.

[4] For *ἀγρέται* (MSS. *ἀγρόται* or *ἀκρόται*) I would read *ἀγέται*. Photius, *ἡγέτης· ἡγεμών*. The interpolation of *ρ* is a frequent source of corruption.

[5] Schol. *οἷον κακὸν ἡ Ἄτη ἐφορᾷ*. But the meaning of this clause is very obscure.

[6] Corrupt.

Cho. You have indeed; terrible is the blow the Persian power has received.

Xer. See you this remnant of my dress?

Cho. I see, I see it.

Xer. And this arrow-holding,—

Cho. What is this you say has been saved?

Xer. Store-place for weapons?

Cho. Small remains out of so much.

Xer. We have none left to aid us now.

Cho. The Ionian people fly not before the spear.

Xer. They are but too brave, and I have seen a disaster I had not looked for.

Cho. Mean you to speak of the route of the naval host?

Xer. And I rent my robes[1] at the sad mishap.

Cho. Alas, alas!

Xer. And more than *alas.*

Cho. For two-fold and even three-fold—

Xer. Are our sorrows; but causes of joy to our enemies.

Cho. And our strength has been maimed.

Xer. I have none left to precede me as an escort.

Cho. Through the losses of your friends by sea.

Xer. Weep for the disaster, weep, and go forward to the palace.[2]

Cho. Alas, alas! Woe, woe!

Xer. Cry out now with responsive beatings of the breast.

Cho. An ill return of ills for ills.[3]

Xer. Wail on in measured notes.[4]

Cho. Oh! oh! oh!

Xer. Heavy in truth was the calamity.

Cho. Ah! greatly do I grieve at it too.

Xer. Ply, ply the quick stroke, and lament now for *my* sake.

Cho. I am drenched in tears, being full of sighs.

[1] See v. 470.

[2] Be my προπομπὸς in default of others. (Here they form a procession off the stage).

[3] Tears in return for misfortunes. (Schol.)

[4] Schol. εὐρύθμως.

Xer. Cry out now with responsive beatings of the breast.

Cho. I have sorrow enough to think about, my liege lord.

Xer. Now raise your voice aloud in groans.

Cho. Oh! oh! oh!

Xer. And there shall be mixed with them a dismal—

Cho. And a deep-sounding blow.

Xer. Beat hard the breast, and utter the loud Mysian strain.

Cho. Grievous, grievous woes.

Xer. And rend and tear the white hair of your beard.

Cho. Yea, with clenched hands, and with many a sigh.

Xer. And utter a shrill shriek.

Cho. That too will I do.

Xer. And tear to pieces your robe across your breast with all the strength of your hands.

Cho. Grievous, grievous.

Xer. And pull the long locks of your hair, and bewail the lost army.

Cho. Yea, with clenched hands and with many a sigh.

Xer. And let not your eyes be dry.

Cho. I am all wet with tears.

Xer. Cry out now with responsive beatings of the breast.

Cho. Oh! oh!

Xer. With cries of ah! ah! go into the palace.

Cho. Alas! the Persian land is full of sad sounds of grief.

Xer. There is a cry of woe in the city.

Cho. Of woe indeed, yes, yes.

Xer. Utter groans as you pace with solemn step.

Cho. Alas, the Persian land is full of sad sounds of grief.

Xer. Alas for those who perished in the three-banked[1] galleys.

Cho. I will escort you with broken sighs.[2]

[1] With three rowlocks, *i. e.* banks or tiers of oars, each above the other,—triremes.

[2] The conclusion of this play, like that of the 'Seven against Thebes,' can hardly be rendered into readable English. In both cases a procession of mourners is described; and the words are merely vehicles for the music of the αὐλὸς, accompanied with the most violent gestures. One difficulty in translating arises from the fact that there are nearly twenty words in Greek to express our commonplace 'alas!'

AGAMEMNON.

PERSONS REPRESENTED.

A WATCHMAN.	AGAMEMNON.
CHORUS OF OLD MEN OF ARGOS.	CASSANDRA.
CLYTÆMNESTRA.	ÆGISTHUS.
THE HERALD TALTHYBIUS.	

Watch. Of the gods I am ever asking a riddance from these toils during the long time of my year's watch,[1] in which, resting by night on the roofs of the Atridæ like a watch-dog, with head on hand, I have become familiar with the host of the nightly constellations, and those bright powers that bring winter and summer to mortals, shining in upper air, (the stars, when they set, and their risings). And now I am looking out for the signal of a torch, a blaze of fire, bringing tidings from Troy, and the news of its capture: for thus firm in its resolve[2] is a woman's manly-counselling hopeful heart. And whenever I have my rest disturbed by night-walking and the falling dew,—a rest unvisited by dreams, for fear is ever at hand to prevent sleep, so that I cannot close my eyelids soundly in repose;—and when, in such case, I have a mind to sing or whistle, throwing in[3] this remedy of song against sleep,—then straightway I fall to tears, bewailing the condition of this house, not now, as once, managed for the best. But now may there come a happy release from our troubles by the beacon of good

[1] Or 'toils of a watch limited to a year in duration' (*Od.* iv. 526.)

[2] κρατεῖ, is superior to all disappointments, and hoping against hope.

[3] ἐντέμνειν is properly 'to shred herbs into a potion.' See v. 1232.

tidings appearing through this gloom.[1] O hail, illuminator of the night, that showest a light even as of day, and the signal for setting up many a dance at Argos through joy at this event. Hurrah, hurrah!

So do I give loud warning to Agamemnon's queen to rise forthwith from her bed, and utter right heartily a joyful strain of thanksgiving in the house for this torch, now that[2] the city of Troy has been captured, as the beacon-light announces to my sight; and I myself will have a dance by way of a beginning, for I shall score a good throw on my masters' affairs, now that this beacon has turned up a sice on the three dice.[3] Well! at least may it be my lot to take in this hand the friendly hand of the lord of the house on his return. As for the rest, I say nothing. A great ox has set his foot upon my tongue. The house itself if it had but a voice, would tell the tale most clearly;—for myself, I speak willingly to such as understand, but I choose to forget to such as do not.

Cho. This is the tenth year since the powerful adversary of Priam, king Menelaus and Agamemnon,[4] that sturdy yoke-pair of Atreus' sons, holding joint thrones and sceptres from Zeus, sent out an Argive army of a thousand ships from this land, a military aid, yelping loud war with all their hearts, like vultures that in solitary grief for their young wheel in eddying circles over their eyries, plying their way with the oarage of their wings, for that they have lost their callow brood, the objects of their toil. But some god on high,—Apollo, it may be, or Pan, or Zeus,—hearing the shrill plaintive cry of these denizens in air,[5] sends to the transgressors a fury, bringing after-vengeance on the deed. And thus it is that the mighty Zeus, the god of hospitality, sends

[1] The scene is at early dawn. After this verse there is a momentary pause, and the Watch resumes his position of rest, suddenly to start up again at sight of the beacon.

[2] Lit. 'if really.'

[3] 'Having thrown three times a six.'

[4] These two brothers are viewed as partners in a joint sovereignty, and therefore spoken of as one. So in v. 602 Menelaus is called king of the Argive land. Compare also v. 112, 115.

[5] The parent-birds are compared to Athenian μέτοικοι, who could obtain redress only through προστάται.

the sons of Atreus for the punishment of Paris, intending to cause[1] Greeks and Trojans alike, in behalf of a woman of several suitors, many a struggle bearing down men's limbs in the fight, when the knee cannot rise from the dust, and the spear-shaft is snapped at the onset of the fight. However, matters are as they now are; and they will be carried out to their destined end. Not by secret tears nor secret libations will Agamemnon soothe the intense rage of a mother for the unholy sacrifice of her child.[2] But we, who have taken no part in the service with our aged bodies, but were left behind in the aid that then went forth, are staying at home, supporting on staves a strength like that of a child. For, as the boyish vigour that holds sway within the breast is equal to that of an old man, and Ares is not at his post;[3] so he that is *very* old, when the green leaf is getting sered, goes his way on three feet,[4] and with no more of Ares in him than a boy, he flits to and fro like a vision of the daylight. But tell me, thou daughter of Tyndareus, queen Clytemnestra, what is this business? what has happened now? What fresh news have you heard, and by the tidings of what message are you sending round orders to sacrifice? For of all the gods who govern the city,—gods supreme and gods infernal, those who are denizens of the field and those who dwell in the agora,[5] —the altars are blazing with offerings. And now here, now there, a torch raises its light to the very sky, fed[6] with the soothing and genuine cordials of pure incense-oil, the goodly essence brought out of the inmost stores of the palace. Tell me of these matters as much as you are able, and as it is lawful for you to impart, and become a healer of this anxiety,

[1] The passage resembles *Il.* ii. 39; but I doubt if *θήσων* is good Greek, and propose to read *Δαναοῖς ἐπιθήσοντας.*

[2] Gr. 'will he soothe stubborn rage for sacrifices without fire.' I have slightly expanded this into what appears to be the more probable meaning of the poet.

[3] *i. e.* the military *ἡλικία* has not yet arrived.

[4] Namely, with the aid of a stick: an allusion to the riddle solved by Oedipus.—Those who were too old to fight ten years ago, are now *ὑπέργηρῳ.*

[5] Where they were represented by statues.

[6] Literally, 'drugged.' The *χρῖμα* (our *chrism*) was *perfumed* oil, *τεθυωμένον*, *Il.* xiv. 172.

which under present circumstances at one time brings gloomy thoughts, while at another you hold out a flattering hope from your sacrifices,[1] to keep away from my mind insatiate care, the grief that preys upon it.

I yet have power to describe,[2] by declaring the full purport of the lucky wayside omens which gave the heroes assurance of success,—for even yet my age retains some of its natural strength, and sheds over me through divine inspiration a strong impulse to sing,—how the twain sovereigns of the Achæans, leaders with one mind of Hellas' youth, were sent against the Trojan land with spear and avenging hand by the warlike bird, the king of birds, the black one and that with the white tail-feathers, when they appeared to the kings of the fleet near to the palace, on the right hand, on perches that could be seen by the whole army, preying on a hare big with young, which they had stopped from running its courses any more. Sing a strain of woe,[3] but let the good prevail. But the good seer of the host, seeing the two warlike sons of Atreus differing in their tempers, knew the meaning of these banqueters on the hare, that they signified the leaders of the expedition: and thus he spake interpreting the prodigy: "In time indeed this expedition captures the city of Priam: but all the public flocks and herds before the walls the fortune of war shall violently ravage.[4] Let them only beware lest some jealousy from the gods[5] should tarnish the great curb of Troy, smitten all too soon in its way on the expedition: for against the house of the Atridae the virgin Artemis bears a grudge because of those winged hounds of her father, which sacrificed the poor hare, young and all, before she had given them birth;[6] and she loathes the banquet of the eagles. Sing a strain of woe, but let the good prevail! So kindly

[1] I read *ἀγανὰν φαίνεις ἐλπίδ' ἀμύνειν*, for *ἀγανὰ φαίνεις ἐλπὶς ἀμύνει* (Med.).

[2] Namely, if too old to fight.

[3] As an *ἀπευκτὸν πῆμα*, inf. 621.

[4] The Geeeks shall consume all the *πρόνομα βοτὰ* (*Suppl.* 672) for their daily subsistence, and so be reduced to great straits.

[5] Provoked by the impious sacrifice of Iphigenia. The 'curb' is the coercing army.

[6] An allusion to the *virgin* Iphigenia, perhaps.

disposed is the fair goddess to the tender whelps of the fierce lions, and to the teat-loving young of all the wild creatures living in the woodlands, that she requires of Zeus that he should give effect to the omens foreshewing these things, the appearing of the eagles both for weal and for woe. But I invoke the healing god (to interfere)[1] that she may not bring on the Greeks unfavourable weather, so as to detain their fleet a long time through adverse winds, in her desire to gain for herself another sacrifice, a lawless one, not to be feasted on,[2] the natural causer of jealousies, holding not in awe a husband; for there abides in that family a mindful wrath, ever rising up in fearful retribution, a crafty housewife claiming vengeance for slaughtered children."[3]

Such were the dread tidings which, with the promise of great glories, Calchas declared that fate had in store for the royal house by the eagles seen on the way. And in harmony with those words sing a strain of woe, but let the good prevail!

Zeus, whoever he be,—if by such a title it is pleasing to him to be invoked, by that do I address him. For I cannot, balancing the whole matter in my mind, refer it to any, save only Zeus, if I am really to throw off this groundless[4] weight of care. Neither could he, who to those of old was a god of power, abounding in confidence to fight with any one, now render any aid, since he is gone by; and he who succeeded him has passed away, having found his conqueror.[5] But if one heartily sings loud songs of victory in honour of Zeus, he will be altogether right in his judgment. A god is he who leads mortals on the way to wisdom, and who has ordained that sufferings, by their own right, should convey instruction.

[1] As ἀποτρόπαιος, and the sister of Artemis.

[2] The sacrifice of Iphigenia, whose flesh could not be eaten like that of ordinary victims. The bloody worship of Artemis, as anciently that of the Italian Diana, was originally a kind of she-devil-worship requiring human victims.

[3] Those of Thyestes as well as Iphigenia.

[4] This boding of which I know not definitely the cause.

[5] Uranus and Cronus, Titan-gods of the old world, are passed and gone, supplanted by Zeus, whose attribute of ἐπινίκιος is also best adapted to the hope of victory at Troy.

For anxiety that is ever recalling past woes, presenting itself to the heart in sleep, instils obedience, and so it comes even to the unwilling: and it may be that this is a mercy of the gods, who sit on their awful thrones with power to compel.

So then the senior general of the Achæan fleet, not putting a slight on any seer, but submitting to the fortunes which befel him;—when the Achæan host began to be sore pressed by the delay in sailing that was exhausting their stores, while they held the coast over against Chalcis in the ever-restless channel of Aulis; and when winds coming from the Strymon, bringing wearisome delay and famine, causing mortals to wander in harbourless seas, unsparing of ships and cables, and doubling the time of their stay, were wearing out by slow waste the flower of the Argives;—when too the seer had plainly told the chiefs that there was another and more painful remedy for the vexatious storm, referring to Artemis, so that the Atridæ impatiently struck the ground with their staves, and restrained not a tear;—then, I say, the elder general spoke thus, addressing the men:—"Grievous indeed is the fate, not to comply; but grievous also is it, if I shall have to slay my child, the darling of my home, defiling a father's hands at the altar's side with gore trickling from a virgin neck. Which of these courses is without evil? How am I to become a deserter of the fleet, and lose my allies? For 'tis natural for them to desire with an eager longing some sacrifice to lull the winds, even if it be the blood of a maiden. May it be for the best!" So when he had put on the harness of necessity, breathing an impious change of feeling, unblest, unholy, from which he conceived a new resolve to dare anything in his heart.—for in mortals 'tis usually a wretched infatuation, counselling evil deeds and the first cause of woe, that emboldens them,—then at last did he dare to become the slayer of his daughter, in aid of a war for avenging a woman's wrongs, and as a sacrifice in behalf of the ships. And her prayers and appeals to the name of father, and even her unmarried life, the chiefs held as nothing, in their passion for war. So the father ordered the ministers after the prayer to summon all their courage and hold her aloft, as one would a kid, over the altar, wrapped round in her robes, in reclining posture;[1] and that a guard over her fair mouth should restrain the utterance of a curse against the house by the forcibly imposed silence of a gag. And as she let fall her long saffron-dyed robes to the earth, she smote each of the sacrificing priests with a pitiful glance from her eye, expressing by her looks, as in a picture, a desire to speak; for ofttimes in the festive halls of her sire she had sung to them, and virgin as she was, with her chaste voice she had been wont affectionately to do honour to the paean sung in happy times at the triple libation of her dear father. But what followed I saw not, and cannot declare: yet the prophetic skill of Calchas is never vain. The descending scale of Justice brings knowledge to those who have suffered; but let that which is yet pending, since we cannot undo it, bring no concern to us beforehand; for that is as good as grieving before it comes.[2] We shall know our fate clearly with the morning dawn. Well! may a happy success result after these horrors, as is the wish of this sole guardian of the Argive land, standing next in authority to the king.[3]

I have come with respectful reverence for your majesty, queen Clytemnestra: for 'tis right to hold in honour the wife of the man who holds rule over the state, when the throne of the husband has been left vacant. But now, whether you have really heard some good news, or whether you have not, and are sacrificing on the hope of happy tidings, I would gladly learn; albeit, if you decline to answer, I have no right to complain.

Cly. Happy tidings, indeed, may Morning, as the saying is, become the bearer of from its mother Night!—But you

[1] That so the life-blood might strike the altar,—an essential part of the cruel rite.

[2] It is best to be indifferent about the future, since we cannot alter it. These remarks refer to the probability of Justice overtaking Agamemnon for consenting to slay his daughter.

[3] Or, 'most nearly related to it.' The Chorus consists of elders, who consider the safety of the country depends on their counsels.

shall be informed of a joy which surpasses the mere *hope* of hearing. The Argives have captured the city of Priam!

Cho. How say you? The word has escaped me through incredulity.

Cly. I say that Troy is in the hands of the Argives. Do I speak plainly?

Cho. Joy steals over me, calling forth a tear.

Cly. Yes, your eye proves that you are pleased.

Cho. Well, but what is your sure *proof* of these events?

Cly. I have one,—of course I have,—if the god has not deceived us.[1]

Cho. But are you paying regard to persuasive visions of dreams?

Cly. I would not accept the mere fancy of a slumbering mind.

Cho. Can it be then that some omen not derived from birds inflated you with hope?

Cly. As if I were a young girl, you greatly underrate my intelligence.

Cho. And pray how long has the city been captured?

Cly. I tell you, in the night that has just given birth to this light of day.

Cho. Why, what messenger could possibly arrive with such speed?

Cly. Hephaestus, sending forth a bright flashing light from Ida. And beacon sent on beacon hither from the messenger fire; Ida first to the hill of Hermes at Lemnos; then a huge blaze from the island was taken up in the third place by the peak of Mount Athos sacred to Zeus; and when, rising high so as to cross the back of the sea, the force of this onward-sped torch with its welcome message,—when the pine-fire, I say, had forwarded its golden light, as a sun, to the heights of Macistus; then did he, without delay or thoughtlessly yielding to repose, pass onward his share of the message. And the light of the beacon, taking a long stretch

[1] By a false blaze, or accidental fire in the woods, &c. The θεῖον ψύθος of v. 462.

to the streams of Euripus, gave notice to the watch on Messapius; while they lighted up in turn and passed it further on, setting fire to a stack of withered heath. And the strong flare, not as yet becoming dim, bounding over the plain of the Asopus like a glorious moon, to the ridge of Cithæron, waked up a fresh relay of the messenger fire. Nor did the guard stationed there disown the light that reached him from far, but set a-blaze a yet greater pile than those described. And now the flame darted across the lake Gorgopis, reached Mount Aegiplanctus, and urged on the succession of the fire not to linger in its course. So they light up anew and speed on its way a huge fire-flake of ample strength even to pass with its distant blaze the headland that looks down on the Saronic gulf. Then at length it alighted, when it had reached the peak of Mount Arachnæus, the watch-post nearest to the city: and so it flashed to this palace of the Atridæ, this beacon-light in long succession from the first signal on Ida. Such was the order of the torch-bearers I had prepared, and so were they passed on in order one from another. And the first in has the prize, even though he started last on the race. Such is the proof and the token I give you, my own husband having forwarded the news to me from Troy.

Cho. To the gods, O queen, I will on a more fitting occasion address my prayers: at present I would fain hear again at length and have my wonder at these tidings, even as you tell them.

Cly. The Argives have gotten their hold of Troy this very day. Methinks sounds that will not blend are heard in the city. For as, if you pour oil and vinegar into the same vessel, you would say that they kept apart in an unfriendly manner; so one may hear the voices of the captured and the conquerors in diverse tones for their different fortunes. For these, throwing themselves on the bodies of the slain,—wives on those of husbands, sisters on brothers, children on those of their aged sires, no longer with a free neck[1] are bewailing the fate of their beloved

[1] Chained as captives.

ones; while the others a hungry and restless toil following the fight is setting down to a meal on whatever the city affords, according to no rule of turn: but just as each drew the lot of chance, they are lodging in the captured Trojan houses, rid at length from the frosts and dews of the open sky, now that the poor fellows will sleep the whole night without having to keep guard. And if they do but treat with religious respect the patron-gods of the captured land, and their statues, the captors are little likely to be captured in turn.[1] But let them beware lest, ere they leave, the lust of plunder should fall on the army so as to harry what they ought not, overcome by love of gain. For as yet they need a safe return home, and to trace back again the other limb of the double stadium. But if the army should return guilty of sacrilege against the gods, the curse of those who have perished[2] may yet wake up against them, even if no sudden reverses should befal them. Such warnings you hear from me, who am but a woman. May the good prevail, so that we see it in no wavering scale! For many are the blessings of which I have received the benefit.

Cho. Lady, you speak with the wisdom of a man in kind compliance with my request. And I, now that I have heard from you trusty proofs, am making ready for a solemn address to the gods.[3] For a success has been achieved that demands our gratitude in return.

O Zeus our king, O thou welcome night, that hast put us in possession of great honours, by having thrown over the towers of Troy a strong covering net, so that no one full-grown nor any of the young could overleap the mighty ring-net of slavery, the curse of a general capture.[4] Truly

[1] *ἑλὼν αἱρεῖσθαι* was said of any person who experienced a reverse, or whose good fortune turned against him.

[2] Iphigenia.

[3] See v. 308. The movement was probably some change of place in the Chorus, introduced by the opening anapæstics, for singing the following *stasimon*. Probably they walk up in front of the stage and back again.

[4] The metaphor is from a stake-net (*ἀρκύστατον*) set round a herd of animals young and old, and too high to be leapt over. See *Theb.* 336. There seems some confusion between this and a fisher's trawl-net, (*everriculum*). Cf. *λίνου παναγρου*, *Il.* v. 487.

the great Zeus, the god of hospitality, do I hold in awe, even him who has been the author of all this, and who has this long time been stretching his bow against Paris so that the arrow might not light in vain by either falling short of the mark or flying higher than the stars. 'Tis from this Zeus that they have received the blow, we may say: *this* at all events one may trace out. They have fared as he decreed it. Somebody once said, that the gods did not condescend to care about mortal men, by whom the sanctity of the marriage-bed was trampled on;[1] but he was impious: for it is made plain to the posterity of those who presumptuously cherish a spirit of rebellion against the gods more than is right, when their houses teem with excessive wealth, beyond what is best for them.[2] But let your lot be such as not to provoke harm, but such as that a man possessed of sound sense may be proof in himself against it.[3] For there is no protection in wealth for a man when once in insolence he has kicked at the mighty altar of justice, intending to get rid of it altogether: but that wretched persuasion forces him on, the irresistible offspring of Atè (infatuation) suggestive of evil.[4] Then all remedy is in vain: the mischief is not concealed, but balefully gleams as a terrible bright light; and he is like base gold that by rubbing and the use of the touchstone becomes dark-grained when tested; for he is as a foolish boy chasing a winged bird, (little caring that) he has brought into his city an intolerable affliction.[5] To his prayers no god lends an ear, but he destroys the unjust man who engages in these things.[6] Such was Paris, who entered the house of the Atridae, and brought shame on a hospitable

[1] *i.e.* adulterers, like Paris. Cf. inf. 1164.

[2] παρὰ τὸ βέλτιστον, Plat. *Phædrus*, p. 233, A. The sense is, that the posterity of the impious find to their cost that the gods *do* regard crime, when too great prosperity and consequent pride provoke the punishment of ancestral guilt. Compare v. 732.

[3] *i.e.* avert it by a sober use of wealth, νόῳ πλοῦτον ἄγει, Pind. *Pyth.* vi. 47.

[4] The same doctrine occurs v. 216 and 1163.

[5] This refers to Paris who has carried off Helen. πρόστριμμα and προστρίβεσθαι (*Prom.* 337) properly refer to the flogging of slaves.

[6] Or, 'condemns the bringer-on of such afflictions.' But καθαιρεῖν seems to refer to the *tugging down* of wrestlers. τῶνδε is perhaps corrupt.

table by the stealing of a wife. And she on her part, leaving to her fellow-citizens the turmoil of shielded hosts and the arming of marines with the spear, and bringing to Troy destruction in place of a dowry, steps lightly through the doors, having dared an unholy deed: and many a sigh was heaved by the seers of the household as they spoke thus: "O house, O house, and O rulers! O marriage-bed, and the impress[1] of her that once loved her lord!" He stands by in silence, dishonoured but not reproaching, perceiving with deepest pain that she has left him. And through a fond longing for one far beyond seas, a vision of her will seem to rule the house: the grace of the well-formed statues becomes odious to the husband, for through the want of living eyes all the marriage-charm is gone. And mournful fancies come to him in dreams, bringing an unreal delight; for unreal is the vision which, when a man sees in fancy pleasing things, passes through his hands and glides away forthwith on wings that attend the ways of sleep.[2] The griefs in the palace are these, and others surpassing these at the very hearth: and in general, in regard of those who have made a common voyage from Hellas' land, a heartfelt sorrow prevails in every one's home; much at least there is that touches closely the inmost feelings. For people remember well whom they sent out: but in place of the men themselves urns and ashes arrive to each man's home. For Ares that barters bodies for gold, and the holder of the scales in the conflict of the spear, keeps sending from Troy to the friends a little[3] scorched bone-dust bitterly bewailed,[4] freighting the urns with well-stored ashes instead of the living men. And they sigh as they praise this man for being well-skilled in the fight, that man for falling gloriously in heaps of the slain on account of another's wife. Other complaints are secretly muttered, and an invidious regret stealthily spreads

[1] *i. e.* no longer the living reality.

[2] The dream vanishes when the sleep is over.

[3] *βραχύ*. It is difficult to render intelligibly the reading *βαρύ*. But perhaps the metaphor is kept up from weighing gold dust in scales.

[4] See *Cho.* 674.

against the Atridae, as the principals in the suit.[1] But others there round the walls lie in tombs of Trojan earth in the freshness of their beauty;[2] and a hostile land conceals the holders of them. And there is talk among the citizens with an angry feeling: and it performs the part of a ban solemnly ratified by the people. And now an anxiety abides on me, to hear of something as yet wrapped in the gloom of night: for the gods are not unobservant of those who have caused much slaughter, but the sable Erinyes in the course of time, when a man has been prosperous without honesty, by a reverse course of life bring him down to obscurity; and when he is among the lost there is no help for him. To be excessively well spoken of is a dangerous fate; for the vengeful bolt is hurled from the eye of Zeus. But I prefer such prosperity as incurs not divine envy: may I neither be a destroyer of cities, nor as a captive myself see my life subject to others.[3]

But now from the messenger-fire a quick report has gone through the city: whether truly, who knows, or whether it be not a deception from the gods? Who is so childish or so distraught in his senses? That any one should have his hopes warmed by a new message of a beacon, and then be distressed by a change in the news! It is natural to the temper of a woman to assent to what is pleasing rather than to what is certainly known. Too credulous, the boundaries of a woman's mind are encroached on by quick inroads; but a report spread by a woman perishes by a quick fate.

We shall shortly know respecting the passing on of the light-bearing torches and of the beacons and bonfires, whether they are real, or whether like dreams this welcome light has come but to deceive our minds. I see here a herald from the shore well-nigh hid under boughs of olive; and the thirsty dust closely joining to the kindred mud[4] upon him attests,

[1] Like ἀντίδικος, the rivals, in v. 41.
[2] Not burned on the pyre.
[3] Or, 'captured by others see life,' *i. e.* live.
[4] Literally, 'the twin-brother of mud, thirsty dust.' The poet does not speak of a distant cloud of dust, as in *Suppl.* 176, and *Theb.* 81, but of the marks of a long journey seen on the traveller's dress.

that we shall not have a speechless messenger, nor one who, by kindling the blaze of mountain wood, will send us tidings by the smoke: but either he will more clearly express to us the joyful news by his words, or—but I deprecate an account which shall be the opposite to this: may an addition happily be made to what has already been happily achieved! If any one prays otherwise in this matter for the city, may he himself reap the consequences of the error of his mind.

Her. Hail, paternal soil of this Argive land! To thee once more I have come in the light of this tenth year; and of many hopes that have been broken I have realized this one. For little did I think that I should die in mine own Argive land, and obtain a share in a tomb dearest to my heart. But now I say, Hail O Earth, hail O light of the Sun, and Zeus supreme over the country, and thou, Pythian king, no longer shooting arrows at us with thy bow. All too hostile didst thou come by Scamander's stream! But now e'en be to us a preserver and a healing god, Apollo our king: and all the gods of contest I hereby address, and my own special patron, Hermes, that friendly herald, the worship of heralds, and the heroes who sent us forth, that they may receive back again in kindness[1] the army that has survived the war. Ye palaces of our kings, abodes dear to my heart; ye august seats, and statues of gods that face the sun; if ever before, now with cheerful eyes receive with honour a sovereign after a long absence: for he has returned bringing a light in the night-time to you alike and to all the citizens here present, Agamemnon the king. Greet him therefore well, for indeed 'tis fitting, since he has razed to the ground Troy with the mattock of Retributive Zeus, with which the soil has been dug over. And the very altars are desolated, and the statues of the gods, and the rising generation is utterly perishing from out of the whole land. Such is the yoke which the elder sovereign son of Atreus has thrown round the neck of Troy; and now he has returned,

[1] The heroes were regarded as infernal and *hostile* powers, unless duly propitiated.

a fortunate man, and most worthy to be honoured of all living men. For neither Paris nor the city leagued with him in guilt can now say that the deed has exceeded the suffering.[1] He has been cast in an action both for rapine and theft; he has lost the prize he had carried off, and he has laid low in utter destruction his paternal land and home. And thus the family of Priam have paid a double penalty for their crimes.

Cho. Hail, herald who has arrived from the Grecian host.

Her. I accept your greeting, and will no longer oppose the gods' decree for me to die.

Cho. Did the love of this your fatherland make you anxious?

Her. Aye, so that a tear now stands in my eye through joy.

Cho. Then it was a pleasing disease, this, that you had upon you.

Her. How so? If informed, I shall master the meaning of what you say.

Cho. I mean that you were smitten with a desire for those who returned the feeling.

Her. You state that this land longed for the army, while the army longed for it.

Cho. So much so, that I oft groaned from a darkly-boding heart.

Her. Whence came this uneasy feeling over you, so distasteful to the army?[2]

Cho. I have long ago learned to regard silence as the best remedy against harm.

Her. You do not mean to say that in the absence of the rulers you had any to fear?

Cho. As you said just now, it were a great joy to me even to die.

Her. Indeed, we *have* succeeded well. But in respect

[1] *i. e.* 'can boast that they have been punished inadequately for their crimes,' according to the Greek notion of exact retribution.

[2] So unsuitable to its present joyful return. See the note on v. 620.

of events that occurred in a long time, one might rightly say there were some which turned out favourably, some too which were to be complained of: yet who, except the gods, is free from harm for the whole time of existence? For were I to speak of our toils and our comfortless bivouacks, the scant room for passing on deck,[1] and the hard lying,—in a word, what was there we had *not* to complain about, or that we did *not* get for our daily share? Then again, for our fare on land, there was a yet greater discomfort; for, as our quarters were close by the enemy's walls, the meadow damps kept drizzling on us from air and earth, a lasting damage to our clothes, and making our hair shaggy as that of beasts. And if one were to speak of the bird-killing cold, such as the snows of Ida produced, too great to be borne,—or of the heat, whenever the sea slept tranquilly reclining on its midday couch[2] unstirred by a wind,—yet why should we mourn for this? Our toil is past; it is past, to those who are dead, so that they will never hereafter care even to rise to life again. What need, I say, to count up closely the lives lost in the war, and for the living to grieve about spiteful fortune? I reckon that we ought even greatly to rejoice[3] for what we have got. To us who are the survivors of the Argive army the gain prevails, and loss does not outweigh it; so that our people may fairly boast to this light of the sun, while they are soaring over sea and land, *The Argive expedition at last, after taking Troy, hung up these spoils to the gods in the temples of Hellas,*[4] *a glory of olden times.* 'Tis now your duty, on hearing such news, to praise the city and her generals; the favour of Zeus shall

[1] Some render παρήξεις 'landings'; but, it more probably means, the difficulty of passing between the rowers along a narrow and crowded deck (σελίς).

[2] An allusion to the *siesta* or midday rest.

[3] Or, 'bid farewell to our misfortunes.'

[4] Whenever the Greeks make expeditions in after times and meet with ancient Trojan spoils in any of the temples, they will recal their ancient glory. If ποτωμένοις be understood of the *present* return, the aorist ἐπασσάλευσαν and the epithet ἀρχαῖον must refer to what will be said of the expedition on some future day.

also meet with due honour for having effected all this. You have heard what I had to say.

Cho. Convinced by your arguments,[1] I do not disown the feeling of joy. For it is never too late for the old to take good lessons. But the house and Clytemnestra are likely to care most about this; albiet you can inform me of it at the same time.

Cly. I raised a joyful cry of thanksgiving long ago, when the first nightly messenger of the beacon arrived, telling the conquest and capture[2] of Troy. And some one then chiding me said, '*Do you put belief in signal-men, and think Troy has now been really taken?* Truly, it is just the way of a woman to be elated in heart.' By such speeches they would fain have proved me to be wrong: but yet I went on with my sacrifices; and taking up the female sacrificial shout, first this man, then that, through the city spoke words of joyful import at the shrines of the gods, as they watched the dying away of the fragrant incense-fed flame. And now,—what need is there for you to give me a fuller account? From my lord himself I shall hear the whole story. But, that I may hasten to receive in the best way my own revered lord on his return home (for what light is so pleasant for a wife to behold as this,—when heaven has brought back her husband safe from foreign service, to open for him the door?), take back this greeting to my spouse; 'to come with all speed, beloved as he is by the city,' (and say) 'may he find[3] on his return his wife faithful to him in his house,—even such as he left her,—a watch-dog of the palace well disposed towards him, hostile to his enemies, and in all else the same as she ever was, having destroyed no seal[4] in all that long time.' Nor know I either pleasure or slanderous word from any other man, more than I know anything

[1] *i. e.* so as to take a more hopeful view of our affairs.

[2] Removal of the people as slaves.

[3] Clytemnestra, conscious of her infidelity, instructs the man to convey a wish, as if the expression of his own hope.

[4] Set on the doors of the royal treasury, perhaps. She wishes to make her πίστις to her husband appear prominently in *that*.

about the dyeing of brass.[1] Such is my boast, and full it is of truth,—a boast which no well-born lady need be ashamed to utter.

Cho. So much for her specious address to you, who know its import by the aid of clear interpreters.[2] But tell me, herald,—and 'tis Menelaus I am asking about,—if he is on his way back and will return safe with your host, the beloved sovereign of this land.[3]

Her. It is not possible for me to tell good news which is false, for my friends to enjoy it for any length of time.

Cho. Would then that you could tell us good news which is true; for when separated these two things are not easily concealed.

Her. The man has disappeared out of the Achæan host, both himself and his ship. What I tell you is true.

Cho. Do you mean, after setting sail in the sight of all from Troy; or did a storm, a common calamity, snatch him from the army?

Her. You have hit the mark like a first-rate archer, and have described a long tale of woe in a few words.

Cho. Was he talked of as alive or as dead by the rest of the sailors?

Her. No one knows, so as to give a clear report, save the Sun who nurtures all life on the earth.

Cho. In what manner do you say that a storm came to the naval host, and in what manner that it ended, by the anger of the gods?

Her. A day of joyful tidings one ought not to sully by the utterance of evil reports. The honour due to the gods is distinct.[4] Now when a messenger announces to a city with

[1] She says this ambiguously, both in reference to her conscious intention to imbrue the sword in Agamemnon's blood, and as a proverb meaning a secret trade or art of staining, enamelling, or perhaps tempering bronze.

[2] The insincerity of which you have no idea of, unless I were to explain it to you. They evade any other comment or remark.

[3] Perhaps this tacitly indicates their resolve never to submit to the tyrant Aegisthus.

[4] *i. e.* deprecations and thanksgivings. The Greeks had a superstitious horror of combining joy and grief. See below, v. 1046. For ὅταν δὲ we should have expected ὅταν μέν.

doleful countenance the misfortunes of a defeated army that are to be deprecated by the people,—to the state one general wound for the public to feel, and that many men have fallen victims out of many private homes, by a twofold scourge such as Ares loves, a double curse of war, a bloody union;—when he brings such a load of woe as that, well may he chant a paean of the furies.[1] But when one comes with the joyful tidings that all is safe and well to a city already rejoicing in its prosperity,—how can I combine the good news with the bad, by describing the storm caused by the anger of the gods against the Achæan hosts? For fire and water, hitherto most hostile, conspired together, and gave proofs of their alliance in destroying the unhappy Argive army. It was in the night that our troubles from the boisterous weather arose; for the ships were crushed and ground against each other by the blasts from Thrace; and they, violently struck in the bows by the storm, with[2] the furious wind and the splashing surf, sank out of sight through the unsteady guidance of the unskilled helmsman: and when the bright light of the sun had risen, we beheld the Ægean sea studded with corpses of Achæan men and fragments of broken ships. Ourselves however and our ship, uninjured in its hull, some one either secretly rescued or successfully interceded for,—some god, not a mortal by his managing of the helm.[3] And fortune our preserver alighted, a willing helper, on our bark, so that it neither felt when moored the force of the breakers, nor stranded upon the craggy shore. And afterwards, having escaped a watery grave, in the clear bright day, hardly trusting our fortune, we brooded in anxious thought over the late disaster of the army that had been destroyed and miserably beaten to pieces. And now, if any of them is yet alive, they speak of us as having perished, why should they not? while

[1] *τῶν 'Ερινύων* MSS. *τόνδ' 'Ερινύων*. Compare *θρῆνος 'Ερινύων* in v. 963. 'The sort of paean (joyful song) he should sing is a paean of woe.'

[2] Perhaps *τύφῳ*, the dative, should be read. Compare *σὺν πίνῳ χεροῖν* v. 750. *σὺν κότῳ* v. 442. *Δὶ καὶ Κρέοντι σὺν Αἰακῷ*, Pind. *Pyth.* viii. 99.

[3] Some superior being begged us off from destruction; not that any human skill saved us by clever piloting.

we suppose that they have suffered the same fate. Well, may it end for the best! To Menelaus' arrival at least first and especially look forward. For if any ray of the sun *does* know that he yet lives and sees, by the designs of Zeus not yet willing to annihilate the race,—there is good hope that he will return home again. Having heard thus much be assured that you know the truth.

Cho. Who was it that named with such entire truth—was it some one whom we see not, directing his tongue with a happy skill by foreglimpses of destiny,—the spear-wooed and jealously-contested[1] Helen? For, suitably to her name,[2] a hell of ships, hell of men, hell of cities, she sailed, coming forth from the dainty precious curtains,[3] with the breeze of the earth-sprung zephyr. And many shield-bearing heroes, hunters on their track, (though already they had put-to at the umbrageous banks of Simois the bark that was never once sighted in the chase,) sailed to win back one who was to prove a cause of bloody strife. But to Troy a wrath that works out its end[4] brought a κῆδος rightly so named, exacting late vengeance for the dishonour done to the hospitable table and its presiding god, from those who with reckless shouts were celebrating the strain in honour of the bride, the marriage song which *then* set the bridegroom's family a-singing.[5] But the city of Priam, wiser in its age, is unlearning that song, and now methinks loudly groans in much mourning, calling Paris *the man of the fatal marriage*, having all that long time before endured a life of much woe for the wretched slaughter of her own citizens. So did a man once rear in his house the cub of a lion,[6] not fed on milk, still fond of the teat, at the outset of its life tame, a favourite with the children, and the delight of the old

[1] The object of contention between two, as Deianira was ἀμφινείκητος, Soph. *Trach.* 527.

[2] Perhaps ἐπείπερ ὄντως.

[3] Namely, that concealed her from sight in the women's apartment.

[4] The wrath of Zeus Xenius. κῆδος has the double sense of 'care' and 'alliance by marriage.'

[5] Lit. 'came (or fell) upon them to sing.'

[6] λέοντος ἶνιν Conington, for λέοντα σίνιν,—an admirable emendation, and, I think, metrically necessary.

men. And many a time it rested in their arms like a young infant, looking brightly to the hand that fed it, and sporting playfully[1] through the cravings of its appetite. But in time it showed the temper it had inherited from its parents: for, by way of returning thanks for its keep, by a surfeit on slaughtered sheep it prepared a banquet unbidden. And the house was soaked with blood, a calamity in vain resisted by the servants, a great mischief causing much slaughter: and by the decree of some god it was reared in the house as a priest of Atè. So at first I should say that there came to the city of Troy a spirit of unruffled calm,[2] a gentle ornament of wealth,[3] a darter of soft glances, a soul-wounding flower of love.[4] But swerving from her course she brought to pass a sorry end of her marriage, having sped as an evil settler and an evil associate to the sons of Priam, sent by Zeus the god of hospitality, a fury bringing sorrow to brides.[5] Now an old saying exists which was of yore current in the world, that a man's prosperity, when it has grown big, becomes a parent, and does not die childless; and that out of good fortune there springs a woe that allows the family no rest.[6] But I hold an opinion of my own apart from others; 'tis the impious deed[7] that gives birth to more such deeds after it, and like to its own race: for it is the fate of righteous families ever to rejoice in a good progeny. But old Insolence is wont to bring forth a young Insolence that wantons in the misfortunes of men, sooner or later, when the appointed time has come; and this young Insolence gives birth to Pride of satiety, and that fiend not to be fought against nor waged war with, unblessed Recklessness,[8]—two black she-devils to a family, resembling their parents. But Justice shines brightly in smoke-dimmed houses, and holds in regard

[1] Wagging its tail.

[2] A gentle-minded creature.

[3] A handsome bride for a rich husband.

[4] These were the complimentary epithets with which the Trojans greeted the advent of Helen.

[5] Such was the changed language of the Trojans when they had begun to feel the miseries of the war.

[6] Compare ἀκόρετος γένει v. 1086.

[7] *i. e.* combined with too great wealth; as before, v. 368.

[8] Ἄτη is the child of Ὕβρις in *Pers.* 817.

the life that is righteous; she leaves with averted eyes the gold-bespangled palace associated with uncleanness of hands, and goes to the abode that is holy, not worshipping the influence of wealth that is stamped with the spurious mark of praise. And she directs everything to the destined end.

Come now, my king,[1] captor of Troy, offspring of Atreus; how must I address you? How can I pay my obeisance, neither overshooting nor coming short of the due mean of compliment? Many mortals prefer the *seeming* to be when they have passed the bounds of justice. Any one is ready to sigh over him who fares amiss; but the sting of grief in no wise reaches to his heart. Men take part too in other's joys, putting on a like appearance by doing violence to unsmiling faces. Yet if any one is a good judge of character, he cannot be deceived by the looks of a man who, under the pretence of a kindly intention, is flattering with a weak and watery friendship.[2] Now you on that occasion, when you were sending out the army on account of Helen,—I will not deceive you,—were depicted to my mind in a very unpleasing way, and as not managing well the steerage of your heart, in that you sought to inspire courage in your dying soldiers by sacrifices.[3] But now not from the mere surface of my mind nor with unfriendly feelings do I say it, toil is cheering to those who have brought it to a good end.[4] And you will know in time, duly distinguishing them, who of the citizens has disinterestedly, and who has unduly, managed state affairs in your absence.

Ag. It is right in the first instance to address Argos and the gods of the country, whom in part I have to thank for my return, and for the retributive justice which I have exacted from the city of Priam. For after hearing the cause not from the verbal pleading of orators, they threw their

[1] With these anapæstics the Chorus go to meet their returning king.

[2] A metaphor from wine mixed with too much water. The σπονδαὶ ἄκρητοι of Homer seem alluded to.

[3] When you slew your daughter Iphigenia to appease the clamours of your soldiers who were dying at Aulis for want. See *Sup.* 101, 190, and 210.

[4] Or, 'brings to us a kindly feeling towards,' &c. A purposely qualified praise.

ballots with one consent into the urn of blood, for man-slaying ravages on Troy: while in the other urn, which did not receive their votes, Hope came near to the brim.[1] And even now the city gives signs of its capture by the smoke. The sacrifices to Atè are yet living;[2] and the ashes as they die out send forth puffs of costly perfumes.[3] For these events we are bound to pay to the gods an ever-mindful gratitude, now that we have thrown round Troy the stake-nets of our vengeance, and in the cause of a woman the Argive beast[4] has razed a city to the dust,—the colt of a horse, a shield-bearing host, having sprung with a bound about the setting of the Pleiades. And the ravening lion, overleaping the rampart, has licked its fill of royal blood. To the gods then I have spoken at length this my opening address. But, in reference to your late sentiments,—for I have not forgotten that I heard them,—I say the same as you, and you have in me an advocate of your views. For to few men does it come naturally to reverence as a friend him who is prosperous; since the venom of malevolence, besetting the heart, doubles the load to him who has the malady; he is not only weighed down by his own misfortunes, but he sighs when he gazes on the prosperity of a neighbour. I can speak with knowledge, —for well am I acquainted with it,—that persons who pretended to be very well disposed to me were but the mirror of friendship, the shadow of a shade. Indeed, Ulysses alone, —the very one who sailed against his will,[5]—was a ready trace-horse to me when working in harness: and I say this of him whether he be now dead or alive. But for other matters that concern the gods and the state, we will hold a general assembly of the citizens[6] and take counsel with them in full meeting; and we must consider how affairs which are

[1] The allusion is to Pandora's box, Hesiod, *Opp.* 96. The Trojans had only hope left, and that not in full measure.

[2] The fires are not yet wholly extinguished.

[3] Compare v. 715. The east generally was regarded as the land of costly scents, which the poet probably here had in view.

[4] There is a double allusion to the lion, as the symbol of the Atridae, and to the wooden horse.

[5] See Soph. *Phil.* 1025.

[6] As distinct from the βουλή, or war-council of the chief.

now prosperous may happily remain so for long. And if in any matter there is need of healing remedies, by applying either the knife or the cautery with friendly hand, we[1] will endeavour to avert the mischief of the disease. At present I will go into the palace and to the central altars of the house,[2] and offer my greetings first to those gods, who after sending me safely out have brought me back. And now that victory has attended our efforts, may it abide with us securely!

Cly. Men and citizens, reverend Argive elders here present! I shall not be ashamed to avow to you my affectionate feelings for my husband; by time people lose something of their bashfulness.[3] Not relying on information from others, (but speaking about) my own self, I will describe the distressful life that I passed during all the time my lord was at Troy. In the first place, that the woman should sit at home all alone without the man, in the constant receipt of many adverse reports, is a tremendous evil: and that one herald should arrive, and another come in after him with some fresh bad tidings worse than the first, delivering their messages at the house. And if my husband here really kept receiving as many wounds as it was currently reported at home, he is pierced, one might say, with more holes than a net. But if he had been really dead as often as the reports represented him, truly like a second triple-bodied Geryon he might have boasted of receiving above him—for I speak not now of that below him—an ample threefold mantle of earth, having been slain once under each form. And as a consequence of such adverse reports, many a noose had to be untied by others from a beam above, when suicidal violence had been applied to my neck. These are the reasons, be assured of it, why our son is not present here,—that dear representative of our plighted faith,—as he should have been, Orestes; and be not surprised at this. A friendly

[1] Myself cooperating with the people.
[2] Lit. 'rooms (halls) by the altar.'
[3] It was not usual for Greek women to speak in public, especially on such a subject.

ally of ours is taking care of him, Strophius the Phocian, who forewarned me of woes that he spoke of in two ways,[1]—your own personal danger at Troy, and the chance that anarchy arising from popular discontents might overthrow the royal council,—as it is natural in men to kick one who is down all the more. Such a reason, be assured, carries with it no deceit. For myself now, the gushing fountains of my tears are dried up, nor is there a drop left in them. For through the late hours of taking rest I have suffered harm in my eyes, ever tearfully watching for the beacon-lights which were to give tidings of you,[2] but which were ever unheeded.[3] And in my dreams I used to be roused by the faint humming sounds of the buzzing mosquito, fancying I saw more evils happening to you than could have passed in the time while I was asleep. Now at length, after enduring all these woes, with a mind free from care I would address my dear husband here as watch-dog of the fold, the saving forestay of a ship, the ground-pillar of a lofty roof, an only son to a father; yea, land appearing to sailors beyond their hope, a daylight most beautiful to behold after a storm, a running fountain to a thirsty wayfarer. For it is delightful to have escaped from all constraint. Such are the terms in which I claim to address him, and let no cavil be made; for many are the evils we have been enduring.[4] But now, dear husband, dismount from this mule-car, without setting on the bare ground that foot of thine, O king! that has ravaged Troy. Ye maidens, why do ye delay, when the office has been enjoined on you to strew the bare ground of his path with tapestries? Let there be made on the instant a pathway spread with purple robes[5], in order that Justice may conduct him into an unlooked-for home[6]. For the rest, care not

[1] See the note on *Theb.* 805.

[2] Or, 'lamenting that the torches were never now lighted, as they used to be, in your house. See *Cho.* 528.

[3] Seemed to my anxious mind unheeded, and neglected by careless watches.

[4] So as to justify now such exaggerated terms of praise.

[5] If the tapestry or carpets be not ready, extemporize with Tyrian robes.

[6] These concluding words have a double meaning, and refer to her intention to kill him

overcome by sleep shall arrange everything as Justice and the gods have ordained it.

Ag. Daughter of Leda, guardian of my house! you have spoken indeed proportionally to my absence; for you have made your address a long one. But, to praise me properly, the compliment should proceed from some other than a wife. For the rest, treat not *my* foot tenderly as that of a woman, and do not, as if I were some Eastern king, open your mouth to address *me* in terms of abject obeisance; nor, by strewing my path with vestments, render it liable to envy: the gods alone we ought to honour with *them*. For one who is but mortal to walk on purples of varying hues is, in my judgment, by no means free from fear. I tell you that *I* would be honoured as a man, not as a god. Without your foot-mats and your purple vests fame finds a voice: and not to cherish a foolish pride is the greatest gift of heaven. Him alone one ought to call happy, who has ended his life in wished-for prosperity. And, if in all things I act with the like moderation, *I* have no reason to fear.

Cly. Nay, but do answer me in this not contrary to my resolve.

Ag. My resolve indeed be assured that *I* shall not alter for the worse.

Cly. Was this a vow you made to the gods, that in a time of alarm you would act thus?

Ag. If any one ever did, I have given this final decision with full knowledge (of consequences).

Cly. And what do you suppose Priam would have done, if he had achieved such a victory?

Ag. I think he certainly would have walked on purple robes.

Cly. Then do not hold in regard what *men* may say to disparage you.

Ag. Nevertheless, what the people say about us has great weight.

Cly. Yea, but he who is unenvied is not an object of emulation.

Ag. 'Tis by no means the part of a woman to be fond of contests.

Cly. But surely even defeat is becoming to the prosperous.[1]

Ag. Do *you* also like that sort of victory in a strife?[2]

Cly. Do comply, allowing me to have my way in this matter.[3]

Ag. Well, if you will have it so, let some one unloose the buskins underneath,[4] that serve my foot to tread in; and as I walk on these purple vestments may no envy from the eyes of the gods strike me from afar! For I feel great shame in spoiling these robes like mere carpets, injuring with my feet costly property and textures purchased for silver. So much for these matters. But this stranger lady introduce with kindness to the house: one who makes a gentle use of victory is regarded by the god from afar with a kindly eye. For no one, if he can help it, takes on himself the yoke of slavery. Now this girl, a flower chosen out of much prize-wealth, was the present of the army, and has accompanied me home. So now, since I have been brought to obey you in this matter, I will enter the hall of my palace treading on purple robes.

Cly. There is a sea,—and who shall drain it?—that breeds the dye of abundant purple, weighed against silver, renewable in all its splendours, imparting its hues to garments. To our house, O king, by the favour of the gods, it belongs to have good store of these, and the palace knows not poverty. Nay, I would have vowed the trampling upon many robes, had it been prescribed to the house by the oracles, when I was devising means for getting thy dear life safely back again. Truly, while the root remains, the foliage returns to the house, stretching over it a shelter against the dog-star's heat. So, by your arrival at the hearth of your

[1] They can afford to give way in minor things.

[2] Namely, which consists in having to give way.

[3] I propose *κράτος μὲν τόδε παρείς*, which I have rendered in the text.

[4] An Eastern custom to this day on entering a sacred place.

home, you show the coming of warmth in winter; and when Zeus is maturing the crude vine-juice into wine, then at once there is coolness in a house, when the male who holds the sway is resident at home. Zeus, even Zeus the consummator, accomplish my prayers; and may you keep in regard whatever end you intend to bring about.

Cho. Why so enduringly does this vision, keeping its place in front of my boding heart, hover before it; why does an unbidden and unhired strain come as a prophet of evil; and why does no confident assurance to reject it, like vague dreams, occupy its wonted throne in my heart? Yet the crisis of the fated time is past, since the fastening of the stern-cables from the bark on the strand, after the naval host had reached Troy; and now from my own eyes I know of their return, being myself a witness of it: and yet my soul, self-instructed from within, keeps chaunting this joyless strain of the fury, not at all feeling the wonted confidence of hope. And my inward parts do not vainly bode,—the heart that whirls in eddies against the midriff,[1] while it justly looks for a fulfilment of its fears. But I pray that, contrary to my expectations, they may prove false alarms, and end in nonfulfilment. Very insatiable in truth is the limit of great prosperity;[2] for calamity ever thrusts against it, like one close leaning on a party-wall; and the fortune of a man suddenly while fair on its way strikes against a sunken reef. Then, if the owner's alarm sacrifices a part to save the rest of his merchandise by a well-calculated throw, the whole ship does not sink, though overloaded with calamity,[3] nor submerge its hull in the sea. Doubtless too a good supply from Zeus, ample in quantity and from a crop sufficient for the year, puts an end to a famine: but if a man's dark life-blood shall first have fallen on the ground by a murder, who shall charm it into life again? Nor would

[1] The pericardium. The passage can only be paraphrased. Literally, 'my heart that whirls in rounds which bring an end fulfilled.' (Davies.)

[2] Difficult it is for people to put a limit to prosperity, and to believe they have had enough of it. Some ellipse should be supplied, as, ('full of danger as it is) for' &c.

[3] *i. e.* when all but lost.

Zeus have put a stop, by way of caution, to him who knew the right way how to raise men from the dead. Now if heaven-appointed fate did not prevent my own fate from receiving assistance from the gods, my heart, outstripping my tongue, would pour out these feelings; but as it is, it frets impatiently in the dark,[1] grieved in the inmost soul, and not expecting ever to unravel anything to the purpose[2] from a mind that is bursting into a flame.

Cly. Go in, you also, Cassandra I mean; since Zeus has allowed you in his mercy to take a part with the household in the lustral water, and to stand among many other slaves close by his altar, as the god of family possessions. Get down from this mule-car, and do not be haughty. Why, they say that even Alcmena's son bore to be sold as a slave, and put his neck to the yoke though sorely against his will. And, if the necessity of such a fate *does* befal one, there is great advantage in having masters of ancestral wealth. Those who, without expecting it, have reaped a good harvest, are cruel to their slaves in all things, and beyond measure. You have from *us* just what is the average treatment.[3]

Cho. 'Tis to you that the lady has just spoken in plain terms: and now that you are within the toils of fate, you will obey her, if disposed to obedience; though perhaps you will disobey.

Cly. Why surely, if she be not, like a swallow, possessed of a strange foreign jargon, I speak within her comprehension, and should move her by my words.

Cho. Go with her: she says what is best for you under present circumstances. Obey, and leave your seat here in the carriage.

Cly. *I* have no time in truth to stay here by her out of doors; for, so far as concerns the ceremonies at the central

[1] *ἄφαντον βρέμει*, Pind. *Pyth.* xi. 30.

[2] To guess successfully the reason of this boding of evil.—*ζωπυρουμένης*, 'kindled with the fire of prophecy.'

[3] Neither cruel nor (as Agamemnon would wish it) specially favourable treatment. The queen puts prominently forward Cassandra's condition strictly as a *slave*. But perhaps *παρ' ἡμῖν*, 'at our house,' is the true reading.

altar, the victims are standing ready to be sacrificed for the fire, since we had hardly hoped ever to attain such a success as this. So, if *you* intend to take any part in these doings, do not cause us delay. But if, from being unable to understand me, you do not take in my words, in place of voice let us know by a sign with your barbaric hand.

Cho. The stranger appears to require a clear interpreter. Her manner is that of a wild creature just caught.

Cly. Rather, methinks, she is mad, or is under the influence of a bad spirit,—as one who has arrived from a city just taken, and has not learned how to bear the bit, before she foams away her fretfulness in blood. I shall not however subject myself to insult by wasting more words on her.

Cho. But I, for I pity her, will not be angry:—Come, poor maid, leave your seat on this car; yield to present necessity, and try on a yoke which is strange to you.

Cassandra. Woe, woe, woe! alas![1] O earth! O Apollo, Apollo![2]

Cho. Why do you utter these words of grief about Apollo? He is not the god to require a mourner.

Cas. Woe, woe, woe! alas! O earth! O Apollo, Apollo!

Cho. Here again she is invoking with ill-omened sounds the god, though he has no right to be present at words of woe.

Cas. Apollo, Apollo, god of the highways, my ruin! For thou hast ruined me in no scant measure this second time.

Cho. She seems about to utter some bodings about her own misfortunes. The spirit of prophecy remains; her mind retains it even in captivity.

Cas. Apollo, Apollo, god of the highways, my ruin! Ah, whither hast thou brought me? To what house?

[1] Greek exclamations, the same in sound as our *tut tut* and *pooh pooh.*

[2] She recognises the Ἀγυιεὺς, or stone pillar of Ἀπόλλων προστατήριος on the stage before the palace door. It was called ἀγυιεὺς from standing in the streets.

Cho. To that of the Atridae. If *you* do not understand this, *I* tell it to you; and that you will have no reason to call false.

Cas. Ah! ah! Rather to a house hated by the gods; many a murder of kindred and many a suicidal noose are my witnesses! A human slaughter-house, and one that sprinkles its own floor with blood.[1]

Cho. The stranger seems to be keen-scented as a hound, and to be seeking whose murders she shall discover.

Cas. Ah yes!—for I have evidences of it here that I trust! these infants bewailing their own murder, and their flesh that was eaten by their own father!

Cho. Of a truth we had heard of your renown as a seer: but we are looking for no prophets now.

Cas. Alack! What is it she is about! What this great and dreadful crime? A terrible evil she is planning in this house, intolerable to her own friends, impossible to heal! And aid stands far aloof.

Cho. Of these prophecies I am wholly ignorant: but those other horrors I understood; for the whole city talks about them.

Cas. Ah! wretched woman! What! will you really do this; will you, after washing and anointing in the bath the husband of your bed,—O how shall I tell the end? Yea, soon shall this be accomplished: hand after hand is stretched forth to reach him by repeated blows.[2]

Cho. As yet I understand you not: for now I am perplexed by misty oracles following close after enigmas.

Cas. Ah! ah! O me! What is this that presents itself to view? A net of Hades? 'Tis the wife of his bed who is the stake-net—who is the accomplice with another in the murder.[3] Now let the company of furies, not yet tired of persecuting the family, raise an exulting shout over a victim[4] to be immolated by stoning.

[1] Enger ingeniously proposes *φονορραντήριον*, 'a sink of blood,' for *πέδου ῥαντήριον*, which is hardly defensible.

[2] 'Is stretching out clutchings at him,' or 'reachings for him.'

[3] Namely, with Aegisthus. See inf. 1622.

[4] At the prospect of Clytemnestra's death. Lit. 'against.'

Cho. What fury is this that you are urging to utter a shrill cry over the house? This speech cheers me not; but to my heart runs the blood-drop, causing deadly paleness; which also, when trickling from a fatal wound, sinks together with the last rays of life's sunset[1]. Mischief is close at hand.

Cas. Aha! See there, *there!* Keep away from the cow the bull. She has caught him in a garment, and is goring him with her crafty black horn, and he falls in a bathing vessel filled with water. I tell you a fatal mishap, even of a treacherous death in a bath.

Cho. I cannot boast of being a firstrate judge of oracles: but I do infer some evil from these words. Yet from oracles what good tidings are ever conveyed to men? Through evils lies the course of those wordy arts; and fears from prophesied ill they ever bring us to learn.

Cas. Alas for the evil fortunes of my own unhappy self! for you speak of *my* sufferings, pouring them into the cup of woe upon *his*. What place is this that you brought me to, wretch that I am, for no other purpose than to die with you? 'Tis surely so.

Cho. You are some crazy-headed person, or possessed by some god;[2] and now about yourself you are uttering an unmusical strain, like a dusky nightingale insatiate in her wailing, that does but cry *Itys, Itys*, in the grief of her heart, for all her lifetime of never-fading woes.

Cas. Alas, for the fate of the clear-voiced nightingale! The gods invested *her* with a winged body, and a pleasant life with nothing to bewail;[3] but for *me* there is in store a cleaving blow with a two-edged axe.

Cho. Whence have you these god-inspired fits of groundless prophecy that come crowding upon you? Whence do you compose these fearful notes in dismal tones, mixed with

[1] Which causes not only pallor, but death, when it runs *out of* the body.

[2] As by Bacchus, Pan, or Cybele.

[3] *i. e.* prospectively, or comparatively with me. See Plat. *Phaedo*, p. 85, A.

shrill piercing strains? What bounds do you put to the paths of ill-boding prophecy?[1]

Cas. Alas the marriage, that marriage of Paris, that has brought ruin on his friends! Alas, native stream of mine own Scamander! Once on thy banks, unhappy maid, I grew up by thy nurture; *now* by Cocytus and the banks of Acheron it seems I shall soon have to sing my prophecies.

Cho. What is this too plain word you have uttered? A child might understand, if he thought about it.[2] But I have received a stroke that brings blood by its bite,—at the dismal fate of her that utters these shrill wild notes, so strange to me to hear.

Cas. O the griefs, the griefs of my city, now utterly destroyed! O the sacrifices of my father in defence of his fortress, causing the death of so many pasture-grazing flocks! But they supplied no remedy to avert the fate that has befallen the city;[3] and now I too shall soon—this fired soul foresees it—fall prostrate on the plain.

Cho. You have uttered this new prophecy consistently with the former. Sure some ill-minded demon, falling heavily upon you,[4] causes you to sing tunefully of these dismal death-fraught sufferings. But what will be the end of them, I am at a loss to perceive.

Cas. Well then, my prophecy shall no longer peer forth from behind a veil, like a newly-married bride, but methinks it will now reach your inmost mind,[5] blowing a clear bright gale against the rising sun, so as to dash up to the brightening sky, like a wave, a woe far greater than this of mine. Now I will inform you no longer by dark sayings; and do you bear me witness, as you run with me in the course, that I scent tracks of horrid deeds long ago perpetrated. I say this roof is never left by a chorus that chants in concert

[1] Either a periphrasis for 'prophecy,' or in reference to *limits* assigned by the god between sense and nonsense, truth and falsehood. The *ὅροι* perhaps were posts to mark distances, like our milestones.

[2] I read *ἂν σκοπῶν* for *ἀνθρώπων*.

[3] 'To prevent the city from being as in fact it is.'

[4] Probably a metaphor from wrestling. Compare Pindar, *Pyth.* viii. 81.

[5] *ἐσήξειν*, namely, *τὰς φρένας*.

indeed, yet in no pleasing strain; for *good* is not the burden of its song. Yea, and after quaffing human gore, so as to be emboldened the more, a revelling rout of sister-furies still stays in the house, hard to dismiss from it. And they chant for their song, ever staying by the palace,[1] the crime that first caused all the woe; and one after another they express their loathing for a marriage-bed that showed no mercy to him who violated it. Did I speak amiss, or do I hit some truth, as an archer? Or am I indeed a false prophetess, like a vagrant tale-teller that knocks at every door? Bear me witness when I am gone, by taking an oath now beforehand, that I know, not by mere hearsay, the ancient crimes of this household.

Cho. Why how could an *oath*, a pledge ever so heartily given, be any remedy?[2] But I *do* wonder at you, that born and bred beyond sea you should rightly speak about a strange city, as if you had been present!

Cas. 'Twas Apollo the seer who appointed me to this office.

Cho. Mean you that, though a god, he was smitten with love for you?

Cas. Until now there was a sense of shame in *me* to say this.

Cho. Every one has more delicacy when in prosperity.

Cas. Well, he *was* a lover who inspired me with great affection.

Cho. Did ye come to the begetting of children in regular wedlock?

Cas. I promised Loxias, and then I deceived him.

Cho. Was that when you already were possessed by the prophetic art?

[1] Not moving off to others, as an ordinary κῶμος.

[2] Cassandra is anxious to avert from herself the stigma of being a false prophetess; and to this end many of her foregoing remarks are directed. She is disappointed that the Chorus will not attest on oath the correctness of her knowledge of the past. They say, that would not remedy evils to come, and merely express surprise at her being so well up with a local story.

Cas. Already I was foretelling to the citizens all their sufferings.

Cho. How then were you made to feel the wrath of king Loxias?

Cas. I could make no one believe anything after I had committed that fault.

Cho. To *us* however you seem to prophesy credible things.

Cas. Aha! aha! O woe, woe!

[illegible] Again does this terrible pang of true prophecy rack my inward soul, harassing it with .... strains. See you those children that haunt the house like the shadowy forms of dreams? Ghosts as of infants slain by their own relations pass before my eyes, their hands filled with the food of their own flesh, and holding their hearts with the entrails, a piteous burden, which their own father was made to taste. 'Tis for this I say there is one that is planning vengeance, a cowardly lion, disporting himself in the lair, *housekeeper*, forsooth,[1] to him that has returned, even my master,—for bear I must the yoke of a slave. Little knows the great admiral of the fleet and the captor of Troy what a subtle speech the tongue of that lewd woman has uttered and has dwelt upon with so blithe a heart, like a concealed Atè, and what an end she will attain with a disastrous success! Such are the deeds she is daring: a woman is the slayer of a man. Oh what hateful monster can I rightly call her? An amphisbaena, or a Scylla dwelling in the rocks, the destruction of sailors, a raging hag of hell, and one that breathes truceless cursing against her own friends? And how the all-daring woman raised a shout of exultation, as if at the favourable turn of the fight: and how she pretends to be glad at his safe return! And if there is aught in all this that I cannot make you believe, 'tis all one: How should it signify? What is destined will come: and even you very soon, when present at my death, will call me in pity too true a prophetess.

[1] Aegisthus is the cowardly lion, opposed to the λέων εὐγενὴς inf. 1230. To his pretended care as *οἰκουρὸς* there is an allusion in 782.

Cho. The banquet of Thyestes on his children's flesh I know of and shudder at; and fear possesses me at hearing horrors described truly and in nothing disguised: but when I hear the other matters, I run on having left the course.[1]

Cas. I tell you you will see with your own eyes Agamemnon's death.

Cho. Unhappy maid, lull to silence that voice of yours.

Cas. But no healing god is at hand to remedy *this* prophecy.

Cho. No indeed, if the fate you predict shall be near: but pray heaven it may not be as yet.

Cas. You are uttering prayers, while *they* are thinking of slaying.

Cho. By what man is this horrid crime being undertaken?

Cas. Surely you must have greatly missed the fatal import of my prophecies.[2]

Cho. For I cannot comprehend what means he has who is to effect it.

Cas. And yet I know full well the language of the Greeks.

Cho. So are Pythian oracles (couched in Greek), but they are still hard to understand.

Cas. Aha! this prophetic fire! how is it coming over me! Alack, destroying god,[3] Apollo, O me, O me! See this two-footed lioness, pairing with a wolf in the absence of the generous lion,—she will slay unhappy me: and as one who is preparing a deadly draught, she declares that she will throw into the cup of her wrath a requital for me also, while she whets the sword against her lord to repay him with murder for bringing me here. Why then do I keep these badges that are but mockery of myself, these staves and these prophetic crowns that dangle on my neck? *Thee* at least I will destroy before I die myself. Away to destruction, lie thou there! Lead on; the way is here; I will follow with you. Enrich some other Atè in place of me. See, see,

[1] *i. e.* without understanding. So *Cho.* 1011.

[2] *i. e.* if you think a man is meant, and not the woman, Clytemnestra.

[3] See note on *Theb.* 132.

Apollo himself stripping me of my prophetic garb, and that too often as he has seen me made a laughing-stock, even in this sacred attire, without any cause, among my friends and by my enemies with one consent.[1] And though I was called crazy, like some fortune-teller, a beggar (wretch that I was) and perishing by hunger,[2] I bore it all. And now the prophet, to wreak vengeance on me whom he had made a prophetess, has led me thus into a fatal plight; where a block awaits me instead of my paternal altar, and I shall shed the warm life-blood butchered[3] with a victim's throat-wound. Yet not unavenged by the gods shall I die! Another will yet come to exact justice for me, a son to slay his mother, an avenger of his father's fate. Yea, though an exile and a wanderer, an outcast from this land, he shall return to set the crowning woe on the heads of his own friends: for a mighty oath has been sworn by the gods, that the overthrow of a prostrate father shall bring him back. Why then should *I* lament thus in piteous strains? As in the first instance I saw the city of Troy faring as it has fared, and the former occupants of it come off thus by the judgment of the gods, I will myself go and fare likewise: I will dare to die: and this door I may address[4] as the gate of Hades. But I pray that I may meet with a mortal blow, that without a struggle, as the life-blood flows away in an easy death, I may close these eyes.

Cho. Maiden, in much to be pitied, yet foreknowing much, you have spoken at length: but, if really you are aware of your own fate, how is it that, like a heaven-directed heifer, you step thus courageously to the altar?

Cas. There is no way of escape, there is none, strangers, any longer.

Cho. Yea, but he who dies last has the advantage in time.

[1] By Trojans and by Greeks alike, though there was no real cause for ridicule, since she was not a *ψευδόμαντις* as they said.

[2] Or, 'a poor beggar dying of hunger I bore to be called' &c.

[3] Or, 'stricken by a reckless blow.' (*Theb.* 599; *Eum.* 530.)

[4] 'By my prophetic knowledge.' MSS. *τὰς λέγω*. I read *τάσδ' ἔχω προσεννέπειν*.

Cas. The day of fate has come: I shall gain little by flight.

Cho. Well, know that you are a patient sufferer of courageous heart.

Cas. Such words are addressed to none of the happy.

Cho. But surely to die nobly is some gratification to a mortal.

Cas. Alas, father, for thee and thy well-born offspring!

Cho. Why, what is it now? What alarm makes you start aside?

Cas. Faugh, faugh!

Cho. Why this *faugh?* unless it be some feeling of horror in your mind.

Cas. The house reeks with blood-dropping slaughter.

Cho. Surely not! *This* smell is of sacrifice at the family altar.

Cas. A stench comes on the senses e'en as from a tomb.

Cho. 'Tis not the delicacy of Syrian odours[1] in the house, that you speak of.

Cas. Well! I will go, to bewail even in the palace my own fate and Agamemnon's. Let me be content with life. Ah, strangers! 'tis not through vain fear that I am distrustful as a bird is of a (limed) bush. Bear ye witness of this when I am dead,—when a woman has died in return for me a woman, and a man has fallen for an ill-mated man.[2] And this I solemnly charge you to attest, as one about to die.

Cho. Unhappy maid, I pity you for your divinely predicted fate.

Cas. Once more, and finally, I would utter an address, but not a dirge on my own fate: and I pray to the Sun, turning to his last light, that my avengers may repay to those hated murderers satisfaction at the same time for the death of a slave, an unheeded victim. Alas for the fortunes of man! When prosperous, one may liken them to a pencil

[1] Very different from the θύος of sacrifices.

[2] When Clytemnestra and Aegisthus have been slain by Orestes.

sketch: but if they are unlucky, a wet sponge being applied to the picture obliterates the design.[1] And the former case I commiserate more by far than this latter.[2]

Cho. Prosperity never comes enough to mortals; and no one keeps it away by forbidding it from his finger-pointed palace, with these words, *Enter not.* And so to this king the gods have granted the capture of Priam's city, and he has returned to his home as one honoured by the gods; yet now, if he is to pay back the blood of those formerly slain, and by his own death is consummating the penalty of other deaths (in requital) for the dead; who can aver that, being a mortal, he was born with a destiny free from harm, when he hears this?

Ag. O me! I am struck a mortal blow in my very vitals.

Cho. Hark! Who is that who calls out about a blow, as if mortally wounded?

Ag. O me, I say, O me! again, struck with a second blow.

Cho. The deed seems to me to have been done, judging by the groaning of the king. But let us impart to each other what may seem safe counsels.[3]

Cho. 1. I for my part tell you *my* opinion; to send orders to the citizens to bring succour hither to the house.

Cho. 2. Nay, but *I* vote for rushing in instantly, and charging them with the deed while they hold the yet gory sword.

Cho. 3. I too, sharing in the like opinion, vote for action; certainly, 'tis no time for delay.

Cho. 4. One may see it: they make a beginning that is a sign of a coming tyranny for the state.

Cho. 5. And here we are dallying, while they, spurning the credit of delay, are not inactive with the hand.

[1] Even if 'painted in,' the whole colouring may be wiped away.

[2] A reverse of prosperity more than a speedy death in misery.

[3] If this scene be assumed to have been acted with very rapid motions and gestures, and highly excited voices, as if all were in terror and dismay, much of the supposed absurdity of it will vanish.

Cho. 6. I know not what plan I can hit upon to suggest. 'Tis the part of the doer to have well considered about the part to be done.

Cho. 7. I too take that view; for indeed I know not how by mere words we can raise the dead to life again.

Cho. 8. And shall we go on living thus in submission to these defilers of the palace as our rulers?

Cho. 9. Nay, 'tis not to be endured, but 'tis better to die. For death is a milder lot than being tyrannized over.

Cho. 10. What! by proofs from groans shall we draw our conclusions about the man that he is dead?

Cho. 11. We ought to speak on these subjects with a clear knowledge; for guessing is quite distinct from that.

Cho. 12. This opinion I am fully prepared to support;[1] to be certain about the son of Atreus, how he fares.[2]

Cly. As I said much on a former occasion merely to suit my purpose, I shall not now be ashamed to assert the contrary. I ask, how could any one, by treating with open enmity those enemies who passed as friends, raise a fence-net[3] of destruction to a height too great for them to leap out of it? Now to me this contest has come, though it has long had in view a victory formerly gained over me,[4] still after the lapse of much time. And so here I stand, where I dealt the death-blow, over the deed done! And I so did it,—this too I am not going to deny—that he could neither attempt to escape, nor avert his fate. I threw around him a net,[5] fastened at the ends, like one used for inclosing fishes,—a robe of fatal costliness. And I struck him twice, and with two groans he dropped his limbs and stirred not from the spot. Then when he was down I added a third, a votive offering to the Zeus of the nether world, the keeper of the dead. And so he yielded up his indignant soul as he lay at my feet: and gurgling forth a sharp blood-spurt as he breathed, he struck

[1] A figure from voting in the assembly: literally, 'I stand in a majority from all quarters of the meeting.'

[2] To be sure that he is as he is.

[3] See the note on v. 350.

[4] In sacrificing Iphigenia.

[5] See the note on v. 350.

me with the deep-red drops of gory dew, yea, and I rejoiced in it not less than a corn-field rejoices in heaven-sent showers, when the green ear is coming forth from the sheath. Such being the case, ye Argives, you may be glad or not, as you please: but *I* glory in the deed. And had it been possible with propriety[1] to pour a libation on the corpse, even that had been justly done, yea, most righteously. Such a bowl of evils in the house has this man filled to the brim with curses, and now drains it himself on his return.

Cho. We are amazed at your language, that you speak so boldly, in making such a boastful vaunt over your slain lord.

Cly. Ye are trying me as if I were a woman without sense: but I with undaunted heart tell you, who know it well,—and whether you choose to praise or to blame me, 'tis all one,—this is Agamemnon, my husband; and he is dead, and this right hand slew him, and it did a righteous deed. That is what I have to say.

Cho. Ah, lady, what poisoned food sprung from earth, or what potion coming from the liquid sea, have you taken, that you have laid on your own head, as a victim, this sacrificial incense, and a people's curse? You cast him from you, you cut him off, and yourself shall be an outcast from the city, an object of stern dislike to the citizens.

Cly. *Now* you sentence *me* to banishment from the city, and to endure the hate of the citizens and the curses of the people, though you *then* brought no such charge against my husband here,—albeit *he*, caring no more for her death than for that of a brute creature, though he had sheep abounding in fleecy flocks, sacrificed his own child to charm away the Thracian winds. Ought you not to have exiled *him* from this land, in retribution for his crimes? But when you are witnesses of *my* deeds, you are stern judges. But I tell you to threaten me thus, with a full understanding that I am

[1] She professes regard for ceremonial customs, which did not allow of joyful acts in connection with death. See the note on v. 620.

resolved on this,—that, if you shall have conquered me by force, on fair fighting terms, then you shall rule me; but, if the god incline to bring about the other result, then you shall know by being taught, however late in life, how to be discreet.

Cho. Thou art a woman of haughty counsels, and haughtily hast thou spoken it,—as in truth thy mind is maddened by thy blood-stained career,—that a spot of blood stands conspicuous, yet unavenged, on thy brow. 'Tis yet in store for you, deprived of the aid of your friends, to repay blow for blow.

Cly. You hear also this solemn form of my oath: I swear by the satisfied justice for my child, by Atè and the Fury, to whom I have sacrificed this man, that I have no expectation of fear, that it shall set foot in my palace, so long as Aegisthus kindles a fire at my hearthstone, remaining, as heretofore, a friend to me. For he is to me no small shield of confidence. There he lies,—the ruin of this woman,[1] the darling of many a Chryseis at Troy; and with him this captive and soothsayer,—this partner of his bed, trusty prophetess and paramour, this lodger with the common sailors on the benches. The worthy pair have met with their deserts: for he died as I have shown you, while she, like a dying swan, after singing her last death-strain, lies dead, dear to his heart, and for me she has brought an extra relish to the enjoyment of my union.

Cho. Alas! Would that some fate would come quickly upon us, not very painful nor from a lingering illness, bringing with it that everlasting endless repose, now that our most gracious protector has been slain,—he who endured so much through a woman, and now by a woman he has lost his life. O thou infatuated Helen, who alone didst destroy those many, those very many lives at Troy! But now thou hast made to blossom afresh a bloody murder accomplished,

[1] Meaning, perhaps, Cassandra; though it may mean, 'destructive of my happiness.'

indelible; for there already existed in the house a heavy woe, that has caused this fall of a husband.

Cly. Pray not that the fate of death may befal thee, through grief at these events, nor turn your anger upon Helen, saying that she was a slayer of men, and that she alone, by destroying the lives of many heroes at Troy, wrought a calamity beyond compare.

Cho. Thou demon, that bearest heavily on this family and the twin descendants of Tantalus, and now by the hands of women holdest a sway of not less haughty pride, grievous to my soul!—But lo, here on the very corpse is he perched like some ill-omened raven, and in hoarse notes glories to sing his strain!

Cly. Aye, *now* you have set right the sentiments you have uttered, in speaking of the thrice-gorged demon of the family; for 'tis from him that a passion for blood-lapping is nourished in the heart;—before the old woe has well ceased, a new shedding of gore.

Cho. Truly a dread and wrathful demon do you describe in this house! Alas! an evil mention of a baneful destiny insatiable. Lo now, 'tis all through Zeus, the cause of and the consummator of everything; for what is there that is brought about to mortals without Zeus? Which of these things is not predestined by Heaven?

O my king, my king, how shall I bewail thee? What shall I say of thee from a loving heart? That you lie there in this finely-woven web, having breathed out[1] your life by an unhallowed murder. O me! a death-slumber it is unworthy of a king, to have been slain by a treacherous fate, with a two-edged weapon from[2] the hand!

Cly. You insist that this deed was mine: but do not regard me as the wife of Agamemnon. It was the old stern avenging demon-spirit of Atreus, that cruel host, which likened itself to the wife of this dead man, and so offered up him in payment, by sacrificing a full-grown for infant victims.

[1] Perhaps, *βίον ἐκπνεύσας*.
[2] The figure is borrowed from discharging an arrow.

Cho. That you are blameless of this murder who shall attest? How can that be? But the demon-spirit of ancestral crime may have had a hand in the deed. For sable Ares is forced onwards by fresh showers of kindred blood to that final point, on reaching which he will afford full satisfaction for the congealed[1] blood of the devoured children of Thyestes.

O my king, my king, how shall I bewail you? What shall I say of you from a loving heart? That you lie there in this finely-woven web, having breathed out your life by an unhallowed murder. O me! a death-slumber it is unworthy of a king, to have been slain by a treacherous fate, with a two-edged weapon from the hand!

Cly. Why, did not *he* too cause a treacherous murder in the house? My own dear sapling that I had reared from him, my ever to be lamented Iphigenia, he dealt with unworthily,[2] and now, when he is himself treated as he deserves, let him not boast in Hades,[3] since he has paid by his own death for crimes of which he set the example.

Cho. I am at a loss, and am destitute of any ready expedient of thought, which way I should turn, now that the house is falling. I fear the loud pattering of the blood-shower that is undermining its foundations; for the first drops are past. Fate is now whetting Justice[4] on a fresh whetstone for another deed of harm. O earth, earth, would thou hadst received me, e'er ever I lived to see this my king laid low in the death-bed of the silver-sided ewer! Who shall bury him, who shall sing his dirge? Will *you* dare to do this,—after slaying your own husband to perform over him the rites of woe, and unrighteously to do a thankless favour to his shade in requital for your daring deeds? And who, in uttering the funeral oration with tears over the god-like man, will grieve with sincerity of heart?

Cly. It is not for *you* to speak of that care: by our hands he died, and we will bury him, not with wailings of the

[1] Not yet washed out of the family.

[2] Perhaps ἀσεβῆ δράσας, for ἀνάξια δράσας.

[3] See the note on v. 516, ἐξεύχεται τὸ δρᾶμα τοῦ πάθους πλέον.

[4] Compare *Cho.* 635.

inmates of the house, but Iphigenia his child,—lovingly as she ought,[1]—shall meet her father at the ford of swift-flowing Acheron, and fling her arms round him to kiss him.

Cho. Here is a case wherein 'taunt has come for taunt,'[2] —albeit my words are hard to interpret,[3]—'plunderer is plundered,' 'murderer pays for his crime.' For the law abides, while time lasts and Zeus is king, for *the doer to suffer:* 'tis the fixed decree of heaven. Who then can cast out of the house its accursed brood? The whole race is fixed fast to misfortune.

Cly. You have rightly touched upon that divine law of retribution. However, my wish is to make a compact with this evil demon of the Plisthenidæ, and to bear what has been done, though hard to endure. And, for the other part, that he shall leave this house, and wear out some other family with unnatural murders. I am content to keep even a small part out of all my possessions, if I shall have taken away from the palace this mania for mutual murder.

Aegisthus. O welcome light of a day of retribution! Now at length can I say that the gods, avengers of mortals, regard from above the crimes of earth, since I have seen this man lying dead in the woven robes of the furies, joyfully for me, since he is paying for the crafty deeds of his father's hands! For Atreus, when lord of this land, this man's sire, banished from his city and his home my father Thyestes,— to give a clear account of the whole matter,—even his own brother, having had a dispute with him about the sovereignty.[4] And the unhappy Thyestes, returning home as a suppliant at the hearth-stone, himself obtained a promise of safety, that he should not die and stain with his blood the soil of his fatherland. But by way of a hospitable banquet,[5] this man's impious father Atreus, with officious zeal rather than

[1] This is said in the bitterest irony.

[2] Proverbs expressing the just law of retaliation, which (they obscurely hint) will fall on Clytemnestra.

[3] Though you may pretend not to see the application. Or, "it is hard to judge between the crimes of Agamemnon and Clytemnestra."

[4] See the note on *Theb.* 805.

[5] Given by Atreus to Thyestes under pretence of ratifying his promise and of forgiving and forgetting the past.

N

with friendly design, did serve up to my father, under pretence of observing mirthfully a day of sacrifice, a banquet on his own children's flesh. The bones of the feet and the top joints of the hands he kept concealed, as he sate apart from the guests at the head of the table: and Thyestes, at once taking without suspicion portions of the flesh that could not be recognised, partook of a repast which thus, as you see, proved fatal to the family. But directly afterwards, when he was made aware of the unhallowed deed, he shrieked out, and fell back vomiting from the cannibal feast. And he imprecated an intolerable fate on the descendants of Pelops, making the overturning the table a symbolical form of curse,[1] that so the entire race of Pleisthenes might perish. 'Tis for these reasons that you may now see this man dead at your feet. And I was the fit person to plot the murder; for he drove me, the thirteenth child, into exile along with my poor father, while I was yet an infant in swathing bands: but I am grown up now, and Justice has brought me back again to my home. And I got this man into my grasp though I *was* an exile, by combining every device of subtle cunning. Thus even death is honourable for me now, since I have seen this man caught in the snares of Justice.

Cho. Aegisthus, I approve not of insolence in misfortunes. Now you assert that you deliberately slew this man, and that you alone plotted this lamentable murder. I tell you that in the hour of justice *your* head will not escape,—do not flatter yourself,—the fate of being stoned amid the execrations of the people.

Aeg. What! do *you* talk thus, seated at the lower oar, while those on the upper benches of the ship hold rule? You shall find to your cost, old as you are, that it is no light lesson for one of your age to be taught discretion, after it has been recommended to him in words. But imprisonment and the pangs of hunger are the best magic charmers for teaching even old age. See you not this, when you have

[1] Hesych. *σύνδικος· σύμφωνος.* I cannot assert the correctness of the above rendering.

eyes to see? Kick not back against the goad, lest by striking it you should suffer pain.

Cho. Lady, you, as guardian of your husband's house when he had recently returned from the war, not only dishonoured his bed, but did also plot this murder against one who was general of the expedition.[1]

Aeg. This speech of yours also shall be to you a source of tears. Why, *you* have a tongue the very opposite to that of Orpheus: *he* led everything through delight at his voice, while *you* think to draw others to yourself by exasperating them with childish barkings. But when put down by force you will show a tamer spirit.

Cho. As if forsooth I would ever have *you* as lord over the Argive people! A poltroon who, not even after plotting this man's death, had the courage to do the deed with your own hand.

Aeg. No, for crafty action was clearly the part of a woman; whereas *I* was suspected by him as an enemy of long standing. However, by the resources of this man's wealth I will see if I cannot rule the citizens; and if any one is disobedient, I will yoke him in a heavy collar, not at all as a barley-fed colt put to run in the side traces: but the much-detested short-fare, with the dwelling in darkness, will soon see him gentle.

Cho. Why then did you not, in the cowardice of your heart, yourself slay this man, but call in the aid of a woman,—the defiler of the country and the country's gods,—to kill him? Is Orestes anywhere yet living, that he may be brought back from exile by kindly fortune, and become the slayer of them both with victory complete?

Aeg. Well, since you are resolved to act, and not merely to talk in this matter, you shall soon know the result. Come on now, my attached body-guards; the time for action is at hand.

[1] Yours was a *double* crime, social as well as political. This sentiment is enlarged upon *Eumen.* 600 seq.

Cho. Yes, come on, let every one get ready his sword with hand on hilt.

Aeg. But I too, be assured, do not object to die with my hand on my sword.

Cho. You say you will die: we take you at your word, and we appeal to fortune.[1]

Cly. Pray let us not, dearest of husbands, do further mischief: to have reaped even these evils, so many in number, is an unhappy harvest. Of calamity there is surely enough already; let us have no more bloodshedding. Go you, and these old men also, to your allotted homes, before you do something that you will suffer for. We ought to have been content with these deeds, as we committed them. And if there ever can be a sufficiency[2] of these evils, we should make the best we can of it, having been miserably stricken by the wrathful onset[3] of the demon of the family. This is what a woman has to say, if any one thinks it worth hearing.

Aeg. But to think that these varlets should thus gather the flowers of a vain eloquence against *me*, and should utter such words, tempting their fate, and should so fail in discreet judgment, and insult one who is in authority!

Cho. Never can this be the part of Argives, to crouch to a bad man.

Aeg. But I in after days will yet make you suffer for this.

Cho. Not so, if fortune should guide Orestes to return home.

Aeg. I know of my own experience that exiled men feed on hopes.

Cho. Go on acting as you do, and fatten by defiling justice: for you have the power.

Aeg. Be sure that you shall be punished by me for this folly of yours.

[1] We choose (or take) the fortune that is in store for us. Compare τύχην ἑλεῖν *Suppl.* 374.

[2] ἄλις, perhaps ἄκος, a remedy.

[3] χηλῇ is probably a metaphor from the fighting-cock's spur.

Cho. Boast and fear not,—like a cock strutting near his dame.

Cly. Care not for their senseless barkings: you and I, who have the command of this house, will set these matters right.

CHOEPHOROE.

PERSONS REPRESENTED.

ORESTES.	A NURSE.
ELECTRA.	A DOMESTIC.
CLYTEMNESTRA.	CHORUS OF CAPTIVE WOMEN.
ÆGISTHUS.	[PYLADES].

Orestes. Hermes, god of the nether world, that dost here survey the royal residence of my father,[1] become to me a preserver and an ally at my request: for I am come into this land, and am returning after a long absence as an exile from my home. And now, summoning[2] my father at this mound of his tomb to hear and attend to my prayers, ... (And I bring as an offering) a lock due to the Inachus for my nurture, and this second lock for a tribute of my grief: for I was not present to bewail thy fate, my father, nor did I raise my hand over the bier at the burial of thy corpse. What is this that I see here? What company of women comes this way dressed in garbs of woe? To what disaster can I refer it by conjecture? Is it that another death has befallen the house, or shall I be right in guessing that these maidens are carrying libations to my father (such as are used) for propitiating the powers below? It can be nothing else: for I fancy this is Electra, even my own sister, advancing, conspicuous above the rest for the sadness of her grief.

[1] *i. e.* as a statue in front of it. Or perhaps, 'who dost execute the commands of thy father Zeus.' I now incline to the former interpretation.

[2] *κηρύσσων*, not *κηρύσσω*. His office of herald is invoked, as well as that of *σωτήρ*. See v. 117.

O Zeus, grant that I may avenge my father's death, and become to me a ready assistant! Pylades, stand we a little out of the way, that so I may learn clearly what is this suppliant procession of women.

Cho. It was by order of the queen that I left the palace to conduct the libations with the accompanying sound of rapidly striking hands.[1] On my gory cheeks the marks of rending are conspicuous[2] through the newly-cut furrow of the nail; but with sighs that are lasting[3] my heart's grief is fed. And the front folds of my garments through the keenness of my sorrows loudly burst into tatters destroying the texture of my robes, as I beat my breasts at calamities that admit not of a smile. For[4] a thrilling fright, making the hair to stand on end, declaring the destiny of the family by dreams,[5] breathing resentment[6] in sleep, caused the utterance of a loud shriek through fear in the dead of night from the interior of the palace, falling[7] like a night-mare in the women's chamber. And the interpreters of these dreams thus declared their import under oath by inspiration from the gods; that those below the earth were exceedingly indignant, and relaxed not their anger against their murderers. Such a bootless offering *to avert harm,* O mother Earth! does an impious woman contemplate in sending me hither: but I fear to utter that word of hers; for what means are there of atoning for blood that has been once shed on the ground? Oh house involved in complete misery! Oh utter ruin of the family! A sunless and loathsome gloom hangs as a dark veil over houses when the lords have been slain. For a majesty that once was not to be contended with, unsubdued, not to be challenged in war, passing through the mind as well as the outer ears of the people, is now removed; and men only fear.[8] But to live in prosperity,—*that* among mortals is a god and more

[1] *i. e.* the sound of the beating of head and breast with the hands.

[2] *παρῇσι φοινίαις ἀμυγμὸς* Hermann and Conington.

[3] Not merely a temporary or external demonstration of grief.

[4] This explains *why* she was sent.

[5] Caused by boding and significant dreams.

[6] That of the dead Agamemnon, who just below is said ἐγκοτεῖν.

[7] See on *Ag.* 1146.

[8] The *αἰδὼς* is gone, only the *φόβος* or *δέος* remains.

than a god.[1] But the swiftly-falling scale of justice drops heavily[2] upon some while yet in the light; the penalty of other crimes awaits those who linger on in the mid space between light and darkness; while others night overtakes without bringing retribution. The life-blood that was drunk up by the earth which nourished it has left a clot of vengeful gore that festers on the surface and will not run through. A lasting woe is in reserve for[3] the criminal, that he may break out with all-consuming disease. For as to him who has tampered with the bridal-chamber there is no remedy, so all the rivers flowing in one course to cleanse the hand-polluting stain of blood wash it in vain. But for me,—for a hard fate by investing my city was sent me by the gods, who took me from my father's house and brought me into the condition of a slave,—the just and the unjust acts alike of violent masters have appeared, since I began this life of thraldrom, proper to be borne without opposition,[4] and by suppressing the bitter detestation of my mind. But yet I weep under the cover of my garments at the forlorn fortunes of my rightful owners,[5] chilled in heart by secret griefs.

Electra. Ye captive handmaidens who have the care of the house, since ye are present as my attendants in conducting this procession, be my advisers also in these my doubts: what ought I to say as I pour these funeral libations? How can I speak words agreeable to him, how address a prayer to my father? Should I do so by saying that I am bringing them *from a dear wife to a dear husband,*—when they come from my own mother? For *that* I have not the present confidence; and yet I know not what I should utter as I pour

[1] They worship Aegisthus for his wealth, and fear him when they cannot respect him. See *Ag.* 1616.

[2] Read ἐπισκήπτει for ἐπισκοπεῖ. The metaphor is perhaps from the game of the Cottabus. If the sense be general, the meaning is that some are punished in youth, some in age, some in the other world. If it be particular, then Aegisthus, Orestes, and Agamemnon are respectively meant. Others interpret these words of crimes known, suspected, and undiscovered.

[3] *Distulit* in seram commissa piacula mortem, Virg. *Aen.* vi. 569.

[4] She alludes to the carrying of the libations against her own feelings and convictions.

[5] Orestes and Electra.

this mixture on my father's grave. Or should I make this petition, as is the usual custom with mortals,—*that he may requite with good those who send these offerings,*—with a gift, forsooth, which their evil deeds have deserved? Or in silence, without paying him honour, as indeed my father perished, should I pour these offerings,[1] a libation to be drunk by the earth, and then go back, like one who has carried out offscourings, after tossing away the vessel without looking behind me? Take part, my friends, in consulting about this; for we entertain a common hatred in the house. Do not conceal it within your hearts for fear of somebody. What must be awaits alike the free, and him who is under the thrall of another's hand. Say on, if you know ought that is superior to these proposals.

Cho. With all the reverence due to the tomb of your father, as a real altar, I will speak, since you urge me, the sentiments of my heart.

El. Speak then, conformably with the respect you profess for my father's tomb.

Cho. Say, as you pour, a devout prayer to such as may be friendly.[2]

El. And who are those of my relations whom I must so address?

Cho. In the first instance yourself, and whoever detests Aegisthus.

El. Then I shall say this prayer for myself and for you.

Cho. Do you yourself consider that, now that you see my meaning.

El. Whom else then should I add to this company?

Cho. Make mention of Orestes, even though he is away from home.

El. Of this also you have reminded me very properly.

Cho. On the guilty authors of the murder now, duly mindful—

[1] Perhaps ἐκχέασα, after 'pouring.'

[2] An intentional caution and ambiguity will be noticed throughout this dialogue.

El. I am to pray *what?* Inform me, who have little experience, and tell me the proper form of words.

Cho. That some daemon may come to them, or some mortal,—

El. Do you mean as a judge or as an avenger?

Cho. Say simply, *to slay them in return.*

El. And are these demands from the gods consistent with my duty as a daughter?

Cho. Of course you may pray *to requite an enemy with evil.*[1]

El. Then hear, thou mighty herald of the gods both above and below, Hermes of the nether world; and summon for me the daemons beneath the earth to listen to my petitions, relating as they do to my paternal home, yea, even Earth herself, who produces all things from her womb, and when she has reared them, receives again the increase from them. And so I, as I pour these libations to departed mortals,[2] say, as I invoke my father, *look with pity on me, and* (shew) *how we may bring back our dear Orestes to his home.* For now we are as it were sold as slaves by our mother and wander as exiles; and she has received in payment Aegisthus for a husband, the very man who took part with her in slaying you. And I indeed am performing the part of a slave, while Orestes is an outcast from his property;[3] and *they* are revelling extravagantly in riches acquired by your toil. But that Orestes may return hither with good fortune I pray to thee,—and do thou hear me, my father! And for myself, grant that I may be far more discreet than my mother was, and more righteous in my actions. For ourselves then we offer these prayers: but on my enemies I imprecate that Justice may shew herself an avenger of your death, so that the murderers may also be murdered in their turn. These petitions I insert in the midst of a prayer for good, uttering against them this prayer for evil.[4] But to

[1] Namely, in merely general terms.

[2] Perhaps here = μορτοῖς.

[3] He is an exile, I am a slave. This in illustration of the above remark.

[4] This is added from the usual Greek dislike of mixing good with bad, and as if by way of precaution to specify distinctly the parties meant.

ourselves be the sender-up of all these blessings from the world below, with the aid of the gods and of earth and of victorious Justice. Such are the prayers with which I pour on the tomb these libations. [But do you, as is the custom, make the paean of the dead bloom with lamentations as you utter it].[1]

Cho. Shed a tear, pattering as it falls for our fallen master, now that the libations have been poured at this (tomb which is a) barrier against evil and good, to avert a curse we were sent to deprecate.[2] And do thou hear me, object of my veneration, hear, my lord, (the prayers uttered) from a gloomy heart. Oh, woe is me, woe! What valiant man is there to prove the deliverer of the house? What god of war to launch arrows in action from his doubly-curved Scythian bow, and wield his hilted weapon in close conflict?

El. My father has now indeed received the earth-drunk libations: but here is a new subject to communicate to you.

Cho. Say on: but my heart palpitates with alarm.[3]

El. I saw on the tomb a lock that had been cut off: here it is.

Cho. From what man, or what deeply-waisted girl?

El. That is easily guessed, so that any one may have an opinion about it.

Cho. Then let me who am old learn from one who is my junior.[4]

El. There is no one but myself who would clip that lock.

Cho. True: they are enemies whose duty it would have been to mourn by cutting their hair.

El. But further,—this lock is, to look at, very closely akin—

Cho. To whose hair? for that is the point I should like to hear.

[1] This last distich is probably spurious. Compare *Pers.* 621. The lines will neither scan nor construe like ordinary verses, which is some objection; and the sense properly ends at v. 142.

[2] Compare *ἀπευκτὰ πήματα*, *Ag.* 621.

[3] They perceive that she is anxious and excited.

[4] Old age is generally slow to learn.

El. It is very much like my own hair to look at.

Cho. Could this then have been an offering secretly sent by Orestes?

El. It most nearly resembles his clustering locks.

Cho. But surely *he* did not venture to come hither?

El. Perhaps he *sent* a clipped lock in compliment to his father.

Cho. This that you say is not less a fit subject for tears, if he is never more to touch this land with his foot.

El. I too had bitter feelings surging up at my heart, and I felt a sudden blow as from a penetrating dart. And now from my eyes there fall draining tear-drops freely flowing from a flood of grief, when I look on this lock: for how can I expect[1] that any other of the citizens is the owner of this hair? Yet neither surely did his murderess clip it from her head,—that mother of mine who entertains against her children an unnatural feeling, anything but motherly. Then how I am to give my full assent to this idea, that the offering comes from that dearest of men Orestes,—but I keep the flattering hope. Ah! had it but the voice of a friend, like a messenger! *then* I should not thus be swayed to and fro by conflicting thoughts; but it would either have clearly warned me to reject with loathing this lock, if it had been cut from the head of an enemy: or, if really related,[2] it would have been able to share in my grief, both as a graceful tribute to this tomb and as an honour to my father.

Cho. We call on the gods to help us, for indeed they well know in what storms, like sailors, we are being tossed: but if we *are* to obtain safety, a great stem may arise from a tiny seed.

El. And see, there are imprints of feet here,—a second proof,—like in shape[3] and closely resembling mine. For

[1] She means, that no citizen would have dared to send it.

[2] *i. e.* taken from the head of my brother.

[3] MSS. *ποδῶν δ' ὁμοῖοι.* qu. *ποδῶν ἀδελφοί?* It is an adjective in *Oed. Col.* 1262, and the words, written in uncials, are as nearly as possible the same. If this be not the meaning, the following *καὶ γὰρ* seems hardly logical, unless we supply some ellipse to make it so.

look,—there are here two outlines of feet,—both of himself and of a fellow-traveller. The heels and the flat markings of the soles when measured coincide exactly with my foot-prints. And an anxiety is present to my mind, and a sinking of my heart within me.[1]

Or. Pray that what yet remains, acknowledging to the gods the fulfilment of your prayers so far, may turn out well.

El. Why, what do I *now* obtain by the favour of the gods?

Or. You have come to a sight of the very objects you have long been praying for.

El. What mortal man can you know that I have been in the habit of calling upon?

Or. I know in my heart that you have often said how much you admired your Orestes.

El. You do not mean then that I am obtaining the object of my prayers?

Or. I am he: seek not for one more friendly than myself.

El. But can it be, stranger, that you are contriving some snare for me?

Or. If I am, I am plotting against myself.

El. But perhaps you are making sport at misfortunes which are mine alone.

Or. At my own then also, if at yours.

El. Do I address these words to you as being Orestes indeed?[2]

Or. Nay rather you see in me Orestes himself, though you are slow to recognise him. Yet when first you saw this clipped lock of mourning hair, and were tracking on my footsteps,—those of your own brother, as of the same size with your own foot,—you were fluttered with hope, and fancied that you saw *me*.[3] Look now, applying the lock of hair to the stump; see too this bit of embroidery, the work

[1] Or, 'bewilderment of sense.'

[2] Perhaps we should read, as better suited to the next verse, ὡς ἂν Ὀρέστης ταῦτά μοι προσεννέπεις;

[3] That it might possibly be *my* footsteps you saw.

of your own hand, and the ridges made by the weaving-blade; and (examining)[1] the pattern of animals woven therein, be self-possessed, and lose not your senses through excessive joy.

El. O dearest object of regard to our father's house,—O long-lamented hope of a stock that should prove its deliverer,[2] trust to your own prowess and you shall regain your paternal home. O delightful name of brother, which to me contains the parts of four,—for I am bound to address you as a father,[3] and my love for a mother falls wholly on you, (for she is most justly detested,) and for that sister who was so ruthlessly sacrificed. And you were ever a brother in whom I had confidence, and who won my respect.[4] Only may Victory and Justice, with him who is third,[5] but the most powerful ally of all, Zeus, assist you in the contest.[6]

Or. O Zeus, Zeus, become a spectator of these things; and look with pity on the orphan brood of an eagle sire that has perished in the folds and coilings of a fell viper, while the bereaved young are pinched by hungry famine, for they are not yet of full size to bring up to the nest the prey of the parent bird. In the same way you may behold me and my sister here, Electra, two children bereaved of their father, and both equally exiled from their home.

El. And if you should have abandoned to destruction these young ones of a sire who sacrificed to you and honoured you greatly, whence will you obtain the festive honours of a like hand? As, if you should have destroyed the young of an eagle, you would not have the means of sending again trustworthy tokens to mortals; so this imperial stem, if wholly withered up, will be of no service to your altars on sacrificial days. Take care of it, and you may yet raise up to greatness from its low estate a house which seems now to have quite fallen.

[1] A verse here has dropped out.

[2] Or, which should perpetuate the family. At this speech Electra embraces her brother.

[3] My real father being dead.

[4] Or, who brought me the dignity I was born to inherit, but which my mother refused me.

[5] *i. e.* Ζεὺς Σωτήρ.

[6] This sentence refers back to v. 229, 'you shall regain' &c.

Cho. My children, on whom depends the safety of your father's hearth, keep silence, lest some one should learn what has occurred, and for the love of gossip report everything to those in power,—whom I hope some day to see lying dead amid the spurting pitch of the kindled pyre.

Or. Assuredly[1] I shall not be betrayed by an oracle of Loxias that carries such weight with it,—which commanded me to go through with this adventure, adding many loud and rousing words of exhortation, and plainly threatening chill horrors in my warm heart, if I should fail to exact vengeance from the authors of my father's death. For he bade me slay them in return in the very same way, exasperated by losses which should deprive me of my property. And he declared that I should myself with my own life pay for (the neglect of) these commands, by suffering many disagreeable maladies. For in shewing to mortals generally[2] the means for assuaging distempers, he foretold to me and my sister these diseases,—a tetter that should spread on the surface of the body and eat out with savage jaws the old constitution; and that white hair should grow upon us as a consequence of the malady.[3] Further, that other[4] assaults of the Furies, to be brought to pass by the murder of a father, were being summoned against me by one who saw clearly though he moved his brow in darkness:[5] (for the dark weapon of the powers below, proceeding from dead suppliants[6] of kindred race, and madness, and groundless fears by night, rouse and allow no rest;) and that my body, tortured by the brazen whip (of the Furies) should be driven from out the city. And that to such there was no portion in the wine-bowl to partake of, nor in the liquor that is wont to be poured in libations; that

[1] This very difficult speech of Orestes appears to be rather a soliloquy than an address to the Chorus.

[2] As ἰατρόμαντις, and as Παιὰν, or god of medicine.

[3] Even when the disease was cured it should leave permanent marks behind it. Or perhaps, 'that the disease should last till old age.'

[4] Beside the νόσον just mentioned.

[5] By Agamemnon, who, though in Hades, had a kind of conscious existence as a δαίμων.

[6] Murdered persons petitioning the avenging powers for justice on the murderers through their surviving relations.

the unseen wrath of an (unavenged) father kept away a son from the altars, and from being entertained by or lodged with any other; and that unhonoured of all and friendless I should at length die miserably, worn out by a general decay. In oracles of such dread import ought I not to put some trust? Even if I do not, the deed (on other grounds) must be done; for many longings combine in one,—the orders of the god, my great grief for my father,—besides the want of means which presses on me,[1]—to rescue the citizens, the noblest of men, the destroyers of Troy with gallant bravery, from becoming subject thus to two women,—for he has but a woman's courage; if not,[2] he will soon know the result.

Cho. Grant, we pray, O powerful Destinies! that from Zeus may come the issue of the matter on the side that Justice is prepared to take. For words of hate let words of hate be paid—so Justice, exacting her due, loudly proclaims—and for a murderous blow let him repay a murderous blow; for *the doer to suffer,* such is the purport of a very ancient maxim.

Or. Father, ill-starred father,[3] what can I say or what can I do to waft to you from afar, to that place where you repose with the dead, a light equal to your present darkness? However, a lamentation intended to do honour is deemed to be none the less[4] a compliment to the former lords of the house of Atreus.

Cho. My son, the consciousness of the dead is not subdued by the fierce consuming flame of the pyre, but he shews his anger even after it. When he that dies is lamented, an avenger is made to appear;[5] and thus the funeral-wail, which is a just tribute to fathers and parents, when raised by both sons and daughters, brings the whole matter to light.

El. Hear then, my father, our tearful mourning in alter-

[1] Means for carrying on the government, and to support my kingly dignity. We must not apply modern notions of money to this passage.

[2] *i.e.* if he will dare to fight, he will find which is the better of the two.

[3] The Schol. seems to have read *αἰνοπαθής*.

[4] Viz., though it should fail in its end.

[5] See *Ag.* 119.

nate strains.[1] This lament of thy two children at thy grave is bewailing thee;[2] and this tomb has received us as suppliants and not less as exiles.[3] Which of these conditions is well, and which without evil? Is not our misfortune too great to grapple with?

Cho. But even out of these moans the god can, if he choose, yet bring about more harmonious sounds; and in place of dirges over the tomb a joyful paean in the royal palace may welcome a newly-made friend.

Or. O that under the walls of Troy you had been slain, my father, gashed by the lance of some Lycian hero! Then you would have left a glorious name in the house, and after founding a course of life to be pursued by your descendants in their career, you would have been laid under a lofty barrow of foreign earth, that would have been no heavy load to the house.

Cho. Dear would he have been to his friends who there gloriously fell, and distinguished below the earth as a ruler of august dignity, an attendant on the mightiest rulers among the shades in Hades; for he was king, while he lived, of those who fulfilled the heaven-appointed lot,[4] and (wielded) in their hands the sceptre obeyed by men.

El. But I would not even wish that you had died under the walls of Troy, my father, and been buried with the rest of the spear-slain host hard by Scamander's stream, but rather that they who slew you had themselves been slain by their own relations, so that some one afar[5] off might learn the tale of their death, without taking part in these troubles.

Cho. These wishes, my child, which you utter, are better than gold and greater even than the great happiness of the

[1] By Orestes and Electra. Compare ἐν μέρει in *Ag.* 1163; *Eum.* 556.

[2] Namely, according to the remarks of the Chorus just made, and with the same object in view.

[3] Whom you are bound to protect, like the god of a temple.

[4] He was king of kings, and as such was supposed to be specially honoured in Hades, as he had been on earth. See *Pers.* 687.

[5] *i. e.* Agamemnon buried at Troy, according to Mr. Davies. But this is hardly consistent with μηδ' ὑπὸ Τρωΐας. The meaning is very obscure. Perhaps, 'that others distant in time and place might learn the story.'

Hyperboreans; for fancy is free. But cease we; for now the heavy sound of the double scourge[1] is reaching the dead: of the one side there are by this time assistants[2] below the earth, while the hands of these detested rulers are unfit to be raised in prayer: so with the children rather the advantage lies.

El. That word went right through earth to his[3] ear, like a dart. O Zeus, who sendest up from below a calamity bringing late retribution on the bold and daring deed of mortals,—(I say not, *punish parents;*) but it will still be accomplished for them.

Cho. Would that it may be my lot to chant the joyful sacrificial strain[4] at the pine-wood pyre, when the man receives his death-blow and the woman perishes.[5] For why should I try to conceal what resentful loathing of my soul,[6] in spite of my efforts, keeps flitting before me, while full in front of my heart's prow blows a gale of sullen resentment?

Or. But is it likely that Zeus, restoring two poor orphans to their rights, will ever lay on them a wrathful hand, cleaving the murderer's heads?[7] (I merely say) may confidence return to the country! and I ask that justice may be given in payment for the unjust. And hear me, Earth, and gods honoured in Hades.

Cho. But the *law* says that drops of blood shed on the ground demand other blood; for the Fury summons havoc to attend on the deaths of those formerly slain,—deaths which bring on calamity after calamity.

El. O Earth, and rulers of the spirits below, behold, [and] ye powerful avenging Furies of those who have been sacrificed, behold the survivors of the race of Atreus deprived of their property and ejected from their home. Which way, O Zeus, can one turn?

[1] The sound of beating the head and breast by the hands of the two children. Compare Soph. *Ajax*, 632.

[2] In the roused spirit of Agamemnon.

[3] *My* ear, according to others: but with little sense.

[4] '*Nuptial* strain,' Davies; *i.e.* as joyful as the strain sung to the marriage πευκαί.

[5] If even by her own hand. (Davies).

[6] I join *οἶον φρενὸς στύγος*, as being most probably what the poet meant.

[7] With his vengeful bolt.

Cho. But now *my* heart is moved for her as she pours forth[1] this piteous plaint: and at one time I am prone to despond, and my heart has gloomy bodings at the word as I hear it; but again when hope has set me on the getting of some help, it removes my grief, shewing itself to me with a fair countenance.

Or. And what subject could we rightly speak of[2] but the griefs we suffer, when those griefs come from parents? She may use fair words (to escape her just fate): but our griefs are not so to be soothed; for, like a savage-minded wolf, we inherit from our mother a temper not to be conciliated.

Cho. I strike an Arian stroke; and in the measures of a Cissian mourner[3] you might behold quickly-succeeding outstretchings of my hands in clenching blows and wide reaches above me and far apart: and to the sound of the blows on my breast responds also the battering of my unhappy head. O cruel and all-daring mother! with the burial of an enemy, a king without his citizens, a husband without mourning, you had the heart to inter him unlamented!

Or. As you say, all was done to dishonour him, ah me! But the dishonouring of a *father* she shall surely pay for, with the favour of the gods and by the agency of my hands. And then, when I have got rid of her, may I perish!

Cho. Yea, and his body was even mangled, that you may know this; and just as she treated him in death, so she buried him, seeking to make his fate too grievous for your life to endure.[4] You hear how ignominious was the sad end of your father.

El. It was a *father's* death that you describe: and yet I was not present, as one held in no honour and of no worth;

[1] Read χέουσαν, namely, for Electra uttering her grief. Compare *Suppl.* 561. κλυούσαν followed closely by κλυούσᾳ is very awkward, to say nothing of the construction.

[2] Namely, what more fit to rouse Agamemnon, than our mother's ill-treatment of us?

[3] Professional mourners known under these gentile names.—It seems best, on the whole, to assign this speech to the chorus. The past tenses appear to describe an action commenced a few moments before.

[4] Hoping to make you commit suicide.

but shut off in the interior, like a mischievous house-dog, I gave free vent to drops that came more readily than smiles, pouring forth tearful sighs in secrecy. When you hear these words, write them on the tablets of your heart; and through the passage of your ears let the tale enter your inmost soul without moving you to frenzy.[1] For what I have told you so took place: the rest[2] do you yourself be desirous to learn. But you must enter the lists with unflinching resolution.

Or. On you I call,—assist, father, your friends.

El. And I, suffused with tears, add my voice in the petition.

Cho. And our company, taking part in it all, echoes the cry. Rise to light and hear, and take our side against our enemies.

Or. Ares must join issue with Ares, justice with justice.[3]

El. Ye gods, decide our claims according to the right!

Cho. A trembling steals over me as I hear these prayers. Vengeance has long been biding its time, and will come at their prayer.

Hemich. A. O troubles inherent in the house! O harsh jarring sound of the bloody scourge wielded by Atè! O grievous intolerable family woes! O pain hard to assuage!

Hemich. B. The true remedy to the house for staunching those wounds is, that they should prosecute this bloody quarrel not by the aid of others from without, but by themselves. So ends our invocation of the gods beneath the earth.

Cho. Hear then, ye powers worshipped below, this prayer, and send assistance cordially to these children so as to ensure them the victory.

Or. Father, who wast slain in a way unworthy of a king, grant me, when you are asked, the possession of a house which is yours to give.

[1] Lit. 'with the quiet step of your mind'; which seems to convey a warning to Orestes not to be carried away by indignation till the time for acting arrives. Such expressions only admit of paraphrase.

[2] Meaning, perhaps, what justice ought to overtake the murderers.

[3] The duty to a mother with the duty to a father.

El. I also, my father, have the like request to make of you; that I may escape after inflicting a terrible vengeance on Aegisthus.[1]

Or. For thus[2] the sacrifices that men are wont to offer to heroes would be founded for you: but otherwise, you will be unhonoured at the savoury burnt funeral-offerings of the country.

El. I too will bring libations at my marriage from my father's home, as a tithe of my entire fortune; and the very first object of my worship shall be this tomb.

Or. O Earth, send up my father's spirit to direct the contest.

El. O Persephassa, grant moreover a seemly[3] victory.

Or. Remember the bath in which you were slain, father.

El. Remember too the strange use you made of the robe she threw around you.[4]

Or. When you were caught, my father, in shackles not forged in brass.

El. Yea, in a coverlet devised for your dishonour.

Or. Are you not roused by these reproaches, my father?

El. Raise you not your head erect to your dearest ones?

Or. Either send Justice to assist your friends, or allow them in turn to get the like grasp of your adversaries, if you desire, after being conquered, to conquer them again.

El. Hear also this final appeal, O father. Behold this brood of yours sitting at your tomb, and pity the daughter and with her the direct descendant of the sire;[5] and do not utterly annihilate[6] this race of the Pelopidae. For thus you are not dead even in death: for children are as voices to a man that keep his memory alive when he is dead; they are as corks that bear up the net, keeping the twisted flaxen line from sinking in the deep water. Hear us: 'tis on your own

[1] This verse is perhaps corrupt.

[2] By our recovering the family property.

[3] An obscure expression, *εὔμορφον κράτος*, perhaps containing a wish to regain her rights without the horrors of a mother's murder.

[4] *ἐκαίνισας* for *ἐκαίνισαν*. (Conington.) In the next line read *γε . . θηρευθείς*.

[5] Males were believed to represent physically the male parent.

[6] Lit. expunge as a picture. Cf. *Theb.* 15.

behalf that such lamentations are made; for you are yourself saved by giving due heed to this petition.

Cho. Your address is long, but you are not to be blamed for it, if it is a recompense for the unhonoured condition of his tomb. For the rest, now that you have made up your mind to the right course of action, act at once, and try if fortune will help you.

Or. It shall be so: but it is not out of course to be told from what motives she sent the libations, and on what account she shewed all too late regard to a malady admitting of no cure. For after he was dead, and when he heeded it not,[1] the sorry offering was sent. I cannot account for this: surely the gifts are too small for the offence. For if one poured out all the libations in the world in requital for a single life taken, the labour would be vain. That is what men say. But tell me this matter clearly, if you know it, since I wish to learn.

Cho. I do know it, child, for I was present: alarmed by dreams and terrors that disturbed her nightly rest, the impious woman sent these libations.

Or. And have you been told the dream, so as to describe it rightly?

Cho. She fancied she had given birth to a serpent, as she herself says.

Or. And what is the end and upshot of the story?

Cho. That she laid it quietly down in its swathing-bands, as one would a child.

Or. What food did it crave, this newly-born monster?

Cho. She herself gave it the breast in the dream.

Or. Surely the teat was not unwounded by the loathsome thing?

Cho. (It was so hurt) that the creature drew a clot of blood in the milk.

Or. 'Twas a dream sent by her husband, and not a vain one.

[1] *ἀτὰρ φρένες οὐκ ἔνι πάμπαν*, says Homer of the state of the dead, *Il.* xxiii. 104.

Cho. And she in her sleep cries out in sudden alarm. And many lights that had been extinguished in darkness were rekindled in the chambers on our mistresses' account. And then she sent these funeral-libations, hoping they might prove an effective remedy of the wrongs she had done.

Or. Then I hereby pray to Earth and to my father's tomb, that this dream may be brought to a full accomplishment in *me*.[1] And certainly I interpret it so, that all the parts hang well together. For if the snake left the same womb as I did,—was wrapped in swathing-bands,[2] and opened its mouth to take in the teat that suckled me, and mixed with a gout of blood the mother's milk, and she in alarm shrieked out through the pain of it,—why, it surely follows, that, as she nursed with violence to herself the ugly monster, so by violence she must die: and I must become a snake, and kill her, as this dream informs me. And I choose you as an interpreter of portents in this matter.

Cho. Then be it so: but now assign your friends their parts in what remains, telling these[3] to do this, those not to do that.

Or. My orders are simple—that my sister should go within; and I charge you to conceal these my concerted plans, that, as they slew by craft a man of royal dignity, they may be caught also in the same snare and die by craft, even as Loxias declared in his oracle, king Apollo, a prophet who has never yet been proved false. For, in the guise of a stranger with complete equipment, I will come with Pylades here to the outer gate of the palace,—I as a stranger, he as a friend and ally of the family.[4] And we will both speak in the dialect of Parnassus, imitating the accent of the Phocian tongue. Perhaps then none of the porters will admit us with a cheerful welcome, on the plea that the house is possessed with evils;[5] we will so linger by it, that persons in passing

[1] Though sent to Clytemnestra.

[2] A corrupt verse.

[3] Probably Electra and Pylades. The chorus are ordered not to raise an alarm.

[4] See *Agam.* 853.

[5] Guests were not admitted in a time of family trouble, Eur. *Alcest.* 751.

the house may make conjectures, and speak thus:—Why does Aegisthus let one who is a suppliant stand excluded at the gates,[1] if he is at home and is aware of it? But if I *do* pass the threshold of the gate into the court, and find him sitting on my father's throne; or if afterwards, coming and meeting me face to face he shall raise his eyes and again drop them; before[2] he has asked, *Of what country is this stranger?* be assured I will make him a corpse, catching him suddenly with a nimble weapon.[3] And the Fury, already satiated with gore, shall drink pure life-blood for a third draught.[4] Now therefore do you, my sister, keep a careful eye on matters within the house, that these plans of ours may fit well together in the result. But you, ladies, I warn to keep a wary tongue,—to be silent where it is needful, and to speak only what is to the point. For the rest, I bid Pylades come this way to watch the issue, and direct for me aright the coming conflict of the sword.

Cho. There are many great and terrible woes[5] that the earth produces; and the all-embracing sea teems with hostile monsters: there approach us also bright meteors[6] between earth and upper ether; and things winged and walking on the plain can tell of the devastating might of windy hurricanes.[7] But the too-daring spirit of man who may describe, or the all-daring loves—so closely bordering on the woes of men—of bold-minded women? For the inordinate love which sways the female both in brutes and among mankind perversely prevails over wedded fellowships. If there is any one not flighty in thought, let him remember the contrivance of the lighted brand which the unhappy daughter of Thestius, that destroyer of her own child, cunningly devised,[8] when she burnt up the glowing faggot coequal in age with her son

[1] Lit. 'have him shut out by (closing) the gates.'

[2] Before he has time to recognize me in spite of my disguise, and so call for aid.

[3] A bold metaphor from a net; but χαλκεύματι really means ξίφει.

[4] The libation to Zeus Σωτὴρ is alluded to.

[5] Poisons, monsters, &c.

[6] Comets and meteors, seen in *upper* ether.

[7] *Atmospheric* commotions.

[8] She knew that her son was destined to die when a certain faggot was consumed.

from the time that he uttered his first cry when he came from his mother, and keeping pace with him through life to the day appointed for his fate. There is another person in story whom we are bound to detest,—the murderous Scylla, who at the instance of his enemies[1] caused the death of a dear father, bribed by the gold necklace of Cretan workmanship, the present from Minos, when she robbed Nisus of his immortal hair as he was breathing unsuspectingly in sleep, audacious that she was: but Hermes overtook her.

And now that I have mentioned relentless family troubles,[2] —but this is not the time (to describe) an unloving marriage, to be deprecated by the house, and the daring plots conceived in a woman's mind against a warrior husband, even a husband who was with reason venerated by his people. (I will only say) I hold in honour the unembroiled hearth of a home, the disposition of a woman that is free from daring. But of all evil deeds the Lemnian takes the first place in story; and it is universally bewailed as an execrable calamity, and every new horror people compare to the *Lemnian crime.* Through guilt which incurs the hatred of the gods, the race of mortals falls into dishonour and is lost; for no one respects that which is under the ban of heaven.[3] Which of these inferences is unfairly drawn? The sword's point is at the heart, and Justice thrusts it right in with a sharply-piercing wound; for the irreligious daring of him who impiously sins against the absolute majesty of Zeus is not passed over in neglect. The stem of justice is firmly planted. Destiny is the armourer that forges the sword in readiness, and causes one murder to bring forth another in families. And in due time the deep-minded Fury when invoked[4] pays to the uttermost the guilt of former murders.

Or. Slave, I say! hear the knocking at the door of the court. Who is within there in the house, slave? I repeat.

[1] Not directly, nor by her own hand, but by betraying him.

[2] She should have said, 'I will refer to the case of Clytemnestra.'

[3] The sentiment is much the same as that in *Ag.* 448—52.

[4] κλυτὰ seems capable of this meaning. Compare θεοκλυτεῖν in *Pers.* 502. But it may be equivalent to πότνια.

(*a pause*). This the third time I call for some one to come out of the house, if Aegisthus keeps a hospitable one.[1]

Slave. Well, I hear. Of what country is the stranger? Whence comes he?

Or. Go and say to the owners of the house, to whom I am come and for whom I bring news,—and be quick, for the dark car of night is speeding on, and it is time for wayfarers to drop their anchor in the hall for the common entertainment of guests,—"Come forth somebody from the house who can acquit a messenger of his charge,—some lady who holds rule in the place,—or for a man to come might be more proper;[2] for then no bashfulness in the conversation makes words obscure. A man speaks with confidence to a man, and makes known without reserve the object of his mission."

Cly. Speak, strangers, if there is ought you require: for there is everything here which is suitable to this house,—warm baths, beds to give rest after toils, and the presence of honest eyes to greet you. But if you have to transact some business that calls for more deliberation, that is the duty of men, to whom we will impart it.

Or. I am a stranger of Daulis from the Phocians. As I was journeying, attended by my own equipage, to Argos, just as I left home to come hither,[3] a strange man met me and said to me, who was not less a stranger to himself, after learning my route and explaining to me his own,—Strophius the Phocian, for I found out his name in the conversation,—"Since in any case, stranger, you are going to Argos, report to the parents, duly mindful of the charge, that Orestes is dead; do not on any account forget it. Whether then the opinion of his friends shall prevail to bring him home, or they prefer to bury him abroad, entirely and for ever a stranger, convey these instructions to us on your return. For at present the sides of a brazen urn contain within them

[1] An ironical taunt, very galling to a Greek.

[2] He disarms suspicion by pretending indifference as to which comes out, Clytemnestra or Aegisthus; but he really wants Aegisthus to come first.

[3] In accordance with my original intention of going to Argos, to which place I have now arrived.

the ashes of the man who has been duly bewailed.[1] Thus much I heard and now tell you: but whether I am speaking to the proper parties and to his relations, I know not; but it is right that the father should be informed of it.

Cly. Alas, your words tell me how utterly we are coming to ruin. O curse of this family, hard to grapple with, at how many things, even lying out of harm's way, do you take sight, bringing them down with well-aimed arrows from afar! And now I am indeed utterly wretched, stripped by you of all my friends. Thus it is then that Orestes,[2]—for he was about making a lucky throw, and just getting his feet out of a deadly slough,—but *now* the healing hope that there was of goodly merriment in the house you set down as present before us (in this urn).

Or. My own wish now would have been to make acquaintance with and receive hospitality from hosts so fortunate[4] on business of a happy nature: for what feelings can be kinder than those of a guest towards a host? But it seemed to my mind a breach of honour not to carry out a matter of this kind for friends, after I had promised it and been solemnly charged to perform it.[5]

Cly. Be assured you shall not meet with less than your deserts, nor will you become less a friend to the family on that account. Another would have come all the same to bring this news. But it is high time that strangers who have been spending the day in a long journey should have

[1] For whom all the proper rites have been duly and respectfully performed.

[2] She should have said, 'has deceived all my hopes by his death.' Of course she is speaking hypocritically, as in the double meaning of the following couplet, where *βακχεία καλὴ* means both the joy of the house at Orestes' safety, and also Electra's ironical account of the present revellings, which she ever hoped that Orestes would return to stop. There is also an ambiguity between 'a hope of merriment' (on Orestes' return), and 'a hope of cure for the merriment' (at Electra's degraded position.)

[3] I propose *ἐγγράφεις* (*i. e.* 'Ἀρὰ) for *ἐγγράφει*, which can only refer to the messenger, *i. e.* to Orestes, possibly with a tacit allusion to Electra—'She now sees her hopes disappointed.

[4] Ironically said.

[5] Compare *ἐπιξενοῦσθαι* in *Agam.* 1291. *ξενοῦμαι* in *Suppl.* 904. There is irony in the words of Orestes. He really means, that it would be impiety to Apollo not to accomplish the murder of his mother.

all that is suitable to their case. Take him into the banqueting-hall for the men, and these attendants and companions in the journey; and there let them receive all that is proper for the credit of the house. And I order you (slave) to perform this, as being responsible to me. But we will communicate with the lord of the house on this matter, and having no lack of friends[1] will take counsel with them about this sad event.

Cho. Come then, handmaids of the house friendly to the cause, when shall we shew the strength of our voices for the success of Orestes? O holy earth, and holy mound of the tomb, that now liest over the body of our loved captain and king, now listen, now bring us aid! For now is the time for crafty persuasion to enter the lists with him, and for Hermes the god of the dead to direct this murderous conflict of the sword.

This man who calls himself a stranger seems to be causing some harm to the house.[2] Why, I see the nurse of Orestes here all in tears! Whither now, Cilissa, are you going past the threshold of the house? Truly grief goes with you as an unhired attendant.

Nurse. My lady bids me summon Aegisthus for the strangers with all speed, that he may come and learn more clearly, as man from man, the newly-brought tidings. To us servants indeed she shewed a smile lurking under scowling looks, trying to hide it at deeds that have been done happily for her—though for the house things are in a very bad way from this news the strangers so plainly report. No doubt *he* on hearing it will cheer up his spirits, when he knows the story. Unhappy wretch that I am! how those sad woes of old, which happened in this house when Atreus had it, combined together to grieve my heart within my breast! Yet never before suffered I a grief like this. For the other misfortunes I endured with patience; but the dear Orestes, the darling of my soul, whom I took and nursed

[1] She intimates that Aegisthus survives, if Orestes is dead.

[2] They now speak for the ears of the nurse, who does not know the plot.

from his mother's womb,—and all those troubles from his cries that kept me restless by nights,—that they should have proved useless to me who had to endure them!—for a thing that has no intelligence one must rear like a brute creature,—of course one must,—according to its humour. For your infant can express nothing while yet in swathing-bands, if hunger or thirst or other want of nature overtakes him; then the young stomachs of children are wont to help themselves. Used as I was to foretel such mishaps, yet I dare say I was often deceived about them; and so, as having to wash the child's swathing-bands, I performed the joint duties of fuller and feeder. I then, exercising these two sorts of handicrafts, took Orestes to be brought up for his father;[1] and now, alack! I hear the news of his death.—So I am going to summon the man who has been the bane of this family. I trow he will be glad to hear of this report.

Cho. How then does she bid him come equipped?

Nur. Do you ask *how?* Tell me again, that I may know your meaning more clearly.

Cho. Whether with body-guards, or walking alone?

Nur. She says he is to bring spear-bearing attendants.

Cho. Then don't *you* tell that with any show of dislike towards your master: but, that he may receive the news without fear, tell him with a cheerful mind[2] *to come directly himself; for it depends on the messenger rightly to communicate a private matter.*[3]

Nur. Can it be then that you are *glad* at the news that has lately been brought?

Cho. Well, now, what if Zeus intends some day to give a favourable turn to our troubles?

Nur. How can that be, pray? Orestes, the hope of the house, is dead and gone.

Cho. Not yet: methinks a bad prophet might know that.

Nur. What do you mean? Have you something to tell beside what you have said?

[1] The male son, as before observed, was considered peculiarly the father's.

[2] *i. e.* looks which indicate a cheerful mind.

[3] That a personal interview with the messenger himself is necessary.

Cho. Go and give the message: do what you were told. The gods have in their care whatever they may care about.[1]

Nur. Well, I will go and obey your orders in this: and may all things turn out for the best with the aid of the gods!

Cho. Now, O Zeus, father of the Olympian gods, grant to me at my request that their fortunes may turn out well for those who have a proper desire to see sobriety prevail. I have spoken justly all that I have said: O Zeus, mayst thou guard him! And set above his enemies our hero within the palace; since by raising him to be great you will receive with gladness twice and thrice as much in return. And take note of the orphan son of one that was dear to thee, that he is harnessed to the car of calamity, and moderate his speed in the race. Would that one could see the strained pace of his steps keeping regular time as they go over this course! You gods also, who within the house are seated in richly-bedizened shrines, hear and be all of one mind. Come now, make atonement for the blood of those formerly slain by new acts of retribution. And oh! when they have been righteously executed, may old murder cease to breed new murders in the house! Do thou also, Apollo who inhabitest the well-built temple at the prophetic adytum, grant that the house of the hero may look up once more in happiness, and see brightly with friendly eyes from out of the dark veil that conceals it. And may the son of Maia rightfully lend his aid with full favour to our cause, and wishing us a happy fulfilment. But what is shrouded in darkness he will bring to light if he pleases; for now, speaking an obscure word, he brings night and darkness over the eyes, and in the daytime he is in no degree clearer.[2] And then we will establish in the city, for the delivery of the house, a continuous[1] beating

[1] The gods have their own schemes to work out. See *Ag.* 947.

[2] Though the result of Orestes' conflict is still obscure and uncertain, Hermes can and will, if he pleases, bring it to a definite and successful issue. But the poet seems to have in view partly the obscure oracles of Apollo.

[3] *οὐριοστάτης* seems a figure derived from a wind 'fixed at a favourable point of the compass.'

of female hands,[1] and with it the mournful strain sung to the fingering of the pipe; for success in this matter brings greater gain to me, and harm is kept aloof from my friends. But do you with good courage, when your share in the action has come, invoking the name of *father* as she utters the word *son*, accomplish a deed of woe for which none will reproach you: and keeping within your breast the resolution of a Perseus, go and perform first for your friends below, and then also for those on earth, the sad duties of a just resentment, by perpetrating a horrid deed of blood within the house, and utterly ridding it of the guilty cause of Agamemnon's death.

Aeg. I have come not unsummoned but at the voice of a messenger: for I am informed that certain strangers have arrived with strange tidings by no means welcome to me. Now as to the death of Orestes,—to attribute *that* also to the house would become a fear-instilling burden to one bitten and still sore from a former murder.[2] How is this? should I consider it as true and real? Or are they but alarming reports spread by women,[3] that spring aloft in air, but die and come to nothing? Which of these alternatives can you allege, so as to make it certain to my mind?

Cho. We heard it indeed; but go in and enquire of the strangers. There is no weight in the reports of mere messengers—nothing like a man's personally hearing the tale from the parties themselves.

Aeg. I wish to see, and as a further precaution to question, the messenger, whether he was himself near Orestes when he died, or whether he speaks of him from some obscure report he has heard. Assuredly they will not deceive a clear-seeing mind.

Cho. Zeus, Zeus, what must I say? At what point must I begin to make my prayers and invocations about these things? And how without saying too much, through my

[1] Perhaps *κτύπον*. The passage is corrupt, but reference was probably made to the professional female mourners spoken of at v. 416. This would be done for the dead king and queen, to avert the guilt of the murders.

[2] That people should say that *I* killed Orestes as well as Agamemnon, would be an alarming prospect to me.

[3] The Nurse and the Chorus.

well-wishing to the cause, can I secure their fulfilment? For now the blood-stained edges of slaughterous cleavers are on the point of causing the ruin of Agamemnon's house for all time, or else he will kindle a fire and a bright light in honour of freedom, and regain the constitutional government of the state and the great wealth of his ancestors. Such is the struggle in which the heroic Orestes is about to engage with two adversaries, being the sole reserve-combatant with both: but may it end in victory!

Aeg. Alas, heaven! help!

Cho. Hark! Hark again! How does the matter go? How have the gods decided the issue for the house? Let us stand aloof while the deed is being done, that we may seem to be guiltless of these evils; for indeed the issue of the fight has been determined by the gods.[1]

Slave. Woe is me, utter woe! my master has been slain! Woe is me again! I call to you a third time. Aegisthus is dead: open directly, and unbar the door of the ladies' apartment; and we want a strong young arm to do it:[2] not however that he can assist one already done for; for how is that possible? Hollo, there! I am calling to the deaf, and talking vainly bootless words to the sleeping. Whither has Clytemnestra gone? What is she doing? It seems to me now that *her*[3] neck is on the razor's edge, and will fall close to his by the blow of justice.

Cly. Well, what is the matter? What means this cry for help that you are setting up in the house?

Slave. I say that the dead is killing the living.

Cly. Ah me! I understand your words though expressed in riddles. We shall perish by craft, as in deed we slew him. Let some one hand me a heavy axe[4] with all speed: let us know at once whether we are to conquer or to be conquered; for to such a crisis have we come[5] in this sad business.

[1] We cannot alter it by interfering, and therefore we are not morally bound to interfere.

[2] The Slave seems to be an old man.

[3] See Soph. *Philoct.* 1369.

[4] Lit. 'man-tiring,' as in *Eum.* 239.

[5] That a mother should have to slay her own son. (Davies).

Or. *You* I have even been looking for: *he* there has had enough.

Cly. O me! thou art dead then, dearest Aegisthus.

Or. So he is *dear* to you, is he? Then you shall lie in the same tomb with him, and so you will never forsake him even in death.

Cly. Stay your hand, my son, and shew mercy to this breast at which you so often slumbered as you drew with toothless gums the nourishing milk.

Or. Pylades, what must I do? Must feelings of mercy prevent me from slaying my mother?

Pylades. Where then is the rest of the oracle delivered by Loxias at Pytho, and our solemn pledges of vengeance? Believe all the world your enemies rather than the gods.[1]

Or. I conclude that you are right, and you advise me well. Follow me; I would take you to the very spot where he lies and slay you there: for even while he lived, you thought him better than my father. With him then sleep in death, since you love this man, but hate him whom it was your duty to love.

Cly. I nursed you; and with you I wish to pass my old age.

Or. What, being the murderess of my father shall you dwell in *my* house?

Cly. Fate, my son, was in part the cause of these woes.

Or. Then 'twas fate that brought this death also.

Cly. Have you no fear of a parent's (dying) curse, my son?

Or. If you are my mother, you made me a wretched outcast.[2]

Cly. I did not make you an outcast by sending you into the house of a friendly ally.

Or. I was sold in more ways than one, though the son of a free father.

[1] Believe that under no circumstances the gods can be your enemies.

[2] And therefore I am the less bound to respect you as a mother.

Cly. Where then is the price, whatever it was, that I received for you?

Or. I am ashamed to reproach you in plain words with that.

Cly. But mention equally the frailties of your father.

Or. Do not find fault with one who toiled (abroad) while you sat idle in the house.

Cly. 'Tis grievous for women to be shut out from the converse of man, my son.

Or. Perhaps so: but the man has to toil to support them in indolence at home.

Cly. It seems you are resolved, O my son, to slay your mother.

Or. Nay, 'tis you who will slay yourself, not I who shall slay you.

Cly. See to it: beware of the vengeful hell-hounds of a mother.

Or. But those of my father how am I to escape, if I neglect this duty?

Cly. It seems that I am wailing in vain, as one living to the dead in a tomb.

Or. Yes, for my father's fate determines for you this death.[1]

Cly. Ah me! *this* is the snake I bare and nursed (in my dream).

Or. Assuredly the fear you had from that dream was prophetic. You slew[2] him whom you should not have slain, and now suffer what you ought never to have suffered.

Cho. I do lament indeed the twofold fate even[3] of these; but since the unhappy Orestes has reached the topmost height[4] of many murders, we still prefer this, rather than[5] that the hope of the house should fall in utter destruction.

Cho. As Justice came to the sons of Priam in the course

[1] *i. e.* it is not in my power to grant your appeals for mercy.

[2] Read *κτανοῦσ' ὃν οὐ χρῆν*, &c.

[3] Namely, hateful though they were.

[4] Climbed to the top of many murders.

[5] Gr. 'so that it should not fall.'

of time, a Justice bringing heavy retribution, so now there has entered the house of Agamemnon a pair of lions,[1] a two-fold god of war: and the exile who consulted the oracle at Pytho gained his end completely, having been well sped on his way by instructions from the god. Raise a shout of joy, ho! at the escape of our master's house from its troubles, and from the wasting of the property by two miscreants, a fate hard to get over. Yes! there came to one who deals in stealthy fight a cunningly-devised retribution;[2] and his hand was guided in the contest,—there is no error in that,—by the daughter of Zeus,—and we mortals call her Justice by a rightful title,—breathing against her enemies a destructive wrath. 'Tis this same goddess that the Loxias who inhabits the mighty adytum of the Parnassian land summons with a loud voice, crafty yet without craft,[3] and now he has gone to fetch her, limping and lingering long in her course. I know not how it is, but the divine power seems restrained[4] from helping the designs of the wicked: we have good cause for worshipping that government that rules even heaven itself. Now at length we may see the light; for we have had the great curb of slaves[5] removed from us. Up then, O house! for too long a time you have lain low on the ground. But now soon will all-accomplishing time pass the vestibule of the house, when once it shall have driven away from the hearth all defilement of guilt by purifications ridding it of its evils. And fortunes falling with lucky numbers uppermost[6], altogether benign in aspect, will turn out contrariwise to the new occupants of the house. Now at length we may see the light.

Or. Behold this joint tyranny of the land,—the slayers of my father, the plunderers of my home! Worshipful were they once, when seated on their thrones; and dear they still

[1] Perhaps, *δίπους λέων*, as *δίπους λέαινα*, *Ag.* 1229. But the 'two lions' may be Orestes and Pylades, the lion being the symbol of the Atridae.

[2] Craft has been met by craft.

[3] Lawfully using craft in executing vengeance.

[4] Namely, by *ἀνάγκη* or Fate.

[5] *i. e.* of slavery.

[6] A metaphor from dice, which have now a *πρόσωπον πρευμενὲς ἰδεῖν*, as before they were unfavourable.

are to each other, as we may infer from their deaths: and their oath abides by its engagements. They swore they would together compass the death of my unhappy father, and that they would die together: this too they have faithfully observed. But behold, ye that have heard the tale of these woes, the contrivance she used, the tie for my poor father,—the shackles of his hands and the couples of his feet. Lay out the body, and then stand close round and shew a hero's funeral pall,[1] that the father may see,—not *my* father, but the Sun, who regards all these woes,—the unhallowed deeds of my mother, that some day he may give testimony in my favour[2] at my trial, that *I* was the right person to execute this murder, that, I mean, of my mother: for I speak not of Aegisthus' fate, since he has (at my hands) the same punishment he would have received from the law.[3] But a wife who contrived this detestable device against the husband by whom she bore beneath her waist the burden of children,—a burden once dear, but now, as it shews,[4] a hostile evil,—what do you think of her? Why, that if she had been a sea-serpent[5] or a viper, she would have caused a gangrene by her mere touch even in one who had not been bitten—such is her daring and her impious spirit. What name shall I give the thing, even if I use the mildest terms? A snare for a wild beast, or rather the pall of a bier covering the feet of the corpse? Nay, a drag-net or a stake-net you might call it, or a garment made on purpose to shackle the feet. Such a device a highwayman might have for his own, who practised the duping of strangers and the life of a robber: and while he destroyed many by such a craft, he might conceive many daring schemes in his heart. May such a wife as that never become an inmate in *my* house: sooner may I perish childless by the hands of the gods!

[1] Ironically.

[2] He seems to identify the Sun with Apollo, who gives evidence for Orestes in the *Eumenides*.

[3] *ὡς νόμου* is used as the genitive is in *Eum.* 398; *Ag.* 1353.

[4] As Orestes has proved himself by the result.

[5] A partly fabulous, and supposed venomous, sea-snake or eel,—perhaps of the *torpedo* kind. There is an allusion to the snake in the dream.

Cho. Alas, alas, these unhappy doings! By a shocking death thou wert slain, woe is me! and to the survivor the calamity is yet only in the blossom.[1]

Or. Did she do the deed, or did she not? Why, this garment is my witness, that she imbrued in his blood the sword of Aegisthus.[2] For the stain of the gore contributes with time to obliterate the many dies of the coloured pattern. Now I speak of it, now I bewail it, as present at the scene;[3] and while I address this garment in which my father was slain, I grieve at the deeds done and the sufferings endured, and the entire race,[4] having upon me the curse of a guilty victory.

Cho. No mortal man will ever pass through an unharmed life in all things.[5] Alas! one toil comes at once, and another will shortly arrive.

Or. But, that you may be aware of it,—for I know not what the end will be,—as a charioteer with his horses I am driving out of the course;[6] for I am overcome and carried away by feelings that are hard to control; and fear at my heart is ready to sing and dance with excitement.[7] But while I am still in my senses I make this avowal to my friends, and declare that I slew my mother with all justice, as a guilty thing, the murderess of my father and the detestation of the gods. And among the chief inducements to this deed I reckon the oracle of the Pythian prophet Loxias, who told me that if I did this I should be exempt from evil imputation, but if I omitted it,—well, I will not mention the penalty; for[8] by guessing no one will come up to the mark of the woes. And now you see how I am prepared to go as a suppliant with this olive bough and woollen-tuft to the

[1] *i. e.* it will yet bear its fruits.

[2] Or, '(all stained as it is,) just as the sword of Aegisthus dyed it (in my father's blood).'

[3] After my long exile. If *αὐτὸν* refers to *φόνον*, it must mean Agamemnon's murder.

[4] The *μὲν* suggests that we should read *γένος δὲ πᾶν . . . . ἔχει*, 'but the whole family incurs the guilt of this victory.' The *ἔργα καὶ πάθη* refer to the maxim *δράσαντι παθεῖν*.

[5] There is some corruption in the text.

[6] He warns them of his coming madness.

[7] The allusion is to the inspiring music of the *αὐλός*.

[8] '(And it is useless to guess) for,' &c.

central temple of the earth, the holy ground of Loxias, and to the light of the fire reputed to be eternal, that I may be rid of the guilt of this kindred blood: and it was at no other altar that Loxias ordered me to take refuge. And I call on all the Argives to witness, how that these unhappy evils were forced on me [by the god] after a long time.[1] But I [shall be] a wanderer and outcast from this land, both in life and in death leaving such reports about me.......

Cho. But you have succeeded in your designs: pray let not your mouth be committed to any ill-omened expressions, nor bode evils against yourself. You have set free the whole Argive state by cutting off by a lucky stroke[2] the heads of two dragons.

Or. Ha, ha! ye captive women, here they come, like Gorgons,—all clad in sable garb, and their hair knotted with clustering snakes! I can stand it no longer.

Cho. What fancies, dearest of mortals to your father,[3] are crazing you? Restrain yourself, fear not, since the victory is greatly in your favour.

Or. They are not mere fancies of these horrors to *me;* for here are visibly the wrathful hell-hounds of my mother.

Cho. As yet the blood is fresh on your hands: from that cause without doubt confused ideas rush into your mind.

Or. King Apollo! see they come in swarms; and from their eyes they dribble loathsome gore.

Cho. There is one way to be purified that is open to you; if you cling a suppliant at the statue of Loxias, he will set you free from these horrors.

Or. *You* do not see these Furies, but *I* see them; I am driven away by them, and can no longer stay.

Cho. Then fare thee well! May the god watch thee with kindly eye, and keep thee safe with favourable fortune.

This then is the third family-storm that has raged and come to an end in the house of the king. First came the sad

[1] There is some corruption of the text, as also in what follows.

[2] The usual metaphor from dice.

[3] *i. e.* if you are persecuted by your mother.

events of Thyestes' children being eaten by their father: next, the tragic fate of the hero-king, when the general of the Achæan army perished, slain in the bath: and now again a third has suddenly come,—we hardly know whence,—a deliverer, or should I rather say, a doom? How far then will the fury of this family curse go in accomplishing its end, —where will it cease, lulled to rest after the storm?

EUMENIDES.

PERSONS REPRESENTED.

PYTHIAN PROPHETESS.	GHOST OF CLYTEMNESTRA.
APOLLO.	ORESTES.
ATHENA.	CHORUS OF FURIES.

Prophetess. In the first place, I address before all other gods, in this my prayer, the primeval prophetess Earth; and after her Themis, who next in succession occupied this oracular seat of her mother's, as is the common story: and in the third turn, with the full consent of Themis, and doing despite to no one, another Titanian goddess, child of Earth, took her seat there, Phoebe; *she* presents it as a birthday-gift to Phoebus, and he retains Phoebe's name adapted to himself as the grandson.[1] He, leaving the lake and low rocky isle of Delos, put-to at the shores of Pallas, where there was way for a ship, and so came to this (Delphian) land and the settlements near Parnassus. Thence he is escorted with solemn worship by road-makers descended from Hephaestus,[2] who caused the uncleared land to be opened for him by a highway.[3] And on his arrival he is greatly honoured by the people, and by Delphus the ruling sovereign of this land. Him then, inspired in mind with the prophetic art, Zeus appoints, fourth in order, to be the present occupant of the oracular seat; and Loxias acts as the

[1] Changed from φοίβη to φοῖβος, and held (with the interval of another name, his mother Latona's) ὄνομα παρ' ὄνομα, or, once removed.

[2] The Athenians, sprung from Erichthonius, son of Hephaestus.

[3] See *New Cratylus*, § 150.

interpreter of his father. These are the gods whom I address in my opening prayers: but Pallas, enshrined before the temple, claims the first right to be honourably mentioned; and I venerate also the Nymphs of the grotto in the Corycian cliff, frequented by birds, the haunt of deities. Bromius also claims the spot as his own,[1] nor do I forget him, ever since the god led his Bacchanalian crew and planned a death for Pentheus like that of a hunted hare. I invoke also the sources of the river Plistus, the majesty of Poseidon, and the supreme god of all, Zeus the Consummator. This being done, I go to take my seat as prophetess. And now may they grant that I may obtain far more favourable responses than from any former entrances! And if there are any deputies from the Hellenes, let them come forward, after determining their turns by lot, as is the established custom: for I give my answers just as the god may dictate.[2] [*a pause.*

Truly a sight terrible to describe and terrible to behold with mortal eyes sent me back from out the shrine of Loxias, so that my steps neither have firm tread nor bear me erect; and I run by the aid of my hands, not by speed of my feet.[3] For an old woman when alarmed is good for nothing; rather she is like a mere child. I on my part was going to the bay-crowned recess, when I saw at the central altar a man accursed of the gods taking refuge there from a deed of guilt, his hands all dripping with gore, and holding a newly-drawn sword and the top-branch of an olive-tree, duly tufted with very large fillets of wool, a white fleece; for on that point I shall speak with certainty.[4] And in front of this man there sleeps a wondrous troop of women reposing on seats: women indeed I call them not, but Gorgons; and yet again I cannot compare them to Gorgon forms. I saw once

[1] It is doubtful if these three verses are genuine. To say nothing of metrical faults, they interrupt the syntax, and they strangely assign to Parnassus events that took place on Cithaeron.

[2] Without favour to individuals or particular nations.

[3] She managed to escape, by taking hold of anything she could find to support her.

[4] The size of the fillets seem to have been a measure of the urgency of the petition for safety.

pictured [figures] carrying off the victuals of Phineus: *these* however are wingless to behold, black, and altogether loathsome in their manners. They snore with laboured breathings not to be approached,[1] and from their eyes they dribble a noxious rheum. As for their dress, it is not fit to be carried to the statues of the gods, nor into the abodes of men. The tribe to which this sisterhood belongs I have seen not, nor [know I] what land can aver that it rears such a race with impunity, and has not afterwards to repent of its pains.[2] What is to be done now must be the care of the lord of this temple, the powerful Loxias himself: and he is both physician-prophet and portent-seer, as well as a purifier of houses for others.[3]

Apollo. Be assured I will not abandon you; but having you in my keeping to the end, either standing close by your side or removed to a distance from you, I will not be lenient to your enemies. And accordingly now[4] you see these rampant witches overtaken by sleep; they have fallen down in slumber, these abhorred virgins, hoary hags,[5] children of ancient birth; with whom no god consorts, nor any mortal, nor even beast, at any time. It was on account of foul deeds that they came into existence at all;[6] for dismal darkness is their home, even Tartarus below the earth, detested both by men on earth and by the gods in Olympus. Nevertheless[7] fly and turn not faint; for they will[8] chase you even across the long continent, wandering ever wearily up and down the land and over the sea and island-cities. And do not forestal your woes by brooding anxiously over this toil; but go to the city of Pallas, and take your suppliant seat there, grasping in your arms her ancient statue; and there having judges to

[1] *i. e.* They breathed fire and smoke. See inf. v. 133; *Prom.* 379.

[2] See inf. 753. The Furies were thought to bring blight to a land.

[3] And therefore he can remove the defilement from himself, and is quite competent to deal with the case in all its aspects.

[4] Namely, as a proof of my power in your favour.

[5] Perhaps *αἱ γῆς παλαιαὶ παῖδες*, for *γραῖαι*, &c.

[6] The Furies were thought to be created as it were, or conjured into existence, by and for the punishment of unnatural murders, &c.

[7] *i. e.* though they are now asleep and seem powerless to pursue.

[8] *i. e.* even though they should chase you.

decide on these matters and arguments in palliation of your crime, we will find means to rid you effectually of these troubles: for it was even in obedience to me that you slew that body which gave you birth.

Orestes. King Apollo, you already know what it is not to act with injustice; and as you know it, learn also not to be neglectful. And your power is sufficient in itself to serve me well.

Ap. Remember! let not fear overcome your resolution. And do you, my own brother born of a common father, Hermes, guard him, and, true to your name, be his conductor, tending with care this suppliant at my temple. Know that Zeus holds in honour the respect due to those out of the pale of the law,[1] when it comes to mortals through safe convoy.[2]

Clytemnestra's Ghost. Sleep on, ho there! yet what need have I of sleepers? I tell you that I, thus slighted by you among other dead, am unceasingly reproached among the shades with being a murderess,[3] and am left to wander in disgrace; and I tell you that I have to bear the greatest blame from them. Yet, though I have endured so dreadful a fate at the hands of those dearest to me, none of the gods is indignant in my behoof, for being slain by matricidal hands. See these sword-wounds of my heart, from whom they came. For the mind in sleep is clear in its eyesight, though in the daytime the fate of mortals is hidden from their ken. Assuredly, many presents of mine have ye lapped up: and wineless libations, sober drink-offerings, and banquets in the solemn hour of the night I consecrated to you at the burning altar, at an hour common to none other of the gods. And all these gifts I now see spurned and trampled on: for *he* has escaped from you and gone off like a fawn; yea, even from the middle of the hunting-toils he has nimbly

[1] *i. e.* suppliants,—if the text can be trusted.

[2] When a murderer is directed or introduced to a temple by some πρόξενος, or guide of authority. See inf. v. 197.

[3] If, while other murdered persons are avenged by the Furies, Clytemnestra is neglected by them, she is taunted by the shades below that her case, as that of a murderess, deserved no redress.

bounded, with gibes and great mockery of you. Hear me, for I plead in defence of my own life:[1] be roused to consciousness, ye goddesses below the earth: for though in a dream,[2] it is I Clytemnestra that summon you.

[*a low moaning is heard.*

Cly. Moan on; but the man is gone far away in flight: for there are those[3] who protect as suppliants my relations, though not myself. [*a moaning again.*

Too deeply do you slumber, and do not compassionate my sufferings: here is Orestes, the murderer of his own mother, allowed to escape! [*a stifled cry is heard.*

Do you cry out? do you slumber still? Get up instantly! What has been accomplished by you,—except to cause harm?

[*a low cry again.*

Sleep and toil, powerful conspirators, have taken out of our fell she-dragon[4] all her strength.

[*a twice-repeated cry, shrill in tone.*

Cho. Seize, seize him, there, there, there! Mark him!

Cly. You are as one that pursues a quarry in a dream, and (idly) give tongue like a dog that never ceases thinking about its toil. What are you doing? Get up! let not fatigue overcome you, nor be unaware of your loss, having your fierceness tamed by sleep. Be pained in your heart with just reproaches; for to the wise they are as goads to the feelings. And do *you*,[5] directing against him your gory breath, withering him with the hot blast, the fire of your inmost breast, pursue, wear him down with a second chase.

Leader of the Chorus. Rouse, rouse up *her*, as I rouse you. Are you asleep? Get up, cast off sleep, and let us see if any word of our opening song is uttered in vain.

Cho. (1) Oh woe, alas![6] We have suffered, friends,—

[1] Namely, her moral existence, or recognition in Hades. Or perhaps, simply, 'about myself.' There seems an allusion to the phrase περὶ ψυχῆς ἀγών, 'on a vital matter.'

[2] Though, as you are sleeping, you fancy you hear me in a dream.

[3] Apollo, Hermes, Pallas.

[4] Ironically said.

[5] Three several Furies appear to be specially addressed in this speech.

[6] The exclamations cannot be literally rendered.

(2) Much indeed and undeservedly have *I* endured,—

(1) Suffered (I say) a calamity deeply grievous, an intolerable evil.

(3) The wild beast has escaped from the nets and is gone: while overcome by sleep I lost my prey.

(4) Fie! son of Zeus; a thief's part you are acting.

(5) And a young god you over-rode us aged deities—

(4) By paying regard to one who was your suppliant, an impious man, and cruel to his parents.

(6) And one that was a matricide you stealthily took out of our hands, though you are a god. Which of these acts will any one say is right?

(7) But to me a reproach came in my dreams, and smote me, like a chariot-driver with a goad grasped by the middle, under the heart, under the liver.

(8) One may feel what is the severe, the very severe smart of the fierce public executioner's lash.

(9) This is what your younger gods do, holding authority altogether beyond what is right.

(10) A blood-dripping gout round the head and the foot,—

(11) One may perceive Earth's central altar to have taken upon itself, so as to endure a terrible pollution of gore.

(12) And though you call yourself a prophet, by a defilement of your own altar-stone you polluted the oracular recess self-impelled, self-invited, contrary to the law of the gods doing honour to human claims, and having brought to nought the goddesses of ancient birth.

(13) Yea, and while to me he gives toil and trouble, yet *him* he shall not release; and even when he has fled beneath the earth he is no more free.

(14) But as a guilty culprit he shall get another foul demon to alight on his head after me.

Ap. Out with you, I insist, out of this temple go at once! be off from the prophetic recess, lest you receive in your vitals a winged glistening serpent[1] speeding from the golden

[1] An arrow, so called from its venomous bite.

bowstring, and disgorge through pain the black froth sucked from men, vomiting the gouts of gore which you have drained from them. Not to *these* abodes is it fitting that ye should approach: but rather where there are punishments of striking off heads and scooping-out eyes and the cutting of throats, and by the destroying of the seed the vigour of boys is impaired, and mutilation of extremities and deaths by stoning, and where men moan forth their horrid misery impaled below the back-bone;—do ye hear the sort of feast ye have a fondness for, and so become objects of disgust to the gods? Why, the whole fashion of your forms suggests it. The den of a blood-lapping lion such as *you* should inhabit, and not inflict a lasting pollution on the temple here close by. Go, ye that are tended without a keeper: for to such a flock as yours no god has friendly feelings.

Cho. King Apollo, hear our answer in turn. You yourself are not partly concerned in this, but you alone did it all, as the sole and entire author of it.

Ap. How was that? Prolong your account to that extent.

Cho. You delivered an oracle for the stranger to slay his mother.

Ap. I did enjoin that he should exact[1] vengeance for his father: of course I did.

Cho. And then you engaged to take on yourself the guilt of recent[2] blood.

Ap. Yes, and I enjoined him to take refuge at this temple.

Cho. And then you abuse us who attended him thither.[3]

Ap. Yes, for it is not fitting that you should come to this sacred temple.

Cho. But on us this duty has been specially imposed.

Ap. What kind of honour is that? Boast of a prerogative that is creditable.

[1] πρᾶξαι, not πέμψαι. Compare inf. 594.

[2] Before it had been removed by ἱλασμοὶ, or ceremonial purifications.

[3] They purposely use προπέμπειν as less invidious than διώκειν.

Cho. We drive matricides from out their homes.

Ap. What! (the slayer) of a wife who has killed her husband?

Cho. That would not be kindred blood shed by the hand of a relation.[1]

Ap. Truly you make of no effect and of no importance the solemn pledges of Hera and Zeus the gods of Marriage; Cypris too is cast away without honour by this argument, source as she is of the dearest joys to mortals. For the marriage-bed appointed by fate for husband and wife is greater than a mere oath, guarded as it is by Justice. If then you are lax towards man and wife, when one slays the other, so that it does not happen that you regard the deed with any anger at all, then I say that you do not justly persecute Orestes. For in his case I know that you are greatly enraged against him; in hers, that you openly act with more leniency. But the goddess Pallas will see that justice is done at the trial of this matter.

Cho. That man I will never, never leave.

Ap. Then go on chasing him—and give yourself trouble still further.

Cho. Do not *you* attempt to abridge *my* prerogatives by your words.

Ap. *Your* prerogatives! I would not even accept them as a present.

Cho. No, for even without them you are held to be great by the throne of Zeus.[2] But I,—for the blood of a mother leads me on,—shall pursue this man with vengeance, and here I put myself on his track.

Ap. Then *I* shall assist him, and rescue my own suppliant: for terrible both among men and gods is the wrath of a refugee, when one abandons him with intent.[3]

Or. Athena my queen, by the commands of Loxias I

[1] The murder of a husband by a wife is not therefore so bad as that of a mother by a son, and does not require the same vengeance.

[2] A contemptuous allusion to his position as one of the νέοι, *i. e.* Ὀλύμπιοι θεοί.

[3] Perhaps we should read, ὃς προδῷ σφ' ἑκών.

here come; and do you receive favourably a wretch, not now with the guilt of blood upon him, nor unpurified in hand;[1] but by this time blunted and worn down at other houses and ways of men, passing alike over dry land and sea, in obedience to the oracular behests of Loxias I am here at thy temple and thy statue, O goddess. Here I will keep my post awaiting the issue of the trial.

Cho. So! Here is a clear trace of the man: follow the tellings of a voiceless informer.[2] For as a hound does a wounded fawn, so do we track out (our prey) by blood and its droppings. And with my long toils to wear out the man in the chase my heart pants: for every spot of earth has been carefully gone over, and across the sea with wingless flight have I come plying my course, not at all behind a ship in speed. And now he is somewhere about here crouching down: the smell of human gore greets my senses.

(1) Look out, look out again, cast your eyes in every direction, lest the matricide should have escaped us by stealthy flight and should go unpunished.

(2) Here we find him again[3] having a safe asylum; with arms clasped round the statue of the immortal goddess,—

(3) He is willing enough to give himself up for justice into our hands![4]

(4) But that cannot be: the blood of a mother is on the ground, not to be taken up again, alas!

(5) The life-blood once shed on the ground is gone.

(6) But you have yet to give me in return to suck the crimson draught from *your* limbs even in life.

(7) Yea, from you would I fain get the feeding on a blood-draught by others loathed.

(8) And after draining you dry I will take you alive to the regions below,—

[1] These two conditions have ceased since his purification.

[2] Namely, the smell of blood; or possibly the blood-drops. See sup. ver. 41.

[3] They catch a glimpse of him at Pallas' statue, but dare not approach to seize him.

[4] Ironically said.

(9) To pay just retribution for the pangs of a slaughtered mother.

(10) And you shall there see if any other mortal sinned,—

(11) By impious conduct to a god, or a stranger, or to his parents dear,—

(12) Having each the punishment that Justice requires of him.

(13) For Hades is a mighty corrector of mortals beneath the earth.

(14) And notices all crimes in his recording mind.[1]

Or. Trained as I have been in the school of misfortune, I know many purifications, and to speak[2] where it is proper, and to be silent alike; but in the present case I was ordered to plead by a wise instructor. For the blood sleeps, and is fading away from my hand; and the guilt of killing a mother is washed out.[3] For while yet fresh it was driven off at the altar of the god Phoebus by purifications made with the blood of slaughtered swine. Long indeed would be my account from the beginning, of how many houses I visited with harmless intercourse.[4] Time purifies all things, as it grows old along with them. And so now with guiltless voice I can invoke in a holy prayer the queen of this land, Athena, to come as my patroness; and she shall gain without war myself and my country and the Argive host, disinterestedly faithful and for ever her ally. Whether then in the confines of the Libyan land, by Triton's stream, the river of her birth, she is setting her foot upright or draped in her peplus,[5] in defence of her friends,—or whether, like a bold general in his ranks, she is surveying the Phlegraean plain,—may she come,—and a god can hear even from a distance,—that she may prove to me a deliverer from these my troubles.

Cho. Think not that Apollo or even Athena's might can

[1] There appear to be fifteen distinct speeches of individual Choreutae, including the Hegemon.

[2] He has learnt, from the various ceremonies he has passed through, what and when to speak or not to speak. To reveal any mystery was regarded as a heinous crime.

[3] The metaphor is from transient colours, called ἐξιτηλοί.

[4] Without bringing upon them any judgment or pestilence after my purification.

[5] *i.e.* she is walking or standing still.

save you from perishing in utter neglect, without one lingering joy left in your heart, the bloodless victim of us deities, a mere shadow. What! not a word of reply? Do you spurn my words, fattened as you have been and consecrated for my victim? Yea, alive you shall make me a meal, and not slaughtered at the altar. And now you shall hear a song that will bind you unto us.

Come now, let us e'en join hands in the dance, since it has been resolved to shew the power of our weird strain, and to declare how our sisterhood distributes the fortunes that prevail among man: and we profess[1] to exercise upright justice. Against the man who holds out pure hands no anger from us proceeds; he goes through life unharmed by us: but when a guilty wretch like this man hides under his robe his gory hands, we come forward as upright witnesses for the dead, and he finds that we exact from him to the full the price of blood.

Mother who didst bring me forth, O mother Night, that I might be a punishment to the living and the dead, hear me! For the son of Latona makes me dishonoured in taking from me this crouching hind, this my own rightful victim for expiating a mother's murder. Such is the strain we sing over a victim that has been sacrificed,[2] a maddening, a mind-destroying distraction, a hymn of the Furies that holds spellbound the reason, not chaunted to by the lute, a blighting to mortals. For this office hath all-pervading Destiny allotted to us to hold for ever; whensoever any mortals have been concerned in the wanton murders of kin, that we should follow them closely till they go under the earth; and when dead they are far from[3] free. It was at our birth that these offices were solemnly confirmed to us: the part of the immortals is not to interfere with us; nor is any one of them a partaker with us of a common banquet. In snow-white robes too I was born to have no share, no allotted right: for I undertake

[1] *εὐχόμεθα* is the reading here rendered. They were *μοῖραι*.

[2] This appears to be said generally.

[3] *οὐκ ἄγαν* represents the prose formula *οὐ πάνυ*.

the overthrow of houses, whenever domestic feuds have caused the death of a relation. Him, oh! do we closely pursue, strong runner though he be, and dim the crimson of the fresh blood. (Yet am I anxious to remove others from these cares;[1] for the gods can only cause the non-fulfilment of prayers offered to me, but they may not come to a quarrel with me. For Zeus has deemed unworthy of his converse this blood-dropping company, deserving only of his hatred.[2]) For, as I said, I take a spring from far above, and bear down on him the heavy-falling force of my foot, my limbs which trip up even runners in the long heat, a check hard to endure. And people who are thought great and grand under the light of heaven fall off and become little and of no account on the earth, when we sisters of the sable robes come suddenly upon them, and move our feet in the hateful dance.[3] But when he falls he is unconscious of it through his fatal folly: such a dark cloud of guilt hovers over the man, and such a murky mist over his house does report speak of with many a sigh.

Yea, 'tis a fixed and abiding law; for we Furies are ready in resource and able to carry out our ends, and ever mindful of crimes; nor are we easily talked over by mortals, while we silently pursue our dishonoured and uncared-for office, kept apart from the gods, with a torch that sees not the light of the sun,[4] chasing over rough roads both the living and the dead[5] alike. What mortal man is there then who does not fear and stand in awe of this our office, when he hears from me the rule which has been ratified by fate, and assigned to us with full powers from the gods? For I bear upon me an ancient prerogative, and I meet not with dishonour even though I have a post beneath the earth, and a sunless gloom.

Athena. From afar I heard the sound of your call for

[1] From Apollo and Pallas in particular.

[2] These epithets are supposed to be applied by Zeus in disparagement of the Furies. The whole passage, which is very obscure, seems parenthetical.

[3] The weird-dance with the *δέσμιος ὕμνος*.

[4] The same idea is repeated, that the infernal is kept apart from the supernal.

[5] 'The seeing and the short-sighted,' cf. 312.

help, even from the Scamander, as I was taking possession of a land which (be it known) the leaders and chiefs of the Achaeans assigned to me as a large portion of the captured (Trojan) property, to be wholly mine with all the trees upon it,[1] a chosen present for the children of Theseus.[2] Thence came I plying my unwearied foot, not with wings, but flapping in the breeze the folds of my aegis, having attached this car of mine to strong young steeds.[3] And now, when I see these visitors to my land, I do not indeed feel fear, but only wonder at the sight, who in the world ye are: and I address myself to all in common, including the stranger who is seated here at my image.[4]. But as for you, who are like no race of creatures born, neither seen by gods among goddesses, nor resembling human forms,—however, to speak ill of others when one has no cause for complaint, is far from right, and justice revolts from it.

Cho. You shall hear all in a few words, daughter of Zeus: we are the children of Eternal Night. In the abodes below the earth we are called *Spirits invoked for Evil.*[5]

Ath. Your origin I know, and the titles you are called by.

Cho. But the duties which are properly mine you shall learn forthwith.

Ath. I might understand them if one of you would give me a clear account.

Cho. We chase homicides from their homes.

Ath. And where does the murderer find an end to the pursuit?

Cho. Where absence of all joy is the law of the place.[6]

[1] Olive-trees were especially sacred to Pallas.

[2] For their share of the prize obtained by the Trojan war.

[3] Hermann would read *κώλοις* for *πώλοις*. The 'steeds' must be supposed to have been unyoked and left elsewhere. But this verse reads like an interpolation. It is perhaps possible *κώλοις ἀκμαίοις* might mean 'holding out the ægis at the tips of my extended hands,' like the wings of a bat.

[4] She wishes to know who is the *ξένος* (Orestes) as well as who are the Furies.

[5] No single English word will render *'Αραί*. 'Curses' conveys no clear idea. But the line is spurious.

[6] Namely, in Hades. See v. 291.

Ath. Are you urging this man also to the like flight?

Cho. Yes; he thought proper to be the murderer of his mother.

Ath. But was there not some other constraint,—some threatened wrath he had to fear?[1]

Cho. Why, what motive is sufficient to goad a man to murder his own mother?

Ath. There are two parties, but the statements of only one side are before us.[2]

Cho. But he will neither take nor tender the legal oaths for a trial.

Ath. You are more willing to be called just than to act justly.

Cho. How is that? Inform me, for you are not deficient in wisdom.[3]

Ath. I bid you not try to carry an unjust cause by oaths.

Cho. Proceed then to cross-questioning, and decide by a direct process.

Ath. Would you commit to me the decision of the cause?

Cho. Certainly, as holding in proper regard the worthy daughter of a worthy sire.

Ath. What do you wish to say, stranger, in your turn in answer to these charges? Tell first your country, your family, and your adventures, and then clear yourself of this slur on your fame, since it is in reliance on the justice of your cause that you sit clasping this my statue close to my altar, a sacred suppliant after the manner of Ixion. To all these questions give me an intelligible reply.

Or. Queen Athena, I will begin by removing a great anxiety expressed in the latter words of your address. I am not a *guilty* suppliant: nor did I take my seat at your statue with pollution on my hand. And I will mention to you a great proof of this. It is the custom that the murderer

[1] The penalty of neglecting some equally strong motive on the other side, namely, the commands of Apollo. See *Cho.* 1021.

[2] *i.e.* let Orestes answer that question himself.

[3] She was the goddess of wisdom. See v. 812.

should not speak nor be spoken to, until, by the ministration of some man who performs expiations for murder, the spurted blood of a slain sucking-pig shall have sprinkled him. Long ago have we had these cleansing rites performed on us at the houses of others, both by slain victims and by running streams. This care then I thus remove by my assurance. But what my family is, you shall hear forthwith. I am an Argive, and my father you know well, Agamemnon, ruler of the naval host; for with him you made Troy, the capital of Ilium, desolate; he perished, on return to his home, not indeed by an honourable death, but my gloomy-minded mother slew him by covering him over with embroidered toils, which bare witness after his death to the murder in the bath.[1] And I returning, an exile hitherto, slew my mother, I will not deny it, by a revenge that required her blood for that of my dearest father. And of this deed Loxias shares the blame with myself, for predicting woes that would be as goads to my heart, if I omitted to do any of these things to those who were in fault. And do you, whether I acted rightly or not, decide the cause: for however I shall have fared before you in this matter, I shall acquiesce.

Ath. The case is too serious, if any mortal being thinks to decide it; nor is it lawful for me (a goddess) to act as judge in a suit about a murder that was caused by keen resentment.[2] Besides, *you* have come to my temple as a suppliant,[3] a broken-down wanderer, purified and incapable of causing harm by your converse: so that (though originally guilty) I receive you to my acropolis as if free from blame. On their parts, these Furies have a duty to perform which makes it hard to dismiss them: and if they should fail to gain their cause in this suit, hereafter poison falling on the ground[4] in consequence of their anger will be a lasting disease causing

[1] See *Cho.* 970.

[2] *i. e.* which had this palliating motive, of just anger, and thus became mere manslaughter.

[3] She could not condemn as a culprit one whom she was bound to protect as a suppliant, now that he had undergone ceremonial purification.

[4] The red blight of vines or corn, (ἐρυσίβη, *rubigo*,) was thought to be the result of poisoned blood-drops left by the Furies. See inf. 998.

barrenness to the land. Such then is the case in this matter: both courses, for them to remain here and for me to dismiss them, are harmful to the land,[1] and perplexing to me. But, as this matter has devolved on me, *I* will appoint judges of murder,[2] bound by oaths, to be an institution for all time: and do you, Furies, call on testimonies and evidences, the depositions on oath for forwarding the cause of justice. When I have selected the best-born of my citizens I will return, that they may decide this cause according to its real merits, having pledged themselves on oath to give no unfair decision.

Cho. Now there will be a revolution that brings in new laws: if the wrongful cause of this matricide is to prevail, then the deed will henceforth reconcile all mortals to an indifference for sin. And many cases of death, no mere fictions, inflicted by children on parents are in store for ages yet to come. For, as no wrath against these deeds is now to proceed from the weird sisters who watch the actions of man, I shall give free scope to every kind of death. And one shall hear from another, while he is predicting the misfortunes of his neighbour, that he is himself obtaining and harbouring in his house[3] the like evils; and the unhappy man speaks in vain of remedies that are no longer to be relied on.[4] And let no one invoke our aid, when smitten by calamity, uttering words of this kind, "O Justice," "O thrones of the Furies." In this strain perhaps a father or a mother who has recently suffered may lament,[5] because the temple of Justice is being overthrown. There *are* cases where it is right that awe should remain enthroned, keeping a salutary watch even over men's minds.[6] It is expedient that they

[1] This verse is corrupt. Perhaps *δυσπήμαντ', ἀμηχάνως τ' ἔχει.*

[2] Areopagites.

[3] We must read *ὑποδοχὴν* for *ὑπόδοσιν*, if any sense is to be made out of this passage; *λῆξιν* will then be from *λαγχάνω*, not from *λήγω*. The Scholiast explains *ὑπόδοσιν* by *διαδοχὴν*, thus pretty clearly establishing the true reading. The Rev. J. Price suggests the following as the meaning: "Each will learn, in different quarters, from an open discussion of his neighbour's troubles, that which will check and diminish his own sorrow."

[4] He talks of the *law* as a remedy, whereas the only true remedy was the vengeance of the Furies.

[5] Namely, in Hades.

[6] As well as over their actions.

should be taught discretion by suffering. For who, if he kept no feeling of awe[1] in gaiety of heart,—whether city or individual,—would equally continue to respect justice? Approve neither of a life that is free from all control, nor of one under the thrall of a despot: the god gives the superiority to the middle course in everything; but other things he regards differently. And I tell you a saying that agrees with this: of impiety bold daring is the offspring in very truth; but from soberness of mind comes that prosperity that is dear to and prayed for by all. And under all circumstances[2] I give you these maxims: Respect the altar of Justice; do not, at sight of gain, spurn and trample on it with godless foot; for punishment will surely follow it. The rightful end is in store for all.[3] Wherefore let people duly put in the first place of honour the respect due to parents, and have regard to a guest-honouring hospitality in their homes.[4] A man who is just without constraint, will not be unprosperous: completely ruined he will never be. But I say that the transgressor who dares in defiance of these laws, and who acts[5] in most things with random recklessness apart from justice, will in time haul down by force his mainsail, when trouble has overtaken him, and his yard-arm is breaking. And then he calls upon powers who hear him not, and struggles desperately for his life in the midst of the eddy. But the god laughs at the rash man, when he sees him powerless from helpless perplexities, unable even to weather the point, though he was so sure that he should never come to this: and so, having dashed against the sunken reef of justice all his former prosperity, he vanishes for ever from sight, and perishes unlamented.

Ath. Make proclamation, herald, and keep back the people; and let the heaven-piercing Tyrrhenian trumpet,

[1] Perhaps *δέος τρέφων*.

[2] *i.e.* generally, as opposed to the *ξύμμετρον ἔπος* or specially applicable advice given above.

[3] Compare *Suppl.* 712.

[4] Those who injured parents or guests were specially the objects of the Furies' wrath, sup. 260. The sense here is, let them hold in honour the *αἰδὼς* due to *ξένοι*.

[5] Read *τὰ πολλὰ παντόφυρτ' ἄγοντ'* &c. with Dindorf, omitting the *καὶ* inserted by Hermann before *παρβάταν*.

filled with human breath, sound forth to the host its loudest tones. For while this my council is assembling, it is to the interest of the people to keep silence, and that my institutions for all time[1] be explained to the whole city, and especially to the culprit here, that the suit may be rightly decided against the guilty party.

Cho. King Apollo, be master of what belongs to yourself.[2] What have *you* to do with this cause? Tell me.

Ap. Both to bear witness I come,—for this man is a suppliant at my temple and a refugee at my altar, and it was I who purified him from the guilt of blood,—and to be his advocate in person. I am thus responsible for the murder of this man's mother. But do you now open the case, whoever intends to lend his name to the present action.

Ath. 'Tis for you, Furies, to specify the charge; for I open the suit. The pursuer, speaking first and describing the case from the beginning, will become rightly our instructor in the matter.

Cho. We are many in number, but we will speak concisely. Do you reply by giving line for line in your turn. And first say whether you slew your mother.

Or. I did slay her: of that there is no denial.

Cho. This already is one of the three points[3] of contention.

Or. You make this boast over one who is not yet finally thrown.

Cho. But you must further say *how* you killed her.

Or. I tell you: it was by stabbing her near the neck with a drawn sword in my hand.

Cho. But by whom were you persuaded, and by whose counsels did you do the deed?

Or. By the oracles of Apollo here; and he is my witness.

Cho. What! One who is a seer gave you instructions to kill a mother?

[1] Namely, the constitution of the Areopagus.

[2] A sort of a challenge or protest.

[3] One point in our favour. A metaphor from wrestling, in which three throws were decisive.

Or. Yes, and up to this time I have no reason to complain of my lot.

Cho. But if the vote shall convict you, you will soon speak differently.

Or. I have faith, and my father will send me aid from the tomb.

Cho. That's right,—trust to the dead, after killing your mother.[1]

Or. For she united in herself two crimes.

Cho. How was that? Inform the judges on that point.

Or. In killing her husband she also killed my father.

Cho. Then the case stands thus: you live, but she has atoned for her crime by being slain.

Or. Then why did you not chase her in flight while she was alive?

Cho. Because she was no blood-relation of the man whom she slew.

Or. Do you call *me* related by blood to my mother?[2]

Cho. Why, in what other way did she nurse you, you miscreant, within her girdle? Do you disown the dearest blood of a mother?

Or. At this point put in *your* evidence, and explain for me, Apollo, whether I slew her with justice. For that I did the deed, as it has been done, I do not deny. But whether this murder seems to your mind to have been justly or unjustly executed, decide, that I may put the matter[3] clearly before the judges.

Ap. I will address myself to you, the great institute of Athena here present, in the spirit of truth, and being a seer I will not deal in falsehoods. I never yet spoke on my prophetic seat, concerning any man, woman, or city, anything but what Zeus the father of the Olympian gods had ordered me. What weight this plea has, I bid you consider, and to fall in with the counsels of my father. For surely an oath has not more authority than Zeus.

[1] Ironical.

[2] The son was believed to be solely the offspring of the father, the mother being only τροφὸς of the fetus.

[3] Perhaps φράσῃς.

Cho. Zeus, as *you* assert, gave you this oracle to deliver to Orestes here, that he must avenge his father's murder and set at nought the honour due to his mother.

Ap. For it is by no means the same thing, that a man of noble birth should die,—one exalted by royalty conferred on him from Zeus,[1]—and that too by the hands of a woman, not by the far-darting war-bow, like that of an Amazon, but as you shall hear, Pallas, and you, judges, who have taken your seats to decide about this cause. For, after receiving him with kindly words of praise on his return from the army where he had made more gains than losses,[2] she extended a garment like a canopy along the side of the laver, as he was going through the bath, even to the very foot of it, and struck down her husband entangled in an endless[3] embroidered robe. Of a husband, I say, the fate was such as I have described to you,—but it was also the fate of one who was held in awe by all, and the admiral of the fleet.[4] And such I have shewn her to be, that the people may be stung with indignation, who have been commissioned to decide with authority this cause.

Cho. Zeus holds in especial regard the fate of a father, according to your account; yet he himself imprisoned his aged father Cronus. Is not that which you say contradictory to this? And I call on you (judges) to take notice of his answer.

Ap. Why, ye creatures universally detested, and abhorred even by the gods, fetters might be unloosed by Zeus; there is a remedy for that, and ample means of getting free from them; but when the dust has drunk up the blood of a man, there is no recalling to life one who is once dead. For *that* my father has not made any charm;[5] but all other things he

[1] ἐκ δὲ Διὸς βασιλῆες, Hes. *Theog.* 96. Compare *Ag.* 43.

[2] Literally, 'made the most profits in the trade' of war. Compare καπηλεύειν μάχην, *Theb.* 540, and for ἅμ' αἴνοις, Eur. *Herc. Fur.* 935, ἅμα γέλωτι.

[3] With the ends sown up,—ἄπειρον, *Agam.* 1353.

[4] Compare *Ag.* 1605.

[5] *i. e.* remedy; the ancient ἰατροὶ using charms, *e. g.* Hom. *Il.* xi.

appoints now in this way now in that, by no certain rule, without exhausting himself by the effort.[1]

Cho. Well, beware how you advocate this man's cause to procure an acquittal. After shedding on the ground the blood of a mother, from whence he derived his own, shall he still inhabit his father's house in Argos? What altars shall he use to which the public have access? What lustral-water of clans-men will admit him to sacrifice?

Ap. This point also I will explain; and take notice how rightly I will expound it. The bearer of the so-called off-spring is not the mother of it, but only the nurse of the newly-conceived fetus. It is the male who is the author of its being; while she, as a stranger for a stranger, preserves the young plant for those for whom the god has not blighted it in the bud. And I will shew you a proof of this assertion: one *may* become a father without a mother: there stands by a witness of this in the daughter of Olympian Zeus, who was not even nursed[2] in the darkness of the womb, but is so fair a bud that no god could be her natural parent. But I, Pallas, in other respects, as I well know how,[3] will make your city and your people great; indeed, I sent this man to the altar of your temple, that he might become a faithful friend to all time, and that you might gain him as a new ally, and those destined to succeed him; and that it might remain a law for ever, that the posterity of this people should adhere to these treaties.

Ath. I now bid the court to give an impartial vote according to the best of their judgment, enough having been said.

Cho. We indeed have by this time discharged all our arrows; and I only wait to hear how the trial will be decided.

Ath. Well, how shall I settle the matter[4] so as to incur no blame from you?

[1] See *Suppl.* 93; *Lucret.* v. 1182.

[2] Much less engendered or begotten.

[3] As μάντις, by giving favourable replies; as ἀποτρόπαιος, by averting evils, &c.

[4] In reference to the permanent establishment of the Areopagus.

Cho. You have heard what you have heard; and when you give in your votes, strangers, respect your oath in your hearts.

Ath. Hear now my institution, ye Attic people, on holding this first trial for bloodshed. And for future time also this court of dicasts shall ever remain in force for the people of Aegeus. But this hill of Ares, once the seat and camping-ground of the Amazons, when they came through jealousy of Theseus on a hostile expedition, and fortified to a towering height, as a counterwork (to the Acropolis) on that special occasion, this newly-built part of the city,—when they sacrificed to Ares, from which event the rock and hill of Ares derived their present name;—in this hill, I repeat, a court held in respect by the citizens, and fear allied with awe shall restrain them from injustice both by day and by night,[1] so long as the citizens themselves make no innovations in the laws. If you sully clear water by foul sewage and mud, you will never procure drink. The mean between anarchy and despotism I advise my citizens to embrace and hold in their regard, and not to cast all restraint of fear out of the city. For what mortal man, if he has nothing to fear, acts with honesty? Be assured that, if you hold in proper respect such an object of your awe, you will find in it both a bulwark of the land and a safeguard of the city, such as no human beings possess either among the Scythians or in the region of the Peloponnesus. Thus then do I appoint this court, untouched by bribes, inspiring awe, keen and prompt in vengeance, for a wakeful guardian of this land in behalf of those who are asleep. Such is the exhortation for their future conduct that I have given at length to my citizens. 'Tis for you now to rise, and each take his ballot and decide the cause with due reverence for your oaths. And now I have done.

Cho. But my advice to you is, by no means to slight this our sisterhood, who can manifest their anger against the land.[2]

[1] It shall be a *wakeful* court, *ἐγρηγορὸς φρούρημα*, inf. v. 676.

[2] Gr. 'This angry company of the land.' See inf. 690.

Ap. Yes, and *I* bid you to fear oracles which are not only from me, but from Zeus, and not to make them fruitless.

Cho. But you are shewing regard for a cause of blood, though that is not your prerogative;[1] and the responses you give, while you continue on the prophetic seat, will no longer be pure and undefiled.

Ap. Was my father too at all mistaken in his counsels in the matter of Ixion, the first applicant for purification from murder?

Cho. You talk: but I, if I fail to obtain justice, will visit this land hereafter with my heavy wrath.

Ap. But among the young and the older gods alike *you* are scouted: *I* shall prevail in the cause.

Cho. That is what you did in the house of Pheres: you persuaded the fates to make mortals immortal.

Ap. And was it not right for me to benefit one who reverenced me, especially when he happened to want it?

Cho. *You* know that you did away with the old appointments, and cheated the ancient goddesses with wine.[2]

Ap. And *you*, let me tell you, when you have failed to get a verdict in this cause, shall spit your poison[3] that will be harmless to your enemies.

Cho. Since you, a young god, are overriding me an ancient goddess, I only wait to hear the issue of this trial, as having half a mind to be angry with the city.

Ath. 'Tis my part now to decide the suit by the remaining vote: and I shall give this ballot to Orestes; for there is no mother who gave me birth, and I approve of the male side,—except that I do not marry,[4]—in all respects with my whole heart, and am entirely in favour of the father's cause. Thus I shall not pay undue regard to the death of a wife who slew her husband, the manager of her house; but Orestes

[1] Namely, as *Φοῖβος*, the god of purity, brightness, and joy.

[2] Apollo was the god of banquets and good cheer, and had violated the *νηφάλια μειλίγματα* offered to Furies and Fates, by inducing them to taste wine. The legend is nowhere expressly recorded.

[3] See the note on v. 557.

[4] She had the especial attribute of *Παρθένος*.

wins the cause, even though he should have equal votes in the trial. Turn out immediately the ballots from the urns, you judges to whom that office has been enjoined.[1]

Or. O Phoebus Apollo, how will the trial be decided?

Cho. O sable mother Night, see you these things?

Or. Now the matter will end for me either in a noose, or in my continuing to live.[2]

Cho. Yes, and it will end for *us* in coming to naught, or exercising our prerogatives still further.

Ap. Count out correctly the ballots turned out from the urns, strangers, with due regard to fairness in the division. For, as serious harm results from the absence of a vote, so a single voter by giving his ballot sets up a household.[3]

Ath. This man is acquitted in the action for murder; for the counting-up of the votes is equal.

Or. O Pallas![4] O saviour of my house! You, even you, when I was deprived of my paternal land, have reinstated me, and every man in Hellas will now say, 'The noble fellow is an Argive once more, and lives on his hereditary wealth by favour of Pallas and Loxias, and that mighty consummator of all things, the saving Third,[5] who, in compassion for the death of a father, is his preserver,[6] on seeing that these Furies were advocates of his mother.' And now I shall depart for my home, after pledging a solemn compact with this land and with your people, to last for the uttermost end of time, that no sovereign ruler of the Argive land shall ever invade this country, or bring against it a well-marshalled host; for we ourselves, being then in the tomb,[7] will contrive for all who may transgress these present treaties, by perplexing disasters, and by making their expedition hopeless and their route discouraged by bad omens, that they shall repent of

[1] An interval of awful suspense here ensues.

[2] In my committing suicide, or holding my political rights as an Argive.

[3] Another pause ensues.

[4] He rushes forward, and clasps the knees of the goddess.

[5] Σωτὴρ τρίτος, a common formula, from the order observed in invoking gods at libation.

[6] Possibly, σώζει σφε.

[7] Having power for evil as a *hero* or δαίμων.

their trouble. But, if the treaties be uprightly observed, and if they honour the city of Pallas in all times by their allied spear, we will be to the citizens themselves[1] more propitious. And now farewell, both you and the people who protect your acropolis: may you retain the art of fighting that allows your enemies no escape, bringing safety to you and victory in the contest.

Cho. Ye younger gods, ye have overridden the old laws, and have taken him out of my hands. But I, dishonoured, (unhappy that I am), who shew my heavy wrath by letting fall from my heart a poison on this land, a poison in return for what I have suffered, a drop causing sterility to the soil,—for from it a blight destroying the leaves, killing the young offspring, (O revenge!) falling on the ground, will cast throughout the country stains[2] destructive of human life,—what, I ask, must *I* do? Should I become a grievous scourge to the citizens for what I have suffered? For oh! terrible it is, ye unhappy daughters of Night, who have to bewail your lot unhonoured.

Ath. Be persuaded by me not to bear your fate with impatient grief; for you have not been beaten in the contest, but the trial came off with equal votes in all fairness, and not to your discredit. The case was this;—a clear testimony from Zeus was given in favour of Orestes: and the god himself who urged him to the deed[3] gave also evidence in person, so that Orestes, by taking this course, suffers no harm. But do you not visit this country[4] with the weight of your anger, by discharging venom-drops from your hearts,[5] unkindly influences consuming the seed. For I engage in good faith for you, that you shall occupy seats in the cavernous recesses of a land made just by your presence, seated at altars that shall be your glittering thrones, and held in honour by the citizens of this land.

[1] Perhaps ἀστοῖσι, 'to my citizens,' the Argives.

[2] See the note on v. 457.

[3] I read ὁ πείσας, which passed by successive corruptions into πήσας and θήσας, the MSS. reading. So in *Ag.* 1602, παίσας is corrupted to πήσας.

[4] Read χώρᾳ τῇδε.

[5] Probably καρδίας is the true reading, as in v. 752, which line is here directly referred to.

Cho. Ye younger gods, ye have overridden the old laws, and have taken him out of my hands. But I, dishonoured, (unhappy that I am), who shew my heavy wrath by letting fall from my heart a poison on this land, yea a return for what I have suffered, a drop causing sterility to the soil,—for from it a blight destroying the leaves, killing the young offspring, (O revenge!) falling on the ground, will cast throughout the country stains destructive of human life,—what, I ask, must *I* do? Should I become a grievous scourge to the citizens for what I have suffered? For oh! terrible it is, ye unhappy daughters of Night, who have to bewail your lot unhonoured.

Ath. Ye are *not* dishonoured: and do not in the excess of your anger, goddesses that ye are, make the land of mortal men unkindly to them. I too have trust in Zeus,[1]—but I need not speak about that,—and I am the only one of the gods who knows the keys of the storehouses wherein the thunderbolt is sealed up. But we need it not; and so do you, in ready obedience to my request, cast not over the land the fruit of a rash curse, causing everything to do badly. Lull the angry force of the dark wave,[2] as being held in solemn honour and an indweller of the land in common with myself. The time shall come when, enjoying the firstfruits of this great land, as offerings for offspring[3] and for the marriage-rite, you shall find reason to praise for ever these my terms.

Cho. That I should be treated thus, alas! *I* of the ancient views,[4] and should have an abode in the land, forsooth, unhonoured and detested! Thereat I breathe out my fury and my full resentment. O Earth, woe is me! What pang is this that enters my side? Hear the cause of my wrath, mother Night! Dispossessed of my ancient honours, the baffling wiles of these gods have made me of no account.

[1] *i.e.* I also could do men harm, if I chose.

[2] The same metaphor occurs in the last verse of the *Choephoroe*.

[3] The Furies were propitiated, not to blight offspring. See v. 755.

[4] The old notions of punishment, as contrasted with the mercy of the νέοι θεοί.

Ath. I will bear with your tempers, for you are older than myself: and in that respect indeed[1] you are doubtless wiser than I; yet to me also Zeus hath granted to be not destitute of sense.[2] But you, if you go off to the land of some other tribe, will some day be enamoured of mine: I forewarn you of this. For the time that is coming on will bring greater honour to these citizens: and you, possessing an honoured abode by the temple of Erectheus,[3] shall receive from men and from companies of women privileges more numerous than you are ever likely to have from other mortals. But do not you throw upon my territories incitements to blood, the bane of young hearts, impassioned by fits of rage not caused by wine; nor, as if you had taken out the hearts of fighting-cocks, set to dwell among my citizens a demon of war, waged between citizens and marked by mutual cruelty. Let war be far away from my confines, coming with no stinted measure to him who may be possessed by a strong passion for glory;—however, I say no more about the fighting of the domestic bird.[4] Such then are the privileges you may receive from me; doing well, you shall be treated well, honoured well, and have a stake in this land which is most favoured by heaven.

Cho. That I should be treated thus, alas! *I* of the ancient views, and should have an abode in the land, forsooth, unhonoured and detested! Thereat I breathe out my fury and my full resentment. Oh Earth, woe is me! What pang is this that enters my side? Hear the cause of my wrath, mother Night! Dispossessed of my ancient honours, the baffling wiles of these gods have made me of no account.

Ath. Be assured I shall not weary of telling you the good you will get; that you may never say that you, an elder goddess, have been made a dishonoured outcast by me

[1] Perhaps, *καὶ τῷ μὲν εἶ σὺ κάρτ' ἐμοῦ σοφωτέρα.* (I rather think this was suggested by Mr. Shilleto.)

[2] Namely, as the goddess of wisdom. See v. 409.

[3] A sharer in the honours of the indigenous heroes.

[4] She compares civil war to cock-fighting, namely, kin against kin, but wishes not to dwell on so ominous a prediction.

who am younger, and by the people my citizens, and have been banished from this land. But if you hold in devout reverence the power of Persuasion, and if[1] the honeyed eloquence of my tongue can calm your wrath, then by all means stay: but if you choose not to remain, certainly you would not in fairness make to bear heavily on this city any lasting anger or resentment or harm to the people. For it is in your power to be a landowner in this country on fair terms, with full honours.

Cho. And what settlement, queen Athena, do you say that I shall have ?[2]

Ath. One unharmed by a single grief; and do you accept it.

Cho. Suppose that I do accept it; what special prerogative is in store for me ?

Ath. That no family may thrive without your favour.

Cho. Will *you* effect this, that I shall have so much power ?

Ath. Yes; for we shall direct aright the fortunes of him who reveres you.

Cho. And will you give me a warrant for all future time ?

Ath. Yes; for I am not bound to promise what I shall not perform.

Cho. It seems that I must yield to your entreaties; and I desist from my anger.[3]

Ath. Then you shall stay in this land and win for yourself new friends.

Cho. What then do you desire me to chant in favour of this land ?

Ath. Such prayers as are directed to a victory that brings no disaster, ... and that too from the earth[4] and from the dews of ocean, and from the sky; and that the breezes of the winds may shed their serene airs as they go over the land.

[1] Perhaps *δ' εἰ* for *καί*.

[2] Probably we should read, *ἄνασσ' Ἀθάνα, τίνα δέ φῄς μ' ἔξειν ἕδραν;*

[3] This is said after a pause for consideration.

[4] Some verse or verses appear to have been lost.

That the produce of the earth and the flocks in teeming plenty may not fail to abound for the citizens for all time; and that there may be a safe rearing of human progeny. But the impious may you be more disposed to root out of the city: for I feel an affection—even as a gardener for his plants—for the family of this just people, spared from mourning. Such are the terms offered you: and I for my part[1] will not rest content without giving honour among men to this city, renowned for national victories in the glorious contests of war.

Cho. I will accept the offer of living with Pallas, and will not reject the worship of a city which even Zeus the all-powerful and Ares rule as the stronghold of the gods, the pride of the Hellenic divinities and the protector of their altars. For her I now pray, no longer with wrathful bodings, that the bright beams of the sun may send up from the earth in boundless profusion the blessings that give enjoyment to life.

Ath. This care[2] *I* undertake in kindly regard for my citizens, in establishing among them the powerful and hardly-appeased deities; for it is their appointed office to direct all that happens among men; and he who has not met with adverse fortune[3] knows not from what source the scourges of life suddenly fall upon him. For the sins of his ancestors bring him into the power of the Furies, a silent destruction, and in the midst of his high boastings level him even with the dust through their anger and hatred.

Cho. But may no evil airs blow causing blight to the trees,—I speak of my own kindly interference,—nor the blast that robs the plants of their young buds, so that they extend not beyond their allotted space:[4] let no dark disease come upon them to destroy the fruit, but may the earth supply

[1] I, as the goddess of war, will do my part, if you, the goddesses of conscience and moral restraint, will do yours.

[2] Namely, the following, which respond to to those just enumerated.

[3] *τούτων, i. e. τῶν κατ' ἀνθρώπους.* The passage is obscure, and perhaps corrupt.

[4] The measured spaces between plants in a row, such as olives, fig-trees, or vines.

food to the sheep thriving with double progeny at the appointed season of the year: and may the wealth produced from the womb of the earth[1] ever pay returns for the lucky gift of the gods.

Ath. Hear ye these words, ye guardians of the land,[2] what blessings she is bringing to pass? For great influence has the awful Erinys both with the gods above and with those beneath the earth; and in their dealings with men it is plain that these bring all things to their end, to some giving songs, to others again a dull life of tears.

Cho. But I deprecate mishaps causing the untimely deaths of men. Grant that our lovely young maidens may have wedded lives, ye gods who have power over marriage, and ye Fates, our sisters by the mother's side, goddesses that direct aright the law, common to every family, at every time exercising due weight in their dealings with men, everywhere the most honoured of the gods.[3]

Ath. I am cheered by your solemnly ratifying these privileges in friendly spirit to my country; and I am grateful to the meek-eyed Persuasion for guiding aright my words and my eloquence in addressing these goddesses when they rudely refused. But Zeus the god of harangues hath prevailed, and our contest on the side of good for all time is crowned with success.

Cho. And that insatiable source of evils, Sedition, I pray may never make an uproar in this city; never may the dust drink the dark gore of the citizens, and in anger exact penalties for slaughter, to the bane of the state. And may they exchange kindnesses with sentiments of common interest, and hate with one mind; for unanimity is the remedy for many evils among mortals.

Ath. Are they not returning to the way of wisdom, and finding out the course of right language?[1] From these

[1] The silver mines of Laurium, which appear to have paid a tithe to the service of Pallas.

[2] The Areopagites.

[3] Fate and Destiny being powers acknowledged by all nations in all times, and thus truly universal.

formidable faces[2] I perceive a great gain to my citizens here; for if you in kindly disposition greatly honour at all times these goddesses who are kindly disposed to you, you will exercise upright justice both in your land and your city, and be distinguished in whatever course of life you may pursue.

Cho. Farewell, farewell! may ye be possessed of all the blessings of wealth! Farewell, people of the city, seated near to Zeus, friends of your friend Pallas, becoming wise in time. For those who reside under the wings of his Pallas are revered by her father.

Ath. Farewell to you also! and now I must precede you to shew you your abodes by the sacred light of these escorts. Go, speedily enter your caves[3] below the earth; keep off all that is hurtful from the land, and send us all that is gainful to the city and leading to victory. And do you, children of Cranaus, guardians of my citadel, shew the way to these new residents among you; and may there remain a good feeling in the minds of the citizens for the good things they have received.

Cho. Farewell, once more farewell,—I repeat it,—all you that reside in this city, whether gods or mortals, ruling the city of Pallas; hold in pious regard my residence among you, and you will not complain of the events of your life.

Ath. I assent to the terms of these prayers, and I will escort you with the light of flashing torches to the cavernous recesses below the earth, with female attendants, and those who honestly[4] guard my sacred image. For the best-born of all the land of Theseus shall come, a goodly company of girls and married women, and a train of ancient matrons in scarlet-dyed holiday vestments. Forward![5] let the light of

[1] The appeal is here to the spectators.

[2] δεινῶπες, Soph. *Oed. Col.* 84. Furiarum *ora* trementem, Virg. *Aen.* viii. 669.

[3] A chasm in the limestone rock under the Areopagus.

[4] In allusion to the treasury of the Parthenon. Mention of women alone appears to be made, as forming the procession.

[5] We must read προβᾶτε for the corrupt τιμᾶτε, τι and π, μ and β being among the commonest errors of MSS. The word προβαίνειν (Lat. *incedere*) is technically used in many passages of starting a procession; and this is evidently the sense here required by the context.

torches also proceed, in order that these friendly dwellers in the land may become noted hereafter for the prosperous fortunes of the male inhabitants.

Escorts. Enter now your abodes, ye powerful goddesses, jealous of your honours,[1] childless children of Night, under this friendly escort,—and do you raise songs of joy, ye people of the place,—beneath the dark recesses of the earth, attended with the honours and sacrifices of fire-worship. Raise the song of joy, ye people of the place. And now proceed, propitiated and rightly-minded towards our country, this way, awful goddesses, rejoicing in being attended on your road with the fire-feeding torch. Shout, women, after our song. And let libations be made as you go, in the rear of the procession, to the light of blazing pine-wood. Thus hath Zeus the all-seeing and Fate together entered the lists in behalf of the citizens of Pallas. Shout, women, after our song.

[1] See v. 854.

THE END.

PRINTED BY J. PALMER, JESUS LANE, CAMBRIDGE.

March 1889.

A CLASSIFIED LIST

OF

EDUCATIONAL WORKS

PUBLISHED BY

GEORGE BELL & SONS.

Cambridge Calendar. Published Annually (August). 6*s*. 6*d*.
Student's Guide to the University of Cambridge. 6*s*. 6*d*.
Oxford: Its Life and Schools. 7*s*. 6*d*.
The Schoolmaster's Calendar. Published Annually (December). 1*s*.

BIBLIOTHECA CLASSICA.

A Series of Greek and Latin Authors, with English Notes, edited by eminent Scholars. 8vo.

*** *The Works with an asterisk (*) prefixed can only be had in the Sets of 26 Vols.*

Æschylus. By F. A. Paley, M.A., LL.D. 8*s*.
Cicero's Orations. By G. Long, M.A. 4 vols. 8*s*. each.
Demosthenes. By R. Whiston, M.A. 2 vols. 8*s*. each.
Euripides. By F. A. Paley, M.A., LL.D. 3 vols. 8*s*. each.
Herodotus. By Rev. J. W. Blakesley, B.D. 2 vols. 12*s*.
Hesiod. By F. A. Paley, M.A., LL.D. 5*s*.
Homer. By F. A. Paley, M.A., LL.D. Vol. I. 8*s*.; Vol. II. 6*s*.
Horace. By Rev. A. J. Macleane, M.A. 8*s*.
Juvenal and Persius. By Rev. A. J. Macleane, M.A. 6*s*.
Lucan. The Pharsalia. By C. E. Haskins, M.A. 14*s*.
Plato. By W. H. Thompson, D.D. 2 vols. 5*s*. 6*d*. each.
Sophocles. Vol. I. By Rev. F. H. Blaydes, M.A. 8*s*.
——— Vol. II. Philoctetes—Electra—Ajax and Trachiniæ. By F. A. Paley, M.A., LL.D. 6*s*. Or the 4 plays separately, 2*s*. 6*d*. each.
***Tacitus:** The Annals. By the Rev. P. Frost. 8*s*.
***Terence.** By E. St. J. Parry, M.A. 8*s*.
Virgil. By J. Conington, M.A. Revised by Professor H. Nettleship. 3 vols. 10*s*. 6*d*. each.
An Atlas of Classical Geography; 24 Maps with coloured Outlines. Imp. 8vo. 6*s*.

GRAMMAR-SCHOOL CLASSICS.

A Series of Greek and Latin Authors, with English Notes.
Fcap. 8vo.

Cæsar: De Bello Gallico. By George Long, M.A. 4*s*.

——— Books I.–III. For Junior Classes. By G. Long, M.A. 1*s*. 6*d*.

——— Books IV. and V. 1*s*. 6*d*. Books VI. and VII. 1*s*. 6*d*.

Catullus, Tibullus, and Propertius. Selected Poems. With Life. By Rev. A. H. Wratislaw. 2*s*. 6*d*.

Cicero: De Senectute, De Amicitia, and Select Epistles. By George Long, M.A. 3*s*.

Cornelius Nepos. By Rev. J. F. Macmichael. 2*s*.

Homer: Iliad. Books I.–XII. By F. A. Paley, M.A., LL.D. 4*s*. 6*d*. Also in 2 parts, 2*s*. 6*d*. each.

Horace. With Life. By A. J. Macleane, M.A. 3*s*. 6*d*. In 2 parts, 2*s*. each.

Juvenal: Sixteen Satires. By H. Prior, M.A. 3*s*. 6*d*.

Martial: Select Epigrams. With Life. By F. A. Paley, M.A., LL.D. 4*s*. 6*d*.

Ovid: the Fasti. By F. A. Paley, M.A., LL.D. 3*s*. 6*d*. Books I. and II. 1*s*. 6*d*. Books III. and IV. 1*s*. 6*d*.

Sallust: Catilina and Jugurtha. With Life. By G. Long, M.A. and J. G. Frazer. 3*s*. 6*d*., or separately, 2*s*. each.

Tacitus: Germania and Agricola. By Rev. P. Frost. 2*s*. 6*d*.

Virgil: Bucolics, Georgics, and Æneid, Books I.–IV. Abridged from Professor Conington's Edition. 4*s*. 6*d*.—Æneid, Books V.–XII. 4*s*. 6*d*. Also in 9 separate Volumes, as follows, 1*s*. 6*d*. each:—Bucolics—Georgics, I. and II.—Georgics, III. and IV.—Æneid, I. and II.—Æneid, III. and IV.—Æneid, V. and VI.—Æneid, VII. and VIII.—Æneid, IX. and X.—Æneid, XI. and XII.

Xenophon: The Anabasis. With Life. By Rev. J. F. Macmichael. 3*s*. 6*d*. Also in 4 separate volumes, 1*s*. 6*d*. each:—Book I. (with Life, Introduction, Itinerary, and Three Maps)—Books II. and III.—IV. and V.—VI. and VII.

——— The Cyropædia. By G. M. Gorham, M.A. 3*s*. 6*d*. Books I. and II. 1*s*. 6*d*.—Books V. and VI. 1*s*. 6*d*.

——— Memorabilia. By Percival Frost, M.A. 3*s*.

A Grammar-School Atlas of Classical Geography, containing Ten selected Maps. Imperial 8vo. 3*s*.

Uniform with the Series.

The New Testament, in Greek. With English Notes, &c. By Rev. J. F. Macmichael. 4*s*. 6*d*. In parts, sewed, 6*d*. each.

CAMBRIDGE GREEK AND LATIN TEXTS.

Æschylus. By F. A. Paley, M.A., LL.D. 2*s.* 6*d.*

Cæsar: De Bello Gallico. By G. Long, M.A. 1*s.* 6*d.*

Cicero: De Senectute et De Amicitia, et Epistolæ Selectæ. By G. Long, M.A. 1*s.* 6*d.*

Ciceronis Orationes. In Verrem. By G. Long, M.A. 2*s.* 6*d.*

Euripides. By F. A. Paley, M.A., LL.D. 3 vols. 2*s.* each.

Herodotus. By J. G. Blakesley, B.D. 2 vols. 5*s.*

Homeri Ilias. I.–XII. By F. A. Paley, M.A., LL.D. 1*s.* 6*d.*

Horatius. By A. J. Macleane, M.A. 1*s.* 6*d.*

Juvenal et Persius. By A. J. Macleane, M.A. 1*s.* 6*d.*

Lucretius. By H. A. J. Munro, M.A. 2*s.*

Sallusti Crispi Catilina et Jugurtha. By G. Long, M.A. 1*s.* 6*d.*

Sophocles. By F. A. Paley, M.A., LL.D. 2*s.* 6*d.*

Terenti Comœdiæ. By W. Wagner, Ph.D. 2*s.*

Thucydides. By J. G. Donaldson, D.D. 2 vols. 4*s.*

Virgilius. By J. Conington, M.A. 2*s.*

Xenophontis Expeditio Cyri. By J. F. Macmichael, B.A. 1*s.* 6*d.*

Novum Testamentum Græce. By F. H. Scrivener, M.A., D.C.L. 4*s.* 6*d.* An edition with wide margin for notes, half bound, 12*s.* EDITIO MAJOR, with additional Readings and References. 7*s.* 6*d.* *See page* 14.

CAMBRIDGE TEXTS WITH NOTES.

A Selection of the most usually read of the Greek and Latin Authors, Annotated for Schools. Edited by well-known Classical Scholars. Fcap. 8vo. 1*s.* 6*d.* *each, with exceptions.*

Æschylus. Prometheus Vinctus.—Septem contra Thebas.—Agamemnon.—Persæ.—Eumenides.—Choephoroe. By F. A. Paley, M.A., LL.D.

Euripides. Alcestis.—Medea.—Hippolytus.—Hecuba.—Bacchæ.—Ion. 2*s.*—Orestes.—Phoenissæ.—Troades.—Hercules Furens.—Andromache.—Iphigenia in Tauris.—Supplices. By F. A. Paley, M.A., LL.D.

Homer. Iliad. Book I. By F. A. Paley, M.A., LL.D. 1*s.*

Sophocles. Œdipus Tyrannus.—Œdipus Coloneus.—Antigone.—Electra—Ajax. By F. A. Paley, M.A., LL.D.

Xenophon. Anabasis. In 6 vols. By J. E. Melhuish, M.A., Assistant Classical Master at St. Paul's School.

Xenophon. Hellenics, Book II. By L. D. Dowdall, M.A., B.D. [*Shortly.*

Cicero. De Senectute, De Amicitia, and Epistolæ Selectæ. By G. Long, M.A.

Ovid. Fasti. By F. A. Paley, M.A., LL.D. In 3 vols., 2 books in each. 2*s.* each vol.

Ovid. Selections. Amores, Tristia, Heroides, Metamorphoses. By A. J. Macleane, M.A.

Terence. Andria.—Hauton Timorumenos.—Phormio.—Adelphoe. By Professor Wagner, Ph.D.

Virgil. Professor Conington's edition, abridged in 12 vols.

Others in preparation.

PUBLIC SCHOOL SERIES.

A Series of Classical Texts, annotated by well-known Scholars. Cr. 8vo.

Aristophanes. The Peace. By F. A. Paley, M.A., LL.D. 4*s*. 6*d*.
—— The Acharnians. By F. A. Paley, M.A., LL.D. 4*s*. 6*d*.
—— The Frogs. By F. A. Paley, M.A., LL.D. 4*s*. 6*d*.
Cicero. The Letters to Atticus. Bk. I. By A. Pretor, M.A. 4*s*. 6*d*.
Demosthenes de Falsa Legatione. By R. Shilleto, M.A. 6*s*.
—— The Law of Leptines. By B. W. Beatson, M.A. 3*s*. 6*d*.
Livy. Book XXI. Edited, with Introduction, Notes, and Maps, by the Rev. L. D. Dowdall, M.A., B.D. 3*s*. 6*d*.
—— Book XXII. Edited, &c., by Rev. L. D. Dowdall, M.A., B.D. 3*s*. 6*d*.
Plato. The Apology of Socrates and Crito. By W. Wagner, Ph.D. 10th Edition. 3*s*. 6*d*. Cheap Edition, limp cloth, 2*s*. 6*d*.
—— The Phædo. 9th Edition. By W. Wagner, Ph.D. 5*s*. 6*d*.
—— The Protagoras. 4th Edition. By W. Wayte, M.A. 4*s*. 6*d*.
—— The Euthyphro. 3rd Edition. By G. H. Wells, M.A. 3*s*.
—— The Euthydemus. By G. H. Wells, M.A. 4*s*.
—— The Republic. Books I. & II. By G. H. Wells, M.A. 3rd Edition. 5*s*. 6*d*.
Plautus. The Aulularia. By W. Wagner, Ph.D. 3rd Edition. 4*s*. 6*d*.
—— The Trinummus. By W. Wagner, Ph.D. 3rd Edition. 4*s*. 6*d*.
—— The Menaechmei. By W. Wagner, Ph.D. 2nd Edit. 4*s*. 6*d*.
—— The Mostellaria. By Prof. E. A. Sonnenschein. 5*s*.
—— The Rudens. Edited by Prof. E. A. Sonnenschein. [*In the press.*
Sophocles. The Trachiniæ. By A. Pretor, M.A. 4*s*. 6*d*.
Sophocles. The Oedipus Tyrannus. By B. H. Kennedy, D.D. 5*s*.
Terence. By W. Wagner, Ph.D. 2nd Edition. 10*s*. 6*d*.
Theocritus. By F. A. Paley, M.A., LL.D. 2nd Edition. 4*s*. 6*d*.
Thucydides. Book VI. By T. W. Dougan, M.A., Fellow of St. John's College, Cambridge. 3*s*. 6*d*.

Others in preparation.

CRITICAL AND ANNOTATED EDITIONS.

Aristophanis Comœdiæ. By H. A. Holden, LL.D. 8vo. 2 vols. 23*s*. 6*d*. Plays sold separately.
Cæsar's Seventh Campaign in Gaul, B.C. 52. By W. C. Compton, M.A., Assistant Master, Uppingham School. Crown 8vo. 4*s*.
Calpurnius Siculus. By C. H. Keene, M.A. Crown 8vo. 6*s*.
Corpus Poetarum Latinorum. Edited by Walker. 1 vol. 8vo. 18*s*.
Horace. Quinti Horatii Flacci Opera. By H. A. J. Munro, M.A. Large 8vo. 10*s*. 6*d*.

Livy. The first five Books. By J. Prendeville. 12mo. roan, 5s. Or Books I.-III. 3s. 6d. IV. and V. 3s. 6d. Or the five Books in separate vols. 1s. 6d. each.

Lucretius. With Commentary by H. A. J. Munro. 4th Edition. Vols. I. and II. Introduction, Text, and Notes. 18s. Vol. III. Translation. 6s.

Ovid. P. Ovidii Nasonis Heroides XIV. By A. Palmer, M.A. 8vo. 6s.

——— P. Ovidii Nasonis Ars Amatoria et Amores. By the Rev. H. Williams, M.A. 3s. 6d.

——— Metamorphoses. Book XIII. By Chas. Haines Keene, M.A. 2s. 6d.

——— Epistolarum ex Ponto Liber Primus. By C.H. Keene, M.A. 3s.

Propertius. Sex Aurelii Propertii Carmina. By F. A. Paley, M.A., LL.D. 8vo. Cloth, 5s.

——— Sex Propertii Elegiarum. Libri IV. Recensuit A. Palmer, Collegii Sacrosanctæ et Individuæ Trinitatis juxta Dublinum Socius. Fcap. 8vo. 3s. 6d.

Sophocles. The Ajax. By C. E. Palmer, M.A. 3s. 6d.

——— The Oedipus Tyrannus. By B. H. Kennedy, D.D. Crown 8vo. 8s.

Thucydides. The History of the Peloponnesian War. By Richard Shilleto, M.A. Book I. 8vo. 6s. 6d. Book II. 8vo. 5s. 6d.

LATIN AND GREEK CLASS-BOOKS.

Faciliora. An Elementary Latin Book on a new principle. By the Rev. J. L. Seager, M.A. 2s. 6d.

A Latin Primer. By Rev. A. C. Clapin, M.A. 1s.

Auxilia Latina. A Series of Progressive Latin Exercises. By M. J. B. Baddeley, M.A. Fcap. 8vo. Part I. Accidence. 3rd Edition, revised. 2s. Part II. 4th Edition, revised. 2s. Key to Part II. 2s. 6d.

Scala Latina. Elementary Latin Exercises. By Rev. J. W. Davis, M.A. New Edition, with Vocabulary. Fcap. 8vo. 2s. 6d.

Passages for Translation into Latin Prose. By Prof. H. Nettleship, M.A. 3s. Key (for Tutors only), 4s. 6d.

Latin Prose Lessons. By Prof. Church, M.A. 9th Edition. Fcap. 8vo. 2s. 6d.

Tales for Latin Prose Composition. With Notes and Vocabulary. By G. H. Wells, M.A. 2s.

Analytical Latin Exercises. By C. P. Mason, B.A. 4th Edit. Part I., 1s. 6d. Part II., 2s. 6d.

BY T. COLLINS, M.A., HEAD MASTER OF THE LATIN SCHOOL, NEWPORT, SALOP.

Latin Exercises and Grammar Papers. 6th Edit. Fcap. 8vo. 2s. 6d.

Unseen Papers in Latin Prose and Verse. With Examination Questions. 4th Edition. Fcap. 8vo. 2s. 6d.

——— in Greek Prose and Verse. With Examination Questions. 3rd Edition. Fcap. 8vo. 3s.

Easy Translations from Nepos, Cæsar, Cicero, Livy, &c., for Retranslation into Latin. With Notes. 2s.

Scala Græca: a Series of Elementary Greek Exercises. By Rev. J. W. Davis, M.A., and R. W. Baddeley, M.A. 3rd Edition. Fcap. 8vo. 2s. 6d.

Greek Verse Composition. By G. Preston, M.A. 5th Edition. Crown 8vo. 4s. 6d.

Greek Particles and their Combinations according to Attic Usage. A Short Treatise. By F. A. Paley, M.A., LL.D. 2s. 6d.

Rudiments of Attic Construction and Idiom. By the Rev. W. C. Compton, M.A., Assistant Master at Uppingham School. 3s.

By A. M. M. Stedman, M.A., Wadham College, Oxford.

First Latin Lessons. 1*s.*

Miscellaneous Latin Exercises. Fcap. 8vo. 1*s.* 6*d.*

Easy Latin Exercises on the Syntax of the Revised Latin Primer and Shorter Latin Primer. With Vocabulary. Crown 8vo. 2*s.* 6*d.*

Easy Latin Passages for Unseen Translation. Fcap. 8vo. 1*s.* 6*d.*

Latin Vocabularies for Repetition. 2nd Edition, revised. Fcap. 8vo. 1*s.* 6*d.*

Latin Examination Papers in Grammar and Idiom. Crown 8vo. 2*s.* 6*d.* Key (for Tutors and Private Students only), 6*s.*

Greek Examination Papers in Grammar and Idiom. 2*s.* 6*d.*

Greek Testament Selections. 2nd Edition, enlarged, with Notes and Vocabulary. Fcap. 8vo. 2*s.* 6*d.*

By the Rev. P. Frost, M.A., St. John's College, Cambridge.

Eclogæ Latinæ; or, First Latin Reading-Book, with English Notes and a Dictionary. New Edition. Fcap. 8vo. 1*s.* 6*d.*

Materials for Latin Prose Composition. New Edition. Fcap. 8vo. 2*s.* Key (for Tutors only), 4*s.*

A Latin Verse-Book. An Introductory Work on Hexameters and Pentameters. New Edition. Fcap. 8vo. 2*s.* Key (for Tutors only), 5*s.*

Analecta Græca Minora, with Introductory Sentences, English Notes, and a Dictionary. New Edition. Fcap. 8vo. 2*s.*

Materials for Greek Prose Composition. New Edit. Fcap. 8vo. 2*s.* 6*d.* Key (for Tutors only), 5*s.*

Florilegium Poeticum. Elegiac Extracts from Ovid and Tibullus. New Edition. With Notes. Fcap. 8vo. 2*s.*

Anthologia Græca. A Selection of Choice Greek Poetry, with Notes. By F. St. John Thackeray. *4th and Cheaper Edition.* 16mo. 4*s.* 6*d.*

Anthologia Latina. A Selection of Choice Latin Poetry, from Nævius to Boëthius, with Notes. By Rev. F. St. John Thackeray. Revised and Cheaper Edition. 16mo. 4*s.* 6*d.*

By H. A. Holden, LL.D.

Foliorum Silvula. Part I. Passages for Translation into Latin Elegiac and Heroic Verse. 10th Edition. Post 8vo. 7*s.* 6*d.*

—— Part II. Select Passages for Translation into Latin Lyric and Comic Iambic Verse. 3rd Edition. Post 8vo. 5*s.*

Folia Silvulæ, sive Eclogæ Poetarum Anglicorum in Latinum et Græcum conversæ. 8vo. Vol. II. 4*s.* 6*d.*

Foliorum Centuriæ. Select Passages for Translation into Latin and Greek Prose. 10th Edition. Post 8vo. 8*s.*

TRANSLATIONS, SELECTIONS, &c.

*** Many of the following books are well adapted for School Prizes.

Æschylus. Translated into English Prose by F. A. Paley, M.A., LL.D. 2nd Edition. 8vo. 7s. 6d.

—— Translated into English Verse by Anna Swanwick. 4th Edition. Post 8vo. 5s.

Horace. The Odes and Carmen Sæculare. In English Verse by J. Conington, M.A. 10th edition. Fcap. 8vo. 5s. 6d.

—— The Satires and Epistles. In English Verse by J. Conington, M.A. 7th edition. 6s. 6d.

—— Odes. Englished and Imitated by various hands. 1s. 6d.

Plato. Gorgias. Translated by E. M. Cope, M.A. 8vo. 2nd Ed. 7s.

—— Philebus. Trans. by F. A. Paley, M.A., LL.D. Sm. 8vo. 4s.

—— Theætetus. Trans. by F. A. Paley, M.A., LL.D. Sm. 8vo. 4s.

—— Analysis and Index of the Dialogues. By Dr. Day. Post 8vo. 5s.

Sophocles. Œdipus Tyrannus. By Dr. Kennedy. 1s.

Theocritus. In English Verse, by C. S. Calverley, M.A. New Edition, revised. Crown 8vo. 7s. 6d.

Translations into English and Latin. By C. S. Calverley, M.A. Post 8vo. 7s. 6d.

Translations into English, Latin, and Greek. By R. C. Jebb, M.A., H. Jackson, Litt.D., and W. E. Currey, M.A. Second Edition. 8s.

Extracts for Translation. By R. C. Jebb, M.A., H. Jackson, Litt.D., and W. E. Currey, M.A. 4s. 6d.

Between Whiles. Translations by Rev. B. H. Kennedy, D.D. 2nd Edition, revised. Crown 8vo. 5s.

REFERENCE VOLUMES.

A Latin Grammar. By Albert Harkness. Post 8vo. 6s.

—— By T. H. Key, M.A. 6th Thousand. Post 8vo. 8s.

A Short Latin Grammar for Schools. By T. H. Key, M.A. F.R.S. 16th Edition. Post 8vo. 3s. 6d.

A Guide to the Choice of Classical Books. By J. B. Mayor, M.A. 3rd Edition, with a Supplementary List. Crown 8vo. 4s. 6d. Supplementary List separately, 1s. 6d.

The Theatre of the Greeks. By J. W. Donaldson, D.D. 8th Edition. Post 8vo. 5s.

Keightley's Mythology of Greece and Italy. 4th Edition. 5s.

CLASSICAL TABLES.

Latin Accidence. By the Rev. P. Frost, M.A. 1*s*.

Latin Versification. 1*s*.

Notabilia Quædam; or the Principal Tenses of most of the Irregular Greek Verbs and Elementary Greek, Latin, and French Construction. New Edition. 1*s*.

Richmond Rules for the Ovidian Distich, &c. By J. Tate, M.A. 1*s*.

The Principles of Latin Syntax. 1*s*.

Greek Verbs. A Catalogue of Verbs, Irregular and Defective; their leading formations, tenses, and inflexions, with Paradigms for conjugation, Rules for formation of tenses, &c. &c. By J. S. Baird, T.C.D. 8th Ed. 2*s*. 6*d*.

Greek Accents (Notes on). By A. Barry, D.D. New Edition. 1*s*.

Homeric Dialect. Its Leading Forms and Peculiarities. By J. S. Baird, T.C.D. New Edition, by W. G. Rutherford, LL.D. 1*s*.

Greek Accidence. By the Rev. P. Frost, M.A. New Edition. 1*s*.

CAMBRIDGE MATHEMATICAL SERIES.

Arithmetic for Schools. By C. Pendlebury, M.A. 3rd Edition, stereotyped, with or without answers, 4*s*. 6*d*. Or in two parts, 2*s*. 6*d*. each.

Examples (nearly 8000), without answers, in a separate vol. 3*s*.

Algebra. Choice and Chance. By W. A. Whitworth, M.A. 4th Edition. 6*s*.

Euclid. Books I.-VI. and part of Books XI. and XII. By H. Deighton. 4*s*. 6*d*. Key (for Tutors only), 5*s*. Books I. and II., 2*s*.

Euclid. Exercises on Euclid and in Modern Geometry. By J. McDowell, M.A. 3rd Edition. 6*s*.

Trigonometry. Plane. By Rev. T. Vyvyan, M.A. 3rd Edit. 3*s*. 6*d*.

Geometrical Conic Sections. By H. G. Willis, M.A. Manchester Grammar School. 7*s*. 6*d*.

Conics. The Elementary Geometry of. 5th Edition, revised and enlarged. By C. Taylor, D.D. 4*s*. 6*d*.

Solid Geometry. By W. S. Aldis, M.A. 4th Edit. revised. 6*s*.

Geometrical Optics. By W. S. Aldis, M.A. 3rd Edition. 4*s*.

Rigid Dynamics. By W. S. Aldis, M.A. 4*s*.

Elementary Dynamics. By W. Garnett, M.A., D.C.L. 4th Ed. 6*s*.

Dynamics. A Treatise on. By W. H. Besant, D.Sc., F.R.S. 7*s*. 6*d*.

Heat. An Elementary Treatise. By W. Garnett, M.A., D.C.L. 4th Edition. 4*s*.

Elementary Physics. Examples in. By W. Gallatly, M.A. 4*s*.

Hydromechanics. By W. H. Besant, D.Sc., F.R.S. 4th Edition. Part I. Hydrostatics. 5*s*.

Mathematical Examples. By J. M. Dyer, M.A., Assistant Master Eton College, and R. Prowde Smith, M.A., Assistant Master at Cheltenham College. 6*s*.

Mechanics. Problems in Elementary. By W. Walton, M.A. 6*s*

CAMBRIDGE SCHOOL AND COLLEGE TEXT-BOOKS.

A Series of Elementary Treatises for the use of Students.

Arithmetic. By Rev. C. Elsee, M.A. Fcap. 8vo. 13th Edit. 3*s*. 6*d*.

—— By A. Wrigley, M.A. 3*s*. 6*d*.

—— A Progressive Course of Examples. With Answers. By J. Watson, M.A. 7th Edition, revised. By W. P. Goudie, B.A. 2*s*. 6*d*.

Algebra. By the Rev. C. Elsee, M.A. 7th Edit. 4*s*.

—— Progressive Course of Examples. By Rev. W. F. M'Michael, M.A., and R. Prowde Smith, M.A. 4th Edition. 3*s*. 6*d*. With Answers. 4*s*. 6*d*.

Plane Astronomy, An Introduction to. By P. T. Main, M.A. 5th Edition. 4*s*.

Conic Sections treated Geometrically. By W. H. Besant, D.Sc. 6th Edition. 4*s*. 6*d*. Solution to the Examples. 4*s*.

—— Enunciations and Figures Separately. 1*s*. 6*d*.

Statics, Elementary. By Rev. H. Goodwin, D.D. 2nd Edit. 3*s*.

Hydrostatics, Elementary. By W. H. Besant, D.Sc. 13th Edit. 4*s*.

Mensuration, An Elementary Treatise on. By B. T. Moore, M.A. 3*s*. 6*d*.

Newton's Principia, The First Three Sections of, with an Appendix; and the Ninth and Eleventh Sections. By J. H. Evans, M.A. 5th Edition, by P. T. Main, M.A. 4*s*.

Analytical Geometry for Schools. By T. G. Vyvyan. 4th Edit. 4*s*. 6*d*.

Greek Testament, Companion to the. By A. C. Barrett, A.M. 5th Edition, revised. Fcap. 8vo. 5*s*.

Book of Common Prayer, An Historical and Explanatory Treatise on the. By W. G. Humphry, B.D. 6th Edition. Fcap. 8vo. 2*s*. 6*d*.

Music, Text-book of. By Professor H. C. Banister. 13th Edition, revised. 5*s*.

—— Concise History of. By Rev. H. G. Bonavia Hunt, Mus. Doc. Dublin. 9th Edition revised. 3*s*. 6*d*.

ARITHMETIC AND ALGEBRA.

See the two foregoing Series.

BOOK-KEEPING.

Book-keeping Papers, set at various Public Examinations. Collected and Written by J. T. Medhurst, Lecturer on Book-keeping in the City of London College. 3*s*.

GEOMETRY AND EUCLID.

Euclid. Books I.–VI. and part of XI. and XII. A New Translation. By H. Deighton. Books I. and II. separately, 2s. (See p. 8.)

—— The Definitions of, with Explanations and Exercises, and an Appendix of Exercises on the First Book. By R. Webb, M.A. Crown 8vo. 1s. 6d.

—— Book I. With Notes and Exercises for the use of Preparatory Schools, &c. By Braithwaite Arnett, M.A. 8vo. 4s. 6d.

—— The First Two Books explained to Beginners. By C. P. Mason, B.A. 2nd Edition. Fcap. 8vo. 2s. 6d.

The Enunciations and Figures to Euclid's Elements. By Rev. J. Brasse, D.D. New Edition. Fcap. 8vo. 1s. Without the Figures, 6d.

Exercises on Euclid and in Modern Geometry. By J. McDowell, B.A. Crown 8vo. 3rd Edition revised. 6s.

Geometrical Conic Sections. By H. G. Willis, M.A. (See p. 8.)

Geometrical Conic Sections. By W. H. Besant, D.Sc. (See p. 9.)

Elementary Geometry of Conics. By C. Taylor, D.D. (See p. 8.)

An Introduction to Ancient and Modern Geometry of Conics. By C. Taylor, D.D., Master of St. John's Coll., Camb. 8vo. 15s.

Solutions of Geometrical Problems, proposed at St. John's College from 1830 to 1846. By T. Gaskin, M.A. 8vo. 12s.

TRIGONOMETRY.

Trigonometry, Introduction to Plane. By Rev. T. G. Vyvyan, Charterhouse. 3rd Edition. Cr. 8vo. 3s. 6d.

An Elementary Treatise on Mensuration. By B. T. Moore, M.A. 3s. 6d.

ANALYTICAL GEOMETRY AND DIFFERENTIAL CALCULUS.

An Introduction to Analytical Plane Geometry. By W. P. Turnbull, M.A. 8vo. 12s.

Problems on the Principles of Plane Co-ordinate Geometry. By W. Walton, M.A. 8vo. 16s.

Trilinear Co-ordinates, and Modern Analytical Geometry of Two Dimensions. By W. A. Whitworth, M.A. 8vo. 16s.

An Elementary Treatise on Solid Geometry. By W. S. Aldis, M.A. 4th Edition revised. Cr. 8vo. 6s.

Elliptic Functions, Elementary Treatise on. By A. Cayley, D.Sc. Professor of Pure Mathematics at Cambridge University. Demy 8vo. 15s.

MECHANICS & NATURAL PHILOSOPHY.

Statics, Elementary. By H. Goodwin, D.D. Fcap. 8vo. 2nd Edition. 3*s*.

Dynamics, A Treatise on Elementary. By W. Garnett, M.A., D.C.L. 4th Edition. Crown 8vo. 6*s*.

Dynamics. Rigid. By W. S. Aldis, M.A. 4*s*.

Dynamics. A Treatise on. By W. H. Besant, D.Sc., F.R.S. 7*s*. 6*d*.

Elementary Mechanics, Problems in. By W. Walton, M.A. New Edition. Crown 8vo. 6*s*.

Theoretical Mechanics, Problems in. By W. Walton, M.A. 3rd Edition. Demy 8vo. 16*s*.

Hydrostatics. By W. H. Besant, D.Sc. Fcap. 8vo. 12th Edition. 4*s*.

Hydromechanics, A Treatise on. By W. H. Besant, D.Sc., F.R.S. 8vo. 4th Edition, revised. Part I. Hydrostatics. 5*s*.

Optics, Geometrical. By W. S. Aldis, M.A. Crown 8vo. 3rd Edition. 4*s*.

Double Refraction, A Chapter on Fresnel's Theory of. By W. S. Aldis, M.A. 8vo. 2*s*.

Heat, An Elementary Treatise on. By W. Garnett, M.A., D.C.L. Crown 8vo. 4th Edition. 4*s*.

Elementary Physics. By W. Gallatly, M.A., Asst. Examr. at London University. 4*s*.

Newton's Principia, The First Three Sections of, with an Appendix; and the Ninth and Eleventh Sections. By J. H. Evans, M.A. 5th Edition. Edited by P. T. Main, M.A. 4*s*.

Astronomy, An Introduction to Plane. By P. T. Main, M.A. Fcap. 8vo. cloth. 5th Edition. 4*s*.

——— Practical and Spherical. By R. Main, M.A. 8vo. 14*s*.

Mathematical Examples. Pure and Mixed. By J. M. Dyer, M.A., and R. Prowde Smith, M.A. 6*s*.

Pure Mathematics and Natural Philosophy, A Compendium of Facts and Formulæ in. By G. R. Smalley. 2nd Edition, revised by J. McDowell, M.A. Fcap. 8vo. 3*s*. 6*d*.

Elementary Mathematical Formulæ. By the Rev. T. W. Openshaw, M.A. 1*s*. 6*d*.

Elementary Course of Mathematics. By H. Goodwin, D.D. 6th Edition. 8vo. 16*s*.

Problems and Examples, adapted to the 'Elementary Course of Mathematics.' 3rd Edition. 8vo. 5*s*.

Solutions of Goodwin's Collection of Problems and Examples. By W. W. Hutt, M.A. 3rd Edition, revised and enlarged. 8vo. 9*s*.

A Collection of Examples and Problems in Arithmetic, Algebra, Geometry, Logarithms, Trigonometry, Conic Sections, Mechanics, &c., with Answers. By Rev. A. Wrigley. 20th Thousand. 8*s*. 6*d*. Key. 10*s*. 6*d*.

TECHNOLOGICAL HANDBOOKS.

Edited by H. TRUEMAN WOOD, Secretary of the Society of Arts.

Dyeing and Tissue Printing. By W. Crookes, F.R.S. 5*s*.

Glass Manufacture. By Henry Chance, M.A.; H. J. Powell, B.A.; and H. G. Harris. 3*s*. 6*d*.

Cotton Spinning. By Richard Marsden, of Manchester. 3rd Edition, revised. 6*s*. 6*d*.

Cotton Weaving. By R. Marsden. [*Preparing*.

Chemistry of Coal-Tar Colours. By Prof. Benedikt. Translated by Dr. Knecht of Bradford. 5*s*.

Woollen and Worsted Cloth Manufacture. By Roberts Beaumont, Assistant Lecturer at Yorkshire College, Leeds. 7*s*. 6*d*.

Colour in Woven Design. By Roberts Beaumont. [*Preparing*.

Others in preparation.

HISTORY, TOPOGRAPHY, &c.

Rome and the Campagna. By R. Burn, M.A. With 85 Engravings and 26 Maps and Plans. With Appendix. 4to. 21*s*.

Old Rome. A Handbook for Travellers. By R. Burn, M.A. With Maps and Plans. Demy 8vo. 5*s*.

Modern Europe. By Dr. T. H. Dyer. 2nd Edition, revised and continued. 5 vols. Demy 8vo. 2*l*. 12*s*. 6*d*.

The History of the Kings of Rome. By Dr. T. H. Dyer. 8vo. 16*s*.

The History of Pompeii: its Buildings and Antiquities. By T. H. Dyer. 3rd Edition, brought down to 1874. Post 8vo. 7*s*. 6*d*.

The City of Rome: its History and Monuments. 2nd Edition, revised by T. H. Dyer. 5*s*.

Ancient Athens: its History, Topography, and Remains. By T. H. Dyer. Super-royal 8vo. Cloth. 7*s*. 6*d*.

The Decline of the Roman Republic. By G. Long. 5 vols. 8vo. 5*s*. each.

A History of England during the Early and Middle Ages. By C. H. Pearson, M.A. 2nd Edition revised and enlarged. 8vo. Vol. I. 16*s*. Vol. II. 14*s*.

Historical Maps of England. By C. H. Pearson. Folio. 3rd Edition revised. 31*s*. 6*d*.

History of England, 1800–46. By Harriet Martineau, with new and copious Index. 5 vols. 3*s*. 6*d*. each.

A Practical Synopsis of English History. By A. Bowes. 9th Edition, revised. 8vo. 1*s*.

Lives of the Queens of England. By A. Strickland. Library Edition, 8 vols. 7*s*. 6*d*. each. Cheaper Edition, 6 vols. 5*s*. each. Abridged Edition, 1 vol. 6*s*. 6*d*. Mary Queen of Scots, 2 vols. 5*s*. each. Tudor and Stuart Princesses, 5*s*.

Eginhard's Life of Karl the Great (Charlemagne). Translated, with Notes, by W. Glaister, M.A., B.C.L. Crown 8vo. 4s. 6d.

The Elements of General History. By Prof. Tytler. New Edition, brought down to 1874. Small Post 8vo. 3s. 6d.

History and Geography Examination Papers. Compiled by C. H. Spence, M.A., Clifton College. Crown 8vo. 2s. 6d.

PHILOLOGY.

WEBSTER'S DICTIONARY OF THE ENGLISH LANGUAGE. With Dr. Mahn's Etymology. 1 vol. 1628 pages, 3000 Illustrations. 21s.; half calf, 30s.; calf or half russia, 31s. 6d.; russia, 2l. With Appendices and 70 additional pages of Illustrations, 1919 pages. 31s. 6d.; half calf, 2l.; calf or half russia, 2l. 2s.; russia, 2l. 10s.

'THE BEST PRACTICAL ENGLISH DICTIONARY EXTANT.'—*Quarterly Review*, 1873.

Prospectuses, with specimen pages, post free on application.

Richardson's Philological Dictionary of the English Language. Combining Explanation with Etymology, and copiously illustrated by Quotations from the best Authorities. With a Supplement. 2 vols. 4to. 4l. 14s. 6d. Supplement separately. 4to. 12s.

Brief History of the English Language. By Prof. James Hadley, LL.D., Yale College. Fcap. 8vo. 1s.

The Elements of the English Language. By E. Adams, Ph.D. 21st Edition. Post 8vo. 4s. 6d.

Philological Essays. By T. H. Key, M.A., F.R.S. 8vo. 10s. 6d.

Language, its Origin and Development. By T. H. Key, M.A., F.R.S. 8vo. 14s.

Synonyms and Antonyms of the English Language. By Archdeacon Smith. 2nd Edition. Post 8vo. 5s.

Synonyms Discriminated. By Archdeacon Smith. Demy 8vo. 2nd Edition revised. 14s.

Bible English. Chapters on Words and Phrases in the Bible and Prayer Book. By Rev. T. L. O. Davies. 5s.

The Queen's English. A Manual of Idiom and Usage. By the late Dean Alford. 6th Edition. Fcap. 8vo. 1s. sewed. 1s. 6d. cloth.

A History of English Rhythms. By Edwin Guest, M.A., D.C.L. LL.D. New Edition, by Professor W. W. Skeat. Demy 8vo. 18s.

Elements of Comparative Grammar and Philology. For Use in Schools. By A. C. Price, M.A., Assistant Master at Leeds Grammar School. Crown 8vo. 2s. 6d.

Questions for Examination in English Literature. By Prof. W. W. Skeat. 2nd Edition, revised. 2s. 6d.

Etymological Glossary of nearly 2500 English Words derived from the Greek. By the Rev. E. J. Boyce. Fcap. 8vo. 3s. 6d.

A Syriac Grammar. By G. Phillips, D.D. 3rd Edition, enlarged. 8vo. 7s. 6d.

DIVINITY, MORAL PHILOSOPHY, &c.

BY THE REV. F. H. SCRIVENER, A.M., LL.D., D.C.L.

Novum Testamentum Græce. Editio major. Being an enlarged Edition, containing the Readings of Westcott and Hort, and those adopted by the Revisers, &c. 7*s.* 6*d.* *For other Editions see page* 3.

A **Plain Introduction to the Criticism of the New Testament.** With Forty Facsimiles from Ancient Manuscripts. 3rd Edition. 8vo. 18*s.*

Six Lectures on the Text of the New Testament. For English Readers. Crown 8vo. 6*s.*

Codex Bezæ Cantabrigiensis. 4to. 26*s.*

The New Testament for English Readers. By the late H. Alford, D.D. Vol. I. Part I. 3rd Edit. 12*s.* Vol. I. Part II. 2nd Edit. 10*s.* 6*d.* Vol. II. Part I. 2nd Edit. 16*s.* Vol. II. Part II. 2nd Edit. 16*s.*

The Greek Testament. By the late H. Alford, D.D. Vol. I. 7th Edit. 1*l.* 8*s.* Vol. II. 8th Edit. 1*l.* 4*s.* Vol. III. 10th Edit. 18*s.* Vol. IV. Part I. 5th Edit. 18*s.* Vol. IV. Part II. 10th Edit. 14*s.* Vol. IV. 1*l.* 12*s.*

Companion to the Greek Testament. By A. C. Barrett, M.A. 5th Edition, revised. Fcap. 8vo. 5*s.*

The Book of Psalms. A New Translation, with Introductions, &c. By the Very Rev. J. J. Stewart Perowne, D.D. 8vo. Vol. I. 6th Edition, 18*s.* Vol. II. 6th Edit. 16*s.*

—— Abridged for Schools. 6th Edition. Crown 8vo. 10*s.* 6*d.*

History of the Articles of Religion. By C. H. Hardwick. 3rd Edition. Post 8vo. 5*s.*

History of the Creeds. By J. R. Lumby, DD. 3rd Edition. Crown 8vo. 7*s.* 6*d.*

Pearson on the Creed. Carefully printed from an early edition. With Analysis and Index by E. Walford, M.A. Post 8vo. 5*s.*

Liturgies and Offices of the Church, for the Use of English Readers, in Illustration of the Book of Common Prayer. By the Rev. Edward Burbidge, M.A. Crown 8vo. 9*s.*

An Historical and Explanatory Treatise on the Book of Common Prayer By Rev. W. G. Humphry, B.D. 6th Edition, enlarged. Small Post 8vo. 2*s.* 6*d.*; Cheap Edition, 1*s.*

A Commentary on the Gospels, Epistles, and Acts of the Apostles. By Rev. W. Denton, A.M. New Edition. 7 vols. 8vo. 9*s.* each.

Notes on the Catechism. By Rt. Rev. Bishop Barry. 8th Edit. Fcap. 2*s.*

The Winton Church Catechist. Questions and Answers on the Teaching of the Church Catechism. By the late Rev. J. S. B. Monsell, LL.D. 4th Edition. Cloth, 3*s.*; or in Four Parts, sewed.

The Church Teacher's Manual of Christian Instruction. By Rev. M. F. Sadler. 38th Thousand. 2*s.* 6*d.*

FOREIGN CLASSICS.

A Series for use in Schools, with English Notes, grammatical and explanatory, and renderings of difficult idiomatic expressions. Fcap. 8vo.

Schiller's Wallenstein. By Dr. A. Buchheim. 5th Edit. 5*s*.
Or the Lager and Piccolomini, 2*s*. 6*d*. Wallenstein's Tod, 2*s*. 6*d*.

——— **Maid of Orleans.** By Dr. W. Wagner. 2nd Edit. 1*s*. 6*d*.

——— **Maria Stuart.** By V. Kastner. 2nd Edition. 1*s*. 6*d*.

Goethe's Hermann and Dorothea. By E. Bell, M.A., and E. Wölfel. 1*s*. 6*d*.

German Ballads, from Uhland, Goethe, and Schiller. By C. L. Bielefeld. 3rd Edition. 1*s*. 6*d*.

Charles XII., par Voltaire. By L. Direy. 7th Edition. 1*s*. 6*d*.

Aventures de Télémaque, par Fénélon. By C. J. Delille. 4th Edition. 2*s*. 6*d*.

Select Fables of La Fontaine. By F. E. A. Gasc. 18th Edit. 1*s*. 6*d*.

Picciola, by X. B. Saintine. By Dr. Dubuc. 15th Thousand. 1*s*. 6*d*.

Lamartine's Le Tailleur de Pierres de Saint-Point. By J. Boïelle, 4th Thousand. Fcap. 8vo. 1*s*. 6*d*.

Italian Primer. By Rev. A. C. Clapin, M.A. Fcap. 8vo. 1*s*.

FRENCH CLASS-BOOKS.

French Grammar for Public Schools. By Rev. A. C. Clapin, M.A. Fcap. 8vo. 12th Edition, revised. 2*s*. 6*d*.

French Primer. By Rev. A. C. Clapin, M.A. Fcap. 8vo. 8th Ed. 1*s*.

Primer of French Philology. By Rev. A. C. Clapin. Fcap. 8vo. 4th Edit. 1*s*.

Le Nouveau Trésor; or, French Student's Companion. By M. E. S. 18th Edition. Fcap. 8vo. 1*s*. 6*d*.

French Examination Papers in Miscellaneous Grammar and Idioms. Compiled by A. M. M. Stedman, M.A. 3rd Edition. Crown 8vo. 2*s*. 6*d*.

Key to the above. By G. A. Schrumpf, Univ. of France. Crown 8vo. 5*s*. (For Teachers or Private Students only.)

Manual of French Prosody. By Arthur Gosset, M.A. Crown 8vo. 3*s*.

Lexicon of Conversational French. By A. Holloway. 2nd Edition. Crown 8vo. 4*s*.

PROF. A. BARRÈRE'S FRENCH COURSE.

Elements of French Grammar and First Steps in Idiom. Crown 8vo. 2*s*.

Precis of Comparative French Grammar. 2nd Edition. Crown 8vo. 3*s*. 6*d*.

Junior Graduated French Course. Crown 8vo. 1*s*. 6*d*.

F. E. A. GASC'S FRENCH COURSE.

First French Book. Fcap. 8vo. 98th Thousand. 1*s*.

Second French Book. 47th Thousand. Fcap. 8vo. 1*s*. 6*d*.

Key to First and Second French Books. 5th Edit. Fcp. 8vo. 3*s*. 6*d*.

French Fables for Beginners, in Prose, with Index. 16th Thousand. 12mo. 1s. 6d.

Select Fables of La Fontaine. 18th Thousand. Fcap. 8vo. 1*s*. 6*d*.

Histoires Amusantes et Instructives. With Notes. 16th Thousand. Fcap. 8vo. 2s.

Practical Guide to Modern French Conversation. 17th Thousand. Fcap. 8vo. 1s. 6d.

French Poetry for the Young. With Notes. 5th Edition. Fcap. 8vo. 2s.

Materials for French Prose Composition; or, Selections from the best English Prose Writers. 19th Thous. Fcap. 8vo. 3s. Key, 6s.

Prosateurs Contemporains. With Notes. 10th Edition, revised. 12mo. 3s. 6d.

Le Petit Compagnon; a French Talk-Book for Little Children. 12th Thousand. 16mo. 1s 6d.

An Improved Modern Pocket Dictionary of the French and English Languages. 45th Thousand, with Additions. 16mo. 2s. 6d.

Modern French-English and English-French Dictionary. 4th Edition, revised. In 1 vol. 10s. 6d.

The A B C Tourist's French Interpreter of all Immediate Wants. By F. E. A. Gasc. 1s.

MODERN FRENCH AUTHORS.

Edited, with Introductions and Notes, by James Boïelle, Senior French Master at Dulwich College.

Daudet's La Belle Nivernaise. 2*s*. 6*d*. *For Beginners.*

Hugo's Bug Jargal. 3*s*. *For Advanced Students.*

GOMBERT'S FRENCH DRAMA.

Being a Selection of the best Tragedies and Comedies of Molière, Racine, Corneille, and Voltaire. With Arguments and Notes by A. Gombert. New Edition, revised by F. E. A. Gasc. Fcap. 8vo. 1s. each; sewed, 6d.

Contents.

Molière:—Le Misanthrope. L'Avare. Le Bourgeois Gentilhomme. Le Tartuffe. Le Malade Imaginaire. Les Femmes Savantes. Les Fourberies de Scapin. Les Précieuses Ridicules. L'Ecole des Femmes. L'Ecole des Maris. Le Médecin malgré Lui.

Racine:—Phédre. Esther. Athalie. Iphigénie. Les Plaideurs. La Thébaïde; ou, Les Frères Ennemis. Andromaque. Britannicus.

P. Corneille:—Le Cid. Horace. Cinna. Polyeucte.

Voltaire:—Zaïre.

GERMAN CLASS-BOOKS.

A Concise German Grammar. By Frz. Lange, Ph.D., Professor R.M.A. Woolwich. In three Parts. Part I. Elementary. 2*s*. Part II. Intermediate. 1*s*. 6*d*. *Now ready.* Part III. Advanced. *In the press.*

Materials for German Prose Composition. By Dr. Buchheim. 11th Edition, thoroughly revised. Fcap. 4s. 6d. Key, Parts I. and II., 3s. Parts III. and IV., 4s.

German Conversation Grammar. By I. Sydow. 2nd Edition. Book I. Etymology. 2s. 6d. Book II. Syntax. 1s. 6d.

Wortfolge, or Rules and Exercises on the Order of Words in German Sentences. By Dr. F. Stock. 1s. 6d.

A German Grammar for Public Schools. By the Rev. A. C. Clapin and F. Holl Müller. 5th Edition. Fcap. 2s. 6d.

A German Primer, with Exercises. By Rev. A. C. Clapin. 1*s*.

Kotzebue's Der Gefangene. With Notes by Dr. W. Stromberg. 1*s*.

German Examination Papers in Grammar and Idiom. By R. J. Morich. 2s. 6d. Key for Tutors only, 5s.

German Examination Course. By Prof. F. Lange, Ph.D. Elementary, 2s. Intermediate, 2s. Advanced, 1s. 6d.

MODERN GERMAN SCHOOL CLASSICS.

Small Crown 8vo.

Hey's Fabeln Für Kinder. Edited by Prof. F. Lange, Ph.D. 1*s*. 6*d*.

Bechstein's Märchen. Edited by Prof. H. Hager, Ph.D.

Benedix's Dr. Wespe. Edited by F. Lange, Ph.D. 2*s*. 6*d*.

Schiller's Jugendjahre. Edited by Prof. H. Hager, Ph.D. [*In the press.*

Hoffman's Meister Martin, der Küfner. By Prof. F. Lange, Ph.D. 1s. 6d.

Heyse's Hans Lange. By A. A. Macdonell, M.A., Ph.D. 2*s*.

Auerbach's Auf Wache, and **Roquette's Der Gefrorene Kuss.** By A. A. Macdonell, M.A. 2s.

Moser's Der Bibliothekar. By Prof. F. Lange, Ph.D. 2*s*.

Eber's Eine Frage. By F. Storr, B.A. 2*s*.

Freytag's Die Journalisten. By Prof. F. Lange, Ph.D. 2*s*. 6*d*.

Gutzkow's Zopf und Schwert. By Prof. F. Lange, Ph.D. 2*s*.

German Epic Tales. Edited by Karl Neuhaus, Ph.D. 2*s*. 6*d*.

Humoresken. Novelletten der besten deutschen Humoristen der Gegenwart. Edited by A. A. Macdonell, M.A. Oxon. Authorised Edition. [*In preparation.*

ENGLISH CLASS-BOOKS.

Comparative Grammar and Philology. By A. C. Price, M.A., Assistant Master at Leeds Grammar School. 2s. 6d.

The Elements of the English Language. By E. Adams, Ph.D. 21st Edition. Post 8vo. 4s. 6d.

The Rudiments of English Grammar and Analysis. By E. Adams, Ph.D. 16th Thousand. Fcap. 8vo. 1s.

A Concise System of Parsing. By L. E. Adams, B.A. 1*s*. 6*d*.

Examples for Grammatical Analysis (Verse and Prose). Selected, &c., by F. Edwards. New edition. Cloth, 1s.

Notes on Shakespeare's Midsummer Night's Dream. By T. Duff Barnett, B.A. 1s. Julius Cæsar, 1s.; Henry V., 1s.; Macbeth, 1s.; Tempest, 1s.

By C. P. MASON, Fellow of Univ. Coll. London.

First Notions of Grammar for Young Learners. Fcap. 8vo. 41st Thousand. Cloth. 9d.

First Steps in English Grammar for Junior Classes. Demy 18mo. 44th Thousand. 1s.

Outlines of English Grammar for the Use of Junior Classes. 71st Thousand. Crown 8vo. 2s.

English Grammar, including the Principles of Grammatical Analysis. 30th Edition. 125th Thousand. Crown 8vo. 3s. 6d.

A Shorter English Grammar, with copious Exercises. 34th Thousand. Crown 8vo. 3s. 6d.

English Grammar Practice, being the Exercises separately. 1s.

Code Standard Grammars. Parts I. and II., 2*d.* each. Parts III., IV., and V., 3d. each.

Notes of Lessons, their Preparation, &c. By José Rickard, Park Lane Board School, Leeds, and A. H. Taylor, Rodley Board School, Leeds. 2nd Edition. Crown 8vo. 2s. 6d.

A Syllabic System of Teaching to Read, combining the advantages of the 'Phonic' and the 'Look-and-Say' Systems. Crown 8vo. 1s.

Practical Hints on Teaching. By Rev. J. Menet, M.A. 6th Edit. revised. Crown 8vo. paper, 2s.

How to Earn the Merit Grant. A Manual of School Management. By H. Major, B.A., B.Sc. Part I. (3rd Edit.) Infant School, 3s. Part II. (2nd Edit. revised), 4s. Complete, 6s.

Test Lessons in Dictation. 4th Edition. Paper cover, 1*s.* 6*d.*

Drawing Copies. By P. H. Delamotte. Oblong 8vo. 12*s.* Sold also in parts at 1s. each.

Poetry for the Schoolroom. New Edition. Fcap. 8vo. 1*s.* 6*d.*

The Botanist's Pocket-Book. With a copious Index. By W. R. Hayward. 6th Edition, revised. Crown 8vo. cloth limp. 4s. 6d.

Experimental Chemistry, founded on the Work of Dr. Stöckhardt. By C. W. Heaton. Post 8vo. 5s.

Lectures on Musical Analysis. Sonata-form, Fugue, &c. Illustrated from Classical Masters. By Prof. H. C. Banister. 7s. 6d.

GEOGRAPHICAL SERIES. By M. J. BARRINGTON WARD, M.A.
With Illustrations.

The Map and the Compass. A Reading-Book of Geography. For Standard I. New Edition. 8d.

The Round World. A Reading-Book of Geography. For Standard II. 10d.

The Child's Geography. For the Use of Schools and for Home Tuition. 6d.

The Child's Geography of England. With Introductory Exercises on the British Isles and Empire, with Questions. 2s. 6d. Without Questions, 2s.

Geography Examination Papers. (See History and Geography Papers, p. 12.)

Helps' Course of Poetry, for Schools. A New Selection from the English Poets, carefully compiled and adapted to the several standards by E. A. Helps, one of H.M. Inspectors of Schools.

Book I. Infants and Standards I. and II. 134 pp. small 8vo. 9d.

Book II. Standards III. and IV. 224 pp. crown 8vo. 1s. 6d.

Book III. Standards V., VI., and VII. 352 pp. post 8vo. 2s.

Or in PARTS. Infants, 2d.; Standard I., 2d.; Standard II., 2d. Standard III., 4d.

Picture School-Books. In Simple Language, with numerous Illustrations. Royal 16mo.

The Infant's Primer. 3d.—School Primer. 6d.—School Reader. By J. Tilleard. 1s.—Poetry Book for Schools. 1s.—The Life of Joseph. 1s.—The Scripture Parables. By the Rev. J. E. Clarke. 1s.—The Scripture Miracles. By the Rev. J. E. Clarke. 1s.—The New Testament History. By the Rev. J. G. Wood, M.A. 1s.—The Old Testament History. By the Rev. J. G. Wood, M.A. 1s.—The Story of Bunyan's Pilgrim's Progress. 1s.—The Life of Martin Luther. By Sarah Crompton. 1s.

BOOKS FOR YOUNG READERS.

A Series of Reading Books designed to facilitate the acquisition of the power of Reading by very young Children. In 11 vols. limp cloth, 6d. each.

Those with an asterisk have a Frontispiece or other Illustration.

Suitable for Infants.

*The Old Boathouse. Bell and Fan; or, A Cold Dip.

*Tot and the Cat. A Bit of Cake. The Jay. The Black Hen's Nest. Tom and Ned. Mrs. Bee.

*The Cat and the Hen. Sam and his Dog Redleg. Bob and Tom Lee. A Wreck.

*The New-born Lamb. The Rosewood Box. Poor Fan. Sheep Dog.

Suitable for Standards I. & II.

*The Two Parrots. A Tale of the Jubilee. By M. E. Wintle. 9 Illustrations.

*The Story of Three Monkeys.

*Story of a Cat. Told by Herself.

The Blind Boy. The Mute Girl. A New Tale of Babes in a Wood.

The Dey and the Knight. The New Bank Note. The Royal Visit. A King's Walk on a Winter's Day.

*Queen Bee and Busy Bee.

*Gull's Crag.

*A First Book of Geography. By the Rev. C. A. Johns. Illustrated. Double size, 1s.

Syllabic Spelling. By C. Barton. In Two Parts. Infants, 3d. Standard I., 3d.

BELL'S READING-BOOKS.

FOR SCHOOLS AND PAROCHIAL LIBRARIES.

Now Ready. Post 8vo. Strongly bound in cloth, 1s. each.

Suitable for Standards III. & IV.

***Life of Columbus.**
***Grimm's German Tales.** (Selected.)
***Andersen's Danish Tales.** Illustrated. (Selected.)
Great Englishmen. Short Lives for Young Children.
Great Englishwomen. Short Lives of.
Great Scotsmen. Short Lives of.
***Masterman Ready.** By Capt. Marryat. Illus. (Abgd.)
***Poor Jack.** By Capt. Marryat, R.N. (Abridged.)

Standards IV. & V.

***Scott's Talisman.** (Abridged.)
***Friends in Fur and Feathers.** By Gwynfryn.
***Dickens's Little Nell.** Abridged from the 'The Old Curiosity Shop.'
Parables from Nature. (Selected.) By Mrs. Gatty.
Lamb's Tales from Shakespeare. (Selected.)
Edgeworth's Tales. (A Selection.)
***Gulliver's Travels.** (Abridged.)
***Robinson Crusoe.** Illustrated.
***Arabian Nights.** (A Selection Rewritten.)

Standards V. VI. & VII.

***The Vicar of Wakefield.**
***Settlers in Canada.** By Capt. Marryat. (Abridged.)
Marie: Glimpses of Life in France. By A. R. Ellis.
Poetry for Boys. Selected by D. Munro.
***Southey's Life of Nelson.** (Abridged.)
***Life of the Duke of Wellington,** with Maps and Plans.
***Sir Roger de Coverley** and other Essays from the *Spectator.*
Tales of the Coast. By J. Runciman.

** These Volumes are Illustrated.*

Uniform with the Series, in limp cloth, 6d. each.

Shakespeare's Plays. Kemble's Reading Edition. With Explanatory Notes for School Use.

JULIUS CÆSAR. THE MERCHANT OF VENICE. KING JOHN.
HENRY THE FIFTH. MACBETH. AS YOU LIKE IT.

London: GEORGE BELL & SONS, York Street, Covent Garden.

CPSIA information can be obtained
at www.ICGtesting.com
Printed in the USA
LVHW042002220323
742311LV00005B/375

9 783382 125769